The Third Generation Series

Book 12

Foreign Agent

I0718871

by

Margaret Gregory

Cover designed by msgdragon
Cover images:
© Can Stock Photo Inc. /innovatedcaptures and Pixabay/xusenru

Also by Margaret Gregory

TYMOREAN TRUST SERIES:
Book 1 - Power Rising
Book 2 - Great Ones
Book 3 - The Return to Earth
Book 4 – Earth Mission
Book 5 – Alien Contact
Book 6 - Invasion

ATAPI SORCERESS SERIES:
Prequel – Korvu: The Beginning
Book 1- The Wild One
Book 2 – Atapi Sorceress

Maeven - Dragon Thief

THE THIRD GENERATION SERIES:
Book 1 - Wanda: From Bad to Worse
Book 2 - Wanda: Choosing Crime
Wanda – Early Days (anthology) Book 1 and 2
Book 3 – Wanda: Risking Life to Live
Book 4 – Erin: The Forcing of Wisdom
Book 5 – Wanda: A New Life Part 1 – Hidden Secrets
Book 6 – Wanda: A New Life Part 2 – First Mission
Book 7 – Wanda: Full Circle
Book 8 and 9 – Erin: The Call
Book 10 - Royal Favour
Book 11 - The Serpent's Shadow

For permission requests, address the request to the author c/o
Permissions,
TAT Indie Publishing
PO Box 2728
Rowville, Victoria, 3178
www.tatindiepublishing.com.au

Chapter 1 - A family emergency

Senator Charles Willard entered his home office and stopped just inside. His hand remained on the door handle. Less than five minutes ago, he had left his chair in its usual side-on position and his desk lamp on. Now the chair faced the French windows, the lamp was off, and the evening sun was providing the only light through the filmy gauze curtains that were no longer billowing in the slight evening breeze.

A quick glance sideways, confirmed that no one was hiding beside the door, or sitting in any of the chairs around the small coffee table. The workstation near the far wall was deserted.

As best as he could tell, his own desk was undisturbed, the files still neatly stacked. It didn't look like any part of the room had been searched. The painting over his safe was still at the same slightly off kilter angle. A collection of green lights, forming part of a metallic wall decoration, glowed unblinkingly.

A suspicion of the identity of the person sitting in his chair crossed his mind. As he thought on the idea, his mind also considered the unobtrusive security on his large property. No alarms had been tripped, since the lights in the decoration were all a steady green. However, an expert infiltrator could elude all the sensors... particularly the highly skilled expert who had set the system up.

None of his live at home or visiting children had come in to the room, they were all having their dinner, and none of them had ever disobeyed the instruction to stay out of this room.

As his alarm subsided, the chair began rotate slowly so that the occupant faced him. Only then, did he move further into the room, turn the light on and close the door.

"I didn't expect to see you," Willard spoke neutrally, but he was thinking that he should not have been surprised. He approached his desk, meeting the blue-green eyes of ... well, she wasn't exactly an intruder even though she had not come in through the front door.

"I am glad you haven't stopped being cautious," was the woman's reply. Then, as she abruptly rose from the chair, and walked out from behind the desk, she stated, "Elisabeth said that you had a confidential problem."

"Gwen..." he shook his head. He had long since given up trying to make her act with his ideas of propriety.

Willard closed the curtains and sat himself where the woman had been, and his guest made use of a second chair. He hadn't been correct when he had thought it wasn't one of his children in the room. It was. However, his eldest daughter Gwen, now called herself Wanda Martin, and he could no longer officially acknowledge any relationship between them.

"So, that is why I have the pleasure of this unannounced visit?" Willard asked wryly. "Do I need to change the locks on my doors and windows again?" He turned his desk lamp back on to see his visitor better.

"Who needs keys?" Wanda shrugged, ignoring his subtle reminder of her past illegal activities. They had a truce between them. They could be civil to each other, now that he could pretend they were not related.

"Dad, Elisabeth couldn't tell me much, only that you were uptight and Vera was beside herself, but wouldn't say why. I can figure that it is hush-hush. What's the matter?"

Only when they were alone together did Wanda call him 'Dad', and even then, rarely. Now, it was to tell him that despite past differences, she still cared about him.

Instead of answering directly, he asked, "How did you get past the guards?"

Wanda smiled faintly, and considered claiming to have sneaked past them. Except that might cause trouble for the men and the situation did not call for flippancy. "I showed them my credentials, and I had called ahead to say I had classified business with you."

The reminder of her 'credentials', didn't get him to open up. He was still deciding whether he should involve her, and had turned away as if thinking on the consequences if he did.

"Vera and the little ones are okay, aren't they?" Wanda suddenly blurted. Vera was her father's third wife, and the mother of her four youngest step-siblings or were there five now?

Willard turned back and quickly assured her, "Yes, they're all fine. So are Stuart and Paul. In fact, Vera did suggest that I call you."

Wanda raised her eyebrows in an exaggerated gesture of surprise. Her mind began working at high speed, as ideas - based on many snippets of information - occurred to her. All she said then was, "Ah...who is missing?"

Willard smiled faintly at the accuracy of her deduction, but even then did not tell her the problem. Instead, he pushed himself up from his chair and returned to the door of the room. Opening it enough to poke his head out, he listened for a moment and then called out, "Daniel?"

Wanda heard running feet and a childish voice answering.

"Can you go and ask your mother to come and see me here, please?"

The child voice said, "Sure, Dad," and its owner trotted off.

A second voice, older and more authoritative, seemed to demand rather than ask, "Have you had some news, Dad?"

Wanda recognised the voice of her oldest step-brother and moved her chair so that if Stuart Willard barged in, he wouldn't immediately see her.

If he was here, Paul probably was as well, and that probably explained the two unfamiliar cars she had observed outside.

Her father was talking quietly, not letting Stuart come in. That was particularly diplomatic of him.

While they spoke, Wanda relaxed and used her own private means of confirming her deductions. In her mind, she thought, "*Lisbeth?*"

Instantly, she sensed her sister's mind. Elisabeth was busy helping Vera with the youngest of the step-siblings. Maddy, the baby, was four and already a wilful handful.

In feelings, rather than words, Elisabeth Willard expressed her relief that Wanda had come.

In the same manner as before, Wanda asked, "*Who's missing?*"

"*Uncle Allan, Vera's brother. You won't have met him. Dad only just came out and told Stu, Paul and me.*"

"*And who is he, if Dad is being tight lipped, and why can't the great detective officer Stu Willard find him?"*

She sensed her sister's amusement at her jibe, and her wordless agreement that their brother was still being stubbornly antagonistic towards the supposedly dead, Gwen Willard. *"Vera's brother is Allan Wexford, and he is currently overseas."*

"Ah," Wanda thought, but ended the unusual conversation when her father shut the door on Stuart.

To Willard, she murmured, "I didn't think Vera really wanted to have anything to do with me. She wasn't exactly enamoured of me when we met last year."

Wanda could, if she chose to dwell on it, recall every word Vera had said to her, along with the exact tone. She hadn't been polite, or even a little grateful to someone who had found and rescued her from the men who had abducted her. It was probably the relief of being rescued, or perhaps the shock of someone she had thought dead appearing out of nowhere and telling her to start moving and helping herself - in some rather strongly worded phrases.

"You and she have never met when the both of you were at your best," Willard chided mildly.

Which, Wanda admitted to herself, was entirely true. The first and only other time they had met was years back when Elisabeth had been critically ill, and she herself had been hiding from both the police and her crime lord boss. Her worry about her sister, along with everything else, had left her in no mood to be polite.

Vera announced herself with a quiet knock on the door. Willard opened it quickly and gestured for her to come in. Wanda swivelled her chair to see her reaction.

Not unexpectedly, it was, "How did you sneak in?" Vera had stopped six feet away and was staring at her with veiled hostility.

Wanda sighed. She might just as well wear a brand on her forehead saying, "Criminal."

Perhaps Vera had been listening to Stuart, the fair-haired eldest son, or maybe, it was just because she was so tightly wound up with worry.

Instead of returning a sarcastic reply, Wanda kept her voice mild as she chided, "I used to live here, and I understood that there was a need for...discretion. Which would hardly be possible if your ghost step-daughter chose to announce her return."

Wanda watched as Vera's face muscles twitched, and she sensed that many impolitic comments were passing through her mind. Finally, the polished Senator's wife persona came to the fore.

"Yes, that is true," Vera managed to sound grateful for the consideration of the delicacy of the problem. Still, she was finding it hard to ask for help from someone who had been a criminal. Perhaps she was having second thoughts, worrying about her reputation...

Wanda tried to sense the cause of her reluctance, as she finally said, "There's a matter...I don't know if you can help...I..."

Having heard the nature of the problem from Elisabeth, Wanda was able to guess what Vera was trying to ask.

"Vera, I will help if I can...and if it needs stealth, sneakiness, and all those anti-social skills - I'm your person. I'm good at what I do."

Vera blushed once again. Wanda's gibe was a subtle rebuke. Criminal she might once have been, but now she worked investigating criminals and criminal acts. The old, "Set a thief to catch a thief."

Then Vera surprised Wanda by admitting, "I never thanked you properly for finding me and saving me last year. Charles told me that it had been you and David who found out where I was, not the FBI. I don't know how you did it, and maybe I don't want to know, but I think we need someone like you."

"Tell me the problem," Wanda said, as she projected a sense of business-like confidence. "Is someone you care about missing?"

"Yes," Vera was startled into admitting. Then she seemed to slump and Wanda quickly stood up and let her father help her to the hastily vacated chair. "My brother is missing, and his daughter. At least, no one has heard from them for days..."

Vera fell silent, and Wanda watched her father's neutral expression as she pieced information together.

"Alan Wexford, the Trade Ambassador," she prompted and Vera looked at her startled when she added, "He's in Germany isn't he?"

"Austria, actually," Vera admitted. "How did you know? It has been kept confidential."

"I hear things," Wanda murmured. "What happened?"

"Nicole, his wife, called me yesterday. From a hospital in Vienna. She had my number in her bag, apparently. She said who she was, but spoke as if she didn't know me. I told her that I was her sister-in-law, that her husband was my brother."

Vera was watching Wanda, trying to determine if her husband's eldest child thought she was hysterical. "I asked her about Allan, and Rachael, their daughter, but she asked who they were."

Wanda glanced at her father, but it seemed that he wasn't going to add anything.

"Go on," Wanda invited, keeping the questions she had, in her mind. She moved another chair near to Vera's and sat so as to be at a similar level.

"I said I would try to reach Allan, and tell him where she was. I expected her to be glad, but she only said, 'He's not there'. The nurse spoke to me after that and said she hoped I could help her get her memory back."

"And you tried calling Allan?" Wanda asked, leaning closer to Vera, and maintaining eye contact.

"Of course I did. He rented an apartment for the month he intended to be there. Nicole gave me the details. The landlord checked for me, when I got no answer. He said there is no one there, but he wasn't worried, because Allan had said he might need to go away for a few days at a time. That's fair enough, but Nicole and Rachael would still be there."

"How old is Rachael?" Wanda asked, she hadn't cared to learn anything about Vera's family.

"Almost six. Nicole is her step mother, but she wouldn't have left her alone."

"No," Wanda agreed, thoughtfully. She had a shiver of disquiet, imagining how she would be if her own two-year-old son went missing.

"So, you are saying that Rachael is missing? You can't know if Allan went away and took her with him."

Vera shook her head. "If he was meeting people and talking trade, he couldn't look after Rachael. And Nicole said, he wasn't there. Surely he would give her ways to contact him."

The details were confusing, and Wanda had no first hand impressions of Allan Wexford to work from.

"I think she's only faking amnesia," Vera added.

"That might suggest she is afraid of something, or hiding something. Do you know what happened to her?"

"Nicole just sounded vague, during the call...until that bit about Allan not being there. The nurse said that it looked like she might have been beaten up."

"What do you think might have happened?" Wanda asked. In her mind was the idea that Allan might have argued with his wife, beaten her up and walked out with the daughter. Things like that happened, and just because Wexford was a trade ambassador, it didn't make him a saint.

"I think that Allan and Rachael were abducted and Nicole knows something she is afraid to say."

Wanda considered that. It was also possible. She would have to ask her father some questions without Vera around. One thing she could ask, "Was Wexford meant to be reporting in on a regular schedule?" She asked her father the question, but he merely shrugged slightly. It was worth a try. She tried another. "Is the State Department looking into this?"

This time, her father answered. "I have alerted them to the possibility of trouble. They have had no indications of a problem. However, I believe they will send through a request to the Austrian Police."

Finally, she was getting the sense of how her father felt on the matter. He wasn't acting as if he thought Vera was making an issue out of nothing. No doubt, he was privy to things that could not be discussed with just anyone. Perhaps there were things he did not want to suggest to his wife.

However, forgetting for the moment that he was a US Senator, and treating him as a concerned relative, she asked, "You think someone needs to go and check things out? Unofficially? On a personal level?"

"I think that Nicole needs a friend," Charles Willard said obliquely. "That is, if you are able to leave little Davy?"

"Jim has hardly had me working since I've had him. David has had most of the fun. It's time he stayed home and played mother. Besides, I can speak German well; David can only speak it as a tourist."

Her mind was already in high gear, planning what she would need to do. She met her father's eyes, as he hovered behind Vera's chair. "I will need to make some phone calls, and see what I can do."

Vera rose then, and in a completely unexpected gesture, leaned over and kissed the top of Wanda's head. "Thank you," she murmured with complete sincerity, before she took herself out of the room.

Charles Willard returned to his desk chair, and waited for his daughter to ask questions. He didn't have to wait long.

"What else can you tell me? You do realise that I have a security clearance that is higher than yours?"

"Do you have to remind me of that contradiction?" Willard murmured. He took a deep breath and began. "Wexford is in Vienna to formalise some very lucrative trade deals. He will be speaking to many people and many organisations. He was chosen for the job because he lived in Vienna for a time and has contacts there."

"Are you able to tell me the nature of the processes, commodities or whatever, that he is talking about?"

Willard did so, adding all pertinent details he had learnt both in his capacity as Senator, and as Wexford's brother-in-law.

"Do you have his proposed agenda? Contact details for the Austrians?"

"I will get you that. Anything else?"

"Do you know if he and Nicole were having marital problems?"

Willard gave her a startled look, but answered, "All couples have the occasional disagreement, they were no different, judging from things Allan said. But, I wouldn't say there was anything that I would call him out for."

Wanda shrugged as if it had been a question she had to ask.

"Anything else?" Willard repeated.

"Use of your phone?" Wanda suggested.

As an answer, her father rose and started to leave the room. He merely commented, "The grey phone is a secure line to Washington."

Her father didn't know exactly what she did as work, only that she now had a State Department ID.

He had guessed she needed 'private use' of the phone. "Will you wait for the agenda?"

Wanda nodded, and began to go towards the phone on the desk. She grinned faintly as she sat back in her father's chair. When she had chosen to sit there before, he had known it as a residual act of defiance against him.

When the door had closed, she did indeed begin to make a call, but it wasn't by the landline. She used her personal mobile, which had a security channel built in. Though for this, she didn't need it. Her first call was to her husband, David Martin. When he answered, she wasted no time.

"Dav, I am going to need a grab bag, a change of clothes, the diplomatic passport and one of the others...make it the Carson one."

"Got it," David confirmed. "Where do you want it?"

"LAX, I think," Wanda considered. "I'll call you back in a bit. I need to talk to Jim."

She hung up without a good bye, picturing David getting what she needed ready. The 'grab' bag was her kit of less than legal tools. The change of clothes, meant an overnight bag and her 'skulking' clothes. David would wait for the rest of the details.

Her second call was to Jim Phillips, her mentor, part-time employer and very good friend. What she needed to have, she didn't have the pull to get fast. She might claim to work for the State Department, but she wasn't officially on their register.

"I have a family emergency," Wanda told Jim as soon as he answered. "A bit like I had last year, but in Austria."

She had no doubt that he had recognised her voice, if not her phone number and she could almost predict how Jim's mind would be putting the information together.

"Wexford?" he guessed.

"And child," Wanda added.

"What do you need?" Jim asked then.

"Visa for Europe, on my d-class passport and the Carson one."

"Who's your back up?"

"Can you line up the US Embassy?" Wanda suggested. "I think I need to do this without help."

She could envision Jim's frown. "Are you sure that is wise?"

"No, but I do think that absolute secrecy is needed, at least until I confirm the facts."

"Very well, where will I send the visa?"

"I am about to arrange a flight to Vienna. Can I pick it up at LAX? Call me when you have it."

"Right!" Jim rang off.

Her next call was to arrange her flight, and then she called David back. This time, she switched on the scrambler function and gave him a brief outline of her 'mission'.

Once, nothing would have stopped him from joining her, but now, it was their unwritten agreement that when one of them went on a mission, the other stayed home with their son. They both knew that their work was often dangerous.

This time, with the information that Wanda gave him, he knew that the mission was also personal. Trying to stop her going would be like trying to stop an avalanche.

Jim called her back almost as soon as she finished talking to David. This time, he was brusque, as if he had other things on his mind. He told her that the visa would be at the airport, wished her luck, and ended the call.

Willard returned as she was wondering at Jim's curtness. Her father had the information he had promised, and Wanda needed to scan through it. Attached to a page at the end, was a picture of the Wexfords, taken when they had visited at the house.

"Thanks," she said, when she tucked it into a pocket inside her loose jacket. "I'll be off."

"You can leave via the front door," Willard suggested. "Vera and Elisabeth are keeping everyone busy in the rumpus room."

He was half smiling.

"Yeah, it's dark enough," Wanda agreed. "I'll be flying out tonight."

Willard merely nodded, and made no move to have a demonstrative goodbye. He was glad they had made peace with each other, but it was best that they kept their relationship professional. He didn't ask to be kept advised of her progress, but knew he would hear if her task was successful.

Chapter 2 - Vienna

Wanda used her diplomatic passport while travelling to Vienna via London, flying business class. At the airports, the customs procedures were streamlined, the service was preferential, and when she was finally in Vienna, she was able to leave the airport quickly.

A commissionaire at the terminal summoned a taxi for her and directed the driver to take her to the guesthouse she had selected from an internet site.

The Pension Handel was a historic building, dating from the early 20th century. The rustic street lighting suggested that the brick façade was light coloured, and the boxes adorning the first floor windows were draping greenery and red flowers.

Perhaps it wasn't the most modern and progressive place to stay, but it suited her purposes. It was close enough to the centre of Vienna, and only a ten-minute walk from the nearest U-bahn station.

What was also to her liking was their policy of paying in cash. That was no problem, for she had arranged to cash travellers cheques in both English pounds and Euros, before she had left LAX.

Her first action after arranging to use one of the deluxe rooms was to ask if she could place certain personal papers in the guesthouse safe. The desk manager didn't even question the request, and within minutes, Wanda's spare cash and her diplomatic passport were securely hidden in the safe.

As far as the guesthouse was concerned, Tatiana Carson, was an American based reporter, on holiday to visit relatives.

The room she was shown to had a 3m high entrance hall, the main room was spacious enough for a family of four, and furnished in traditional Viennese style. She told the young man who had escorted her there, that the room was 'absolutely lovely', and staying there was going to be 'delightful'. She emphasised her enchantment by twirling around to look at everything.

Once she was alone, she sobered and went to explore every part of what actually was a suite. Two bedrooms came off the main room, as well as a private bathroom. She took her small case into the nearest bedroom, and tossed it on the bed.

She assumed that her hosts would expect her to be ready for sleep, since she had travelled a long way and it was after 9 pm local time. However, retiring for the night was not her immediate intention. One thing that she never failed to do when she was in a new and unfamiliar place was to thoroughly explore - checking out the alternate exits, the fire exits, stairs, lifts and the general layout. Her look around also took in the unobtrusive security features and her mind instinctively calculated the blind spots.

On her walk through, she also went back to the ground floor and stopped at a wall rack containing brochures. She took a folded street map of Vienna, a bus and train route map, public transport timetables, and one with various 'must see' attractions and a brochure about the guest house.

Back in her room, she changed out of her 'business' outfit of shirt, skirt and jacket, and into more casual slacks and blouse with a light lacy-look woollen jumper. The only oddity in her appearance was her rubber-soled shoes. Then she studied the map she had collected.

Despite the eleven-hour flight from LA to London, and the 2-hour connecting flight to Vienna, Wanda wasn't tired. She had slept during the long flight and her body, still on LA time, was telling her it was about noon. That being so, she intended to get to the hospital and ask to see Nicole Wexford.

From the map, she discovered that the guesthouse was in the sixth district and that the apartment Allan Wexford had rented, and the hospital where Nicole was, were both in the ninth district. Easy enough to get to by train, but considering the late hour, she decided to take a taxi. If she left the hospital before the last train, she might return that way. She had no intention of renting a car in this foreign place.

Wanda walked to the train station to seek a taxi, rather than calling to arrange for one to take her from the guesthouse. She had several reasons for this - firstly, to start learning her way around. That was the one she would admit to. The other reasons were probably needless precautions. She was deliberately not linking herself directly to her current lodgings and the station provided a venue for her to change her appearance. Both things she had habitually done when embarking on her former illegal jaunts. This current outing wasn't for any illegal purpose, but some intuition was telling her the matter would not end when she had seen the woman and spoken to the police.

The hour was late, her immediate glance around took in the departure boards, the ticket windows, the escalators down to the platforms with their ticket checking men and machines. All was orderly, and the people still moving around the concourse all seemed intent on their own business. Wanda observed the locals while she made her way to the ladies' toilets. Once there, she was pleased that there were no other women in the facilities. She went to a cubicle and locked herself in and wasted no time making some changes to her appearance. This was such a well-practiced art, that she was ready to emerge a mere eight minutes later.

When she left the station in the hired a taxi, she looked quite different from the person who had left the Pension Handel. Now, her mid-length brown hair was tied back in a ponytail, with two strands on each side of her face falling loose. These she had treated with a chemical dye, so they appeared bleached blonde. The effect could be neutralised later with a second chemical. The other change was the use of coloured contact lenses to change her eye colour from blue-green to brown.

The taxi driver took her to the main entrance of the hospital, and told her where she needed to go to ask about her relative.

Wanda thanked him in fluent German, and paid him more than the trip fee in thanks. She was acting the part of a travelling American, though less blatantly. The driver had been friendly and helpful, more so since she did not insist on speaking English.

The woman at the reception desk saw a completely different sort of person walk in the front entrance. She saw a young woman, a foreigner by her clothes, and the hesitant way she moved and stopped to study various signs. She sighed, as the woman finally spotted her desk and approached.

If the woman spoke little German, and needed to have simple instructions explained more than once, she was going to be late finishing work. However, as soon as the woman started to speak, her vague annoyance vanished.

"I am here to visit the woman who doesn't know who she is," Wanda said, making her German hesitant, and stilted as if she had translated her words one at a time from English.

The receptionist had heard about that patient, and had instructions to alert the hospital administrators if anyone came asking about the woman.

While pressing an alert button under the desk, the receptionist asked as if it was a standard question, "Do you know what room she is in?"

"No, sorry, the woman rang my Aunt Vera, in London, because she had found her number in her bag. Aunt Vera said the woman didn't recognise her name, but that we might know her. I came here straight from the airport."

The receptionist smiled and commented, "It is very late, past the end of visiting hours, but I will just call up and find out where this lady is and if you can see her."

Wanda wasn't fooled by the offer, though she maintained an earnest, worried and hopeful expression. She could hear some of the conversation from the other end, and realised the receptionist was getting instructions from someone.

"The lady is in ward fourteen, on the second floor. You may go up and talk to the ward nurse," the receptionist finally told her. Then, she was kind enough to indicate the lift that would take the young foreign woman up to the second floor.

Wanda expressed her thanks and followed the directions she had been given, deciding to forego her usual scouting foray on the way up.

Nurse Theobald, sat behind a curved desk, where two other people were reading through patient files. They had desk lamps directed at the papers, since the main overhead lights were off.

Wanda was quizzed in detail. The nurse no doubt wishing to be certain this late arriving stranger did not mean to harm her patient. Having satisfied herself, she led Wanda to a private room two doors down from the desk and eased open the door. The lights were out, and the nurse used a small hand torch to find the join in the curtain surrounding the bed. She moved the curtain slightly, and disappeared, but her voice was audible as she spoke softly, waking the woman sleeping in the bed.

Wanda waited outside the curtain, studying the layout of the room or what she could see in the dim light reflecting in from the passage. Then the nurse turned on the bed light and gestured her in; she saw only the bruised and battered face of the woman.

The nurse introduced her. "This is Tatiana, she says she knows your friend Vera."

"Aunt Vera asked me to come," Wanda added in English, after she had glanced around at the equipment within the curtain.

"Do you know me?" Nicole Wexford asked, her voice sounded hopeful, but her face was creased as if in confusion. "I don't recall your name, or your face."

"You may not have met me personally," Wanda admitted, "but you may have seen me at some of Aunt Vera's parties, before I moved to London."

Nicole was shaking her head, and Wanda sensed she would become difficult unless she was convinced her late visitor was there to help her.

"Aunt Vera said you rang her," Wanda said as she delved into the small handbag she had with her. She brought out the photo of the Wexfords that her father had given her.

"I did ring someone," Nicole admitted. "But she spoke of people I don't remember."

Wanda turned back to the nurse and asked, hesitantly, "Can I stay here a while and talk to her?"

Her mind was thinking, forcefully, "Privately!"

The nurse reacted to the mental hint, without thinking it odd. "Call me if I can help."

Once they were alone, Nicole Wexford dropped the vague act,

and hissed, "Who are you!"

"I do know Vera and Charles Willard," Wanda admitted. She sat on the visitors chair and pulled it close so she could whisper, "I work for the US State Department."

"Oh, thank God!" Nicole almost wept with relief.

"Hold together, Nicole. We won't have much time before the nurse finds a reason to come back. Tell me what happened."

"Rachael and Allan are missing! Allan went away, it was only meant to be overnight, but I didn't hear from him for three days. Then I had a message from him, for me to join him at the Heinrich's place. I would be able to bring Rachael because other wives would be there."

"This message was from Allan? Are you sure?"

Nicole nodded. "I was so relieved, he said that his phone had gone flat and he had to find a new charger. He wouldn't use public phones."

"So, you went there?" Wanda prompted.

"I took a taxi to go there, but I think I blacked out."

Wanda asked urgently, "And Rachael was with you?"

"Yes, and she was still with me when I woke in some rank smelling house. We were locked in a room, and Rachael wouldn't wake up."

"Then what? How did you and Rachael get separated?"

"Two men came into the room, with guns. One went and picked Rachael up. I screamed and tried to stop him but he punched me several times and growled for me to shut up. Next thing I knew, I was in a park somewhere, and then here."

"Then why the act? Why not tell all this to the police?"

"They will kill Rachael if I do, they said so."

Wanda's first instinct was to think this was an abduction, but if it was, there had yet to be a ransom note. Surely if there had been the state department would have been buzzing.

In spite of the careful questioning, that seemed to be all that Nicole knew. There were glaring oddities in her story, but Wanda sensed that her fear for her husband and daughter were genuine.

"I want to get you away from here, to the US Embassy, will you agree?"

Nicole nodded. "Will you be helping to find Rachael and Allan?"

"You bet!" Wanda assured her. "I think that you should tell them that Allan and Rachael are missing. By now, the Embassy may suspect it anyway. You are in no condition to do anything to help, and I am sure that the Viennese police can be discreet."

Wanda's sense of time running out peaked, just as she heard the door to the ward opening further. It did not feel like the nurse returning, so she glanced around and greeted the strange man who poked his head through the gap in the curtain.

"Are you a doctor?"

The man smiled apologetically. "No, Vienna Police, Investigative Bureau."

Wanda did not change her expression immediately, pretending once again to need time to translate.

He flashed a badge, and added, "My name is Otto Donau. I was advised that you might know our mystery patient." He casually replaced his ID by clipping it back onto his belt. He stood at the end of the bed glancing from the patient to the visitor.

His glance went from her to Nicole and back.

"Um, yes," Wanda agreed cautiously. She wasn't getting bad vibes from the man, but she had yet to decide how far she wanted to trust him.

"Um, yes?" Donau prompted, waiting politely for her to continue.

"I was about to call the American Embassy, Kommisar Donau," Wanda said, fumbling the language. "This is Nicole Wexford. She's from California."

Donau gave a slight bow in greeting, and then asked, "Were you in Vienna by yourself, Frau Wexford?"

"I...still don't remember, but this woman knows me."

"She rang my aunt," Wanda said quickly, in English, and then translated it. "She had the number in her pocket or something. My aunt recognised her voice, and was worried that she didn't know her. I was in London, so my aunt asked me to come. I had met Nicole a couple of times some years ago."

Wanda was willing to play along with Nicole's ploy of amnesia, for a while longer.

"What else can you tell me?" Donau invited.

"Her husband is Allan, and she has a daughter Rachael, who is six." Wanda shrugged. "That was why I was going to call the Embassy. They should be able to check her ID, if she has it here. They might be able to tell you more."

"I will do that for you," Donau offered. "And you are?"

"Oh, sorry. I am Tatiana Carson." Wanda made the claim, looking directly at the policeman, as if she was absolutely telling the truth.

"You have some ID," he suggested.

Wanda obediently felt around in her handbag for her passport. The photo in it matched her current appearance, and she passed it to the man with no sign of concern.

He studied it, and Wanda was not deceived by his casual manner when he handed it back. Still, he would have found no discrepancies. Jim's forgers were experts. The document had stamps from London, and several other European countries, including Austria.

"Where are you staying, Fraulein Carson?"

Once again, Wanda looked directly at the policeman and lied. "Um, I haven't worked that out yet. I came right here. I didn't know if I would need to stay or not. Will I be needed?"

"Perhaps for a day or so. May I suggest a guest house?"

"Oh, could you? That would be a help. Though I can't afford anything fancy. I am hardly rich. My Aunt had to pay for my fare here."

She smiled as if grateful, and mentally projected 'grateful, relieved, young and innocent'.

"Pension Waldorf, Freidrichgasse 15, Immerstadt," Donau spoke carefully, adding the phone number.

Wanda immediately scrambled in her handbag for a pen and notebook, she didn't want to betray the fact that she had an eidetic memory. She asked, if Donau could repeat the address, and he did so with a slight smile, then added, "They close the desk at 11pm."

After a deliberate pause, as if mentally translating the last statement, Wanda glanced at the clock that was above all the equipment surrounding Nicole.

"I would like to talk to Frau Wexford alone," Donau told her, nodding politely at her."

"Ah...I will go and give this place a call," Wanda tacitly agreed to leave. To Nicole, she said, "I will come and see you again."

Wanda did not think Nicole would tell the detective anything, and felt it was safe enough to leave. Her original thought that Nicole needed to get the local police involved was still valid, but her own mind was considering what she now knew, and wondered why the men had abducted her, and Rachael, and then let her go. Why had Allan Wexford been targeted? Because he was an important American? She had too many questions, and her mind created suppositions of maybes that might be adverse to American interests.

Her own reasons for not talking to the policeman were more complex. At first it had merely been caution, now, it was because she had decided to investigate things for herself, before the police made anyone nervous. She gave the policeman a quick smile as she left through the gap in the curtain, and made a quick gesture to swipe some of the examination gloves in the rack by the door before departing the ward. In no way did she betray that she knew the policeman was watching her as she walked to the payphone near the nurses' station.

She did use the phone, but not to call the guesthouse that Donau had mentioned. Instead, she called the US Embassy and asked for the man who was the contact that Jim had arranged.

"Neil? Wanda Martin. I have located Mrs Wexford, and the police will probably get in touch shortly. She is afraid to talk to the police, and her husband and daughter are definitely missing. I need an hour to check out the Wexford apartment. I want to be out before they think of it."

Neil Thompson did not ask why. "I will organise a delay, though they might have other means to find out the address."

"I am aware of that," Wanda accepted the warning. "I will let you know if I find anything."

She disconnected and dialled the number for the guesthouse and spoke to the owners. Then, she glanced around as if checking her bearings, shrugged the strap of her bag over her head and strode towards the stairs.

Though she had seen no one but the policeman and the nurses, she soon had the feeling that she was being followed. She trusted the feeling, and if she was right, it was a complication. The most likely scenario was that Donau had a colleague, but what if it was someone related to the abductors of Allan Wexford and his daughter? That group had given Nicole a frightful warning.

She would need to find out, but she needed to check the Wexford place first. Well, she had a ready-made detour that should enable her to shake the watcher.

When she reached the ground floor she returned to the reception desk, noting that the woman had left and a man was now on duty. She asked him if he would call a taxi for her, so she could go to the address that Donau had given her. He obliged, and one arrived within minutes.

Once she was seated in the back of the taxi, she used a tiny torch to check the map to see how far the second guesthouse was from the Wexford apartment. She estimated a ten-minute walk and noted a nearby bus route. She memorised the information as she read it.

That she was being followed still, she was sure, but she doubted that whoever it was would expect her to be an expert at losing such shadowers.

As the taxi drove off, Wanda glanced along the street before going inside. She memorised the look and number of three cars that followed the taxi. One of them pulled in outside a building further down the street. That made her decide that having a second place to stay would be an asset.

Inside, a man waited at the reception desk. He looked up and smiled, greeting her by name, though with a questioning tone. Wanda admitted to being Fraulein Carson, and answered the man's questions about the type of room she required. Wanda chose one of the budget rooms, paid for two nights, and explained that she had left her luggage at the airport because she had not been sure she needed to stay.

The man smiled and accepted her explanation. He was kind enough to offer to supply her with some basic hygiene necessities, and Wanda thanked him. She feigned huge yawns as the man showed her up to a room on the second floor, and managed a polite goodnight in response to his parting words.

The last thing the man would have expected would be for his tired, late arriving guest to leave again almost immediately. Wanda waited until she was sure he would be out of sight, and paused only long enough to draw the curtains on the room's windows, and turn off the light. A brief glimpse out onto the back yard of the guesthouse, revealed no watchers there. Then she slipped out of the room, found the back stairs, ghosted out the back door when the man from the desk locked the front door, and quickly made her way over fences and through to the next street. The feeling of being watched had disappeared.

She walked quickly, without needing to check the map, and arrived in the street behind the apartment block she needed to enter. Slipping back into stealth mode once she was off the street, she worked her way to the back of the Wexford's building. Her outfit wasn't exactly best suited to climbing fences, since she had to be careful not get the lacy wool top snagged on fences, or any part of the outfit dirty. However, once she was inside the building, she would simply seem to be one of the current residents.

Entering via the rear door was a simple exercise, and the back stairs were in plain view. She saw the security camera, but was not concerned. The small device she had taken from her bag would ensure that the camera was frozen on a deserted back foyer for long enough for her to be upstairs out of sight. Similarly with any other security device she passed.

She met no one, and on reaching the top floor apartment, forced the lock, wiped it and entered in a very short time.

Now she took out a pair of the flexible latex disposable gloves that she had swiped form the hospital, and set to work. Her first move was to confirm what her senses were telling her - that the apartment was indeed deserted, and then she set to searching it with a thoroughness honed by Jim Phillips. She used the light from her tiny torch, and did not touch the room lights.

The apartment was one of the more modern kind, as the décor was late 20th century, and it was relatively Spartan like most rented places. The exceptions were a doll that was lying casually on the couch, and several soft toys in a pile on a side dresser. There was a TV guide on top of the TV, with the latest show list being for two days previously. In the little kitchen nook, a child's cardigan was draped over the back of a chair.

Wanda memorised all she saw, without trying to make sense of it. That was a refinement that she had no time for. Once Donau learnt that Nicole's husband and daughter were missing, they would arrive at the apartment in force.

The contents of every cupboard and every drawer were examined. In the kitchen, there was only the supplied utensils, cooking equipment, glasses and crockery. The cupboard in the main part of the apartment was empty. Wanda went into the first of the bedrooms, and found child sized underclothes in a drawer, small clothes hanging in one side of the wardrobe, and a hamper for dirty clothes in the other. For reasons she didn't stop to consider, Wanda found one of the laundry service bags and placed several articles of the child's dirty clothing in it.

Wanda surveyed the rest of the room, another doll was made into the bed, as if waiting for Rachel to return. The bedside cabinet held several storybooks, a colouring book and pencils, a small box of sweets and several local coins.

The second bedroom was bigger, having a double bed, larger bedside tables, the wardrobes and a desk with writing materials provided. This received special attention, as Wanda imagined Allan Wexford working there but the drawers and desk top held nothing of a personal or business nature.

A second phone extension sat on the desk, twin to the one in the main part of the suite.

Once again, Wanda checked the wardrobe and drawers. Nicole's clothes filled one side of the wardrobe, the other side contained only one suit, still in the plastic used by drycleaners, and two shirts on hangers, but with the creases from being folded still apparent. Only one suitcase rested on top of the wardrobe, and a quick lift of the front edge suggested it was empty.

The drawers showed a similar story. One bedside cabinet had a drawer filled with Nicole's underwear, handkerchiefs, some jewellery and her passport. Allan's side was empty.

Unpleasant ideas were forming in Wanda's mind as she began to check the apartment for a safe. She didn't find one, but the building might have a safe for the tenants to use.

About then, Wanda had the sense of time running out. She glanced at her watch - she had been in the apartment fifty minutes. It was more than time that she got out. On impulse, she returned to the bigger bedroom and took an item of Nicole's, and wrapped it in a second of the laundry service bags. There was nothing of Allan's that she could use, not even sleeping clothes from under the pillow of the bed. Too bad, but she was out of time.

That inner instinct had never failed her and she acted on it. Touching the security nullifier before she opened the door, she took a last glance around, and left. The door relocked behind her, and she walked briskly down the passage and around the corner. Behind her, coming from the direction of the elevator, she heard voices; she increased her pace and deactivated the nullifier.

She left the way she had arrived, and made her way back to the adjacent street. It was likely, she decided, that the police would have someone watching the street at the front of the apartment building.

Before she emerged onto the street, she rolled the purloined clothing into as small a bundle as possible, and took her jumper off to drape over it. A short time later, she was able to hail a taxi and directed it, not to Freidrichgasse, but back to the first room she had rented. She needed to use her key to get back into the building.

Chapter 3 - Unanswered questions.

Once back in her room, Wanda sat back in one of the comfortable armchairs and thought through her observations. In her mind, it was like she was repeating her recent actions exactly.

One point seemed apparent - Allan Wexford had moved all his clothes out of the apartment, except for those that had been at the laundry. Yet nothing that her father had said, or her step-mother, had hinted at trouble between Nicole and Allan.

Nicole was genuinely distraught about Rachael's disappearance, even though she was actually the child's step-mother.

The missing clothes may just have been because Allan planned to be away. Nicole had said it was meant to be just overnight, but she didn't hear from him for three days. She hadn't been able to reach his phone...but surely he should have left info as to where he was going to be...in case of some emergency. Wanda realised that she had seen nothing with any such information on.

And then Allan hadn't told Nicole where he had been, and the message he gave her about joining him had been a trap.

Trying to think outside the obvious, Wanda still came up with only two options - either Allan Wexford had been abducted, or he had chosen to leave his wife. The latter might explain Rachael's disappearance - he might have wanted to keep his daughter and hired someone to get her, and that would be why she was taken but not Nicole. But, had he wanted his wife beaten and left to die?

If the former, was Rachael taken to force Wexford into agreeing to some action. Wouldn't having both wife and child be a bigger lever? But if so, why dump Nicole and risk her going to the police?

Maybe they thought she would die, but she was found and was now able to talk...and the abductors would have to realise the police would come looking for the American. Or were they sure Nicole was too terrified to dare?

Wanda pushed the questions to the back of her mind. There still might be a third explanation, but she couldn't think of it at the moment. She was beginning to feel very tired, and there were some things she needed to do before she went to sleep and she forced herself up out of the chair and went to where she had put her grab bag.

Her hand rummaged in it and pulled out an android tablet and its charger. Then she checked the brochure on the guesthouse, and confirmed her memory of seeing that it had free wi-fi. That suited her, since she wanted to connect to the internet.

While the tablet loaded up, and the connection to the internet was established, Wanda changed into her jersey track pants and long sleeved t-shirt. Then she opened up Skype and established a connection to David's computer, back at her home in Crystal Brook, California. It was after midnight local time, so LA would be a bit after three pm. David might be busy about their farm, or doing something with Davy, but she hoped he was waiting for her to call him.

He was.

She could see David's face as he looked towards the small webcam, he smiled at her then had to twist to avoid a small fist that shot up at his face. Wanda could hear him talking, and realised that he had Davy on his lap.

"Look, see, there's mommy."

Wanda made some funny faces as she looked at the screen of her tablet. She heard her son laughing and then his face came close as his nose almost touched David's webcam. She spoke to him, and told him she'd be home in a few days, and she wanted him to be good for 'Daddy'.

The little face disappeared, after David told him to sit quietly while he talked to Mommy.

"What's progress?" David asked her.

"Vera was right," Wanda said obliquely, knowing he would connect that with, "I found Nicole Wexford."

He didn't ask for details, for they had agreed to keep the Skype sessions to comments that would mean nothing if they were intercepted or overheard. She would type the details, encrypt the file and send it via email.

"What's been happening?" was her way of asking what he had found out from there.

David twisted around and freed one hand to pick up a manilla folder - his mime for sending her a file. He had been researching the companies and the people who were mentioned in Wexford's itinerary. There was a lot he could do via the internet and by sneaking into supposedly secure government and corporate sites.

"I will pick it up and read it in the morning. Later this morning," she corrected herself with a yawn. "It's past midnight here, but I will send that other stuff before I sleep."

"I'll see ya, then," David told her before closing the Skype connection.

Wanda did the same, and then went to her email program to retrieve and save the encrypted attachment that came with David's "Hope you are well" message.

That could wait; she needed to type a summary of her 'research' so far. Not that she had much to report, but she mentioned all she had done, what she had learned from Nicole, and referred to the policeman, the probable follower who may or not have been the police, and her visit to the Wexford apartment. When she finished, she encrypted the file using a program her cousin Erin had devised and sent it to David. Then she saved the encrypted file on her tablet, deleted the original plain text version and turned the tablet off.

Taking the tablet into the bedroom, she set it to charge, and went to take a shower. She wanted to wash the blond streaks out of her hair before she went to bed.

She was awake early, revved up for the job she had given herself and also quite hungry. Breakfast at the guesthouse was from six to eight am, so she had half an hour to wait. So instead of wasting the half hour, she read the file David had sent, read through Wexford's itinerary again, and planned how she would do her own checking of all the places and people.

By her estimation, Wexford should have been about half way

through his schedule of talks and visits. It was a realistic chance that one of the people, or places where he had been, was related to the reason for his disappearance. She did not want to alarm anyone and become the next to disappear, so her initial visits to the places would be by stealth. The police would soon be involved, and they could openly question the contacts, but might still learn nothing. She aimed to see if any of the contacts were hiding secrets. When she went back again, it would be as a representative of the US Embassy.

First thing after breakfast, she found her way to the nearest large shopping precinct and bought a number of gift items, then had each wrapped by the helpful shop assistants. While selecting those items, she found a stationers that had some excellent quality writing paper, along with ink pens, envelopes and gift tags.

Before heading back, she also called the US Embassy from a public phone and spoke to her contact.

He was able to tell her that the police had indeed contacted them, and they were able to confirm Nicole Wexford's identity, and Nicole herself was now safely installed in a guest room at the Embassy. He added that no mention had been made that her husband and daughter were missing, but only that the police offered to tell her husband where she was, and had been curious as to why her disappearance had not been reported. Thompson, expected a call back when the police could not find Wexford.

Wanda returned to her room, having spoken like a cheerful tourist to her hostess, and claimed she had been buying gifts for the relatives.

In the privacy of her room, Wanda set to work, first pulling on some close fitting gloves and then setting out her pens and stationary. She turned on her android tablet, in case David had sent more information through, and to retrieve some names he had sent her. With exquisite care, Wanda began to write on the gift tags, using neat, Slavic style calligraphy.

David knew how she worked, and had provided, amongst the other information, the names of the secretaries or Personal Assistants of the important men that Wexford was to speak to. All of her addressees, had been checked and seemed to be perfectly legitimate, and would be the recipients of her gifts.

They were anonymous 'thank-you' gifts, that would give her an excuse to visit each place, 'to deliver it personally', and cause a degree of office 'flutter' whilst she glanced around at the security set-up. If she was going to return at night, she needed the information, and she wanted to get all twelve places scouted during business hours.

With those preparations complete, Wanda carefully packed her gifts into one of the bags from the gift shops, and then stowed some other things into her small backpack. As she left the guesthouse, she smiled and waved at her hostess and headed for the nearest train station. In some shops nearby, she bought a greyish jacket that at a glance would pass as a uniform for a small courier company. At another shop, she bought a 'courier' style shoulder bag. Each of these went into the large plastic gift shop bag until she was alone in a cubicle in the ladies rest room of the station.

There, she set out the small personal grooming kit, and a selection of unlabelled opaque bottles.

In the ten minutes that she was occupying the cubicle, she gathered her loose hair into a severe style, part plaited, part coiled and pinned. Then she lightly rubbed a lotion over the top layer, to make it seem reddish-brown. She kept in the brown eye lenses, but used greasepaint to skilfully change the apparent lines of her face, put the jacket over her white shirt, and inverted her slacks so they were black, not fawn.

The woman who left the rest room and caught a train into the first district, looked nothing like the tourist from the 6th district.

Wanda's first destination was the furthest from the train station, and so she opted to take a taxi to the location. This was not the first place on Wexford's itinerary, nor one of the places on her mental list of possible enemies - it was a seemingly safe place to start her scouting forays, and practice her deception. Her plan was to make her way to the floor where her target worked, politely and insistently ask to see the recipient of her gift, deliver the attractively wrapped package, thank the person for seeing her, and withdraw before anyone thought to look at her. The distraction of the unexpected gift, and any waiting around time, would give her more than enough time for her to see what she needed to know about the security. Then she, a mere courier, a forgettable once off visitor, would be gone.

With her eidetic memory, Wanda had no need to record her observations at each place. Her memory for details was still as sharp as it had been when she had been doing this sort of work for crime lord Harrison Franklin. Neatly stored in her mind was each building, each business, names of people, the layout, the security and the ways in and out. If need be, she would be able to recall other details of each place as if she were back looking there.

After several deliveries, Wanda had begun to see a trend. All of the first four buildings, the furthest from the centre of Vienna, were older buildings. In each, the level of security was adequate for the types of businesses within, but nowhere near as sophisticated as she would have found in Los Angeles or San Francisco. She could not tell if the buildings had nightwatchmen either inside, or patrolling outside, but when she returned, she would be ready for both.

As she progressed, she came to more modern buildings, which were three or four stories high. The first two of these had manned reception desks on the ground floor. The first had been no trouble, the security man had been politely helpful. She had needed to sign a visitors' ledger, and sign out on her departure. For this, she had used an alias, and signed left handed.

The second of these, a four-storey building set back from the street, was the opposite. The guard at the desk was adamant on accepting the delivery, and refused to listen to Wanda's insistence that she had orders to deliver the package in person. He finally compromised by ringing the recipient, explaining the situation, and requesting the man to come down.

Wanda continued her innocent, naïve and polite manner as she waited, glancing around as if she had never seen such opulence in a building. She saw enough while she was waiting to know that the security here was 'ultra' and the switchboard for alarms was right behind the reception desk.

She spotted a man coming out of the elevator, heading towards the desk. Something about him raised her hackles. When the guard indicated her to the newcomer, he spoke to her civilly enough, but she had the sense of being looked down on, examined like an insect specimen, and after a long minute, disregarded as unimportant.

None of that feeling showed on her face, as she chatted like an animated doll, thanking the man for coming down, presenting him with the present, and turning to go.

"Who sent you to give this to me?" the man asked, holding the wrapped parcel as if someone had handed him a something totally useless.

"Sir, I am afraid that I have no idea. I am simply the courier. I expect that the information will be on the inside. Though sometimes, I think they must be some advertising thing." Wanda shrugged. "No matter to me if I am paid to bring it."

The man waved her off, and turned to stalk back to the elevator. Wanda wondered if he was going to toss the package in the first bin he came to, or if curiosity would get the better of him.

Since the man had been close to rude to the security guard, she made a point of thanking him for helping her, and then promptly departed towards the way out. Behind her, she heard the phone on the guard's desk ring, and inexplicably felt the urge to increase her casual pace. The wide-open foyer suddenly seemed to have a hundred cameras on her not just the four she had seen.

Her 'danger' sense had roused when the man had come from the elevator. It did not ease after she had left the building, but she forced herself to maintain a casual pace, as she returned past the stone statues of men and animals that adorned the forecourt. However, she went to the nearest bus stop and caught the first bus to arrive. After four blocks, she alighted and began to walk in a random direction. After two more blocks, she entered a building, also at random and studied the directory board. No one followed her in, and when she emerged, no one seemed to be watching her. Still reacting to what now seemed to be an irrational sense of being followed, she walked to the next building and repeated her action of scanning the directory board. This time she picked a name at random and since there was no reception desk in the building, she went to the elevator as if she had found the place for her next delivery.

The floor where the elevator delivered her had a ladies room, so she made use of it before returning to the ground floor.

Her danger sense had not fully abated, but it was now only a niggle, not a full scale alarm. She allowed herself a few minutes to recall all of her actions that morning, finally returning to the last delivery. From when she had left the building, to when she had caught the bus, there had been too little time for the man to have sent someone after her, unless he had recognised her 'gift' immediately, and used his mobile phone to activate someone. Maybe the guard had rushed to the door and seen her catch the bus? But he wouldn't have come after her. Someone else may have.

Wanda did not ignore her danger sense, and her immediate concern now was to be sure that no one was following her, but if she did feel someone was, to locate and identify them. She decided to do three more random, false deliveries, walking and using buses to move from place to place. After the third, the sense of being followed was gone. It seemed that she had convinced whoever it was, that she was of no importance.

Her mental map of Vienna enabled her to stay located during her diversions, and now, as she headed to her next actual destination, she considered what the alarm meant.

She had been thinking that Wexford had deliberately disappeared, and arranged to keep his daughter. Now, she wasn't so sure. No one should have been that alarmed by her little gifts, unless they had a seriously sensitive guilty conscience. So maybe, the other possibility had merit.

All the places that Wexford should have visited before he disappeared had been on a mental list that she had labelled as possibly related. Now she shuffled the list of places she had been to so that the place of that last delivery was at the top of the list, she deleted the locations of two of her deliveries, since they were later on his itinerary and he probably hadn't been there. Those that were left she kept in mind.

The scenario that made best sense to her was that someone in one of those companies had been spooked by her delivery, and for some reason called on people at that ultra security conscious place. That man may have scorned the caller until he too, received a similar delivery.

Did that man initially link her to Wexford, or had she hit on two businesses that were up to something illegal? Two apparently impeccable companies. Wanda made a mental note to get David to do some deeper digging into those people and places.

Whatever the reason, she was on the alert as she did her next four deliveries. After the last of these, she again had the sense of being watched. This time though, she spotted her tail easily. It was a woman about her age, and Wanda decided to make things easy for her by heading for some nearby shops, finding herself something to eat and drink, since it was well past lunchtime, and went outside to where she could sit in plain view, surrounded by hopeful pigeons. After half an hour, the woman gave up, and when she was out of sight, Wanda stood and headed for the train station and lost herself in the crowds. She took the train to the place that was last on her mental list - choosing to reverse the order of the rest of her delivery list.

At first, she didn't recognise the man talking to the receptionist. Then he half turned as if looking where he was being directed and she saw his face clearly. It was the policeman that she had met the previous night.

Without missing a step, she approached the desk but stopped a polite distance back from the speakers. As soon as the policeman moved towards the elevators, she scooted forwards and asked where her delivery recipient could be found.

"Second floor, at the end of the corridor," the woman said brusquely. She was busy patching in a line to call someone - probably to warn them that a policeman was coming up.

Wanda trotted to the elevators and called a request to, 'Hold it," as he was about to step in.

He did so, courteously preventing the doors from closing, so she could enter first. She knew he was studying her, but if she was simply who she was pretending to be, she would have nothing to worry about. However, she had the perfect way to ignore the policeman when she spotted the German shepherd in the elevator car. She stopped in the opening as if uncertain about the dog.

The policeman, Donau, murmured, "Back," and the dog obediently backed into one corner.

He added then, "My dog is called Alex. He won't hurt you. What floor did you need?"

"Second, thanks," Wanda used a voice that was slightly huskier sounding than her own and gave him a brief look as she edged in and away from the dog. She was in no way scared of it, just pretending.

Still trying to innocently ignore the policeman, she concentrated on the dog and tentatively extended her hand for it, no him, to sniff. She was rewarded with an enthusiastic lick, and she quickly withdrew her hand and wiped it on her slacks. The creature seemed to know darn well that she truly liked dogs. Just as well he couldn't talk.

Donau chuckled quietly. "He likes you."

"Yes, but I hope it is not so much that he is eyeing me for his dinner," Wanda responded quickly, giving the policeman a brief smile. "He's nice."

The door swept open then, and Donau gestured her out first. She gave him another smile for the courtesy, but stopped after getting out to look around as if uncertain where to go. The policeman strode past, the dog trotting at his side. She gave him a few moments to get ahead, and followed, but glancing from side to side at the closed doors as if looking where she had to go.

She entered the door at the end of the corridor about a minute after Donau, but she stopped inside the door to look around. She saw the policeman across the room talking to a woman at a desk, who was probably the person she herself wanted. It would not be wise to head directly there.

She noticed that the dog was not with the policeman and glanced around. Alex was flopped on the floor nearby, watching her. She merely looked back, and then turned her attention to the girl at the nearest of four desks who was busily typing in front of a computer.

"Excuse me. I have a person to person delivery for Heidi Lowenbach."

The girl looked up, took an earbud from her ear and apologetically asked Wanda what she had said.

After repeating it, the girl directed her. "Over there, talking to the man who just came in."

"Thanks," Wanda said dismissively, and as she strolled towards the woman, noticing everything.

She saw the 'big man' emerge from an office as he came out to greet Donau. While she waited politely for the woman to turn her attention from the men, so she could continue her courier act, she was aware that the 'big man' was staring at her. She sensed a definite surge of interest, but he had the policeman to deal with, and the two men went into his inner sanctum.

Wanda decided that he wasn't alarmed, but neither was he surprised. It was as if he had been told that a courier might arrive. This was the man Heinrich, who had supposedly invited Nicole Wexford to join her husband on the evening of her ordeal.

Some subtle tendril of warning shimmied down Wanda's spine, and she studied the woman as she presented the gift and gave her short explanation. Her instincts were on the alert, but the woman seemed to be what she was meant to be, although somewhat distracted by having the police visiting her boss. The arrival of a useless trinket, while giving her a thrill of surprise, was dismissed as soon as the courier girl started to leave.

Wanda paid extra attention to the signs of security in the big office, as she left without looking back. The business, according to David's notes, was a scientific supply company that also manufactured glass items for various uses. Wexford was scheduled to visit here during the three days he was out of contact with his wife. When she recalled the date, Wanda made a note to double check it as something didn't seem to add up. The American trade envoy may not have even got to this place, but she placed this business second on her 'hit list' for her upcoming night's work. Number one was the place that had the ultra-security, and third was the place that had warned number one about her. Though, she still had to identify which place it was.

Wanda finished her deliveries and headed back to the guesthouse. Her mind was only partly on her surroundings, the rest of her mind was revelling in the exhilaration of the brush with the policeman. That Donau didn't seem dull witted, but he had never even suspected that he had met her the night before. That he was completely ignorant of her planned night's work was an even greater boost to her ego. However, it also sent a warning through her whole being, that heightened her perceptions, prepared her mind for the need for extreme stealth and absolute attention to details.

At Neubaugasser station, she once again made use of the ladies room to brush most of the reddish tinge from her hair, and then used a moistened piece of paper towel to remove the final traces. She left her hair loose, and finally removed the courier jacket, and re-inverted her slacks so that once again, they were fawn in colour. Before putting the jacket and courier bag back into the gift shop bag, she removed her small backpack and put it on.

With one last mental check over, Wanda emerged and went looking for a light energy snack to eat as she returned to the guest house.

Chapter 4 - Night work

After typing and encrypting a report of her day's activities and all her observations, then sending it to David, she wandered down to the guesthouse office and found a young woman on duty. She guessed it was one of the hostess's daughters, and that suited her.

Casually, Wanda asked, "What can you do around here for fun? I have had enough of visiting obligations."

She returned upstairs with the addresses and directions to two nightclubs that were both in the first district, the film list at the Mariahilf theatre complex and the name of a dress boutique that sold evening and cocktail dresses.

Wanda made sure she was seen leaving by taxi, wearing her new evening clothes, a glittering tunic over black leggings. What no one would notice was the hood connected to the filmy black skivvy she had under the tunic. She changed her small backpack for an even smaller drawstring bag that she could later make into a lightweight carry bag. In it at that moment were the basic tools that she needed for lock picking, deactivating alarms and blanking security cameras as well as a pair of black gloves and light flexible shoes - both being made of light but strong non-slip rubber. The only other thing she added was her android tablet and a few short computer leads. They sat under a small purse with a tiny supply of makeup and some local currency.

She had not let any of her former skills lapse for lack of practice, and she felt as ready as she had ever been to do the task she had set herself. Now, the familiar pre-job anticipation was making her hyper-alert. The stakes were high in terms of personal danger, but the reward this time would not be money but personal satisfaction. She would find Rachael and Allan Wexford.

She went to one of the nightclubs until it was past ten o'clock, ensuring that the barman at least would recall her, then, before leaving, spent a few moments adding make up to her face to change her facial appearance. She went out and caught the first of several busses that would take her to her first destination. The bus took her past the building that was top of her list, but her scrutiny as she went past told her that the offices she wanted still had lights on. The building had internal security guards and she did not want to be rushed for time. She continued onto her second target - the place where she had seen the policeman.

Even at that time, the bus was a quarter full, and the people were orderly and polite, and the streets the bus traversed were quiet. Acting the tourist, Wanda struck up casual conversation with several of the passengers. She was told that Vienna was not like her American cities; it was safe to walk the streets. To her observation that she hadn't seen any police patrols, she was told that they weren't needed, but they were there.

She thanked the driver when she alighted near a hotel, and walked slowly until it was out of sight. Then she walked to where she could cut through to the adjacent street, where the Heinrich Scientific Glass premises were.

On the way, she slipped into a convenient shadow and removed her glittering top and rolled it up. Within moments, it was in the fully expanded drawstring bag. After that, she became a black shadow, flittering on the edges of the dim security lighting and avoiding the brighter streetlights.

In her mind was the data David had found about the company. It made specialised glass products for high tech companies, as well as medical and analytical labs. It was the sort of place that might hold corporate secrets in the form of their product specs.

Wanda crouched in a dark shadow just inside the boundary fence at the back, and watched for a time, seeing a guard come out, do a circuit of the building, checking all doors and windows, before returning inside. The light she could see from the back, must be where they spent time between patrols.

Wanda sprinted to the door and arrived just after it closed, when the guard pushed it fully shut, he would have assumed that it was locked. Her own extra senses told her when it was safe to sneak inside, and she had reclosed the door behind her when she heard the faintest of clicks. She moved her hand just over the lock mechanism and it tingled. The alarm had just been reset. That was not a problem. She could neutralise that before she left. And while it was armed, the guards would be feeling secure.

It was easy for her to scout the building, to get her bearings and locate additional ways out. The ground floor was mostly the storerooms and manufacturing, which explained why the offices were on the second floor. She activated the camera interference device, which had the effect of freezing the image on the recording screen until she was past it. It was very effective unless the monitoring guard saw someone there that suddenly stopped and then was feet away a moment later. She didn't plan to make such a mistake.

She went to the door leading into the large open plan office. The double glass doors were closed now, and only dim security lights illuminated the deserted office. Before entering, Wanda checked for alarms, her small sensor device detected a slight current, and she went to work to provide a bypass circuit. Within a minute, she was through the door, leaving the bypass in position.

Her first action was to go to the desk used by the boss's personal assistant and check all the drawers - forcing the two that were locked. She flicked through the files in one, and the personal trivia in the other, and then re-locked both. She used the earphones to listen at random to several Dictaphone tapes, and then began to boot up the computer with the screen off. Now she put to use the teaching of her cousin Erin, who was highly skilled at infiltrating computer systems. An unobtrusive cable went from an output jack on the computer, to an input jack on her five inch tablet.

While she waited, she crawled under the desk, where she was in shadow, and so the light from her tablet was blocked from chance observation.

From her device, she ran a 'force open' program, which her cousin had created for her. In simple terms, it was a quick and nasty backdoor bypass of any system security. It would definitely be frowned on if anyone legal learnt the purpose of the tiny program, and she could be killed for it if a criminal did. When time was at a premium, as it was this time, she felt the risk justified.

Within a very short time, Wanda was free to rifle through the contents of the computer, accessing and sampling company files, correspondence, the boss's calendar, and the PA's private calendar.

She was able to confirm that Wexford had indeed visited the company, and the date, which she estimated to have been the day before he disappeared. She found a copy of the draft agreement between the company and the US Department of Industry. Proof of these things she saved onto her tablet, in an encrypted form. As an afterthought, she saved the diary entries from both the boss, Heinrich and the PA. The latter had a cryptic 'meeting with AS' entry for the evening of the day of Wexford's visit.

Using her tablet to control the computer, Wanda told it to shut down, and withdrew her cable before it finished. Her intrusion there had taken less than fifteen minutes, and she was wondering if the guard would be patrolling the second floor. If they did, she would hear him trying the door and have warning, but for now, she wanted to get into the bosses office and look around.

With the camera freeze device activated again, she crawled to the door of the inner office, had the lock opened within moments, and went inside. She locked the door behind her and quickly set to work. While the computer there was waking up, she searched the office checking the drawers, the desk, opening the safe and checking there. Finding nothing of interest, she repeated her hacking of the computer security and found the boss's private correspondence and emails. Her first randomly chosen entry made her body go tense, and without reading further, copied the whole file of correspondence, did a bulk forward of emails to one of her prearranged hotmail addresses, and quickly shut the computer down again, and removed her cables.

Just as that finished, a slight sound at the door alerted her and she ran for the office 'ensuite' that she had found in her initial search. With that door locked behind her, she shoved her tablet and cables into her bag, and shrugged it on her shoulders. Then she stood on the toilet and forced open a window above it. It wasn't easy to slither out, but her memory recalled her scan of the exterior done at her earlier visit. There ought to be a pipe going up close to this window. There was, and she clung to this and eased the window almost fully closed.

She hoped that as the window was small and on the second floor, they would not consider it a security threat or possible breach. She glanced down and around. She was in shadow, at the side of the building, so not directly visible from the road, and while she stayed still she should not be noticed. A light breeze was moving the branches of a leafy tree that grew between her and the nearest street light. That was a piece of luck.

She was about to climb down when she heard the sound of car doors opening and closing. Changing her position slightly enabled her to see the end of a dark coloured car. As she watched, two uniformed men strolled into view. Either they were police or more security men, but they did not think to look up. One flashed his light at the doors and windows on the ground floor, as another rattled the front glass entry door.

An inner prompting told her to keep still and keep watching. She was rewarded by seeing a third uniformed man, one she had not expected, lighting a cigarette, and then moving back out of sight. Another prompting told her to get down, fast, and get away. She never ignored those subtle feelings. And as soon as her feet touched the ground, she trotted towards the road, using every bit of shadow, and listening out for the cigarette smoking officer.

Just before she stepped out onto the footpath, she replaced her glittering top. When the car emerged from the front carpark of the scientific glass place, she was waiting with two other people at the nearby bus stop. Now she could tell that it was a security company car, not the police.

As she took buses to get her across the city, Wanda prioritised her intended missions. There was no way she could visit all twelve places in one night. The three in district one, in particular, were going to need time. If the way was clear at her primary target, she intended to infiltrate it that night. If it wasn't, that would be her goal for the following night - a Saturday.

There were still lights on at midnight, Wanda noted, so tomorrow it would be. She stayed on the bus and headed for where she had done her first four deliveries that morning.

At each place, she became like a shadow - removing the glittery top and hiding it then pulling up the black hood so it covered most of her face. The first of the buildings was very easy to enter, there was no security guard, and the alarms were outdated. Within an hour, she was finished. She learnt nothing of use, except that Wexford was due to visit there in two days' time. She once again hacked the computers, and saved random files.

The second place was not far away, and she slipped through the darkness to get there. Checking it out was a repeat of the previous foray. She found no mention of Wexford in the computer diary, and once again sampled files and emails. She noted with interest that both this place and the last, sourced hard to get items for high tech companies. The first had been an import-export company, the second a commodities trader.

The third place out of this group of four was the headquarters for an electronic parts manufacturer, and Wexford had been there on the third day of his tour. While sampling files and electronic correspondence, she found nothing to make her think this place was doing anything illegal.

The last of the places was little more than a two-room office on the fourth floor of a slightly more modern building. David's research indicated that the building had eight tenants, two on each floor. When she had visited in her guise as courier, she had assumed that the door behind the secretary had led to a larger area.

Mentally, she reviewed her impressions of the place. The other business on the floor had wide glass fronted doors, leading into the reception area, and glass walls for half the distance along the passage giving a view of a number of product displays - white goods and household appliances.

There were similar windows along the other side of the passage, but these were blocked with opaque material. From the passage, the view through the glass entrance doors was blocked by a decorative screen with the company name. Wanda, using her habitual precautions, forced the doors open after checking and finding no alarms. A faint shiver of warning made her extra cautious.

The lock had been modern, but inside the reception area was as empty as before - several chairs, a table with the sales brochures for a wide range of entertainment equipment, the secretary's desk with the oil-filled puzzle and paperweight in a prominent position.

There were no locked drawers or cabinets. The desk held necessary stationary, the cabinets had more of the brochures that were on display, along with order forms and invoice forms. The computer was not even password protected, and the files on it were dull - import and export documents for televisions, stereos, computers and the like or routine correspondence with customers.

Wanda looked for the appointment calendar for the boss, it was nearly empty, and she memorised the few entries. All the dates were in the future, and Wexford was not mentioned. Or was the secretary in the habit of erasing the details of visitors after they had been?

An oddity, to add to the question of why Wexford had this place on his itinerary. Perhaps the inner office would tell her why.

She stiffened when she realised that the door had not even been locked, but although the oddness of the place was giving her warning shivers, no one was in there.

She entered and shone the narrow beam of her torch around the room. It was smaller than the reception area, and even emptier. The bookshelf was empty, the filing cabinet was only for show, the desk had no drawers to hide anything and all that was on it was an ashtray with two types of cigarette butts and a phone unit. What was glaringly obvious was the lack of a computer.

Now, Wanda's danger sense was rousing. She continued her survey of the room and found the built in cupboard. She forced open one side and the other wouldn't budge. It seemed that it had never been used and when it had been painted, it had been sealed shut.

The side of the cupboard that was used had shelves with catalogues from wholesale suppliers, as opposed to the retail supplier catalogues on display in the outer area.

A narrow slit, no more than a quarter inch wide, was all that could be seen of the other side of the wardrobe. Wanda shone the torch in and saw what seemed to be a coat hanging on a rack. She left there and considered what the absence of a computer could mean.

She checked the phone with her gloved hands, confirming it had a dial tone. That suggested that the business hadn't recently moved away. The phone didn't have a way to connect a computer to the internet, but these days a computer could use wi-fi for that. A laptop computer...that could be taken away with the boss and so leave no potentially incriminating information lying around.

Considering what she had been doing that night, Wanda thought, whoever this man was, he had the mind of a criminal.

That made Wanda's mind switch into a higher gear. What she had seen of the two rooms suggested that he was a middleman between customers and suppliers - in all things electrical. Were his suppliers drop-shippers? Possible. But there were those displays across the passage...

Her mind was intrigued by the mystery, and she still wanted to know why Wexford was to come here.

She shone the torch on the cupboard again, and decided to try to get the other side open. She used a narrow file, to feel up and down the slit, and this time found out why the door would not open. There was a tiny bolt at the top and the bottom with a flap in the dividing panel that moved enough for her hand to reach them. Once each bolt was moved out of the hole, the door swung open easily.

Wanda saw the panel with many glowing green LEDs and one that was red. She recognised it as an alarm panel, and used the torch to read the labels. The red light had 'main office', the others were labelled by room.

He danger sense roused fully. She rechecked the room, and still saw no movement sensors or cameras. That didn't rule out pressure sensors, but surely, if these alarms were monitored, someone would have come by now? It was time to go. With a final quick flick of the torch into the area around the alarm board, Wanda rebolted the door, and took herself out of the inner office, back through the outer office and into the passage.

The other business's area, now interested her, because the other lights on the board had to refer to somewhere. With more speed and less finesse, Wanda let herself into the area on the other side of the passage. Once through the inner door, her quick survey with the torch beam gave her the impression of a warehouse - the boxes probably held electrical goods, but they were unlabelled. She withdrew, and returned to the passage. Now she was ready to leave, using the back fire-stairs, by which she had arrived.

On the next floor down, once she had checked she was alone, she took a few moments to check out the businesses on that floor. The layout was the same as on the level above - receptionist desk in plain view, and instead of a boss's office behind, there were storerooms. One side had wine and cigarettes, the other had DVDs, CDs and computer software.

As she emerged, she caught a flash of light - the number of the floor on the elevator. She saw it flash from three to four. Time she was gone!

Wanda retreated with every sense alert for trouble, but no one challenged her. She left via a back driveway, avoiding a car that was parked in the small car parking area. When she was well away from that place, she resumed her 'nightclub' clothing, and minimised her drawstring bag, and shrugged her arms back through the strings, the way she had carried it all night.

The busses had ceased running about an hour before, but Wanda knew she was not far from one of the stations, and there she found a taxi to take her back to the guesthouse.

None of the staff saw her return, and she used her key to get in.

Even though she did not believe anyone could have guessed her night's activity, Wanda checked her room thoroughly, comparing what she saw now with her memory of how everything had been when she left. Nothing had been disturbed, and her little tell tales - such as the cotton strung across doorways a fraction of an inch off the floor, or a wisp of fluff caught in a closed door, were not disturbed.

Such precautions were an instinctual habit, especially when she was working on her own. And only after assuring herself that her bolt hole was secure, did she change from the black outfit and glittery top into her sleeping clothes. After taking her tablet from the pack, Wanda stuffed the pack in amongst the clothes in her case. Not the most secure of places, but okay if no one suspected her activities.

As soon as she turned her tablet back on, she saw it needed charging, and after seeing to that, she sorted all of her copied files into folders, compressed the files and sent them in an email to David. Then she checked for messages and activated Skype.

The receipt of her email, resulted in David's face appearing on the screen of her tablet.

He moved back and she heard him ask, "Busy?"

"No, had enough of nightclubs for one night." David would know it was four am where she was, and he knew what she had intended to do.

"Any recommendations?"

"I can see why items 15 and 2 are on the list, but not 7, 9 and 4."

Wanda saw David's start of interest as he checked the references. She added, "Number 7 is something to do with the never ending back paddock problem."

"A fence?" David silently formed the word and let his wife read his lips.

"Number 4 maybe as well. That being the case, I can't say I am much further ahead."

"What's next?"

"More of the same. See if you can make anything of what I sent you. Have you had luck with the officials?"

David shook his head. He had been trying to get a line into the Vienna police computer network. "I think I need your cousin's help - they must be cagey blighters. However, the USE," David stressed the word and waited for Wanda to nod, she had his meaning - the United States Embassy, "Has things safe, quiet and co-operating but unhelpful."

Wanda took that to mean that Nicole Wexford was still claiming amnesia.

She asked then, "Number 3?" That was to indicate that she wanted to know if he answers to the third thing she had asked him to check.

David showed her an image of a police official, it was Donau.

"What does he know?"

In answer, David held up a file folder and pointed at the webcam. The info would be in what he had sent her.

"I'll check that," Wanda told him and then gave the cut the

connection sign. Not that she really wanted to, because talking to David over Skype was as close as she could get to being with him. However, they had agreed to keep the sessions short, in case of intentional or inadvertent eavesdroppers.

Wanda shoved aside any regrets; they would only distract her. Instead, she opened the file David had sent and read his answers to her questions, and his comments on what she had given him. He had not suggested anything she had not already thought of, but maybe he could make something of the latest lot of miscellaneous files.

At least, if she had to be alone, having David available via internet was a bonus. He was able to do research for her.

That made her recall the file on what the police were finding out. Since he couldn't get into the official police site, what had he discovered?

Most of it, Wanda already knew - that Nicole was settled in at the embassy, and the diplomatic aides had confirmed her identity and advised the police of the names and descriptions of her husband and daughter. They passed on the address where the family had been living, and Allan Wexford's reason for being in Vienna - basically described as trade talks. The policeman, Donau, had asked for and received a copy of his proposed itinerary. He had kept his promise to keep the embassy advised of his progress, but so far, he had only confirmed the places he had visited and those he hadn't.

However, knowing that meant that she did not need to return to all the places and ask those obvious questions.

Her own forays of the past night had actually netted more information than the policeman's face to face visits.

Wanda wondered if Donau shared her confusion over some of the companies Wexford was to visit. Though that last one, the fly-by-night place, David had checked. His business name and the website hype seemed legitimate. There had been no apparent complaints against the company.

The one where she had seen Donau, was legitimate, and there was enough content on the web to confirm it was a reputable business.

What she would dearly like to know was how Donau went when

speaking to the contacts at the Alpha Prime building. She doubted if he would discover any more than if he had been there or not. He should have been there in the first week of his trip to Vienna.

After a huge yawn, Wanda decided to go over the rest of David's replies after she had caught up on some sleep.

Chapter 5 - The Prime Target

Her sleep brought on no revelations. Except for the sense that Wexford's trip wasn't what the US Government thought it was and her feeling that some of those businesses were fronts for shady or criminal enterprises, she was no closer to finding him.

She was still in two minds about whether this was an abduction, as Nicole believed it to be, or if Wexford had walked out on her.

Maybe if she could get Nicole to talk about Allan, and their marriage and home life, she might get a better feel for the kind of man Wexford was.

Wanda knew that Nicole would be waiting to hear back from Tatiana Carson, but she did not want to see the woman until she had a better idea of what might have happened. She could delay talking to her a day or two, and then she would question her again.

Her only hope to finding Wexford was to track his movements, and that brought her back to her plans for the day. She wanted to scout the outside of the building that was at the top of her list. So when she went down to breakfast, half an hour before they finished serving, she asked her hostess about the building with the statues. She had to explain where it was, but then her hostess was full of information about the statues, what they represented, the story behind them, praise for Herr Wessler, the owner of Alpha Prime, because he had created many low cost housing places for the poorer people of Vienna.

Wanda managed to change the subject to places she really should see whilst in the city. She listened to the suggestions, and managed to sound excited. Therefore, her hostess was not surprised when she left with a backpack containing food, water, and a camera, and her clothes and shoes were suited to walking.

Used to cities like Los Angeles or San Francisco, it had not occurred to Wanda that so many places in Vienna would be closed on Saturdays, and that many more would shut in the afternoon.

She became aware of the difference as she travelled by bus into the first district. The pedestrians she saw walking along the streets had a more casual air about them - they were not hurrying to or from their jobs. Many were strolling along, looking at the architecture of the buildings, others were shopping, either for necessities if they were locals, or souvenirs if they were visitors.

Wanda was thoughtful, and decided to change her plans. She could see how this more casual attitude would work in her favour.

Instead of going to Alpha Prime first, she made her way in turn to three of the nearer places. Two of these were very modern buildings, but on the weekend, they were practically deserted. At the first, the on duty guard sat at the reception desk, alternately reading and staring out the front glass doors, and only left his station to go to the gents toilets. Wanda walked in, brazenly, and was out of sight before the guard returned. The alarm system was cursory, for several other people had gone in and passed the guard without question.

She easily avoided these few people, none of which were interested in the office that was her target. She had plenty of time to work uninterrupted, copy random files and correspondence, even do a little surfing the internet to find where she could get some equipment she might need. On her way out, she simply walked out.

To enter the second place, she needed to neutralise the alarm on a side entrance, but again, she worked undisturbed and left the same way, to go and mingle once again with the weekend strollers, and stop every now and then to take unimportant pictures with her digital camera.

Wanda arrived outside Alpha Prime near half past eleven, and studied the building whilst she meandered around the stone statues - taking photos of each, from several angles. In time, she worked her way to the glass doors, and glanced inside. There was still a guard at the reception desk, and the occasional person crossing the huge open foyer to go the elevators or to leave the building.

The front door was not going to be her way in; it was too open. She needed to find a less obtrusive way, and she had two options. On one side of the building was the entrance to a carpark. That attracted her attention first. She saw a car approach via a short driveway, moving slowly because some people seemed oblivious that they were walking on a piece of road. It began a turn, into an opening in the side of the building. The drivers arm reached out and touched a card to a sloped panel on a pillar. She saw a boom go up, and the car drove in. She glanced up at the side of this lower building - at the front, the arched windows were glazed. At the side, they weren't - the building was the carpark. Moving nearer, Wanda saw there were two booms, one to stop people going in, another to stop people coming out. She considered ducking under the boom to go in and look around, but when she changed her position, the sun reflected off a small round object attached to the wall. There were three in a vertical line there and three matching ones on the other side of the opening. To her experience eye, they would send an alarm if someone broke an invisible beam.

Changing her focus, she glanced through the gap between the buildings. Above the gap was a sign relating to the carpark fees and hours. There was an electronic billboard above that, level with the second floor...right next to the office she intended to visit. She considered it. There was a gap between the frame and the wall of the building - she could slip through. The board could hide her actions - if she were to break in through the window.

To see what was behind it, Wanda went openly into the gap, past the carpark entrance, and rested her back against the wall, pretending to need to get a stone from her shoe. Further in was a garden, but a glass fence blocked her from walking to it. Beyond that, she saw two covered in crossovers between the Alpha Prime Building and the carpark building - she estimated one was on the second floor and the other on the third floor.

As her eyes scanned the area, memorising every detail as she considered ways to enter the building, she glanced up and realised that this side area was covered over with clear glass. It wasn't enclosed, for she could feel a breeze funnelling through the gap. She could make an approach to the second floor from the ground, but... there might be a better way on the other side of the building.

A ten-foot wide driveway that led to the rear of the building, separated the Alpha Prime building from its other neighbour. A sign in German, when translated, indicated that deliveries went to the rear.

Moving casually, and pretending to be mostly interested in the traditional architecture of the older building, Wanda moved along the driveway. Glancing now and then at the more modern building, as if to contrast the hexagonal tessellated concrete slabs that formed its side walls with the large windows and decorative ledges, her mind considered how easy it would be to climb up or down the side of the older building. She casually glanced up to assess the gap between the two buildings.

Continuing her stroll, she noted the external security cameras attached to the Alpha Prime building, they covered the driveway, but she gave no sign that she was anything more than a casual explorer.

At the rear of the two buildings were yards where goods could be picked up or delivered, but only a relatively small van could turn around in the restricted area.

Wanda noticed the oddity of a pest control van parked at the back of the modern building. She saw two men in long sleeved white coveralls carrying gear inside and contemplated sneaking in. In fact, she had begun to move that way when she saw the grey uniform of a guard. It was a timely observation, for she did not have all the equipment she needed to explore that building. But an idea had begun to form, and she backed into the yard of the older building until she was out of sight. From there, she studied what she could see of the upper section of the wall of the Alpha Prime building.

The back and sides were vastly different to the glass frontage. On the sides, of the upper level, there was a row of rectangular windows, seemingly in pairs, but set into the same unclimbable flat concrete wall segments. Each pair fitted into one of the hexagonal blocks. At the back, the windows were smaller - probably they were in rooms used as rest rooms or staff lunchrooms. There were some similar windows on what was probably the third level - along the side of the building.

In terms of forcing entry, the older building beside her would be absurdly simple to get into, but the Alpha Prime building would take all her skill - or would it? She wondered what the roof of that building was like. Often the security there was the least stringent, particularly when it seemed impossible for anyone to get onto the roof without going through the building.

But, ten feet across, and one storey up - coming from the old building to the new - for her, it was do-able. She had most of what she needed, and could get the rest without rousing anyone's suspicions. However, she would need to see what the roof of the older building was like, and scout it so she knew her way around.

It was the work of moments to open the door. Cards that had been tucked into the frame during the guards' rounds of the previous night fell down, but she didn't let that worry her. It was merely another way by which the two buildings differed - the other building had electronic punch-ins - something she had noted subconsciously or her visit as courier.

Once in, she began to scout the building, floor by floor. As well as learning all the routes through the offices and other rooms, she confirmed that the building was deserted. The roof was accessed by the fire stairs, and she found no alarm on the door leading out. But, now she had to be careful. Some of the windows in the side wall of Alpha Prime, overlooked this lower roof. Keeping low - she moved behind the safety wall of the roof until she was behind one of the air circulation ducts.

She could now study the top edges of the hexagons, but still not see the roof itself. The tops and dips in the hexagon pattern, would make her plan easier, but she still wanted to get a picture of what to expect over there.

While she sat hidden by the duct, she took out her Android tablet, to see if she could find a wi-fi connection she could tap into to check Google Earth. She hoped people in Vienna were not as security conscious as those back in the US.

The strongest signal was encrypted, the next one wasn't, but it was weaker. She tried it anyway, and was rewarded with connecting to the internet. She brought up Google Earth and homed in on her position. She studied the roof of Alpha Prime, though on her small 5 inch screen, she could only get the overall picture, not a great deal of detail. She identified the air ducts, the two lift housings, the fire stairs, a communications tower and other unidentifiable objects. There was no hope of determining if they had security cameras up there but it was more information that she had before, anyway.

On a whim, she opened Skype and then sent an email to David, just a 'hello' message. He might not yet be awake, but if he was, he would hear the message tone and guess she was waiting on Skype.

A few minutes later, when his face appeared on her screen, he did look as if he had just risen from bed.

"Hiya, sleepy," she greeted.

David yawned as he said, "Morning. Anything for me?"

"Nah, it's a nice warm day and I am out enjoying the sunshine."

Wanda saw her husband grimace. "It has been pouring down here."

She replied, "We needed the rain."

"Yeah, but Davy has discovered mud!" David told her, with a wry shrug.

Wanda grinned back at him as the connection wavered. "I'll be in touch later. I have some research to finish and a busy night of hitting the high spots of Vienna."

"Be careful," she was told in turn. "And check the weather before you go out. There is a cold front heading your way."

David closed the connection before she could, and Wanda considered his warning. She found a local weather site and the forecast there reassured her. Vienna was meant to remain fine until Sunday. Before she thought to do more, the wi-fi connection dropped out.

As she thought about leaving the roof to return to her lodgings, she considered the powerful wi-fi signal. The answer was in her sight. Alpha Prime had an ultra-modern building, with the latest high-tech mod cons. That powerful encrypted wi-fi source had to be from there.

Before acting on the rash idea that had occurred to her, she sat back and recalled everything her cousin Erin had taught her about wi-fi, computer security and computer hacking. Generally, she left the computer stuff to David, but here was an unparalleled opportunity to use a highly secret little program that Erin had sent her before she had left LA. She called it a 'quick-hack' program.

She copied the wi-fi source name and link into the program and ran it.

Moments later, a multi-character string of digits appeared on her screen, and she saved it. Then she copied it into the space for a password, when trying to link to the wi-fi source. She grinned when she saw the bright green logo of Alpha Prime appear on the screen.

Before she tried anything else, she strengthened the firewalls on her tablet, to prevent return intrusions or attacks from Alpha Prime's computer security. She was right inside the firewall of the company, and all files appeared open to her probing. Yet, she decided not to try prying into Wessler's files. He may have extra protection on them that would activate if a distant computer tried to read the files.

Instead, she probed carefully, first finding and bringing up floor plans of each floor, and getting a security overlay that had rooms coloured green, orange or red. She saved the pages and retreated, making certain to break the wi-fi connection by turning her tablet off. It was time for her to leave until nearer night-time.

Chapter 6 - Unexpected events

In the privacy of her room, Wanda checked her gear as she packed it into a compact backpack. The bulkiest part was the high tensile rope she had purchased on her way back. It wasn't very thick, but she had twenty feet of it. The heaviest part was the folding grapple hook that she would shoot across from the old building to the new. She had two of the compressed air canisters that fit the modified flare gun. In a smaller bag, one that strapped around her waist, she had her collection of illegal tools, several cards that looked like credit cards, but which would allow her to override the electronic locks used around the Alpha Prime building, and a collection of different computer leads that should enable her to connect her android tablet to any computer. Her tablet was placed in a padded pocket on the side of her dark coloured, close-fitting trousers.

The waist bag, she hid by pulling on a lightweight, hooded, zip-up jacket. It was bright red and dark blue, but she shoved a very light weight black hooded skivvy, into the top of the bag along with her tiny makeup kit - refilled with all she needed to change her appearance for the night. In her pocket was a small amount of cash, but no identification.

When she walked through the guesthouse foyer, she returned the greeting of the man on duty. This was the son of the owners, but not the one she had met on her arrival, but she chattily told him that she was meeting a cousin for a picnic on the banks of the Danube.

He kept his response to, "It's a nice night for it," and went back to reading a magazine at the counter.

A couple of tourists arrived, with luggage, and headed for the reception desk. Wanda smiled at them, and let them in before exiting the front door.

As she walked towards the bus stop, anyone seeing her would think she was off for a hike. Her feet were wearing strong walking boots, which had the advantage of hiding the thick rubber-soled climbing shoes. No one looking at her would think she was planning a daring infiltration into one of Vienna's newest buildings.

The bus took her to one of the riverside stops, near to a block of public toilets. This was where she planned to change her appearance to a dark haired, Slavic-featured woman. Then, when she left, she would work her way to the building beside her target. It was her intention to be in place there well before the first rounds of the nightwatchmen. Once she was there, she would wait and hide until it was dark enough for her to be next to invisible when crossing from roof to roof.

With the change in appearance, Wanda became like a different person. When she stopped for a coffee and bagel, she spoke in flawless German, imitating the local idiom perfectly. The vendor had no suspicions, and chatted to her as if she were a local. He spoke differently to those who were obviously tourists.

She walked from there to another bus route, and rode the bus into the centre of town. Here she saw her first police patrol, eyeing off a trio of rowdy young men. She stopped, as if reluctant to go near them.

"Do you have a problem?" a polite voice asked her. She turned sharply and saw one of the police officers.

"Trying to decide if I should detour around that group," she claimed.

"I will have a word with them," he offered. "Where are you headed?"

Without needing time to think, Wanda recalled the mental map of this area and named a street a few blocks further on. "Wintergarten Strasse. I am meeting my boyfriend. We're going hiking in the forest tomorrow."

Since she looked the part, and was in no way nervous in the policeman's company, the man never suspected she was anything but a law abiding woman. He escorted her past the three men, and went to speak to them after he left her.

When they returned to their car to resume their patrol, Wanda was well out of sight, on a bus heading towards Alpha Prime.

The first part of her plan went without a hitch. She slipped into the yard behind Alpha Prime, from the service alley behind it, and then dashed into the smaller yard of the adjoining building.

In passing, she noted that the pest controller van was there again. They were extra people she would have to avoid. In moments, she was inside the older building, having noted that there were no new security cards in place yet. She stopped just inside to get the feel of the building, and give her other senses a chance to work. This was one factor that made her a 'lucky' thief.

Wanda knew it wasn't luck, she could sense when other people were nearby. Now though, she sensed she was alone, and went quickly to the top floor, choosing to wait inside until it got dark.

Taking off her pack, she used it as a seat and took out her tablet. The first thing she did was reduce the brightness of the screen. When she needed to use it, she also needed to keep the glow from betraying her. Then she used the 'quick hack' program to get the password for Alpha Prime's wi-fi network again. It was as well that she did, the password had changed.

She inserted herself into the security program once again, observing the various screens, but not trying to change anything.

She had thought the building would be deserted. It wasn't, and she decided that all the orange areas, that indicated people, could not be due to the pest controllers. Much of the building was green - deserted, but there were red indicators around the rear loading dock. She found the meaning of that as being a security breach, and assumed it was red because at this time, that entrance should be locked.

In the back of her mind, she was amused by there being pest controllers in that building. What ever they were dealing with, they were not prepared for the kind of pest that she was.

Wanda allowed herself to smile as she brought up the security schematics, and looked for cameras on the roof. There was one, but it was focussed on the door to the stairwell, and took in the lift housings as well. It made sense - if people were up here for a nefarious purpose, they would probably be entering or leaving by the stairway. There was an alarm there too, but neither that or the camera would be a problem.

As it grew darker, Wanda mentally rehearsed her intended actions. First, pulling on the strong flexible climbing gloves, and then removing her climbing equipment from the pack. She filled the empty space with the bright coloured jacket and the boots that were hiding her climbing shoes. Once she emerged from the stairway, she immediately went to work.

One end of her line was tied to a stanchion she had noted on her earlier visit. The grapnel was attached to the other end of the line, and the end of the hook was protruding from the flare gun.

Taking a precautionary look over the edge of the roof, down to the ground below, Wanda saw no one walking along the lighted road, but a car was paused at the roadway with its lights adding extra illumination. She considered that the light would blind the driver's night vision, but she waited to see what the car would do. When it began to move along the road, she counted slowly, and when she estimated that it would be below, she fired the gun, sending the grapple soaring across the gap. The sound of the car engine, soft as it was, covered the whoosh of the gas canister decompressing and the clunk of the metal catching on the concrete.

Giving the rope a sharp tug, Wanda tested the result. The hook had opened up and was holding firmly. Now she pulled in the slack, and re-tied her end of the rope. Then she donned a rope harness, with a second line attached to it. She ran the line out so that when she began to climb, it would be pulled behind her. Once the converted flare gun was put in her bag, and that pushed into a dark shaded area, she was ready. Without more than another precautionary look below, she climbed onto the top of the roof wall, grabbed the line and began to pull herself upward along it. She had prepared this line with hand loops at half-metre intervals, to help her climb. If anyone looked up, the security lights would make it difficult to see a dark shape moving along a dark line.

It might have been five years since she had last done this, but she hadn't lost the knack, or forgotten any of the precautions drilled into her by her one time partner Harry. She was still as fit now as she had been then.

When she reached the other roof, and pulled herself over with the skill of an Olympic gymnast, her mind was in high gear, and focussed on what she needed to do.

She arrived out of the camera's field of view, and prepared her way back. The line attached to the grapnel was untied, and retied to the base of one of the air conditioner units, but it was now tied so that a tug on the second line would release it when she was back on the other roof. All she needed to do was keep tension off that second line until she was ready to release it. The grapnel was folded up and placed near the second line and her harness, for her to collect on her way back. For now, it was extra weight.

The roof was deserted, she was sure of that, and now she needed to blind the camera eye, but so her tampering was not immediately noticed. She was counting on the person who monitored the camera feeds, to ignore the roof, since it was the least likely place for an intruder to want to be. Still, she moved carefully, not wanting a shadow to be noticed by the camera. She approached from behind it, and ever so slowly, moved its field of view so she had a narrow field of approach.

During that stealthy approach, she had found a piece of metal that had fallen off one of the air-con housings. It would be useful if she needed to jam the stairway door during her getaway.

Then, when she could work there unseen, she created a wire bypass for the alarm circuit, and opened the door just enough for her slim frame to edge in.

The first thing she did once in was to check the security picture. There was no red colour for the roof, so her bypass was working. The fourth floor was green - deserted, the third had orange areas - possibly guards and maybe some were the pest guys. The second floor was the same and someone was in the office she wanted to visit. Maybe it was a cleaner who would be finished soon.

Still, she had work to do on the third floor first, creating alternate ways out. On the side where she had climbed over, she wanted to open a window just below, as she had already opened one in the other building. Then, she needed to do the same on the far side of the third floor, in whatever office was directly above that which was her target.

Before moving down the stairs, she activated the camera interference device, so that any camera within a circle of three metres around her, would freeze its image. She still instinctively looked for them, but that distance was usually far enough for her to be around a corner before the effect was ended.

fter opening the first window and leaving that area - a tearoom, judging by the tables, chairs and mini kitchen - Wanda proceeded cautiously, but quickly along a deserted passage way that passed closed offices, meeting rooms, storerooms, and the lift-wells and stairs. She was careful approaching the corner, for her senses were warning her that someone was nearby. The echo of voices over the guard's radio warned her that he was close. Without needing to stop and consider, she rapidly forced the lock on the nearest office with a swipe of her override card, and slipped inside. The mental map in her mind of the green and orange areas, combined with her instincts, told her the room was safe. She locked the door behind her, and put her ear to it, trying to listen for when the guard moved away.

The man seemed to have stopped by her door, and now Wanda began to question her choice of rooms. This one had dim lights still on, where all other offices were completely dark. Why?

Then the door knob moved under her light touch and the guard's voice came plainly, as he spoke to his controller. "The pest guys have cleared this floor. I'm going to open some windows, the smell is too strong up here."

Wanda stopped listening and trotted to the door of the inner office, forced it using the override card again and entered. She kept the door open a crack to see what the guard did. He mentioned opening windows, and the outer office area she had dashed through had windows that opened facing the delivery road. This inner office, was one that faced the main road, had the floor to ceiling windows which did not open.

She eased the door closed, and allowed it to lock as the guard came near. The handle rattled once, and Wanda was sure that guard was moving away, but something warned her to stay where she was.

Curious about the office and why it had the security lighting, Wanda moved from the door to the desk. She was safe enough from being seen from the outside for the windows had vertical blinds that were already closed.

The user of the office was Rudolf Fischer and the name meant nothing to her. The outer door had listed no business name, but it was apparent from his open organiser, that he was a busy man.

His appointment calendar for the previous few weeks indicated that he travelled frequently. The places he went, Amsterdam, Antwerp, and others, suggested he was a gem trader or diamond broker.

The idea occurred to her that if she wanted a distraction from her actual target, this was a prime one. If her intrusion were discovered, this would be a more logical place for a thief to intend to be.

She did not find the impulse to find and open the safe to be at all foolish. Her reasoning seemed sound. In fact, finding the supposedly well-hidden safe was child's play - not behind the unimpressive modern painting, but in the wall at the end of a storeroom, that had shelves of boxes and mailing envelopes and other packaging needs.

The safe itself was modern, but not the newest kind, and she had it open before she stopped to reconsider. To see inside, she needed to use her tiny torch, but there was no worry about that being seen. Her hand touched the collection of soft leather bags, feeling the hard stones within. She grabbed one of the bags, but pulled two out. Putting the torch in her pocket, Wanda opened one of the bags, but dropped the other. The first bag held small industrial sized diamonds, and she closed that carefully and reached down for the one she'd dropped.

Barely had she touched them than her danger sense kicked in. She dropped the first bag and pushed the door of the safe closed. Before leaving the storeroom, she pulled out her tablet and checked the security diagram. Fischer's office and the outer office were green, the way to the office above Wessler's was green. The cause of her alarm was not apparent, but she never ignored her sense of danger. Her mind went back to her task, and it seemed the way was clear for her to continue.

The guard had done her work for her. Windows were open on the other side of the building too, so Wanda did not stay on the third floor. She needed to go down a level and check out Wessler's office.

Rather than retrace her steps to the back stairs, Wanda forced open a door that said maintenance, and came off the inner side of the passage near the lifts. She had guessed correctly. There would be a way down to the lower floor that by-passed the actual lifts and the stairs. It had the extra advantage, of bringing her down close to the office she wanted.

Wanda checked her tablet and saw that the front of the building was now green, but the passage accessing the back offices had sections of orange. When she emerged, she heard some kind of motor running, and guessed the sound was coming from where the orange sections were. She wasted no time running to the front corner office, noticing in passing a cart she thought was a cleaner's cart. She paused when she found the outer door to Wessler's office propped open, but when she saw the open windows, assumed it was to clear the smell. That made her task both easier and more dangerous. She could not guess when the guards might return to close the windows, or if they would spend more time in this corner. That thought, made her decide to ignore the PA's desk in the outer office and go straight to Wessler's private domain.

Wanda used the furniture to screen her from view as she approached the inner door. This office had glass windows facing the passage way - and a guard simply had to glance in...

Maybe that was why her danger sense had not abated. Once again, she checked her tablet. The office still showed green, but there was something amiss.

As she was crouching behind the PA's desk, she only needed to reach out to touch the handle for the inner door. Very slowly, she tested it...it turned.

Wanda held her breath, and listened, trying to hear if there were any sounds within. Caution warred with her belief that the office was empty and this was the chance she needed. Ideas flicked through her mind, but she finally concluded, that if someone was in the office, they were in there for some un-official reason. She would enter, in an unexpected way, and she would be ready to overcome them.

Instead of standing and walking in, she remained crouched and slowly pushed the door open. In her hand was her only weapon, a sharp knife that she carried in case she had to cut one of her ropes in a hurry. She had the advantage of the light coming in through the glass window, and saw a shadow waiting inside the door, pressed against the wall.

The arm that reached out at standing height, met nothing. The man who glanced around the door, saw nothing, until the point of a blade just touched his chin. He went rigid as Wanda stood up, but spoke calmly and quietly.

"I will have to remember that trick."

It was Wanda's turn to go still. She knew that voice.

"Nicholas? What are you doing here?"

The man didn't answer until he had pulled her into the office. "Jim didn't say you would be here! What are you doing? Does he know?"

Aware that time was precious, she said quickly, "Yes and no. I need to access the computer. You do what you were doing."

Wanda set to work at once, connecting the computer to her tablet, and starting the computer with the screen off. She was not surprised that it started fast, for surely a man like Wessler would have the latest and best of everything.

After she sampled random files, she set the computer to copy file after file to the tablet. It would take some minutes, and during that time, Wanda checked the office, and found that Wessler had an ensuite. Was that the latest thing in executive office design? The idea amused her, as she looked in and saw the window that faced the side of the building.

As her tablet gave a soft ping, she heard Nicholas curse. He was trying to open the safe, and had just realised he had failed. Before detaching her tablet, she ghosted up to Nicholas, whispered, "Let me," and edged him aside. She had the safe open in minutes, almost as if she had used magic to do it. Nicholas moved back into place and Wanda disconnected her tablet and closed the computer down. Her senses were telling her she needed to hurry. She voiced a warning to Nicholas, but he was already hurrying, removing files from the safe, selecting certain ones, and adding pages from a folder he must have had inside his white coveralls.

A whisper of a voice, suggested he had an earpiece in and was getting a warning from another of Jim's team.

"Hurry," Wanda urged again, waiting near the door.

The safe was shut, everything back in place. She let Nicholas out the door, began to follow, but her danger sense peaked again, and she ducked behind a desk and watched.

The guards came by when Nicholas was back at his trolley, and had hoisted a spraying hose over his shoulder. When she saw one guard starting to frisk him, she slipped back into the inner office, locked the door and made for the en-suite. At least Nicholas had a cover - as a pest controller - she didn't. She had a few moments while they checked him, and maybe they would not come this far in, but it was not safe to assume it.

With a fleeting awareness of the irony, Wanda stood on the toilet and opened the small window - recalling a similar escape the previous night.

The sense of danger was strong as she pulled herself out the window by holding onto the frame. Her feet had only just disappeared when she heard the door open and saw the glow of the light.

Outside, she had to contend with the strong wind that had sprung up, for it was rushing through between the buildings, and trying to scrape her off the wall. As she inched along, concentrating on feeling with her fingers and toes for the gaps between the hexagonal panels, she heard the voice of the guard. She doubted that he would be able to look out far enough to see her, but she was moving into the alcove of the next window.

"Did you check this window earlier?" A pause, and another voice was muffled. "Well it's open. So it was probably the wind that caused the signal."

As soon as she heard the window shut, Wanda began edging back towards it. She wanted to get up a level, but the glass that covered the gap between buildings was between her and the open third floor windows. She recalled her observations from earlier in the day and her belief that she could fit between the electronic billboard and the wall. That was her quickest way up, but was it the best? She was hidden from the road at the moment, but she might be seen as she climbed up onto the glass roof. Maybe, she wouldn't have to go right out. Maybe there would be a gap between the board and the glass roof?

Her progress was slow, but at least the en-suite window was dark, as she edged past it. When she reached the electronic board, she wanted to laugh. There was a maintenance ladder, going up. The board must be serviced by people who approached via the glass roof. It eased one concern, that of whether the glass would hold her weight.

The smell of rain on the wind accompanied a stronger wind gust as she stepped onto the glass. All the windows along the building were dark, she passed a small window like the one below in Wessler's en-suite, and moved to the first of the larger windows, that would be in his outer office. The vertical blinds were rattling due to the wind, but the darkness reassured her. She slipped in, moving with the blinds, and then moved out from behind them. The noise of the wind, and the distant rumble of thunder, made it impossible to hear any quiet sounds, but there was no reason for guards to be waiting here in the dark for her, or for anyone else. Yet it felt like the hair on her neck was trying to stand up.

The room was too dark. The dim lights in the passages were off! She kept moving around the edge of the room to the door; the darkness was a bonus, it would make her escape easier. She glanced to where she had seen movement sensors - the red lights were off! The power must have gone off.

Suddenly, Wanda felt the need to run, and she did - through the propped open door, and along the passage. Her direction was instinctive, and she went back towards the jewel merchant's office, and slowed before she ran into the wall. Then, she began to hear muted clicks and the usually unnoticed hum of the air circulation system.

In that instant, the knowledge hit her. The power had gone off, and now a generator had cut in. It would only power essential systems - security? Dim lighting came on, she had to get out!

It was only an instinct, but she guessed that with the mains power off, the wi-fi link between the sensors and the security board might revert to wired. Her interference device may not work. As soon as she turned into the far passage, an eerie wailing almost deafened her. She sprinted the final way to the fire stairs, entered the stairwell and ran up to the roof. Once there, she shut the door and jammed it with the piece of metal, and removed her wire alarm by-pass.

The wind felt even stronger up on the roof, and now she could see the lightning as well as hear the thunder. Subconsciously, she counted the seconds between the lightning and the thunder. Not too bad, it was still several miles away, but there was dampness in the wind. She had the wind at her back as she ran to her line and re-tested its hold. Then she felt for the grapnel, and shoved it in her pocket. Her retreat was doubly dangerous in the wind, and getting over the edge of the roof the most perilous part, but she had the loops to help her.

There was no time to worry about how long it would take the guards to figure out where she went. She needed to concentrate on her hold on the rope.

A third of the way across, she began to hear a noise above that of the wind. Someone was pounding on the door, trying to force it open.

Wanda told herself, "Don't think of that. It will hold. They won't see you..."

She didn't stop moving, kept her eyes on the roof ahead, and her hands moving her along as she dangled down from the rope.

Lightning flashed overhead, and she heard, "There he is!" She hoped they didn't have guns ready to fire, but she pushed such thoughts aside.

A sharp jerk on the line tied to her harness, almost made her fall. Instinct made her grip the rope tighter, as a surge of adrenaline gave her the energy to move faster. If the men yanked on that line, in the other direction...

All tension went off the rope, and Wanda's body acted instinctively as she began to fall. The wind was blowing from her right, but gravity was taking her down, the end or the rope still fixed to the older building turned her into a pendulum but she twisted so that her feet took the jarring shock. The grapnel fell from her pocket and landed with a loud clang below.

The flash of light had shown her where she was in relation to the open window, and as the thunder rumbled loud and close, she turned her motion into a climb, and walked the few feet sideways so she could dive feet first inside the building.

In a fluid motion, she removed the harness, took her knife from its sheath and cut the release line free. It would fall to the ground, but even if found, it would not be connected to her. She tossed the end of the shortened mainline out the window, and closed the panes, just as a torch played over the side of the building. She ducked down, out of sight, and scuttled a few feet before straightening.

She had to leave, fast, before they sent anyone to watch the building - her pack on the roof would give no clues, all the incriminating equipment was on her - in the waist bag, or her pockets.

On the ground floor, she glanced towards the street entrance, and saw the flash of blue lights coming through the glass of the main doors. She backed away, towards the rear, but heard someone shaking the door, trying to get in. She was trapped!

Wanda ran back upstairs, knowing that she needed to hide any evidence that would connect her to the fleeing intruder. First to the roof to get her pack, and to retrieve the rest of the line. She took out her jacket and donned it, pulled the hiking boots over her suspicious footwear, and shoved the harness and the short length of line in with the flare gun.

Her mind then recalled the janitor's closet on the upper floor. Such a bag would not look obviously out of place there and she was acting on the idea even as she thought on it.

That room wasn't even locked, and she dumped the bag almost in plain view. She used her torch to see what else was there that might help her. She located the source of a particularly strong smell, and found a pile of rags that must have been used for polishing woodwork somewhere in the building. She was reaching for them as she considered where to hide her tablet.

Selecting the least strongly smelling cloth, she un-wadded it and then drew out her android tablet and turned it off. Now, even if it were found, even the cleverest IT expert would not be able to break her password protection. However, she did not want it found, and so she wrapped it in the rag, hoping it would not be damaged, and placed it at the back of a head high shelf. Then she threw the other rags bag into a pile on top, and put the tins of polish in front of them. That left her waist bag, and the loose equipment still in her pockets.

As she emptied her pockets, she considered whether to hide these things in the room as well, or somewhere else. The latter, she decided, as she began shoving the loose things into the waist bag. Her hand touched something soft, and she turned her torch on the object, expecting it to be another of the rags, but it wasn't.

It was like someone had just forced the air from her lungs. She recognised the bag, felt it over and confirmed there were hard objects with in.

"Shit!"

For a moment she was too stunned to move. The realisation that she had taken the stones, and even now she could not recall doing so, was unbelievable. She had never, ever, taken things without meaning to - without remembering.

The sound of more sirens finally penetrated her shock. It meant more police were arriving. The stones, she had to hide. If she were to be found, they would damn her. In a frenzy of activity, she returned to the shelf with the rags, and found one to wrap the bag in. She put them where her tablet was, and then decided to take that with her. She placed the waist bag in a bin filled with miscellaneous cleaning equipment, and pushed it to the bottom. She deliberately spilled a little disinfectant, to provide an off-putting smell.

Now her mind turned to the best place to hide. The roof, she decided. Any normal thief would be trying to dodge the police. The guards assumed she was a man, but since she wasn't, and was also smaller and slenderer than a grown man, she could hide in places that might be disregarded.

Her sense of danger was at full alert, and that meant she had little time. Indeed, as she began to run up the stairs to the roof, she could hear noises below her within the building. She ran faster, reaching the roof and locking the door behind her. Instinct took her to a small corner, behind an air con unit, but another thought intruded. She had to hide her tablet, and if she left it here, and it rained, it might be damaged. She also had her knife, and she didn't want to have that if she were found. It was a dangerous weapon. However, it was also very useful. She used it to pry up a section of the housing, on the far side from her intended hiding place - just enough to slip her tablet out of sight, and then she tossed the knife from the far side of the roof from Alpha Prime.

She dived into cover, just as the door to the roof opened, and the wind made it bang against the wall. As the footsteps trotted out onto the concrete, she made herself as small a heap as possible, and became still. Clearing her mind, she imagined a deserted roof and hoped that the searchers would get that idea.

It seemed to work, for after an initial look around, when a torch narrowly missed throwing light on her, they police officers began to retreat, talking amongst themselves about where to look next. They had instructions to search the building, but did not believe they would find anyone.

Wanda began a mental mantra, "There is no one here. There is no one here."

Her relief when they returned to the stairs was short lived. A voice, full of authority and somehow familiar, directed the other officers to look for where the intruder had tied the line.

He went on to say, "Most of it was in the laneway, but he was seen crossing back to here. Those thoughtless fools, untied the rope, but there is no sign that anyone fell. It was still attached this end. The intruder must have returned here, because the rope they found down there was cut."

For a time, the men were scouring the roof near where she had tied the rope, but there was nothing to find.

The lightning showed a tall man standing back, watching the search, when Wanda dared a peek from her hiding place. She felt a few heavy drops of rain and changed her mental mantra to, "Pour down, rain like hell."

It was probably coincidence, when the rain did indeed begin to come down in torrents, but she was elated. The police were running for shelter, and her coat was providing her with some protection.

Somehow, the identity of the ranking police officer had not occurred to her, but when a moist, cold object forced its way into her hood, and an even wetter floppy object licked her face, she controlled the urge to curse aloud. She turned to see glistening eyes at the other end of a dark snout, looking quizzically at her.

"Go away!" she whispered, also telling the creature, mentally, to leave her alone.

The dog gave a quiet whine, but didn't move.

The damage was done. The fool creature had been followed, and a torch shone down into her hiding place.

"Stand up and keep your hands where I can see them," the familiar voice that she now knew to belonged to Kommissar Donau, was polite, but held a note of warning.

Wanda quashed the 'gone' feeling. She might be caught, but she had no intention of staying that way. At least, her makeup made her look nothing like the people she had been playing when they had met on either of the previous times, though, the rain that was still drenching them, might be playing havoc with it.

"Come out of there. Slowly."

Deciding that for now, compliance would be a valuable diversionary tactic, she obeyed. When Donau realised that she was a female, what would he do?

The dog had woofed softly, when she had been told to come out, as if he agreed that she should. To give her time to think of a story, she acted as if her legs needed to have the circulation return to normal. She stamped her feet a few times before moving. The dog licked her hand, and she gave his nose a quick rub.

She sensed, the hand that flicked the hood from her face, allowing the light to shine in her eyes. It went down at a quiet command from Donau, but in the movement, she saw that a second police officer held a gun.

"Do you wish to stay in the rain all night?" Donau enquired. "I asked you to come out."

This time the dog nudged her leg and one of the officers grabbed her arm, and began to pull her forward.

When she was out of her awkward corner, Wanda felt her wrists being grabbed and forced behind her. She was hustled towards the door, as if the officer was keen to get out of the rain. Donau and the other officer followed, close behind.

As soon as he was inside, the dog, Alex, shook himself vigorously. Donau made a sound like a disgusted growl, and told his dog, "I didn't need to be any wetter! And I can't shake it off like you can."

In spite of her predicament, Wanda turned her head away to hide a smile. Donau had a coat on, and would not be as wet as she felt herself to be.

"We will go downstairs," Donau decided, and Wanda was led to the stairs and warned by the man holding her, "Don't try anything."

Wanda volunteered no speech, and Donau asked no questions on the way down. However, she sensed he was studying her, as if he felt he should know who she was.

Once they were on the ground floor, he walked around to face her. "Nothing to say?"

He had a handkerchief out of his pocket, and was holding it

casually, still studying her.

"Why were you on the roof?"

Wanda scrunched her shoulders and in perfect idiomatic German, and the Austrian dialect, volunteered, "I was hiding."

One of the officers gave a laugh, and said, "That's for sure, but why?"

Another man hurried towards then demanding, "How did you get in?"

Wanda looked at her feet, and shrugged, "Snuck in, Friday night."

"Why?" the same man demanded, his face an angry shade of red.

"Needed somewhere to sleep."

When Wanda wasn't expecting it, Donau reached out and held her chin, forcing her head up to look at him. He wiped her face with his handkerchief, preventing her from ducking away. When he released her, he studied the flesh coloured marks on the cloth, before returning it to his pocket.

"Maybe you did," he decided to say. "But you are unlawfully on private premises, and we are looking for a daring intruder who crossed to this building by rope, from the building next door."

Wanda's did not try to look away now. "That's why I was hiding. I didn't want to be seen." She knew that by keeping eye contact, the man would think she was telling the truth.

"Maybe so, and it seems that Alex here, likes you. What can you can tell us about the man you saw?"

Wanda considered what facts were irrefutable, and which were not and spun her story.

"I was in the little kitchen room, where they keep biscuits, and I heard someone moving around. Thought it was the guy who owns the place. So I hid. But the steps went up. I stayed where I was, and curled up in a corner. Must have slept and when I woke I needed the loo, real bad. I was in there when I heard noises in the office room with all the books. Sounded like someone had jumped on the floor and fallen over. It got quiet for a bit, and I peeked out. Saw a figure come out and go downstairs, I dashed back to the kitchen, but then he came running back up like you lot were after him. Didn't see where he went, but I heard noises like he was moving junk around. I figured he wouldn't want to go to the roof and be cornered, so I snuck up there. Didn't realise it was going to rain."

When Donau gestured to one of the officers, and Wanda felt herself being frisked, she wondered if he believed her.

"Take her in. I will talk to her again later."

The impersonal hands finished their job, and reported, "Clean."

Donau nodded, and shrugged towards the front door. "Bring in enough men to search this building."

Wanda breathed a sigh of relief. It seemed that Donau believed her, or at least found her story plausible, and was not expecting her to give trouble. Yet, she had followed a narrow path between truth and fiction. She hoped that he would not find her waist bag, for though she could replace the tools, the cards for the electronic locks were custom made. She didn't care about the backpack, and its contents. Maybe if they found that they would stop looking. Or the damn stones. She didn't want to touch them again. Trouble was, Donau had that brown-eyed sniffer with him. Those dogs were too smart by half. What if he found where she hid her tablet? Or would the rain wash the smell away? With any luck, if they found the pack, and the stones, they would stop looking.

Either way, she didn't intend to get to wherever she was supposed to be going, and would be keeping a low profile, in her guesthouse bolt hole.

Chapter 8 - Worried friends

"That's it, Jim," Nicholas finished. "They must have found her. She didn't follow me out."

Behind the two men, Max Hart lowered binoculars from his eyes, but continued to scan the view down the street from within the dark coloured van. "Then why did the police rush into the other building?"

"She couldn't follow you out," Jim Phillips said quietly, he did not want anyone outside the van to hear them talking. "Wanda always has more than one escape route. The important thing is that you, Max and Grant were out before the police arrived. Are you absolutely sure that they think diamonds were stolen?"

Max answered that. "I heard them mention an open safe on the third floor, and that the thief had dropped a bag of diamonds...I think that was why we were frisked before they let us leave, and wouldn't let us take the equipment."

"We were in plain sight when the alarms began," Nicholas reminded his friend.

The fourth member of the team, who was listening to the police radio frequencies, removed the earbud from his ear and said, "The power went off, and the alarm started after the generator cut in. The alarms might have reset. Some of the guards did suddenly race upstairs."

Nicholas Black asked the question that concerned him. "Are we going to do something to help her?"

Jim shook his head. "We have work to do."

None of them were comfortable with the idea of leaving a friend, one who had often worked with them, in trouble. However, Jim was right. The mission came first and Wanda was doing her own thing.

"Let's go," Jim directed.

Wanda allowed herself to be pushed into the police car, and since it hadn't stopped teeming down, took perverse delight in making the vinyl seats, slippery wet. It also gave her an excuse to wriggle, claiming her hands were cold and she was trying to warm them.

When her escort slipped in after her, she flung her head around, and showered his face with flying drips, and then quietly apologised. She knew that the man was not thinking her dangerous, and tending to believe her 'homeless' story. He did not seem alarmed when she continued to wriggle, though he did suggest that she sat still. Wanda chose to obey, for by then, the real purpose of her unsettled movements had been achieved. She had worked a short piece of wire from her belt, one of several she had along its length, and used it to pick the locks on the handcuffs. Now, though she appeared docile and yawned for effect, she was keenly watching where they were going, and waiting for a chance.

The officer next to her reacted fast, but Wanda had been faster. As the car turned left, and the officer caught a hint of activity outside the car, she opened the door, flung it wide and she dove out in a seemingly suicidal move. But she had timed it to perfection, there were no cars beside them, as she hit the road, rolled, and after springing to her feet, raced across the rest of the road and into a crowd just about to enter a train station.

The police car screeched to a sliding stop, and the two officers came racing after their prisoner, but they had to avoid cars first, and the heavy rain and the people soon precluded sight of the woman.

They returned to the car and called in reinforcements, but they second car arrived too late. The bus pulled away as the extra officers arrived.

Wanda was soaked, but so were most of the other passengers. She was lucky that her bus ticket was still legible, lucky that she had left it in her pocket, and lucky that she had found those damned diamonds and not still had them on her, unrealised.

The euphoria of a successful raid, bubbled up inside her. It didn't matter that she had been caught for a short while, she had got free. She recalled that this feeling had once been like a drug to her, and her mind asked whether she had taken those diamonds to feel this thrill again.

Then the thrill abated abruptly. Those damned stones. Whatever had possessed her? She didn't need money, she didn't have to do it to obey the dead and damned Harrison Franklin, and she was no kleptomaniac. If the police didn't find the stones, she would have to get the things to the police - as soon as possible.

A different kind of mirth overcame her, at the audacious idea her mind had just given her. She would go back there, tonight. She didn't need fancy tools to get back into that place, and it was the last place that the police would expect to find her right now.

There was no hurry, Wanda knew, as the number of passengers decreased in ones, twos and threes. It was late, they all wanted to get home. She waited until the rain eased, and then buzzed to alight at the next stop. When the bus drove off, and its lights disappeared around a corner, she crossed the nearly deserted side road, and walked two blocks back to the main road. She took another bus that was heading back to the city. From the route number on the bus sign, she knew it passed within two blocks of Alpha Prime, and when she was at the closest point of approach, she alighted and began to walk.

An occasional car passed her, spraying up water from their tyres, adding to the rain. She heard a truck engine and glanced over her shoulder. A dark van was slowing, but it didn't have Polizei emblazoned on the side, so she kept walking, though watching for trouble. It pulled in a few car lengths ahead, where there was space at the kerb, and she slowed her pace.

An umbrella poked out the passenger door, and then a woman stepped out. She stayed next to the van, turning so that the streetlight lit her face. Wanda slowed further, but she had recognised Casey Randall, and understood the slight shoulder shrug that meant, "Get in."

With a shrug of her own, Wanda approached, and when the rear door opened right beside her, she changed direction and stepped up.

She was not surprised to see Jim Phillips inside, and she knew him well enough to sense he was not pleased. However, before he could speak, Casey did.

"I thought Jim was mad to think you would come back here."

Mad is correct, Wanda thought as Jim voiced his first question. "What were you doing, you little fool?"

Wanda chose to misconstrue his question, wondering what he

knew of what she had done. "Going where you would find me," was her instant response.

As the van pulled back out into the traffic, she heard a faint chuckle from the driver's seat. Max, she decided. She watched Jim as he closed his mouth and seemed to be mentally counting to ten. She dared to take a seat next to Casey, and Jim relaxed enough to sit on the bench seat opposite.

"We need to talk," he told her. "But first, why were you headed back to the Alpha Prime Building? The police are still there in force."

"I wasn't going back there," Wanda stated, no longer being smart mouthed. "I was going back to the building beside it. I left some stuff there."

"The police found a backpack with some rope and a flare gun," Jim told her. "That is all they said on the radio." He watched Wanda closely, and saw her alertness. "Was there anything else?"

She nodded. "My little bag of tricks. I hid that separately, in the trolley in a cleaner's room on the top floor. And my tablet is shoved under the metal side of one of the ducts on the roof. I chucked my knife off the far side of the building."

"Casey?" Jim queried.

"I will go in tomorrow," she promised.

"If the police haven't found them," Jim reminded her. "What about the diamonds?"

Wanda opened her mouth to say, "What?", but squirmed instead and admitted, "I wrapped them in some smelly polish rags and shoved them to the back of a shelf in the cleaner's room."

Jim simply shook his head, refraining from further comment on that topic. "Where are you staying?"

She told him.

"Do you want to go there?"

"I don't have my key. I was intending to return in daylight when the door is open."

"Max, take us back to the hotel."

Jim gave Wanda time for a hot shower, in the suite that he was using as his headquarters. Max had coffee ready for her when she emerged wearing one of Casey's lounging robes, and with her hair wrapped in a towel turban. Her clothes were draped over the heater, drying.

Once Wanda was sipping hot coffee, Jim got straight to the point. "Have you found Wexford yet?"

She sat down so she could put the hot cup down on a low table. This room was as impersonal as the apartment she had searched, except for some cases placed on a table and a case rack.

"No, all I have done is check the daily schedules of some of the men he was meant to see, to try to confirm who he saw just before he apparently disappeared. I was checking their computers, for appointments, correspondence, and any indication of odd behaviour.

"The first day I was here, I visited each place as a courier and checked the security. Well, except Alpha Prime - that place was next thing to a fortress."

"So Nicholas said," Jim admitted, sitting down in a second chair. "It was fortunate that you were there, but why was it so imperative for you to pay that place a visit?"

"When I was playing courier, the guy that is Wessler's PA, was an arrogant, condescending so and so. Also, when I left there, I was followed."

Jim nodded, as if her observations confirmed some theory he had, but he didn't explain. "How many places have you got back to?"

"Eleven. In most places, the security was basic."

"Wexford's itinerary, tell me your impressions of each place."

She didn't quiz Jim, or demand to know why he wanted the information, because his mission was 'need to know' and she was coming to the conclusion that Wexford and his disappearance was connected to it.

"I haven't studied all the files I copied, but I sent them to David to go through," Wanda began, with perfect seriousness, and she sipped at her coffee to give herself time to reorder her memories. "I haven't heard back from David on last night's stuff, or sent what I got tonight. From what I have seen though, I don't know why Wexford was to speak to some of those people. Two I would swear were just high volume fences, and one keeps all his business on a lap top. That is Franz Lunn..."

Wanda reported in detail, relating her observations of each place she had been to.

Jim watched her while she spoke, concentrating and adding all she said to the information in his own mind.

"It agrees with the information we have," Jim commented once she had finished. "So it is your gut instinct that we have encountered some sort of criminal cartel here?"

"I hadn't quite gone that far," Wanda admitted. "I was trying to decide if Wexford hadn't just walked out on Nichole and taken his daughter."

Jim tapped his chin a few times, and came to a decision. "We are here to break up a criminal trade cartel. The head man is believed to be Wessler of Alpha Prime. The second in command is Franz Lunn. Our information is that they are planning a coup that will seriously affect America's trade relations and well as destabilising the Euro. It might also throw the world's economy into a major recession."

"And Wexford is involved?" Wanda asked.

"No, he was the one who warned the State Department. He was going to allow himself to be drawn into the conspiracy. We think he was taken because he was onto them. His reports stopped the day that we think Nicole and the daughter went missing."

"Why take them both, and let Nicole loose?" Wanda asked, rethinking her ideas. "I mean, if they wanted to force him to do something, wouldn't having them both be greater leverage?"

"You have some doubts?" Jim probed, knowing Wanda's intuition was often acute.

"Yes, but I can't really say why. It's nothing I can really point to. I mean, they knocked Nicole out when they took Rachel, but they didn't kill her. She got away, and could tell the police about them. Admittedly, they scared her silent, but they might not have."

"They might have thought she was dead," Jim suggested. "She was beaten severely and unconscious for three days."

"Oh..." It was Wanda's turn to think. "So Wexford has been gone longer than I thought. Nicole said he had been gone three days with no contact, then he rang to tell her to come to the Heinrich's place with Rachel. She was attacked that day, was unconscious for three more after she was found. And it's been what - another four since then? Nicole knew he was going to be away, and he had given her a contact number, but she couldn't reach him there. When he rang about going to the Heinrich's he claimed his phone had been flat, and he'd forgotten his charger. Maybe he lost it, because it wasn't in the apartment when I searched. So when was it that he contacted the State Department about this crime thing?"

"A week ago," Jim said. "I can understand why you are uneasy."

"We are only guessing the timing," Wanda countered, staring at Jim before asking, "What do you want me to do?"

"Keep trying to find Wexford."

For a long moment, Wanda considered how she would need to change her tactics, but then the question surfaced, and she blurted it out, almost challengingly. "When the cartel disbands, can you guarantee that Wexford and his daughter will be freed?"

"If we find them we will get them away," Jim promised.

"In other words, no guarantee," Wanda stated.

"Wexford knew the risks."

"Crap! If he did, and he decided on this insane plan, he should have sent his family home."

"His wife might have refused," Jim countered.

Wanda had an idea he was right, but Nicole hadn't mentioned anything risky. "What time frame do I have?"

Jim considered. "Three days."

Wanda swore under her breath, she was already chafing at her lack of progress.

"I think you should present your credentials to the local police and work with them," Jim advised, standing up.

"And you called me a fool for going back to get my stuff," Wanda muttered.

"Go as yourself, not one of your alter-egos." He looked down at her with a serious expression.

"I will think about it, Jim, but I really don't think it is a good idea. It would limit me too much. As a free, unknown agent, I can do things and find out things that the local police couldn't."

"Perhaps," Jim admitted. "But we also need to find out what they know."

"I'd rather have someone else liaising with them. I would trust Donau, I think, but right now he probably has a five star manhunt out for me, and I think he half suspects that he had met me before. I know he is asking about Wexford's movements, doing what I was going to do next. However, I don't think anyone who is part of your cartel will tell him anything besides, 'yes he was here', 'he didn't show', or 'who do you mean?'"

Max Hart, who was listening, while slouching against one wall, interrupted the conversation by remarking, "You do have a way of stirring up policemen."

"Yeah, somewhat," Wanda agreed, she took a sip of the coffee that was now at a drinkable temperature. Her mind was considering ways to go on looking for Wexford that didn't involve the police and would keep her away from the people Jim was 'investigating'.

"I think I need to talk to Nicole again. Last time, I was just off a 15 hour trip and she was probably doped up."

"A good idea," Jim agreed. "Why don't you get some sleep, and organise that tomorrow?"

Wanda understood that was a tacit dismissal, and stood up, glancing around for a couch to crawl onto.

Max seemed to read her mind. "There's a spare bed in there. I won't be needing it tonight." He gestured with his thumb at one of the doors leading off this main one.

Returning from his nights work, Max brought with him a copy of the first edition of one of Vienna's daily newspapers. He showed it to Jim, who had risen early and was preparing for his role that day by getting Casey to change the look of his face. They both studied an artist's sketch in the paper, which was a very good likeness of one of Wanda's 'faces'. Jim sighed, and asked, "What does it say?"

Max translated the text and summarised it. "Basically, the police are hunting a jewel thief who stole gems worth thousands of Euros, but left behind some industrial diamonds worth only hundreds of Euros. They mention the escape and suggest that the person is a jewel thief the police have been hunting for some months."

"No way," Wanda blurted, having emerged to hear the last of the translation. "They are not going to try to hang that on me." She held out her hand for the paper to read the article in full.

"I suppose your exploits will serve as a distraction to those I am to meet today," Jim murmured.

"Maybe," Wanda agreed. "I'm more concerned that they don't think I went into Wessler's office, or that I might be looking for clues to Wexford...I would rather they worried about something else."

Jim twisted away from Casey's attention, and she made a disgusted sound. "Do you think they might connect you to Wexford?"

Wanda considered what she had just said, "I still don't know if it was the police who tailed me after I saw Nicole, or some other group, and the fact that my innocent deliveries caused someone to have me followed. They might think that I, or someone I work for, is onto their cartel - not sussing for Wexford."

"Wanda, be very, very careful," Jim warned her. "Seriously!"

"I know I was acting like a hyped up teenager last night, but believe me, I am now remembering that I am a mother - seriously."

"Do that, and keep in touch with David or Neil Thompson. If I need to get a message to you, I will do it through them. You don't have a cell phone do you?"

"No, just my tablet." Wanda grimaced, remembering she didn't even have that at the moment.

"Stay here until Casey gets back," Jim told her.

Chapter 9 - Hiding the traces

Casey spoke to the owner of the historic little building where Wanda had left her things. She produced a laminated ID card, made that morning by Grant Collier, and introduced herself as a representative of the pest control company that had dealt with a beetle infestation in the neighbouring building.

From the moment she began to speak, she sensed that the man, Ernst Hilbert, was paying scant heed to her story, but willing to go along with it so that this beautiful woman would stay around. It was exactly the reaction she had set out to achieve.

"So you see, we have to find where the horrible things were coming from. So I need to check dark, cluttered places," she spoke in a husky voice, which hinted at gratitude for his help.

She glanced at the back yard with a stack of shipping crates, stacked up, and suggested that the creatures might hide around such things.

Hilbert glanced from the decidedly feminine company rep to the heavy crates and gallantly offered to check there for her.

"You should really check inside as well," she suggested, "Do you have many dark enclosed rooms?"

He told her that most of the building was open, except for the janitor's rooms, one on the ground floor and the other on the top floor.

"If it is fine with you, I will check there while you do out here. I have a lot of places to check today."

After receiving an immediate agreement, Casey went inside, making a show of looking down into the angles between doors and walls. She carried a brief case, and had taken out a clipboard before she had rung Hilbert's door chime. She had also taken out a plastic bag of dead black beetles and strewn them around the back yard, amongst the crates. Finding them should make him hunt more carefully.

Since she knew exactly where to go, Casey went immediately to the top floor janitor's room, but wasn't hopeful of finding anything.

The room showed signs of a search, and they had found Wanda's backpack here. She rifled through the rubbish bag on the cleaner's trolley first, found a couple of x-rated magazines under the top layer of trash, and the smelly rags Wanda had said she put in there. She dug deeper and found the small, soft drawstring bag, and felt the laminated cards, and the long thin tools within. This went into her case, under a false bottom. Then she checked the high shelf, and found the rags used for polishing. Again, she found the soft bag containing the hard marble sized lumps. That joined the other bag. She sniffed her hands, and confirmed that the polish smell clung to them. Her nose wrinkled in distaste, but it would prove that she had searched diligently.

She went to the roof next and found where Wanda had pried up, and then pressed back, a section of the metal duct cover. She had the hidden tablet out, and in her case, by the time she heard doors on the lower floor slamming open.

When Hilbert rushed out onto the roof, panting like a dog after a long run, she was making comments on her clipboard. "What is it, Herr Hilbert?"

"I found a whole lot of them, dead, amongst the crates."

Casey was ready to reassure him with, "You saw none that were moving?"

He seemed to need time to consider that, so Casey went on, "If they were dead, they probably came out of next door, to die. I found no signs of any as I checked the rooms. I have seen nothing up here either. I am told they sometimes come in and climb through the ducts. I am sure that you have nothing to worry about, but if you find any live ones, please call the company."

She gave the man a business card, and slipped the clipboard back into the case. "Thank you so much for your help. I am sorry that I needed to disturb you."

Hilbert gruffly said, it was no trouble. None at all, not like last night.

"Last night?" Casey asked innocently. "When that dreadful storm came through?"

It was all the introduction that the rotund, out of condition little man needed to begin a recap of the previous night's events. He wanted to keep the beautiful visitor around, and Casey was the perfect audience, horrified at the terrible events. She learnt very little that the papers hadn't reported, and she wasn't sure if Hilbert was elaborating on the facts when he claimed that, the thief was believed to be a famous international crook and Interpol was to be consulted.

Wanda returned to the guesthouse mid-morning, with several shopping bags full of clothes, which hid her odder purchases. The matronly wife of the owner remarked on her absence at breakfast and she acted coy and said, "I spent last night with a friend."

The woman arched her brows in a knowing fashion, and Wanda merely grinned, unrepentantly.

Once in her room, she put her bags near the door and went to check her tell tales. The one on the main room and the one into the bathroom were broken. She checked both rooms; saw nothing out of place, then checked the bedroom. There were fresh towels on the bed. The woman must have gone in earlier.

Wanda found nothing else amiss, and made a mental note to tell the woman to leave the towels for a week, not a mere two days.

Satisfied that she was alone, Wanda went back and locked the door. She dug into one of the bags, and found her tablet, no longer wrapped in the foul smelling rag. It needed charging before she could use it, so she plugged it in before retrieving her illegal entry tools, and the electronic override cards. The little drawstring bag was pushed into a corner of her suitcase.

When she emptied the new clothes she had bought, from the bag, a large envelope dropped out. Wanda stared at it.

"Damn!" The envelope contained the soft bag with the diamonds inside, and Jim had told her to drop them in the mail, addressed to the gem trader, Fischer. She had promised him that she would do it on her way back. That meant a trip out later, or a visit to the post box on her way to the Embassy to see Nicole. Actually, it would be better to get a mailing box for them - less chance that they would be lost in transit. She would stop at the post office, get a box and send it right away.

Meanwhile, she was keen to Skype David. He might be worried, since she hadn't contacted him last night. She calculated the time in LA - 3 am, David was likely asleep.

He had, however, left the computer on, and the webcam focussed on a note that read, "Davy said, nite-nite."

She grinned, her spirits rising, now she had a reason to stop second guessing her actions of the previous night. All the same, things like that note were reminders to be careful.

David's email was delivered as she prepared the information packet to go to him. He would know that she was okay, once he got that. She sent the encrypted files off, deleted the original files, and opened the zipped file David had sent. While the decryption program ran, she went to get a drink from the bar fridge and a couple of muesli bars she had bought for snacks.

She moved the second shopping bag, and dumped the rest of the clothes onto the bed with the others. If she went to the police, and offered her help, she needed to have a completely different look. The clothes that she had worn already, would need to be thrown away.

Then she had a thought. If she went to see Nicole, it would have to be in her Carson persona. She would need to keep the clothes she had worn that night. Those should be safe enough, but would Nicole expect to see the blond front locks? Yes, it would be better, except that she had opted for that look to stand out, now she wanted to stay low-key. She added the need to detour via some public toilet to her day's itinerary.

First though, she really needed to see what David had sent and see if his ideas suggested another way to look for Wexford. Jim was working the cartel angle, and she needed to stay clear of that. He hadn't said how he was going destroy the cartel's function, but she knew how he worked. In this case, he would probably aim to foment trouble between the leader and the deputy, maybe even cause one to kill the other, and have enough evidence for the killer to be proven guilty. No doubt, there would also be a trail of evidence for the police to find on the cartel's operations.

Wanda chose to look at David's updated report on Wolfgang Wessler, the CEO of Alpha Prime. There was a picture of the man - smiling faintly, as if he knew his Aryan good looks would always get him his way. His eyes were cold. Wanda had seen such eyes on other powerful and unscrupulous men.

He had a sterling reputation, owned a long list of properties including a mansion outside the city, and was on the boards of three philanthropic trusts. Still, Wanda memorised all the addresses on his properties. If he were involved in Wexford's disappearance, one of these places might be where he and his daughter were being kept. Too bad, she needed to keep away from him while Jim was working.

Frank Lunn, the one Jim said was the second in command and the fly-by-night guy, was still an enigma. David had found nothing more about him, and only a sketch likeness on his website. The two men were very different, and from what she knew so far, were a good representation of the two sides of the cartel. The legitimate public façade, and the underhanded activities.

She went through the rest of David's commentary, while she considered how to search for Wexford without impinging on Jim's work. Her husband was as good as Jim at picking up on details.

"You should follow up that glass guy. The email you saw was the first in a series between him (no. 3) and no. 1. He proposed that our guy was open to monetary incentive. No 1. proposed private discussions, outside business hours."

No 3 was Heinrich, and it fit with the arrangement for the meeting at his house. Wanda read on.

"Most of the records you sent, indicated that the bosses were out at meetings - four nights in a row after that. Looking at the timeline, it looks like our guy was still following his schedule all that time. He was reporting in until three days before you heard about Nicole."

Wanda considered that again, considering what Jim had told her. She still couldn't decide if Wexford had gone missing well before Nicole and Rachel were taken, about the same time, or after.

David's next comment was, "This might sound odd, the glass guy's PA, Lowenbach, sent off some emails in Russian, but to an IP address in Austria. I had the emails translated. Seems to me, she knew Wexford from before he left Austria to return to the States. According to her resume, that you also managed to copy, she once worked in the same company as Wexford did, though in a very junior capacity."

Now that, Wanda decided, was very interesting.

David's final words were, "Are you sure Nicole doesn't know any more? Obviously, our man must have told her he'd be away, or surely by three days she would have been worried and called the embassy or the police and like you said, all his stuff was gone. Why don't you check with No 3's people, his wife, or servants or neighbours, rather than the man himself? Does anyone know where Wexford's embassy loan car is? Has the embassy reported it missing?"

All were good ideas, even the last idea which was an echo of Jim's. "I think it is worth the risk of talking to that policeman - if you are sure he won't connect you to Carson. We need to find Rachel, she shouldn't be involved in this."

Wanda spoke to herself, "Damn it, Dav, I agree with you, but I don't want to stay too close to the man. Though it isn't him connecting me to the Carson persona that I am worried about. It's some blasted stones, and a little matter of being caught where I wasn't meant to be."

She made a promise to herself to post the damn stones at the first opportunity, but even as she thought that, another idea occurred to her.

"I need to check out where Nicole was found and try to back track from there."

That thought drove all concerns about the stones from her mind.

Chapter 10 - American agent

Wanda walked into the train station in her Tatiana persona. In the ladies' rest room, she used a cubicle to change from 'tourist clothes' - a loose short sleeved floral blouse over tee shirt and slacks - to a business suit, by adding a white shirt and jacket. To further change her appearance, she braided her hair in a complex style, added subdued make up, and exchanged her flexible soled runners for a pair of low heeled, black leather shoes.

Her black, 'business satchel', was flatter now, without the jacket and shirt, and she was able to zip up the un-needed extension. By opting to carry it by the handle, rather than the shoulder strap, it looked a completely different bag.

Apart from the running shoes, she had her tablet, diplomatic passport, and some miscellaneous things, but not her non-legal tools. The smallest of those were in a bundle back at the guesthouse in their safe. The rest of her tools were wrapped in clothes and hidden in her case.

The final touch, in changing her identity, was to remove the contact lenses that made her eyes seem brown, rather than their normal blue.

When she emerged from the station again, it was within a crowd of people that had arrived on the most recent train. She was lucky enough to get a taxi within minutes and she directed the driver to take her to the United States Embassy.

She was surprised when the driver took the taxi onto what looked more like an open plaza than a street, for they seemed to be the only car in the wide paved area between two stately buildings. Her attention was caught by a milling group of youths, and the flashing lights of a police car approaching from the other direction. However, the taxi stopped short of the group and announced her destination.

She paid the driver, and opened her door, noticing four marines standing alert, two either side of the unassuming security door in front of a white painted door of the embassy. Two of them stepped forward, coming down two of the wide semicircular steps as she approached, one asked politely, "What is your business here, Mam?"

She flicked another glance at the youths, now having a mock argument with the two uniformed policemen, as she introduced herself. "Wanda Martin, I am here to see Neil Thompson, the diplomatic attaché." Her hand was feeling in her bag for her diplomatic passport, but she noticed that the marine was watching the movement.

After taking and examining the document, he nodded to his comrade, and handed her passport back. "This way, Mam,"

"Do you have trouble here?" Wanda asked, shrugging a shoulder at the youths.

"They are keeping their distance," the man told her, without adding any other comment.

Wanda glanced at the other three marines, they were alert, keeping part of their attention on the milling young men, and the rest on the general area.

Her escort took her up the paved stairs and opened the door for her, and then followed her in. He had a radio earpiece, and she heard one of his colleagues announcing her arrival.

The entrance hall was opulently impressive, but Wanda had little time to appreciate it. A tall, brown haired man, in business attire, without the jacket, strode into view and came to greet her with a wide smile.

"Mrs Martin, I'm Neil Thompson. I am so pleased to finally meet you."

"As am I," Wanda replied automatically, but in a quiet voice. She was wondering why her danger sense had given her a jolt. "Thank you for seeing me. Are you expecting trouble from the people outside?"

Thompson, nodded towards a corner of the entrance hall, and said quietly, "The Ambassador spoke to the local authorities. They sent a representative of the Investigative Bureau. I don't think that group intends trouble, but we are being careful."

Wanda glanced in the direction Neil had indicated, and saw a man looking at her. She recognised Otto Donau, but gave no sign. He had just called his dog back, for Alex had started to move towards her.

Thompson spoke softly, "The Ambassador wishes to speak to you before he sees the policeman. I was told to bring you up right away."

They had to pass close to Donau as they went towards the stairs. She glanced at him as she would a stranger, and merely murmured, "Good Day," to him as she passed.

Then they actually went to an elevator, which surprised her, but Thompson explained that it was installed for the Ambassador, who was nearing retirement age and finding the steps hard to manage.

However, once they were within, Wanda demanded, "What's going on?"

"Ambassador Browning will brief you, but the Inspector wishes to question Nicole Wexford. He had his superiors arrange the visit. Did you know to expect him here?"

"No. So he didn't come about that group outside?"

Thompson shook his head, "He has promised to look into them. The regular police will get names and addresses of that group. We wish to avoid another minor terrorist incident."

Wanda raised her eyebrows. She had thought Vienna was a quiet city, unlikely to be the target of terrorists or major criminals. With her own work to consider, she pushed any other concerns aside.

"I actually came to talk to Nicole myself. How is she?"

"Borderline hysterical," Thompson admitted as the lift arrived at the second floor, and the door opened. "Our doctor has her sedated, but she wants to talk to Tatiana Carson, but all we have said is that the young woman hasn't been in touch."

Wanda smiled faintly. Thompson knew that Carson was her alias, but she asked, "Does the Ambassador know Miss Carson?" She turned her head enough to see her companion shake his head.

"Ambassador Browning was advised that you would be coming to Vienna. He is very concerned about Allan Wexford. I believe he met the man some years ago, and again when he arrived in Vienna recently."

That was all he had time to tell her, for they had walked from the elevator and had arrived at the Ambassador's office. Thomson knocked, and opened the door, entering first, and then introducing her.

"We are very pleased that you are here, Mrs Martin. It is a very bad business, Wexford being missing. I understand that you are to liaise with the local police?" Browning was seated at his desk, and did not try to stand.

"Yes, Sir," Wanda confirmed. "I will help in any way that I can to find him. However, would there be anything that I need to refrain from mentioning?"

"Are you aware of why he was here?"

Wanda nodded. "To speak to various business men, Sir. The details, no,"

"That's about it," Browning agreed. "Trade matters." He waved the topic aside, like brushing a fly away. "Important thing is finding him. His wife can't tell us much, poor woman. The doctor thinks the amnesia is from shock and the beating up she suffered. However, she is insisting on seeing some woman named Carson. Tatiana Carson. Do you know her?"

"Not well," Wanda lied. "The name was mentioned. A relative of some kind, I believe."

"So Mrs Wexford claimed. We've no record of her. The woman told Mrs Wexford that she would help find her husband."

Wanda shook her head. "Unless she told Carson more than she told you, I doubt there is much chance of a stranger to Vienna, succeeding. Have you been able to add anything to help the police?"

"Not a great deal. We had his itinerary, his address, and gave them a description of him and young Rachel. They are looking for his car. We arranged the hire of it for him. Neil, give Mrs Martin the reports, will you?"

"Yes, Sir," Thompson agreed. "And Sir, Inspector Donau is waiting downstairs."

"Right," Browning looked at Wanda. "Did you have word that he would be here?"

"No, but then I haven't checked my emails this morning. I came to speak with Nicole, and I believe the Inspector wishes too as well, so we can do that together. Much better for Nicole as well, more discreet, and I am more confident of the security here than at the police building."

"Discreet, yes," Browning agreed, as he heaved himself to his feet. "We had best not keep him waiting any longer. There is a meeting room downstairs where we can talk.”

“Sir, if it isn’t an imposition, could I have a moment to visit the ladies room?”

Browning gave Thompson a look, and he immediately offered, “I’ll show you where to go, and wait to bring you down.”

Wanda watched Browning’s deliberate movements as he walked from his office to the elevator. Thompson directed her in the opposite direction.

One of the female secretaries was repairing her make-up when Wanda entered. They both exchanged polite greetings, and she entered one of the cubicles, and made use of it until the other women left.

Once she was alone, Wanda quickly removed her jacket and shirt, so that her forearms were bare. Had there been an observer, they would have found her next move odd. She scratched at each wrist in turn and brought up a flap of skin. It was plastiskin, but a thicker version of what actors wore to change their facial features. In this case, the material was hiding her ‘ultimate’ tool kit - a specially created set of burglars tools, the individual pieces were flexible enough so that anyone gripping her forearm would not feel them. When the matching two pieces were put together, the tools were rigid.

Wearing this false skin was so much of a habit now, that removing it made her feel exposed. However, for this next meeting with Donau, the removal had a deeper purpose.

It wasn’t because she thought he would notice it, but that without the plastiskin in place, the old scars at her wrists would be noticeable. If the policeman had any vague suspicions that she and Tatiana were the same person the wrist scars and the different eye colour would convince him otherwise. And he might indeed have a few, since her Tatiana face was her natural face - undisguised. She had done her best to minimise similarities, but the man was sharp eyed and sharp minded.

With the plastiskin rolled up and pushed to the bottom of her bag, she re-dressed and went out to wash her hands and repair her own make up.

Thompson returned about then and handed her a 'visitors' tag to clip on her jacket, and gave her a slender manilla folder containing various documents. He then he led her down to the ground floor meeting room.

Donau rose from a chair as she entered, his dog raised his head to look at her. He gave her a slight bow and extended his hand in greeting. As the introductions were made, he studied her, and Wanda made no secret of doing the same. She made it seem she was meeting him for the first time, and returned his hand grip firmly. In her previous encounters, she had been acting shy or vaguely nervous.

Before the policeman could ask, Wanda explained who she purported to be. "I am employed by the US State Department as an investigator. Usually, I deal with domestic matters. I had business here, which I can deal with easily enough, even though I have been reassigned to liaise with you. The US Government wishes me to help you expedite the locating of Allan Wexford and his daughter."

"What have you been told, Mrs Martin?" Donau asked.

"I have only just arrived," Wanda explained, as she moved to a spare seat that Thompson was positioning for her. She turned the file folder slightly, enough for Donau to glimpse the "Confidential" stamp that was on the front cover. "All I was told was that Allan Wexford and his daughter are missing and that his wife is here. I was hoping that you might know more."

Browning, who had been quiet since Wanda had entered, spoke up. "They have found Wexford's car, the rental we arranged, over Florisdorf way."

"It has been examined?" Wanda asked, looking from Browning, back to Donau, who was reseating himself in a chair opposite Browning.

"Yes, a forensic team has gone over it. There is nothing to give us a lead, as it was wiped clean. We believe it was driven there and the driver picked up."

"So you do not know if Wexford drove it there or someone else?" Wanda stated.

"That is so. Do you know if Wexford smoked?"

Wanda glanced at Browning, who quickly answered, "Yes. American ones, naturally. Virginia's. Is that relevant?"

"Possibly not," Donau admitted. "The car had a smell - cigarettes we believe - probably from smoke absorbed by the fabric lining. Our scientists could not identify the brand. I will suggest that they find some of those."

Thompson, standing back by the door, offered, "I will see if our commissary has some."

"Later," Wanda suggested quietly. She went on, talking to Donau, "Inspector, I am told that you wish to speak to Mrs Wexford, and that you have spoken to her once before. Was she able to tell you anything?"

"No, not much. Her memory of events was blank. I am hoping she has remembered more now."

Wanda had no sense that Donau was withholding anything. She looked back at Browning, to ask, "Ambassador, would we be able to talk to her now?"

"Of course. Dr Witcombe says that she is calmer this morning."

Donau rose, keen to get to work. Wanda rose as well, but she had a request. "Inspector, if you don't mind, I would like to have a few words with her first, and some with the doctor."

"May I ask why?"

Wanda smiled faintly. "Of course. Before coming to Vienna, I spoke to several people who know her and her husband. I want to get my own impression of her and reassure her that she has my support, and that of the US Government. I will encourage her to help as much as she can and to make my own evaluation of her condition. I am also a trained paramedic."

Donau's eyes widened in surprise and he seemed to be re-evaluating her. He relaxed enough to admit, "I have been told that I must follow your foreign customs whilst I am here. Will I be allowed to bring Alex with me?"

"Alex? Oh, your dog? Is he a police dog?" Wanda asked.

"Indeed." Donau smiled. "I have found that he has a way with distressed victims."

Wanda glanced at the dog who was aware of being talked about, his tail was wagging gently. "I can see why with those big brown eyes. I gather he has other specialties too?"

"Yes. Drugs, explosives, bodies, tracking," Donau confirmed.

"A handy partner," Wanda murmured. She gave her attention back to Browning and asked if he would excuse them. The Ambassador merely nodded, and gestured for Thompson to escort them.

At the door of the infirmary, Wanda requested, "If you would just give me a few minutes."

She went in and found that the doctor was talking to Nicole, who was dressed casually, and sitting in a chair by the neatly made bed.

"Hello, Dr Witcombe, Mrs Wexford, I am Wanda Martin, US State Department Special Investigator. Doctor, I need to speak to Mrs Wexford. How is she doing?"

"Improving," the doctor said tersely. "I hope you will not upset her."

"It is not my intention. I am here to work with the police who are trying to find her husband and daughter. We need her help."

Witcombe shrugged and left the room.

"Where's Tatiana Carson?" Nicole hissed in a whisper. "She said she was looking for Allan and Rachel."

Wanda was looking at Nicole, and had her back to the door. She winked deliberately at Nicole as she said, "I haven't met her, and she has not been in touch here. However, I would not expect a foreigner, stranger to this city, to get far. I am a State Department investigator, and I will be working with the Vienna Police. They are being very discreet."

"You look like her," Nicole challenged quietly.

Wanda grinned faintly and merely said, "I am told that looking average is a good thing. Now, I have Inspector Donau here. He needs to talk to you. Will you cooperate, please? I am sure that Rachel wants to be with her mother."

Nicole's eyes began to fill with tears. Wanda knelt down and took her hands, sensing both guilt and fear. She knew why, she was afraid to talk. "We will get them back," Wanda assured her. "I'll ask the Inspector to come in."

Wanda returned to the door and beckoned. She was almost positive that he had been listening from the doorway. It didn't matter though. He would not have heard Nicole's questions, only the answers she had given her. And the dangerous question had been settled.

Wanda chose to stay standing beside Nicole, resting her arm on the back of the chair. Donau pulled up a second chair. Alex crept up to Nicole, as if sensing she was upset. He sat up, but rested his head on her knee. Nicole began to pat him, as if it were an automatic response.

"I hope you are better today, Frau Wexford," Donau asked gently. "How are you?"

"I am still sore, all over," Nicole told him, glancing briefly at him.

Wanda sensed that she had gone tense, and gently patted her shoulder. "Do you remember what happened?" She asked the question, and caught Donau's look of surprise. He had been about to ask the very same thing.

"Some," Nicole admitted in a low voice, that Donau had to lean forward to hear.

"Tell us," Wanda urged, giving Nicole's shoulder a gentle squeeze.

"Rachel and I were going in a taxi. To the place of a Mr Heinrich - out in eighteenth district. Mrs Heinrich invited us, since Allan was going to be there, as were the wives of some of her husband's other business friends."

"Had you met Frau Heinrich before?" Donau inserted the question.

"No. I haven't met any of Allan's contacts here. I thought it was very nice of her to think of us." Nicole looked up at Donau.

"What did her voice sound like," Wanda asked, interrupting Donau's next question.

"Why...nice, I suppose."

"I mean, how did her voice sound? Educated? Cultured? Common?" Wanda suggested.

"Polite...a bit tentative, but then she didn't know me. And she was a bit 'that's thatish' as if she expected me to agree."

"What about accent? Did she sound Austrian?"

"I suppose so...maybe a bit harsher sounding than the women at the apartments, but nothing really different."

"Did you get there?" Donau asked, then he clarified, "To the Heinrichs?"

"No. On the way, I started feeling sleepy."

"And then?" Donau prompted gently, noticing that Alex was now licking Nicole's hand.

"I woke up, and I was in a strange old house. Rachel was still asleep and I couldn't wake her up."

Wanda asked, "Can you describe the house?"

"It was dark. But there was some light coming in from outside, through the window. There were no curtains. I was on the floor, and the room was pretty empty."

Nicole was looking down at Alex now, but not stopping him from licking her hand.

"What happened next? Can you remember?" Donau urged. He was taking notes in a small notebook, but discreetly.

"Two men came in. One went to Rachel and picked her up, slung her over his shoulder. I got up and tried to stop him..." Nicole stopped talking, she was rigid with fear, realising that she had been warned against talking to the police.

"And," Donau prompted, as Wanda was whispering in Nicole's ear. "You're safe here Nicole. Can you describe the men?"

"No. Just that they were big, and solid, and their faces were covered." Nicole looked away from Donau, and her free hand sought for Wanda's hand where it touched her shoulder.

"Did they speak?" Donau suggested.

"I was screaming at the man who had Rachel, trying to grab her back. The other man dragged me away, and threw me to the floor. He said I was trouble and he wouldn't take me to Allan, and it would serve me right if both Allan and Rachel were killed. He was horrible. His voice was harsh and accented. He said if I wanted to see them again I had to keep quiet. Not to talk to the police or anyone."

"Have you any idea what they wanted?" Donau persisted, still gently.

Nicole shook her head, but Wanda felt her tense even further. She did know something, but Wanda decided not to push that question. She gave Nicole some time, to see if she would say anything.

Donau spoke next. "Did your husband tell you anything about his work?"

Nicole shook her head.

"Did he seen worried about anything?"

Another head shake, but this time, Wanda sensed that the unspoken negative was a lie.

"When did you last speak to your husband?" Donau asked.

"He'd been away for three days, having talks with people. That's why I decided to go to the Heinrich's. I wanted to see him."

Nicole covered her face and began to shake.

Wanda gave her shoulders a squeeze, and whispered, "You have been very helpful. We will let you rest for a while, but we are going to find your family."

Nicole reached for Wanda's hand and gave it another squeeze, before letting it go.

Alex moved as Wanda edged back around Nicole's chair. Donau took the hint and rose to leave the room with her. The dog gave Nicole a final lick, before trotting after his master.

Neil Thompson, who had been a silent observer, led them out.

"You can use the meeting room downstairs if you wish to talk."

Donau accepted, and Wanda murmured the suggestion of coffee.

Back in the meeting room, Donau chose to move a chair near the table. He sat side on to it so that he could stretch out his long legs. He rested one arm on the table, and the other reached down to scratch Alex's ears.

Wanda ignored his casual pose, she pulled out a chair further along the table and sat so that she could open the folder that she had been carrying.

"Just give me a minute, will you?" she murmured as she began to look through the papers. She was reading parts of one when Thompson brought in coffee and biscuits, and then quietly departed.

When she put the last paper back in the folder, she glanced back at Donau, who was sipping coffee, and caught him giving Alex a biscuit.

"Sorry, I didn't know if any of that stuff was relevant."

"Is it?" Donau asked casually.

"Most of it is need to know," Wanda gave an apologetic shrug. "Transcripts of Wexford's reports, details of several signed off deals, and so forth. Looks okay at a glance, but I would have to see what our legal department says. I am not sure what level of discretionary power he has. He has sent several draft proposals, with a personal comment that he thinks the figures asked are excessive."

"His words or yours?"

"Mine," Wanda admitted. "He said extortionate."

She wasn't ready to suggest 'criminal cartel' yet.

"Tactful," Donau agreed. Then he asked, suddenly, "Why did you stop Frau Wexford from talking?"

"Apart from promising the doctor that I would not get her agitated, I could feel her tensing up. Your pooch did a marvellous job of keeping her calm, until then. I intend to talk to her again later, and see if I can get anything more."

"I will hold you to that. We need to move fast on this." Donau's face took on a stern aspect, and it reminded her of when she had met him the third time.

"I know, Inspector," Wanda said, meeting his gaze. "I can imagine what Nicole is going through. I have a two year old son at home, and his Dad tells me that he has just discovered mud. I want to get back to both of them."

Donau gave her a quick grin, but returned to serious by asking, "Have you any ideas on where to look for clues?"

"I have been told that you have been checking Wexford's itinerary. That would have been my first task. With that Heinrich invitation..." Wanda paused to look through the folder, although she knew Wexford's itinerary by heart. "Wexford was scheduled to talk to him on the day of the invitation...if my calculations are correct. He's into scientific glass products, and..." Wanda checked another page. "Wexford's last recorded report was that day. Timed at four pm."

"What was that part about having talks for three days before the invitation?" Donau asked. "It sounded like she couldn't reach him during that time."

"It did," Wanda agreed. "I will follow thiat up. Have your people checked the apartment they were using?"

"Yes," Donau admitted. He glanced away and his hand began tapping the table as if that subject was annoying or frustrating.

Finally he admitted, "When we got there, it had been ransacked. Nothing personal had been left there."

Wanda stiffened and stared at him. She hadn't expected that. When she had left, she had thought it had been the police arriving.

Donau's next question came as a sharp interrogative. "I had asked to speak to Tatiana Carson."

Wanda didn't even twitch. She had expected that question.

"Who? Oh, yes. Neil mentioned the name. You will need to speak to him. I don't know if they have a record of her."

"She implied that she was American, and showed me a United States passport." Donau relaxed his sharp gaze, and added. "There is no record of her entering Austria."

With a shrug, Wanda dismissed that factor, and distracted Donau by asking, "Have you questioned taxi drivers? Asked about missing taxis?"

Donau was momentarily confused, thinking taxis and Carson. Then he realised that she was referring to something else and his expression changed. Wanda decided it was a bit of arrogance showing.

"Naturally we checked if anyone picked up a man near where the car was found, and we will ask about the taxi that took Frau Wexford that evening."

Wanda decided that there was something common to policemen the world over - they though they knew better than mere civilians. She decided to challenge his ego. "Have you found her handbag?"

Donau jerked, and stared at her. That idea had not occurred to him.

"Where would you suggest to look, Frau Martin?"

"I'd try to backtrack from where she was found."

Donau moved in his chair, sitting upright and bringing his legs in. "The ground was gone over. It looks like she was dumped in that park, and it has rained since then."

"Does that affect Alex's sniffery?" Wanda's tone was serious, but she caused Donau to chuckle.

"It can, sometimes. Do you think you can find something we missed?"

Wanda shrugged. "Merely a hunch. Would you let me view the scene with you?"

"Hunch?" Donau queried.

"In trying to think like a criminal," Wanda eyed at Donau as she spoke. "I wondered why, if Nicole was knocked out in a taxi, woke in a house, and Rachel was taken away from there."

Donau suddenly stiffened as if the thought had not occurred to him. "Ambassador Browning suggested that I could take you with me when I work on this case. My superiors have asked me to concentrate on it. It might be dangerous."

Wanda stood, tied up the file she had rifled through, and considered her answer.

"So is crossing the road."

Donau suddenly leant forward and caught her left wrist. He turned it over and rubbed the scar.

"You've seen trouble before."

"Yes," Wanda agreed, not pulling free immediately. "And State Department agents are trained to handle it. I won't be a liability."

"What happened?" Donau asked, rubbing the scar again.

"Nothing that is relevant to now," Wanda told him, giving her wrist a flick, and freeing it.

Donau studied her a moment longer than was polite, then asked, "Are you free now?"

"Yes. Just let me return this file. I'll meet you and the pooch in the front hall."

Alex woofed softly, and as Wanda left the room, she heard Donau speaking quietly to him.

Once out of sight of Donau, Wanda took a deep breath and let it out slowly. If she had read the man correctly, she had impressed him. However, her mind recalled, all too vividly, the diamonds in her bag back at the guest house. She had intended to send them to the police that morning, but that would have to wait. Right now, she needed to keep convincing Donau that she was a serious investigator, so that he would never connect her to any robberies.

She found where Neil Thomas had his office, recovered her bag, gave him the file and a brief outline of what she was going to do.

Donau drove from the embassy and went first to his headquarters. There he arranged for a temporary ID for Wanda, for while she was working with him. While that was being prepared, he returned to his office, where three other officers were busy at their desks. He requested one of them to begin an enquiry into missing taxis, asked for the latest information on the previous night's robbery, and then sat down to read through the half dozen files on his desk.

Only then, did he assuage his colleagues' curiosity and introduce Wanda, for it led to him briefing each of them on his other cases that they would have to take over.

Wanda was only half listening to the conversations. That they had no new leads to the diamond thief's location, amused her, but she hid her faint smile by looking out the window, down into the busy street below. She remained that way until Alex came over and dropped a ball at her feet. When she ignored him, he nudged her leg with his nose and gave a small woof.

"He wants you to throw it," Donau said to her, as he reached to answer a phone.

With nothing better to do, Wanda complied - rolling the ball in all directions around the room until the messenger arrived with her temporary ID. Donau rose from his chair, called Alex to order, and gestured for Wanda to precede him down to where he had earlier parked his car.

Alex made his habitual dash to the front seat, and growled when Donau chided him for a lack of manners. Wanda decided he was claiming it was his turn, for she had travelled in the front from the embassy. He did, however, move to the rear seat, even if slowly.

Donau decided to visit Mrs Heinrich first, and that gave Wanda time to think on all she had discovered so far. It hadn't yet given her a clue to Rachel's whereabouts, or her father's. She hoped, intensely, that Jim's mission went well and he found Wexford alive. Yet if he was indeed a prisoner, she doubted that he would be with the cartel leaders.

During the drive, Wanda appeared to be looking at the buildings and scenery, and she was - putting places on her mental map of the city. Then they moved out into a less built up area. It appeared that Heinrich was quite well off, and could afford a large block of land on the edge of some kind of wilder land.

"I will just listen and observe," Wanda told Donau just before they exited the car. "They don't need to know how well I understand the language here."

Her reasons were not questioned; Donau seemed to intuit that she would be observing everything that he might otherwise miss.

So while Donau questioned Frau Heinrich, in the front parlour of the large single storey dwelling, Wanda concentrated on the body language of the woman, her speech, and the actions of the few house servants who hovered near the door to the parlour.

While appearing to listen intently to the conversation, she was actually sensing the reactions in a way that Donau would never guess. The general sense she received was that they were genuinely shocked that the Heinrich family name had been used for such a vile purpose. Yet, amongst the horrified reactions, she had the feeling that someone there did know something and was keen to go off and report to someone. This was not something she could prove, so she did not mention it to Donau.

After leaving the Heinrich place, Donau drove to a park in a district nearer to the centre of Vienna. He parked at the roadside, and led the way into the neatly landscaped area.

"Frau Wexford was found here, by cyclists," he explained. "Just over there."

Wanda looked towards the group of trees, and Alex ran ahead to sniff there again. As they walked closer, Wanda looked around, noting everything she saw. She had a general idea of the placement of trees and shrubs, and watched Alex nosing around.

Where Donau indicated, the trees were only a few strides from the path. There were no bushes there, so if Nicole was dumped there - there was no intention to hide her. But was she dumped?

They were not far from either of the roads that edged the park...

her eyes strayed to the phone and an idea occurred to her.

"What injuries did Nicole Wexford have?" she asked Donau. Nicole had not mentioned going anywhere from the house, so how had she got here?

"No broken bones, but plenty of scrapes and bruises. Concussion too. What are you thinking?"

"What led you to think she was dumped here from a car?"

"Alex followed her scent from the tree to the road."

"What if...Nicole woke up from that beating, and knew she had to get help. She found her way out of the old house, and began walking...possibly only vaguely aware of what she was doing. What if someone offered to help her, and she simply insisted on getting to a phone, so these Samaritans took her to here, where there was a phone." Wanda pointed to the one she could see. "She walked from the car to here, and collapsed again."

Donau looked thoughtful. "Let's follow that idea. How would we tell where she came from?"

"I doubt that it would be far," Wanda considered. "If we work on that phone being the nearest. Are there some older type houses around here?"

"Too many to count. Vienna is a much older city than any of your American ones." He turned slowly in a circle, as if looking through the trees, but said then, "East of here probably has the oldest houses."

They returned to Donau's car, where Wanda asked to have her shoulder bag locked up, and then began to walk along the road in an easterly direction. Alex was happily sniffing the path, but showing no signs of having caught a familiar scent.

Wanda looked for possible clues, and kept one eye on the dog, as they walked without finding anything. When they had gone about two miles, Wanda began thinking that the proposed car might have come out of a side street, or her idea was flawed, when Alex suddenly began to trot faster. She and Donau had to run to keep up with him. Then he dived through the gate of a property where the garden was dead and uncared for, and the house had a vacant look. That there was no car parked outside, may have meant the owners were out, but there were no curtains in the front windows either.

"Stay here," Donau ordered her, as he drew his weapon. He made several hand gestures to Alex, as he cautiously approached the door, with the intention of scouting the house.

Wanda was sure the place was empty, and let him check anyway. She studied the dirt on either side of a footpath. When Donau returned, she pointed out some ground out cigarette butts, several boot prints and a piece of white fabric.

He had his mobile phone out and nodded at her discoveries. When he had finished giving instructions to his subordinates, he returned the phone to his pocket and asked, "How did you know?"

"I didn't. I was following a hunch."

"Is there more to your hunch?"

"Only conjecture."

"I would like to hear it."

Wanda considered her thought process. "Nicole remembered blacking out in a taxi. What if they needed to hide the taxi, or return it somewhere, so unloaded their captives here, believing that they would be out cold for long enough, and then brought another car here to collect Rachel."

"Her handbag was inside," Donau decided to reveal. "If, as you seem to be implying, Frau Wexford woke up and left - why didn't she take it with her?"

"If she had concussion, she may have only been barely conscious."

Sirens were coming nearer, and two cars pulled up outside the house soon after. When the officers emerged and strode up to Donau, he gave them instructions.

"Keep people away from the house and the edges of the path. I have a forensic team coming. This is to be treated as a crime scene."

Donau gestured Wanda towards the house, but she glanced towards the street where a small crowd had already started to form.

"Do you wish to look inside?" Donau invited. "You will refrain from touching anything of course."

At first, she had thought it unnecessary, but at that moment, she sensed a thread of alarm from someone in that small group. She reviewed the faces she had memorised in her earlier glance, but no one had seemed to be acting oddly. Had she and Donau stumbled onto somewhere that Nicole's captors had not expected them to find?

"Yes, though I doubt that I will see anything you did not," she murmured.

Wanda stopped just inside the door. She had smelt a whiff of something. "Cigarette smoke? Does it smell like the smell in Wexford's car?"

"You're good," Donau commended. "What else?"

She let her eyes scan the passage, and saw nothing obvious, but a breeze came into the house behind them, rousing the smoke smell.

"When was Nicole found?" she asked abruptly, without considering the question first.

"Over a week ago - she was unconscious for three days before she woke up and knew who she was."

His answer confirmed her vague feeling. That the abduction had been more than four days before. Donau distracted her from her thoughts.

"You were going to make a comment?"

"Yes. If it has been that long, surely the smoke smell would have been aired out of here by now. Perhaps this place is used on a semi regular basis for various reasons."

"Yes, I had thought that too. I can certainly see why you were asked to help on this," Donau commended.

"I haven't found Rachel or her father yet," Wanda demurred, and she looked into all of the rooms in the house before returning outside. Only one room had any sign that someone had been in there.

"I am going to need to be here for some time," Donau apologised. "Do you wish to stay, or would you like someone to drive you back to the embassy?"

"I will not be much use here, now, so I will head back. If someone could take me back to your car for my bag, I can find my way from there."

"Nonsense!" Donau objected.

"Fine. The Embassy then. I do have other tasks to do, and my other bag was meant to be sent there. I might as well see if they have a bed I can use while I am here."

The police driver dropped her at the side gate of the embassy, and she showed the guard her passport and was allowed in. She reported the recent events to Thompson, and said she needed to go out again. She asked him to organise a taxi for her, and asked him to tell Donau, if he should get in contact, that she had gone off on another matter.

She told the taxi to take her to the nearest major shopping precinct. She wanted to buy a mailing box to use to send off the dratted diamonds. Being with Donau had reminded her of the folly of holding onto them any longer than necessary. However, her first priority was to turn herself back into Tatiana Carson and to that end, she merged into the crowd of late afternoon shoppers, and looked for a ladies room. There was a short queue, and by the time the she was able to use a cubicle, several more people had joined the line behind her.

It made her intention more difficult, since it was a fiddly job to reapply the plastiskin, and she did not want to occupy a cubicle for too long. Plus, the smell of the adhesive might cause comment. So she, simply changed back into her Tatiana clothes - the noticeable floral shirt, and the dark slacks, changed her eye colour, and hair style. It was a risk, although slight, that anyone would notice her wrists, if she kept her hands in her pockets, and held her bag on her shoulder. On her way to look for a mailing box, she stopped at a small boutique and bought a long sleeved knitted jacket, and changed into it in the shop.

Now, she was ready to go on, but the smell of food made her hungry, so she stopped to get a sandwich. She ate as she walked, and found herself heading for the bus stop. With an inward curse, she recalled the need for a box and turned abruptly, causing a hurrying man to have to swerve to avoid her. He gave a sharp comment, and kept going, not waiting to hear her apology. He was, she realised abruptly, dressed in a similar fashion to the youths who had been hanging around the embassy.

Her spurt of alarm didn't last long. The man could not have been one of those youths; he was older and just wearing the same style of clothing. Still, she decided on caution as she went back into the main concourse. She studied the people around her with increased attention, moved randomly in an attempt to spot if anyone was following her. She was uneasy, but her danger sense was at a low level.

"I have a very guilty conscience," Wanda thought to herself. She pictured the little bag with the diamonds in, which she hadn't even looked at. And she still couldn't explain the compulsion that had made her take them or why she had forgotten to send them off that morning. She could have used the envelope Jim had put them in...

On the way out again, she seemed to see casually clad youths everywhere. She berated herself for seeing danger even when there was none, and forced her mind to find the differences in the outfits. So they were wearing shirts, long pants and casual jackets, but they were not all the same style, or the same colour. None of them seemed to be paying her any attention. None began to follow her to the bus.

She kept alert, but part of her mind was wondering if she had caught a bug, and would be coming down with the flu or something. Then she told herself sharply, "Paranoia is not a symptom of the flu."

Another idea occurred to her, as she recalled that she had felt queasy that morning. Then, she had put it down to the after reaction of being caught, but that wasn't right. She had been feeling the familiar euphoria of outwitting policemen by escaping, even while listening to Jim's disapproving comments.

The bus left the shops, but stopped again a short way along the road. Two young men, got on there, and sat nearby, but they paid her no attention and discussed video games. She considered it a coincidence that they left the bus with her at the nearest station, since quite a few other passengers did the same.

She dawdled and watched them walk to one of the platforms before she ducked into the ladies room again. This time, she was determined to replace the plastiskin, because if she was going to meet trouble, she wanted the security of her 'last ditch' tool kit.

As she undressed enough to have her forearms bare, and then

dug into her back for the plastiskin roll and the adhesive, she realised that if she had been followed from the embassy, the only link between her Martin dress up and her Carson one was the bag. No, she amended, her hair colour was the same, but she did not have any hair dye with her. But, first things first, get the plastiskin back on.

In the past two years, she had practiced the procedure often enough to be able to do it in all sorts of circumstances. First, the alcohol swab to clean the skin. Then the adhesive around the edge of the stretched out rubbery material. Then the fiddly part, arranging it on the closed down lid of the toilet, with the flexible tools facing up, squatting down and rolling her arm onto the patch and adhesive.

It took a few minutes for the adhesive to dry, and that gave her just enough time to smooth the material so it looked perfectly natural.

Once both pieces were back on, her nerves were steadier. As she re-dressed, she considered how she could change her look again. She could, tie her hair back and roll it under a soft beret, which had been an afterthought when she had prepared to come out and one of her cover purchases that morning. Then, if she removed the floral blouse and just had the knitted jacket over the black tee shirt, it would be enough. However, she would need to ditch the bag...

Her passport went into the extra pocket in her slacks, her small wallet into another pocket. Then she took out the plastic bag that the knitted jacket had come in and wrapped her android tablet in that. Since it was only a small one, she tucked it into her underwear. The rest of the stuff in the bag would not give a clue to her, so when she walked out of the cubicle, she left the bag there.

She had the urge to get back to the guesthouse quickly, so instead of taking the train, she went back through the evening commuters, to the street, and hailed a taxi.

In the taxi, as it pulled away from the kerb, Wanda finally began to relax. Still, the habit of caution was still strong, and she gave the driver the address of a place a block away from the guesthouse. She glanced at the traffic behind the taxi several times, but had no sense of being followed. When she arrived and had paid off the driver, she paused to watch children playing ball on the footpath, before beginning to walk on. Nothing seemed out of place. The few cars that drove up and parked, disgorged men just home from work. Children stopped playing and ran to meet them.

Berating herself again for her paranoia, Wanda hurried past the last few premises to the guesthouse, and was ready to greet her host.

"How was your day, Fraulein?" he greeted with a smile.

"Tiring," Wanda supplied immediately. "There are so many places here that I want to see while I am here, but I forgot my camera."

"Then you will need to go around again," he chuckled, but in a friendly way. Then he added, "You are just in time for dinner, my wife had made her delicious schnitzel with salad."

"Sounds like what I need. After I wash up."

What she really wanted to do was to see David's face, and talk to him, and so she hurried upstairs, but did not forget to check her telltales to be sure no one had entered her room in her absence.

Even then, she could not do it immediately, as her tablet was dead flat, and would need to charge a bit before she could begin to use it. After setting it to charge, she took the time to have a quick shower, and to change into looser, more casual clothes.

When Wanda opened the Skype session, she had a view of David sitting at the kitchen table. He seemed to be finishing his breakfast, and lingering over a cup of coffee. She could hear Davy's childish squeals in the background, and the barking of a puppy. They didn't have a puppy!

"A dog?" Wanda greeted when David came back to the computer.

"Tell you about it ...later. How was your day?"

"Mixed. I made a good impression on Inspector Donau, I managed to get Nicole to talk a bit more, until she began to get upset. Said I would talk to her again, but that will have to be tomorrow. They found Wexford's rental car - wiped clean of prints, but with a lingering cigarette smoke smell."

David suddenly stood up and said, "Hang on a minute..." His image moved out of range of the webcam, but Wanda heard him scolding Davy, and yips from the puppy.

"Sorry, go on," David told her when he got back.

Wanda had a moment of homesickness, and wanted to find out what was happening at home, but she continued her report. "I had a look at the place where Nicole was found, and Donau's dog picked up a scent. We found the house where Nicole recalls waking up in - the place where they took Rachel from her."

"Any clues to who took them?"

"No, just men with faces covered and rough ways."

In that moment, Wanda felt her danger sense kick in. She went rigid, listening, but not to what David was saying.

"What's up?" he repeated sharply, and the second time, Wanda turned her attention back to him. "I know that look of yours..."

"I am not sure - there were some young men hanging around the embassy, all wearing a kind of uniform, dark trousers, khaki shirts, but the police were dealing with them. But later, I saw more in a shopping centre, similar style, different colour shirts - told myself it must be the popular fashion, and I am sure I wasn't followed back here. But...I may have been followed from the embassy - I sensed someone near the house that was too interested in us."

David's expression changed to one or fear, "Get out of where you are. Now!"

Her own mind was telling her the same thing, and she wasted no time, not even saying goodbye to David. She yanked the charger from the wall plug, turned the tablet off and shoved both into a black backpack. Her case was within reach and she opened it on the way to empty the drawers and cupboards. She hadn't kept much out of her case, but now she sorted her stuff into essential - which went into the backpack, and other, which went into the case. Money, Carson passport and the diamonds went into her pocket.

She left the case in her room, but took the backpack with her when she went downstairs to talk to the owner about retrieving what she had in the guesthouse safe.

When she knocked at the office door, she had forced her body to appear calm, and to act as if she had nothing more than the evening meal to worry about. She endured the casual chat, said she would be in for dinner shortly, thanked him for retrieving her package, and tried not to run back to her room. She was already planning her route out the back door, and had just picked up her case when the door from the passage slammed open. A black clad man with a large handgun rushed in, as a second figure smashed in through the window. She didn't stop to think how he had managed that, simply made a dive of her own towards the bathroom, where she could escape through that window and onto the roof. A silenced bullet passed narrowly in front of her, and a harsh voice warned her that he would not miss the next time. The window intruder needed only her momentary pause to reassess her intentions, and he grabbed her. Wanda felt a prick as he slapped his hand against her neck. She barely had time for that fact to register, and her world went dark.

Chapter 12 - Helpless

Wanda woke up feeling odd - a mixture of stiff, woozy, and breathless. She rolled over, and realised that she was on the floor. Memory returned along with a rush of adrenalin. She recognised her room in the guesthouse, but when she changed position, she saw the mess. She was a mess. Someone had searched her thoroughly, for she saw her tablet, passport, room keys and wallet on the floor.

The room had all the contents of her case strewn around, as if someone had been in a tearing hurry to find something. Her first thought as she pushed herself up, was that no one could possibly have thought she would have anything valuable. But she had!

"The diamonds!" she said aloud, and with a groan, managed to get to her knees, and to feel her pockets. They were still there! Odd...

Wanda stood unsteadily and began tossing things back in her case or backpack. Her roll of tools was still there, although it too had been looked at and re rolled without care. She tossed that in the case, and zipped it up. Then her mind registered the one thing she had not found - her diplomatic passport! She had put it in her backpack, tucked into an inner pocket. With a sinking feeling in her gut, she took a moment to check there. It was gone.

"I don't like this..." she spoke to herself. Then she silently considered, "I was knocked out, the whole place, including me, was searched. But they left the diamonds, my wallet with money in, my tablet, and took my passport, but only the diplomatic one..."

She glanced at the window, someone had drawn the thick drapes. "And how come no one had come to investigate the smashed window?" Perhaps it wasn't noticeable with them drawn?

When she moved the curtain, she caught a flash of blue light. Down in the street, was a police car and two smashed cars.

The hairs on her neck wanted to stand out straight. Whoever had worked her over was a pro. Were Austrian gangsters that good? Well, she needed to get away before they decided to come back. She grabbed her pack and shrugged it on her shoulders.

"Going somewhere?" a nasal voice challenged from the doorway.

Wanda spun around, reacting to the new threat, and wondering why her danger sense had not warned her. Maybe it had been trying to, and she was too dopey to think?

The short lean man who held a gun aimed at her, was wearing a suit, his expression was malevolent. However, in spite of never having seen him in person before, she knew who he was from a sketch David had sent her. It was Franz Lunn, the man she had dubbed 'fly by night'.

She stood still, studying how the man moved as he drew closer.

"I was told that there was a thief here. One who had some diamonds, stolen from me. I want them back."

Wanda briefly considered giving them to him, but she didn't like bully boy tactics, and decided that as soon as he had them, she'd be dead. Anyway, her memory supplied, if they were his, why were they in a safe at Alpha Prime?

"I honestly don't know what you are on about," she claimed, and she watched his approach, and glanced at the door.

"You won't get out that way. I have two men out there."

Wanda shifted her weight as if she intended to dive into the bathroom; Lunn turned his body, as if anticipating that move as well. She feinted in that direction, he moved to block her, but realised his mistake when he felt the solid kick on his left thigh. He went down, cursing, but before he could get up, or re-aim his gun, Wanda had disappeared behind the thick window curtain. She was counting on him not knowing that window had been so thoroughly shattered.

She was already on the roof and moving over the tiles, when he jerked the curtains open, and swore. She heard, after the initial curse, "She's gone over the roof!"

Wanda already had her escape route planned; she would climb down at the rear, the furthest end from where the driveway came around to the rear. There was a small garden in that corner that was not lit during the night, and a drainpipe to help her down.

She heard someone coming after her, a heavy man from the way the tiles were cracking under his feet. Without looking around, she increased her pace to the edge of the roof, skilfully scrambled down, and raced into the darkness. It wasn't just the man she wanted to avoid. There were more police sirens approaching, and something told her they were going to be looking for her too. Her best course of action was to retreat to a park that was two blocks away, and climb the big old tree she had noticed on one of her trips to the station. She ran as fast as she could, wasting no time wondering how she had been found out.

Earlier that day...

Johann saw the car drive up and the man, woman and dog emerge. He moved his wheel barrow closer to the front door and pretended he was weeding under the bushes. The visitors ignored him, and knocked on the front door.

Old Hubert, who considered himself like a butler, opened the door, listened to their self-introduction and asked them to wait. He would have shuffled to get Frau Heinrich, for her voice came clearly to the gardener, as she invited them in.

Johann intended to listen to the conversation, so he wheeled his barrow around to the rear door and took himself into the kitchen to help himself to a glass of water. He smirked at the outrage in Frau Heinrich's voice. He couldn't hear the conversation directly, but when the policeman left, the two women servants began cackling like chickens. He caught the words, "United States, State Department - that woman was." That sounded important and he wondered what she wanted. He listened a bit more and was rewarded.

As soon as he was able to slip away, not having learnt more than the fact they were looking for someone, he strolled down the road to use the public phone.

When his call was answered, he drawled, "Heidi, darling, is your boss man in?"

"No, he's in a meeting. What do you want?"

"Tell him that the police spoke to his wife, Leibchen, and a female investigator from the US State Department. They were looking for someone and asking if she knew someone called Wexford." He went on to tell all he had gleaned from the clucking women.

"Really? Fine, I will tell him."

Heidi Lowenbach hadn't let on to Johann that she knew what he was talking about, nor that his news had alarmed her. She did not like the idea of an American official nosing around. When she made a phone call, it wasn't to her boss.

"Aleksi?" she checked when the phone was answered. Sometimes it was the nosey servant at his father's house that answered.

"Heidi! Is there a problem?"

"The boss's wife just had a visit from the police and a woman from the US State Department - probably an investigator. Do you think they are on to you? They were asking about you and your whore."

"Calm down, Heidi. We knew the police would go there, and there is nothing there to find."

"But...an American investigator?"

"Heidi dear, as far as they know, I have been abducted. Of course they have to investigate! They will naturally assume it was by someone I spoke to."

"What if your whore told them something?" Heidi persisted.

"She knows nothing. And she has been frightened into silence. She will be too afraid to say anything in case the kid gets hurt, or her all American dream man," Aleksi's tone was derisory.

"Why did you keep the kid?"

"She's Wexford's, but as far as she knows, I am her father. Besides, like I said, while I have her, Nicole won't talk. Anyway, why do you worry? The family won't harm little girls."

"Is that why your whore wasn't killed? Are you going to keep that bitch in my place?"

"Heidi darling, she only thinks she's married to me. You know I can't be married twice. Father doesn't know about us, and as far as he is concerned, she married into the family and must learn to be obedient. She is useful at the moment to keep the police busy, looking for her darling Allan, but I don't need her anymore. Now, tell me about that American woman."

Heidi gave him as much information as Johann had given her, and as much of a description as the lecherous creep had provided.

At the other end of the phone connection, Aleksi was thoughtful. Finally, he said, "She's no one that I recognise. So she is probably some yuppie graduate that they appointed to appease Nicole. She's probably meant to suck information out of the police. She won't be able to do much on her own."

"What will I tell Heinrich?"

"Tell him that they visited. That's all he needs to know for now. He can find out the rest from his wife, later. He knows I am hiding out until the deal with Wessler goes through. And he won't mention that because he will lose too much if he does."

"He's edgy as hell about that robbery at Alpha Prime," Heidi spoke indiscreetly about her boss. "He says Wessler and Lunn are practically spitting nails at each other. Wessler reckons Lunn put the thief up to it, because how else would the thief have known which bag to take. He also says Lunn must be trying to destroy him...that makes me think the diamonds were stolen."

Heidi heard Aleksi laugh, and was obliquely reassured. "Those stones probably were stolen in the first place, all Wessler's group are crooks, including your boss. If having the police around asking questions keeps them worrying about all their other little intrigues and guilty secrets - all the better for me. I will be able to screw them for more than they realise."

Reassured, Heidi ended the conversation.

At a luxurious mansion on the outskirts of Vienna, Aleksi put the phone down and turned to an older man who had just demanded, "What was that about?"

He spoke Russian, and his tone demanded an answer.

Aleksi, known for the past five years as Allan Wexford, switched to his native language and repeated the gist of the conversation.

"What were the names of those officials?" the older man demanded.

"Donau, from the Austrian Investigative Department, and the American was Martin," Aleksi supplied.

The old man searched his memory. "Donau, he's sharp. I haven't heard of the woman. I would have, if she were dangerous. I presume she was the one seen at the American Embassy."

Aleksi knew that the family had branches in many places, and whilst there was a high degree of rivalry, they were also firmly united for mutual protection from outsiders. No doubt, his father would ask questions of the American based cousins.

An hour later, Theo Stephanovich was in an icy rage. He went in search of his son and snarled, "That American woman led Donau to our halfway house."

Aleksi, relaxing in a small side lounge, proposed, "There won't be anything there. You said Dimitri and Sergei were pros."

"Not professional enough. Donau found your woman's bag and a kid's nosewipe. Plus they found tracks and cigar butts."

"They can't link that to us. Why not just send those two out of the city?"

"If I am feeling merciful," Theo said coldly. "I will have them here to explain their stupidity. Do you know that Martin woman?"

Aleksi thought for a moment. "No. Do you want her watched?"

"I have sent someone out to the halfway house, to follow her when she leaves. I want to know where she is staying."

"Surely it would be at the Embassy," Aleksi suggested.

"No, she was seen to arrive there in a taxi, without luggage. And there was another woman who saw your wife two or three nights before. We need to know who that one is too."

Aleksi watched his father alternatively pace and stand scowling. It was a sure sign that he thought that his plans might be compromised. When the phone rang an hour later, Theo answered it himself.

He growled his usual greeting, and listened for several minutes before questioning the caller.

Finally, he gave an order, "Find her and report again."

After hanging up the phone, he was thoughtful, and then asked, "What do you make of this? The woman goes to the Embassy, stays a short while, takes a taxi to the nearest shopping precinct. There she goes to the toilets, and comes out looking different."

"She is up to something," Aleksi said immediately.

"Then she left there, taking a bus to a train station, and did another change trick there. It was only luck that Feodor, didn't lose her. Then she took another taxi."

"I would say she spotted a tail," Aleksi commented.

"If she did, it means she is good," Theo stated. "No. She is good. That double change act is a pro's trick."

"Where did she go?"

"We will know soon. Our contact at the taxi company said that she went to the 6th district to Theogasse. Then she walked."

"Then what do you intend?"

"I'll send a team to give her the treatment. That might tell us enough. I want to know what she knows about you. If she won't cooperate, I'll have her brought here for questions. However, if we do, you had best not be here."

"That is obvious, father," Aleksi retorted quietly.

They didn't have to wait long; the next call had Theo issuing orders for a shock assault on the Pension Hotel. The team had not needed much time to prepare, they had already been moving into the 6th district.

Their report had Theo in a thoughtful mood. He told them, "Leave everything except that diplomatic passport, and withdraw and watch."

Aleksi recognised the look of calculation on his father's face. "What?"

"That woman from the embassy, Martin, is also the thief from last night."

"Oh, interesting," Aleksi murmured. "That was a slick job, and a slick escape. A pro indeed. Do you think she is after the cartel?"

"I would say, yes. You intimated that you thought your contacts were crooks, and part of some cartel. Those diamonds though, she had to have known they were there, but how?"

"Heidi told me that Heinrich heard Wessler and Lunn arguing. Wessler thinks that Lunn is trying to upstage him and that Lunn put the thief up to it and compromised the security."

"Lunn? It's possible...The diamonds were from a robbery in France, two weeks ago," Theo considered that information. "Tell me, if Wessler and Lunn were out of the picture, could we work with Heinrich?"

"He is already coveting the top position," Aleksi assured his father. 'What are you thinking?"

"Have your little Heidi tell Heinrich that you think the Martin woman is onto the cartel. That the woman took the diamonds as evidence. Then let on that you know where she is living, and he should tell Lunn."

"What? Let Lunn and Wessler settle their argument?"

"I think the cartel will want to find out what the woman knows. They can take her out of the picture."

"If Lunn doesn't kill her first," Aleksi warned.

"Either way will work for us. However, to add a further layer of confusion, I will have our team place an anonymous call to the police as soon as Lunn gets there. A tip that the diamonds are there. If Lunn is caught too, well and good. If he escapes, he will blame Wessler. As for the woman, I wonder how she will explain having the diamonds. The police want that thief very badly. She won't be able to claim any immunity, for I will have her diplomatic passport."

"What if she escapes?" Aleksi asked. "Or Lunn finds the diamonds and simply leaves?"

"He won't have time, and she's had a dose to knock her out. She should be out for at least another hour."

"Father, you always tell me - never assume anything."

"And that is why I have the team watching still."

Aleksi smiled. His father still had his mind working at top speed.

Chapter 13 - Capture

Otto Donau was almost home when a message over his car radio destroyed his contemplation of a productive day. He had just finished promising Alex a gourmet dog feast, when any idea of continuing home left him.

"Car three, request from Leonard Christian. Meet him at Fredrickstrasse, Pension Handel.

"On my way, Control," Donau acknowledged. As he turned around, he told his dog, "Food will have to wait. Sixth district. Something important or Christian would not have called me."

Alex woofed softly.

"He's on that diamond robbery from last night. The one with the thief you liked. I hope you don't intend to consort with all thieves from now on."

Donau glanced at his dog who appeared to be dog-grinning.

"I wonder if I should have Frau Martin with me? I wouldn't mind having her observations to add to mine. And that robbery was at a place that her compatriot, Wexford, visited."

Alex woofed again as if agreeing.

Donau put the request through to control, and a short time later had the reply that Frau Martin was unavailable.

"Probably just as well. I enjoyed her company and she has a very shrewd mind. Plus, she was tactful enough to let me know she was married."

Donau pulled up between two patrol cars that were blocking the road. When he spotted Christian, thanks to the strobing blue lights, he got out and strolled over.

"What do we have here?" He shrugged further into his jacket, for the breeze was chilly.

Christian commented, "We had a tip off that the diamonds from last night were here. In room 11."

"Indeed? Were they?"

"No. But just before we arrived a group of masked raiders, tied up the owners and two of the staff - terrified any guest that saw them. We have been pulling the guests out of cupboards, and from under beds…"

"Christian…stick to the point!"

"There is no one in room 11. Signs of intrusion, broken window, smashed in door, one bullet hole in the wall. It looks like the occupant was about to leave - but if so, took off leaving a case behind."

"Took off, or taken off?" Donau asked aloud.

"Took off. We have a witness that saw a figure climbing out of the window and going over the roof. Two figures - another one followed soon after."

"What was the name of the person in room 11?"

Christian consulted a small notebook. "Tatiana Carson." He repeated the description that he had been given by the owners. "They said she was a really nice, polite, young American."

"Did you ask how long she has been there?"

"This is the fourth night. I checked the register."

"In…deed," Donau remarked. "She was at the hospital, and identified the mystery woman from the park. At the time, she said she hadn't arranged a place to stay, so I recommended one close to the hospital. She went there, booked for two nights, but never stayed there."

Christian's eyes went wide. "So, she didn't want you to be interested in her."

"So it seems, and perhaps we know why. I will have a look in room 11."

During his talk, Alex had hopped out through the car window, and trotted up behind Donau. When his master walked off, he was close behind.

They went past huddles of onlookers in the street, and groups of frightened guests inside. He found the stairs and followed the brilliant glare to room 11. The forensic team was still busy, dusting for prints.

One of the technicians, recognising Donau, predicted his question. "Lots of good latents, but only one person. The staff must really clean between guests."

"Can I look in the case?" Donau asked.

"Go ahead. We've dusted that already."

Squatting, with Alex's nose sniffing the case, Donau used his pen to push the latch. One side fell down and a jumble of things tumbled out. "Packed in a hurry," he murmured, using the pen again to move items. He called to the technician who had recognised him. "Have you made an inventory of all that is in the case?"

"Not yet Commissar, but we will. All the cupboards and drawers are empty." The man went back to his task.

"I wonder if she was intending to leave anyway, or knew the masked men were after her." Donau spoke quietly to Alex. He dragged out an item of clothing and let the dog sniff it, then he woofed softly, confirming he had a scent.

"Have you a medium plastic bag?" Donau asked the technician. The man pulled one from his kit, open on the floor, and passed it over.

"I will remember to include that garment in the list, Sir," the man promised.

"Thanks, and when the list is done, let Christian have it, will you?"

Donau gave Alex a hand signal that meant 'search', and watched as the dog moved around the room. Finally, the dog put his paws on the windowsill.

"Alex, heel!" he called softly. The dog came over, and Donau returned to the stairs.

The dog found the scent in the front hall, and followed it to the door leading out to the street. That was to be expected, but the woman had not left that way. He needed to find where she had come down from the roof. He went to the driveway that went to the rear, and gave the command to seek.

There was just enough light to make out the drainpipe, and see that it had come away from the wall. He doubted that the woman, Tatiana, had caused that. It must have been whoever followed her.

"Where did she go?" he asked Alex, who, with a woof, headed off into the darker sections of the yard. He stopped and barked at the back dividing fence.

It was apparent from Alex's stance that the woman had jumped the fence, and Donau regretted that he was still wearing the suit he'd worn for the visit to the American embassy. With a sigh, he helped Alex over the fence and climbed after him. After the sixth fence, the state of his suit took second place to his determination to catch the thief. He expected that she was long gone, by bus, taxi or train, but for as long as Alex had a scent, he would see where it led.

If the woman was an American, Donau thought as he followed his dog, how well did she know Vienna? Did she have a third rented room somewhere?

The scent Alex followed finally reached a road, and Donau saw a bus stop, and began to go that way. His dog, however, stared across the road, and waited for him to cross. As soon as they were on the other side, Alex raced directly up the driveway of a private residence, and Donau had to follow.

At the rear of the house, a huge man challenged him. "Who are you? What are you doing here? This is private..."

Donau ended the tirade by reaching for his police badge, and holding it up in the dull light of the back door lamp.

"Police. Investigative Bureau," he announced clearly. "Go back inside and lock your door."

The man turned and ran for his door, like he was a dog headed for a fox hole.

Alex was barking from the darkness at the rear of the yard.

"This woman knows how to make it hard to follow her," Donau spoke to his dog. "I wonder...was she running from the other men, or did she expect you to follow her?"

He helped the dog over yet another fence, and as he followed he continued his thought. Carson had met him when Alex wasn't around, but if Carson was the thief, was she also the woman he had found in the neighbouring building? Or were the two women different people and this Carson's native cunning?"

Alex took Donau through another property, and out to a second street. Again, the trail crossed the road, but this time there was a park opposite. Alex went off at an angle and finally stopped and began sniffing around a big old tree.

Wanda was settled, high up in the tree, and felt safe enough to relax and doze. The man who had come out of the window after her had lost her, and she was well away from the Pension Handel and the police. The downside was, she'd had to leave her case, with the garments that she had taken from the Wexford apartment, and enough of her toolkit to prove to them that she was a thief. Most of those tools could be replaced easily, though some would be difficult.

With a wry thought, she realised that the first intruders had done her a favour - by taking her other passport. However, the amusement was fleeting as she wondered what they intended to do with that document. At the very least, she would be in for pointed questions by the powerful people in the State Department. Some of those people still disliked her.

That, however, was not the immediate problem. What she should do next, was. In the morning, once the police presence had died down, she could take a taxi back to the Embassy, after taking her brown lenses out. Even without a passport, Neil Thompson would vouch for her and let her in. She needed to go there, since she had promised to talk to Nicole again.

With several hours at least, to wait, Wanda curled into a tighter ball, to keep warm, and began to doze. She was in no way scared that she would move and fall, and for now, no one would expect her to be in the tree.

Sometime later, and she dared not use her tiny torch to check her watch, Wanda woke - instantly alert, and aware of danger. Knowing at once where she was, her senses told her to keep perfectly still and quiet. She listened, tuning out the whisper of rustling leaves and picking up the quiet voice talking to a dog. Was that all? Some local walking a dog? No, there was also a tinny sounding voice, like from a portable radio, acknowledging some instruction.

"Damn, damn, damn," Wanda thought to herself. She tried to think, "Go away, there is no one here," but it was too late. The damn dog knew. Donau knew. She hadn't a hope in hell of outrunning them. Staying silent was her only chance and that was slim.

They would have her out of the tree, one way or another. It would be easier if she simply gave up - but she had the diamonds on her.

An idea occurred to her, she could hide them up in the tree first...

then what would they find on her? The rest of her tools, her ready money, her tablet...damn! She would have to hide her whole bag, somewhere up higher than any solid policemen could climb. Just keep money and passport. Putting her thought into action, she began to climb higher, moving as quietly as she could, trying to make her sounds blend into the wind. She ignored the polite invitations from below to show herself.

She was listening, sensing that two more officers arrived, and they had doubts that anyone was up the tree. Donau, however, knew! He trusted his dog. Would he be tricked if she pretended not to understand the language? No, he had spoken to her in German that first night in the hospital, and she had spoken back in German, although haltingly. Could she pretend she was running from those men, and if they had found anything there, it was because it had been planted?

Well, someone had called the police, though how they had known about the diamonds was a mystery. Those first men, who had searched her room, her things and herself, and left the diamonds, were her first suspects. They had drugged her, and probably expected her to still be unconscious.

That fly by night guy, Lunn, had known the diamonds were in her room. Odds on, those others told him. But who were those others? The people who had followed her earlier? The young loiterers? Were they related to the cartel? And that was why Lunn was told? No...or they would have recovered the diamonds and got clear.

They had left her alive...for Lunn to find...and he would probably have killed her once he had those damned stones. They wanted her out of the way, but not linked to them. Unconscious, or arrested would probably satisfy them too. So who were they, and what plan of theirs was she threatening?

Whatever it was she had done, that second group were a totally unexpected complication. She needed to find out who they were and if they had anything to do with Wexford.

She felt a stirring of wry laughter. Here she was considering that second group a complication, as if her impending inevitable arrest was not. She did not want to tamely give herself up. She had Wexford and his daughter to find. But, the police would get her, and she would have to be ready to take any chance to escape that offered. And it would not be as easy as the first time.

If it wasn't Donau down there, she'd have more of a chance, but she didn't want to disable him. She liked him, and although his dog liked her, he wouldn't stand for her, hurting his human.

Donau though, had studied her as herself, Wanda Martin. However, she did not want to reveal that identity, so, she would have to act differently. As Carson, she had used halting German, but as the dark haired squatter in the building next to Alpha Prime, she had used idiomatic Austrian. If she wanted to blend those two, could she pretend that German was her native language? Possibly... and claim her father was American...and the reason she came to see Nicole. He would ask about that, but it would be the least of his questions. The rest of his questions she didn't want to answer. Couldn't answer.

She still had her mission - to find Wexford and his daughter. Or hope Jim found him...but what if he did and Wexford's daughter was somewhere else? Damn! Damn! Damn! Jim needed to know about that rival group, whoever it was that followed her. He hadn't mentioned anything like that.

"Why don't you come down and make things easier on yourself?" Wanda heard Donau say. She mentally commented, "Since when?"

No, the longer this took, the more time she would have to figure out how to escape. Then she admitted to herself, "And more police will come to stop me."

In her mind she told herself, "You sure know how to get into trouble, Wanda Martin!"

Still, she had been in worse trouble, and even now she did not want to recall that time. "This is nothing compared to that. Nothing!"

More back up had arrived, a police car drove closer - over the path and lawn, and kept its lights aimed at the tree. Two officers emerged. Donau spoke to them and within minutes, she was the squirrel caught in the spotlight.

The newcomers repeated Donau's polite requests for her to come down. Wanda stayed silent, trying to move out of the beams of the powerful torches. That made five men and the dog. She hadn't forgotten the dog.

They tired of polite very quickly, and first one and then the second of original officers began to climb the tree. Neither were as slender or tree nimble as she was, but they were fit.

Wanda looked down and saw the other two officers standing next to Donau watching the progress of their colleagues. There was her chance...when both of the climbers were occupied, she slipped down from her perch, on the far side of the tree from the climbers, and eyed the final drop to the ground. Her mind took in the scene, she prepared to drop from the tree on the far side from Donau and run off in the shadow caused by the tree.

Or, that was her intention. The initial drop, roll and spring to her feet had been perfect, but after three steps, she went light headed, stumbled and fell.

"That was a stupid trick," Donau said as he held the woman down and applied handcuffs. He rolled her over as his backup arrived with one of the torches. Alex began licking the woman's face and although her eyes were open, she wasn't reacting. He told his dog to move away, as he felt for a pulse. Alex had moved away, but he was inching back, until his nose nuzzled the woman's face.

"What has got into you, Alex!" Donau spoke sharply. His dog whined softly.

"We need an ambulance here," Donau spoke loudly, and the officer ran to the car.

"Concussion, maybe," one of the tree climbers suggested. "That lowest branch was seven feet up."

Donau shone the torch on the woman's face. Her eyes remained open, fixed and staring.

"Did she have a bag or anything with her?" Donau asked the other tree climber.

"Sir, she was high above us, and we never saw her coming down. But if she had, surely she would have it on."

"If this is our jewel thief, then she is a very clever piece of work. And she couldn't miss knowing we had her cornered. Last night, the thief had a small, black, drawstring backpack. See if you can find it. Look around here, and backtrack the way she ran from the guesthouse. Bring a map and I will show you the way she came. You should also check the guesthouse roof and the back of the grounds there."

One of the officers who had earlier climbed the tree, took a torch, tucked it in his belt and headed back for the tree, with a marked lack of enthusiasm.

When the officer returned from making the call for an ambulance, Donau directed, "When it gets here, I want you to go with the prisoner. Have the hospital test for drugs and alcohol."

Then, feeling pleased with himself, he called his subordinates and reported the capture. He suddenly thought about frisking the unconscious woman for weapons. His hands were gentle, since he did not know what injuries the woman had, but when he felt the thick wide seams of the trousers, he felt sure that something was in them. He made a note to check more thoroughly at the hospital.

He felt her pockets, pulled out a flat folder...passport, Tatiana Carson...but he had already recognised her. Money clip - enough money to get a long way away.

The ambulance arrived, lights flashing, siren silent. They too drove over the grass and paths. The attendants checked the patient, listened to what had happened, and used a cervical collar and backboard as a precaution. They allowed Donau to switch the handcuffs from the back to the front of the prisoner-patient.

"The prisoner is slippery enough when awake, but someone was after her as well. There was a bullet hole in the wall of her room at the guest house," Donau warned the officer who was to accompany the prisoner. He promised that he would send reinforcements.

Alex let the attendants move the woman, and then woofed at his master.

"I'll get you something on the way home, Alex, but I am not finished here." Donau returned to the tree and listened to the cursing of the climber.

"Anything?" he called up.

"No, Sir, not so far," was the answer. "But this tree goes up higher than my weight can be supported. The leaves get in the way of seeing anything up higher."

"Come down then," Donau sighed. "We will have a look tomorrow, in daylight." Once the man was down, he added, "Keep a watch here. I will see that you are relieved."

With that, Donau used his phone to call Christian and request a ride back to his car.

On the way, Donau told Christian, "I'll be at the hospital, when you finish here, bring me a report."

"Will do," was the promise. Then he growled as Alex stuck his head between the front seats, and tried to nuzzle his pockets. "Haven't you fed him?"

"You called me before I reached home," Donau admitted. "I will stop on the way to the hospital."

Alex was out of the car as soon as the door was open, and ran to jump into Donau's, going in through the still open window. It was his way of saying, "Hurry up."

His master was suitably prompt, for now that the action was over, he was feeling very hungry too.

Donau chose a small café, ordered hamburgers on rolls, two for him and two for Alex. When they arrived, he ate quickly, but even so by the time he had eaten one, Alex had gobbled two and was looking up hopefully, wanting more.

"That's enough of that!" Donau scolded. "When we get home, I will give you some of the good stuff."

The tail thumped the floor, and one of the chairs moved slightly.

"When we get to the hospital, you will have to wait in the car again. That's hospital rules. I am not allowed to break them!"

Chapter 14 - Aftermath

Wanda woke again and realised she was in an ambulance. She could hear the siren, although it was muffled inside. Her eyes opened then closed, but there was the attendant leaning across her to check something, so no one noticed. Her mind considered what she could sense of her situation. She sensed two people near by - one attendant, and probably a policeman. In her present condition, they'd have her before she could sit up, let alone leave. It wasn't even possible.

By the feel of it, they had put a cervical collar on, and had her on a backboard. She discounted them - she could wiggle her toes and feel the blanket...damn that meant they had taken off her shoes. The hand restraints were in front of her...that was a bonus, but they had put restraints across her chest and legs. She didn't have the energy to fight any of it.

When she tried to recall how they had caught her, she couldn't. She recalled dropping from the tree, starting to run, feeling giddy... she must have passed out. It had to have been an after effect of that knock out drug. Her body reacted oddly to drugs. Once she had realised that, she had (under medical supervision) experimented. In her line of work, she needed to know what would happen if she were given any.

The truth drugs, incapacitated her body, but freed her mind. The knock out ones had a variety of effects, depending on what class of compounds they were. The worst of them would rev her up to unstoppable, and then she would collapse. Others would knock her out for a short time, like the one she'd been given, and then she was fine.

Tonight, she had felt okay when she woke in the room, more than fine once the adrenalin rush had flushed the lingering effects from her system. She had calmed down from the fight or flight feeling, once she had perched in the tree. It was when she had dropped and rolled, that it had hit her again. What she needed to be sure of was what would happen if she got active again now. Would she collapse again, or was the effect almost over? An abortive escape attempt would be disastrous; she would only get one chance.

Perhaps, for now, it would be better to seem vague, and to look for a chance at the hospital. The doctors might insist that the hand restraints came off.

Wanda kept her eyes closed, relaxed her whole body, and waited.

The twitching started as they transferred her to a trolley to wheel her inside. A second policeman joined the parade. The first one kept with her, right into the treatment room. The other waited outside the door.

Wanda felt the twitching, as tremors in all her limbs, and the rapid beating of her heart. She hoped it would ease, but it grew so intense that only the restraints were stopping her from racing off.

She had felt like this before, but in controlled circumstances, and then it was from the drug - and the reaction had come on fast. It had not been this long after the injection. Then, she had worked through it with extremely physical activity - now, she had an overwhelming desire to escape, so that she could work it out again.

They knew she was awake, even though she wasn't responding to their questions. They wanted to know what she had taken. She couldn't tell them that she had been given something. She couldn't make her mouth work to warn them of what might happen. They probably wouldn't believe her anyway.

It took three strong pairs of hands to hold her still enough for them to get blood samples, and to put in an IV drip. They needed to take off the handcuffs, so they could keep her arms restrained. Then they tied them to the trolley with bandages, whilst the xray machine was brought in and used on her.

The twitching was an issue with the xrays, but they were satisfied with the results, and so the annoying collar came off, and they removed the backboard, but they refastened the chest restraints.

All the while, Wanda felt the twitching increasing in strength.

The lab results had been rushed, and the preliminary report was through. The emergency doctor explained things to the policeman, but he understood a great deal less than Wanda did. She, after all, had trained as a paramedic.

No, she hadn't been drinking. The twitching was a hyper-adrenalin reaction - she had very high levels of that. They found traces of a knock-out drug - the name they used was unfamiliar, so Wanda could not predict which group of drugs it was from. The levels of that were still high enough that she should have been unconscious.

It confirmed what Wanda had already deduced. She knew what was building up in her, and tried every trick she knew to relax and calm herself. But it seemed that the harder she tried, the more energy built up inside her. She hoped the restraints were strong enough.

The twitching reached a crescendo, and she was beyond controlling it. Her mind fixated on her last coherent thought - escape.

Donau entered the room just as Wanda's body arched in a kind of spasm. She rocked and twisted in the restraints, unbalancing the trolley. When it hit the floor, the restraints released, and she wrenched free and scrambled up and began to run. Her mind was not in control, for she ran blindly, bounced into a trolley of equipment and knocked it over, she ricocheted into a cupboard with glass and wood doors, turned again and ran to the door. Hands grabbed her and tried to stop her but she wrenched free with seemingly superhuman strength. She erupted out of the treatment room and ran straight ahead, knocking into two nurses, pushing past them and angling now towards the exit. A cleaners cart was in her way, and redirected her towards some stairs, going up.

The policemen were chasing her, aware that the steps went right up to the roof, and they did not want her to fall from there. They were slowed by having to jump over the fallen nurses, and swerve around the upset trolleys and avoid the scattered equipment. They were losing ground.

Donau voiced the urgent need to stop the woman before she reached the roof. He feared she intended suicide. All three men put on a burst of speed, reaching the roof seconds behind her, and seeing her heading directly towards the wall around the edge of the roof. Donau knew very well how agile the woman was, she could be up on that wall in a flash. He tried to hurry faster, but his breath was coming in harsh gasps.

Instead of climbing, the woman bounced off the wall and ran straight back at them. Three pairs of hands grabbed her, managed to contain the frantic mindless struggles and force her down on the concrete surface of the roof. It took all three of them to keep her there, none dared relax as much as a hand to get their handcuffs.

A doctor came out onto the roof, puffing from the run up the stairs. He knelt beside the woman, made an attempt to get a pulse, gave up pulled a bottle and a syringe from a small bag he carried. Within seconds, he had injected the woman with a small dose of a clear fluid. He took and held the patients right wrist, and watched as the struggles eased, and the twitching decreased. The police continued to hold her as the doctor called for a trolley. Two attendants came with it out onto the roof, and lifted the now unconscious woman onto it, and secured her.

Donau, watched the woman as he questioned the doctor. "Is that likely to happen again?"

The doctor admitted, "I don't know. I have never seen a reaction like that before. That injection should counter the adrenalin, but I will need to watch her carefully overnight." He put the used syringe and the partly emptied phial back in his bag.

"Do you have a secure ward," Donau asked, not happy with the turn of events.

"I will see if there is a room in the psych unit," the doctor proposed. "Or we can use full body restraints." He watched Donau's face, and saw the muscles in the jaw twitch.

That would have to do, Donau decided. "I will arrange for a police guard to stay with her. How soon will I be able to question her?"

The doctor began to follow the trolley downstairs. "When I have re-evaluated her condition, I will be able to give you an estimate. Not before morning at least. She will likely be weak and woozy after that counter drug, and she may not be coherent for a while."

"Keep me advised," Donau instructed, taking a card from a small card holder, and handing it to the doctor. He let the doctor go off, and followed at a slower pace. When he was allowed into the emergency room, a different one to where the patient had been first, new blood samples were just going off to the lab, and a new IV had been inserted. The vital signs were still alarming, but were better than they had been before the escape attempt.

Donau went out of the room, gave orders to the two policemen, and summoned two more. Then he returned to his car. Alex met him with a face lick and tried to remind him of the promise of more food.

"I just have to go back to the office, Alex. I won't be long there, then we can go home."

He was no longer feeling pleased about his day's work, and he wondered if Christian had finished at the guesthouse and made a report.

After letting himself in through the night entrance, Donau took the elevator up to his office, rather than the stairs. Alex, refused to enter the elevator, woofed and raced for the stairs. He was canine grinning when the elevator door opened on the next floor up.

Donau had to grin, as he pretended to race his dog to his office. Alex had run to where he kept one of his noisy toys, while his master went to his desk. The message he found there had been left several hours earlier, but it told him to call his superior as soon as he got the message.

The clock on the wall told him it was eleven-thirty, Kolbe, his superior, would be at home. Did he really want to be woken? Reaching for the phone, Donau checked the relevant number, he had it programmed into his phone, and dialled - ready with an apology if the man had been asleep.

Kolbe sounded wide awake, for after Donau announced himself, he said, "I hoped you would call. Good work this evening, catching that diamond thief. Where have you got her?"

Donau related the events surrounding the capture and at the hospital.

"Trying to escape?" Kolbe queried.

"I am not sure," Donau admitted. "The doctor says her behaviour was a drug reaction. Someone administered a knock out drug, and from the levels in her, she should have been unconscious."

"Could she have taken it herself, on purpose?" Kolbe asked.

"I doubt it, though we should not assume she didn't. If she

intended to escape, she would not want to be incapacitated. And she couldn't know we would take her to the hospital, not directly to the remand prison.'"

"If she is an American, she may not know our procedures," Kolbe reminded him. "Were you able to question her?"

"No, she was unconscious when I first got to her, and she was pretty well out to it even when she was running."

"What about the diamonds? Do we have them?"

"No, Sir. They were not at the guesthouse."

"But you are sure that she is the thief?"

"There is little doubt, Sir. She left a case in the room at the guest house. There were tools in there that could be used for illegal entry. I have the people working under Christian looking for a small backpack, but we may have to repeat the search in daylight." Donau reported all he knew, adding, "Christian should have a report for me by morning."

Kolbe accepted that, considering the time, and told Donau in turn, "I have sent a request to Interpol for any information they have on international jewel thieves. I heard the media speculating that last night's thief was one. Was there anything else?"

"Yes, although it is just a feeling. I think she was fleeing from the men who attacked the guesthouse."

"Then double the security at the hospital, and arrange to get that woman to the prison first thing tomorrow," Kolbe directed.

Donau gave the expected, "Yes, Sir," and tried not to yawn.

"I want to know as soon as she is able to be questioned."

Donau repeated his, "Yes, Sir," and was glad when Kolbe rang off. He was just finishing the arrangements for extra security at the hospital, when Alex barked a warning. He turned and saw Christian walk in, with a bunch of folders under one arm, and biting into a roll with ham and cheese.

Alex slunk around the room to approach from behind. A second bark, louder this time, caused Christian to drop his roll, in preference to losing the folders under his arm. The roll never even reached the floor. Donau pretended to shuffle things on his desk to hide a smile. His expression was serious when he looked up again.

"Didn't expect to find you here. I was going to do my report and leave it on your desk," Christian said, after giving Alex an 'I'll get you.' glare.

"What have you got?" Donau asked.

"Nothing on the bag search," Christian began. "I have the list of things in that room, and the case. That's in the evidence locker downstairs. There were some interesting things in that case. I highlighted them on the list." He had the folders on his desk, and selected one.

Donau took it and began to read, but was still listening to his subordinate.

"They found nothing in the room to identify the intruders, though we had security footage showing them in the upper level passage. The bullet they took from the wall is of Russian manufacture. The fingerprints have no match in our files, do you want them sent to Interpol?"

"Kolbe has already contacted them for information," Donau spoke almost absently. Something interesting had caught his eye in the list. "Certainly, send them through. What did you make of this list."

"Little doubt that she is a thief," the younger man shrugged. "There is enough theatrical make-up to turn her into just about anyone. Some of the stuff explains how she got into and out of Alpha Prime."

"No, I mean the two laundry bags. One has a child's clothing inside. The bags have the name of the apartments where that missing American was staying."

"I kept them separate. They may be useful," Christian shrugged.

"She must have gone there straight from the hospital," Donau explained. "Though by the time we got there the place had been cleaned out."

"She must have been intending to find the man," Christian suggested. "She might have considered how your food thief could use them."

"Alex wasn't with me in the hospital," Donau told him. "She wouldn't have known of him. So why did she take the stuff?"

"I am out of ideas," Christian yawned. "Do I need to stay? I'll have the report for you in the morning."

"Go home!" Donau agreed. "But I want it as soon as I can. Kolbe wants to be kept up to date. Though I intend to be up early. He wants that woman at the prison, first thing. I want to oversee the transfer - in case those masked men from this evening, make another try for her."

Donau, Leonard Christian, and a third member of his team, Rudolph Bauer, met the relief team of guards at the hospital. They were waiting at the ambulance entrance as he had directed, and the car they would use to transport her was in an ambulance slot. Only Donau went up, after commanding Alex to stay in the car.

He went up to the psych unit, and presented his identification before being allowed in. A nurse directed him to the private room where his prisoner had spent the night. Once inside the room, he nodded to the two police guards and waited until after a nurse had completed taking the usual observations of blood pressure, pulse and temperature, before interrupting her. In the meantime, he studied the woman on the bed, noticing how pale she was, and how her wrists were tied to the side of the bed. His own presence did not seem to have registered on her. As he walked closer, he saw the woman's eyes, watching the nurse. They did not even flick in his direction. Compared to last night, she seemed totally lethargic.

"How is she?" Donau asked the nurse.

"Vital signs are normal," he was told. "She is weak, but that is to be expected."

"I am here to escort her into remand. Are her clothes here?"

"In the drawer," the nurse gestured.

Donau recalled the ideas he'd had the previous night, and went to the drawer and took out the trousers that woman had been wearing. He checked the wide seams, but nothing resisted his bending. He did discover that the trousers were reversible.

Clever, he thought, as he checked the pockets of both sides and found only a few small coins. He still had her passport and the rest of the money she'd had when he arrested her. He was keeping an eye on the woman via his peripheral vision as he examined her clothes. She gave no sign of a reaction to what he was doing, and he decided that his suspicions of the previous night had been groundless.

Hard on that thought, he reminded himself not to be fooled. The woman, in her black haired guise, had been deceptively docile two nights ago, and had fooled him into thinking he had not met her before and that she was merely a squatter. And then she had freed herself and jumped from the car.

He studied her face again. Was this her real face? It had to be, for the pallor was too real, and the brown eyes were slightly bloodshot.

He went to the bed and asked, "How are you feeling?" He kept his tone neutral, though he wondered what her reaction would be. Did she recall that it was he who arrested her?

"Like an effing truck ran over me," she said in American English. "Have you figured out who spiked me?"

"What can you tell me?" Donau replied in English, wondering if she knew why he was there.

"Some creeps burst into my room and tried to kill me," Wanda claimed, deciding to pretend she was an innocent victim.

"What did you do?"

"Ran like hell," was her claim. "Climbed out the window and got over the roof. The creeps didn't expect that - they had the door covered."

"How many were there?"

"Four, all masked."

"Who were they?" Donau asked.

"How do I know. I just came her to help my Aunt's friend. So why am I tied up here and why are you taking me to some jail?"

Weak she might be, Donau thought, but she wasn't going to admit anything.

"We will talk about that at Speilsburg," Donau said carefully. "You won't have to worry about the masked men there." He turned to the nurse. "Can you see that she gets dressed?"

"Yes, Sir. If you would be so kind as to close the curtains?"

"What if she tries something?"

"You'll be right there, and I have been dealing with psych patients for a long time."

Donau didn't like it, but he pulled the curtains shut. He heard the undoing of the Velcro wrist restraints and the nurse saying, "I will help you sit up. Just sit in the side of the bed for a bit first. You will still be feeling light headed and weak. While you do that, I will take out the IV drip."

Donau gestured to the two guards, still watching from the doorway. One of them approached, and he asked, quietly, "Any trouble during the night?"

"None, Sir. Woman woke an hour ago and has been quiet since then."

Wanda took the nurses advice. She remembered how she had been after the tests she had made with various drugs. Still, 'weak' was an understatement, but her mind was clearing.

Her danger sense had kicked in, albeit mildly, just before Donau had entered. The two guards she had noticed earlier had not bothered her. In fact, she had found their presence comforting. In her current condition, and as she had been the previous night, she would be no match for those masked gunmen, or that creep Lunn.

She caught the question Donau asked of the guards. She had been awake for more than several hours, but had not wanted to show it. In that time, she had learnt exactly what her situation was. She was indeed under arrest, suspected of the diamond robbery. The two guards had warned the nurse when she had come on shift. What she didn't know was if they had found her bag and those cursed diamonds. If they hadn't, she might convince them she was a victim, being framed.

"Let me help you get dressed," the nurse interrupted her thoughts. "The top first."

Wanda tried to help, but raising her arms was a torment, she felt like she had no energy.

"Now, I will help you off the bed. Hold onto me if you feel unsteady."

Again, Wanda followed the directions, easing down onto her feet and gradually putting her full weight on her legs. Yes, she was weak, but it was not as bad as she had feared. Still, she intended to mislead the policemen, so she let her legs collapse under her.

The nurse had an arm supporting her, so although she fell, it was against the bed, and not onto the floor. She sensed Donau reacting to the noise.

The nurse held her upright and used her foot to lower the bed.

"Just sit for a bit longer and I will get you something to drink."

Wanda waited until she was alone behind the curtain to check the waist of her trousers. Her fingers felt for the flexible metal bits in the band, and was gratified to feel they were still there. That was all she had time for; the nurse returned with a beaker full of water, and Wanda received it gratefully. Her throat was as parched as a desert.

"Feeling better?" the nurse asked when Wanda had finished the entire beaker full.

"I need to use the toilet," Wanda spoke softly. The nurse simply helped her to the small side chamber, and let her do what was needed. The window in there was small and the glass reinforced. She did not close the door, but only she would be able to see into the room.

Wanda was moving with deliberate slowness, but as she began to move, she felt her body begin to unstiffen. Once she had food, she would feel even better, but she doubted if the police would think to give her any.

By the time she had finished her personal need, she was able to cooperate with the nurse to finish getting dressed. Her mind had cleared of the last of the fogginess, and for this, she was glad. She had to think of a way out of her predicament.

Since waking at four am, she had been trying to recall the night's events. Parts had been unclear, and still were, but she recalled the ambulance, and the treatment room, and the twitchiness. That's when her memories were a blur - as if her mind had been working a thousand times faster than normal and her body had been trying to keep up. And the weakness she had felt...after the twitchiness...oh, she knew what had happened, she'd freaked out.

Had she babbled? No, or Donau would have betrayed the fact. She was sure...yes, sure...that Donau only thought she was Carson. That was bad enough, but had been the reason she had come with two identities. So, she would let the policeman think she was still very weak. He might not be fooled by docility, but maybe he would by the weakness. Maybe he would be slightly less alert, and she would have a chance to get away. She had to get free, but she did not dare admit to being a US agent. If the police discovered that, the shit would hit the fan.

The nurse helped her secure her belt, noticing nothing odd about it. Wanda checked her pockets, but already knew they had been emptied.

"Where's my effing stuff?" she asked, just loudly enough to be heard beyond the curtain.

"I have that," Donau admitted.

Wanda muttered a curse. "I don't know what you are trying to pin on me, but you had effing well better pay for a phone call."

"Why?" Donau asked, as the nurse moved the curtains back.

Wanda saw that two more policemen had crept into the room. She hadn't heard them arrive.

"Aren't I allowed one?"

"One can be made for you," Donau suggested.

"Bastard," she muttered, being deliberately rude. She turned to the nurse and asked politely, "Do you have something I can use to comb my hair?"

A comb was produced from the little bag of frequently needed items that the nurse wore at her waist, and Wanda was helped over to the washbasin, which had a small mirror, protected by a wire screen.

As she combed her hair out, so that it dangled down around her face, she used the mirror to confirm that the brown eye lenses were still in place. She was also able to confirm that the plastiskin on her forearms was undisturbed.

They had put the drip in a vein in the back of her hand; probably they could not find one in her arm because of the false skin.

She has surreptitiously confirmed that her ultra flexible, and very sharp knife, was still in the seam of her trousers. She was, therefore, not out of resources, just temporarily out of ideas. She was in no condition to take on five others, six if she included the nurse, so she would just have to play weak and watch for a chance.

Chapter 15 - Assisted escape

From overhearing things whilst she was thought to be asleep, Wanda had a very good idea of what the police thought they knew. However, unless they had found her stuff, they couldn't prove it, but if they were taking her to some remand place, it meant they had either arrested her for something or wanted to hold her until they could prove their theories. Donau had tried to imply going there was for her safety, but that would not explain why he had taken her Carson passport and her money. And the extra guards...to her it meant that he thought she would escape.

Well, she would pretend to be cooperative innocent victim...

"Hey!" she protested when one of the police officers moved behind her and grabbed her wrists.

"What are you doing?" she spoke in English, but then translated it.

"You are under arrest!" the policeman informed her.

Wanda glared at Donau. "What on Earth for?"

Donau humoured her and spoke in English. "For the diamond robbery at Alpha Prime."

"What the heck is Aplha Prime?"

"Fraulein Carson, we found tools for burglary at the guest house - in your case, and make-up."

"So?" Wanda challenged. "I am looking for Nicole's family. Why would I rob a place I have never heard of?"

"Your friend's husband went there." Donau was watching her as closely as she was watching him.

"Wow, how did you get to be an Inspector of Police?" Wanda said derisively. "I was attacked, probably by thugs who were told the same lies that you were. Someone doesn't want me to look for the Wexford's."

"And who might that be?" Donau asked, rhetorically. "We can discuss this at Spielsburg."

"But why the handcuffs? You have no evidence I did anything wrong?" Wanda insisted.

"What about the clothing you took from the Wexford apartment?"

"What about it?"

"How did you get in? Did Frau Wexford give you a key?"

"She gave me permission to go there."

Wanda lied, but kept eye contact with Donau.

"You broke in there."

"Is Nicole pressing charges?"

"No, but I am," Donau a told her to end the standoff. "And when the fingerprints taken from the police car that transported the thief from Alpha Prime are compared to yours, your lies will be useless."

Wanda saw the tiniest muscle twitch in Donau's cheek, and she knew he was lying. He had only just thought of that possibility.

"Enjoy your fantasy," Wanda invited. The idea had given her a moment of alarm, but she had better control of her reactions than Donau had, and he was good. When she had opened the door, she had done it with her fingers in the sleeve of her jacket. There would be no prints there.

"I am going to get a lawyer and I am going to sue the whole damn Vienna Police force," she added, as she decided she had better say nothing more.

Even though she had given Donau a legitimate reason to hold her, though that would have been true anyway, her protests had given Donau pause. He gestured to the policeman, and the handcuffs were secured in front of her, a more comfortable option. She had half expected to be secured to one of the two hefty officers. For now, there was nothing more she could do. No doubt, Donau had been given orders.

Her vague ideas for escape looked impossible once she emerged into the early morning air, and was led past an ambulance and gently forced into a dark coloured car. Two more officers were waiting with two men in plain clothes, beside a marked police car and a dark blue sedan. She saw Alex leap out of the latter, and try to poke his nose into the car after her.

She wished he'd leave her alone. If Donau needed convincing that she and the woman at Alpha Prime were the same, the dog had just given it to him. The only good thing was it was not likely to be believed in court.

Mentally, she sent out a plea, "Don't let them find my stuff."

All the same, she thought, who did they think she was? Would a slight female jewel thief warrant a seven person escort? Did they really think those masked men would come back after her? She didn't. They had their chance and left her for Lunn to find. Damn! She had to get away.

From the car, she saw her escort sort themselves out. One police officer sat beside her in the back seat of one dark car, another officer took the front passenger seat and one of the plain clothed men went to the driver's seat. Donau took his dog to the dark blue sedan, and had the other plain clothed man with him. Two officers went to the marked police car.

By the time the car began moving, Wanda had already worked one of the wire pieces free from her belt, and had it in her right hand. Then, she used the pretext of looking to see where they were going, to test the door handle.

"No use trying to open the door," her nearest escort warned her. "They won't open from the inside."

Wanda slumped back into the seat with a sense of frustration. Damn them! She closed her eyes to mere slits and pretended to doze. She didn't think she was fooling them, they were too alert.

Besides, even if she did get out, she wouldn't get far with Donau following behind and the other car up ahead.

Her mind was on ways to escape, and she thought to herself that some back up now might be really useful. But she had relied on her own wits for a long time...there would be a way.

The crack of a shot and the veering of the car were completely unexpected. Instinct made her grab the front of her seat companion's uniform and pull him down, just ahead of the shattering of the side windows as another bullet screamed past.

Donau had been right, the bastards were trying to get her, and she muttered to herself in English, "I'll get the bastards."

The driver was trying to control the wildly spinning car, but in the next moment, the front of the car hit something solid and the two men in the front were thrown forward, even with the seat belt, and fell back.

Wanda raised her head slowly, to look around. She was hearing more gun fire, and wanted to work out where it was coming from. She could not see the sniper. Quickly, she reached out and checked the man beside her. He had a graze on the back of his head, where the bullet had narrowly missed him, but he was alive. As she reached to check on the others, the door beside her was wrenched open and a rough hand grabbed her by the fabric of her clothes.

"Out!" was all she heard, and the voice was muffled by the face covering ski mask. She heard a gun discharge close by, and did not try to fight the man who held her. His grip on her clothing was making the neck opening cut into her throat. He dragged her out, and forced her to run.

At first she was half dragged, but then she found her feet, only to stumble in instinctive reaction to a bullet that whizzed past her ear. She found her feet, and ran, while her mind was repeating, "Please don't let them shoot me." She wasn't sure if she meant the police or the masked men.

It seemed the invisible powers she prayed to heard her, for she was dragged to the back of an anonymous white van. There, without warning, her captor picked her up and tossed her into the back, just as he might have tossed a sack of vegetables or a side of beef. He was in the van with her, and shouting, "GO!"

The van's tyres shrieked on the tarmac as the engine revved, and then the van took off at high speed. In the distance, Wanda could hear sirens, and her captor was staring out a small window in the back.

She willed him to keep looking out, to stay contemptuous of her as a threat, and in moments she had freed her hands. Then she stood, silently, and steadied her breathing as she planned her attack. The freight space of the van was empty, it was tall enough for her new captor to stand, and long enough for Wanda to make a short run.

Although she moved softly, the man sensed her attack at the last moment and began to turn towards her. Before he could shout a warning to the driver, Wanda's kick boxing attack stuck him in the neck, and he fell heavily against the door, knocking his head. He was unconscious and breathing with difficulty, but Wanda wasn't going to stay and do first aid. She shoved him away from the door and opened it. The van was still going fast, and the police cars had been forced back by a truck that was skewed across the road. She had little time to consider her next move, one that most people would think was suicidal, but she knew exactly what she was doing.

She had to act while the road behind the van was free of cars; she leapt, curled into a ball, and rolled. The landing was still a hard jolt, but the immediate roll, slowed her momentum. Before the pain kicked in, she was up on her feet and running for the nearest cover; her mind in survival mode.

She ran into the driveway of a private house, raced through the back garden, to the back fence. She scrambled over, into another garden, and this time went to the side fence and worked her way along the row of houses until she came to one with a locked shed. She had the lock opened in seconds, went inside, and curled into a ball on the dirt floor. Some of the gardens she had fled through had lock up garages, but the shed had seemed a safer option.

She didn't care if she only had a few square feet of space, and that the shed smelt of garden chemicals. She was out of immediate sight, and needed to deal with the waves of pain, that seemed to be making her whole body throb and the blood pound in her ears.

Her position was still perilous. The truck might still be racing away, but then men in it had friends, lots of friends, some may have seen her escape and even now be looking for her.

"Don't let anyone find me," Wanda repeated over and over, as her abused body sent shooting pain messages to her brain.

After a while, the intensity of the pain dropped, and she could think again. The first thing Wanda told herself was, "That was damn stupid." Then she began a series of increasingly vile curses, as she tried to think the pain away.

When she had forcibly relaxed, and eased the pain enough to be functional, she began to plan. She needed help, and the last helpers had not been the cavalry she had wanted. Now the police would be convinced that she was in league with a gang of violent thugs, as well as being a thief. She would have to ditch her Carson persona. Then perhaps there would only be one group of hunters after her.

But she had no ID, and no money. If she could get to the US Embassy, that could be rectified.

Just then, she heard voices that seemed to be just outside the shed. She froze in place and began her, "Don't let anyone find me," mantra again.

She listened, and closer than the screaming sirens, a car door opened and closed. A car started, revved a bit, and returned to idle. A second door opened and closed. Wanda forced herself to stand, and look edgeways though the tiny side window. A red car was reversing out of sight along the side of the house to the street. The sound of its engine soon faded.

While part of her was reluctant to leave her shelter, Wanda wondered if the house the people had left had a phone, and if Austrians made a habit of locking their doors. As she thought it, whatever power sent her warnings, was giving her an urgent one. Without questioning it, and without neglecting caution, Wanda glanced through the slit in the doorway, saw no one and raced stiffly towards the back door. That the door was locked, was only a momentary inconvenience. She went in, and relocked the door behind her.

An odd sounding bell rang in the front of the house. Wanda nearly jumped out of her skin, knowing that she had not thought to check for other occupants, or for signs of an alarm. The bell came again after a moment, and now Wanda realised it was the front door bell, and her sense of danger was like a snake crawling around her body. She realised, that whoever was ringing might be looking for her. If no one answered, the caller might well walk around the house checking windows and doors, and might even look inside.

She was in the laundry, and the window had no curtains, but if she huddled on the floor, no one would see her, not even if they looked through the glass in the back door.

The back door rattled as if someone was trying to open it. It didn't. Then she heard a thump at the window, and it rattled but didn't open. As much as she wished to know who was outside, she didn't try to look. It was more likely the friends of the masked men, rather than the police.

It seemed like a long time before the sense of 'people nearby' receded, and Wanda felt it was safe to move.

Once she did, she found that the pain was back. Her whole body had gone tense. Now, she had to force herself to move, to search for a phone, to call for help.

The house was scrupulously neat, and she did nothing to disturb that state. She wanted no one to realise that she had been there.

On a table near the front door, Wanda found an elegant hand piece on an equally elegant phone base, she lifted the hand piece and used the old style finger dialler to call the US Embassy.

The calm voice of the telephone operator relieved her. She asked for Neil Thompson, and he came on the line seconds later.

"It's Wanda Martin. I need your help."

Her contact was quick on the uptake. "Where are you?"

The answer to that was on an envelope next to the phone. The thrifty owners had a neat pile of used envelopes to use as notepaper.

Thompson whistled softly and said, "Do you realise that the police have a huge manhunt going on in that area?"

"Woman hunt, and yes," Wanda admitted. "Can you pick me up?"

"Fifteen minutes, if I don't get held up. I will have the embassy work van. It's dark blue."

"Don't get held up," Wanda urged him.

It was nearer twenty minutes when the van stopped outside the house. Wanda was out of the house, the door locking behind her, and into the passenger seat in less than twenty seconds. Thompson drove off immediately.

"There's an embassy jacket behind the seat, as well as a brush and comb. And take the brown lenses out."

Wanda reached for the items and wasted no time donning the jacket, even though it was awkward, before clipping in the seat belt. Thompson glanced at her as she groaned faintly.

She used the small mirror under the sun visor to brush out her hair, and was relieved to find no trace of her ordeal on her face. Everywhere else felt battered and bruised. In the plastic bag that had held the brush were hair ties and hair pins. Since Donau had last seen her with it tied back, and then out, she just took the side hair and tied that back. After that, she removed the brown lenses and wrapped them in a tissue from the glove box and slipped them in her pocket.

"I have never in my life been so glad to see anyone," Wanda told Thompson. "Thank you."

"Pleasure, but don't relax yet. I was searched on the way here and the van may be checked again on the way back. I am going a different way, just in case. Who is after you? The police?"

"Them, yes, and the people who pinched me from them."

Thompson gave her another sharp glance, but asked no more questions. "Well, my job is to help prevent major diplomatic incidents," he said instead. "I did warn the marine guards that I might be in a hurry on my return."

"And you might not be joking," Wanda warned him. "Were those youths still hanging around the embassy when you left?"

"Uh-huh."

"Well, I think they are related to a nasty bunch of gun wielding masked men."

"Maybe you should hunker down in the back when we get past the road blocks."

"A very good idea, I think."

In the back, lying prone against the front seats, and covered with a dark canvas, she wouldn't be noticeable. The windows at the back of the van were tinted, so anyone looking in would not be able to see her unless she made a silhouette. With that idea in mind, she told Thompson to return at a casual pace, as if he had been on a routine errand.

As she had expected, the van was surged by the dozen young men, as they tried to see in the front and the back of the van. They began to move away even as the marine guards and police approached to move them. After exchanging a few pointed remarks to the guards, Thompson drove the van around the back of the building, out of sight. Wanda crawled out of hiding as soon as the van stopped.

"You can use the Ohio Room on level three," Thompson told her. "Do you need anything else?"

Wanda took him literally. "I need to get a message to Jim, a completely new wardrobe, and a new android tablet."

"Dare I ask?" Thompson began, but Wanda cut him off.

"Not just now."

They were entering the embassy, and two more marine guards were acting as door men. A subtle sign of the heightened state of alert. Once they were out of earshot, Wanda continued.

"I need a long soak in a hot bath, but will make do with a shower. I need to find a suit, and all accessories, and I need it before that Inspector Donau thinks to come looking for me. I need a new passport, money, the works."

"The passport will be problematical," Thompson warned her. "But if you give me a list of what you want, I will authorise one of the girls to get the things."

"Can you order them by phone and have them delivered?"

Thompson nodded, "Anything else?"

"A huge breakfast and a litre of vitamin water."

"And then you will tell me what happened?"

"Mmm," Wanda hummed without committing herself. "Could you, if anyone asks, say I came in very late last night, around eleven. And, I am tied up in a meeting until further notice?"

"Very well. What do you need to tell Jim?"

"Come upstairs shortly and I will give you my list, and encrypt the message for Jim."

Wanda left Thompson at the foot of the stairs, and found her own way to the Ohio Room. It was one of the rooms equipped for guests and on the bed next to towels was an ankle length terry robe. Wanda grabbed it and the towels and went directly to start the shower, and strip off the foul clothing she had spent the past day in.

She gave herself five minutes under the hot water, feeling her muscles relaxing. During that time, she washed her hair and made liberal use of the bodywash provided. She saw bruises already turning black, on her arms and legs, though fortunately she could hide them all. They were the result of her leap from the truck.

If Donau came, and she was positive he would, she now had a chance of acting normally, and not as if she had been knocked out, come to, scrambled over fences, climbed a tree, fallen from it, gone berserk in a hospital, got tranked and restrained, dragged from a car and jumped from a moving van.

She had the dressing gown on and was using a hairdryer when Thompson knocked on the door. He had one of the kitchen staff with him, and there was covered tray on a trolley. He was carrying an odd looking box and a coil of telephone cable. Wanda let them both in, and closed the door once the embassy chef had retreated out of the room.

Thompson was busy, inserting the box in the line between the telephone wall plug and the handset.

"Jim has a secure mobile, he leaves it on to retrieve messages. I thought if he was listening it would be faster than getting a message to him."

Wanda agreed, but she asked, "Can I call home too?"

Thompson grinned. "If the boss don't like it, he'll charge you for the call. Go ahead, I will let you know when your necessities arrive."

Wanda thanked him and passed him the list she had hastily scribbled after leaving the shower.

Wanda called the number that Thompson had written on a sticky note, pasted to the box. It answered immediately with Jim's brief repetition of the phone number.

"W," she said first. "I have proof of a second cabal, working on the first. They know the state department is sniffing around. Not sure where they fit in. Looking at."

She didn't expect a reply, but within seconds of hanging up, she got a call back.

Chapter 16 - In plain sight

"Go home!" Jim's voice said immediately. "Have you seen this morning's news?"

"I don't have to," Wanda told him. "I can't leave. I haven't got a passport."

"Then don't stick your nose out of the Embassy."

"Jim, I can't find Wexford or his daughter from here. Do you know where they are?"

She heard Jim inhale. "No." He seemed to sigh and then he directed, "Tell me what happened."

Wanda reported tersely, with no unnecessary words. She left out nothing, including how the second group knew both her identities and had taken her diplomatic passport.

"I do not like this," Jim stressed before asking, "Do you have any theories?"

"Apart from them not wanting me to find things out - possibly about Wexford, no."

"You still think he is up to something shady," Jim quizzed her.

"Yes."

"Do whatever you need to, to get Nichole to open up. See if she has any idea, any suspicions, that Wexford is involved in an illegal deal. The cabal is to meet tonight, and I will be going. If I see Wexford there, I'll try to talk to him."

"Won't that be dangerous?"

Jim didn't answer that, but commented, "That little business of yours has helped a great deal. Did you send those items off to where you said?"

Wanda didn't want to answer, but Jim insisted. "Did you?"

"I was going to get a better mailing thing when I spotted the watchers."

"So no?"

"Uh huh."

"Where are they now?"

"Either up a tree or the police have them."

"I hope...this doesn't blow up in our faces," Jim told her, then added, "Stay at the Embassy."

"That would be smart," Wanda agreed before hanging up. And then she admitted to herself, "If I had any smarts."

She knew Jim was right, to a point. However, this was her mission, and she had made little progress, and was running out of time.

Maybe her smarts would return after she had eaten. Certainly she would start to feel stronger, and the smell of a hearty cooked breakfast was making her empty stomach growl.

The chef had also brought in a copy of the morning edition of Vienna's main newspaper. She read the headline on the front page, saw her 'Carson' face, taken from her passport and with the white hair streaks touched over. She read the article as she ate, but it told her nothing of what she really wanted to know, and it did not mention that she had escaped. At least, the officers in the car were not badly injured.

She finished breakfast and considered calling David. She calculated the time difference, it would be very late in LA, but there was a chance he would be up still, more than a chance that he would be worried, since she'd had no chance to tell him anything since she'd had to flee.

The phone was answered on the first ring.

"Dav?" She heard an exhalation of relief.

"Thank God!" David Martin said fervently. "What happened?"

"I got away from the armed men, away from the police and I am snug in the embassy."

"Do you have a report to send? I have got nothing."

"Ah...no. I don't have my tablet. I left it up a tree. How's Davy?"

"Do not...change the subject," David warned her. "Davy is asleep and your sister is here. She says you're in trouble."

"I'm fine Dav, really."

In the background, very clearly, she heard her sister's voice. "Tell her to think again."

"Wanda?" David queried, for she had gone quiet.

"I'm fine," Wanda repeated, but with less insistence. Speaking to David was making her lose control. She wanted to cry...an irrational after reaction. It did not take much more insistence to get her telling David everything she had told Jim.

Then David went quiet, and Wanda knew that he was thinking.

"It's Wexford. Something he is doing."

"I have figured that much," Wanda agreed, trying to sound normal.

"Have you thought it might be someone like Jackie and Les had to deal with last year?" David said unexpectedly. "When Vera was in trouble too?"

"What? Here?"

"Why not? A different branch of the family."

"Oh God!" Wanda exhaled. "Could they know I interfered then?"

"We told the FBI not to mention us, so the risk is slight. But I agree with Jim. Get out! I'm not there to back you up."

"No, I can't. I have to find Rachel and her father."

"He might be a traitor!" David argued.

"Rachel then, she's innocent."

"Damn it," David cursed. "What about Davy? What if they know and plan to kill you?"

"Davy has you. And if they wanted to kill me, they'd have done it last night, or this morning. I am still alive and I have a chance to unmask them. I'm the perfect bait, and they don't know me."

"They won't let you trick them again, like that," David warned her.

"I won't use the same tricks," Wanda promised, feeling her mind and body returning to full function.

"I'm going to fly there," David decided abruptly. "You had better be there to meet me at Vienna Airport."

"I will, I promise," Wanda said with mental finger crossed. However, the thought of having David working with her was a relief.

Less than half an hour later, Neil Thompson let himself into the Ohio Room, when his discreet knock went unanswered. His presence woke Wanda from a power nap in the chair.

"What time is it?" she asked, taking in the half dozen large bags from some of Vienna's leading stores.

"Nine thirty. You have an appointment in half an hour. Donau is insisting that you clear your schedule to see him. Also, you may like to watch the satellite news. There is a report on the man hunt for the masked gunmen who fired on two police cars and rescued a dangerous criminal. Your Carson face is being shown prominently."

"Thanks," Wanda said calmly. Talking to David had purged her mind, returning it to full working order. "Did Donau ask what time I returned yesterday?"

"No, just if you got back safely. I said you had."

"Page me when he arrives, will you? If I am not here, I will be down with Nicole."

Thompson nodded and retreated so that Wanda could dress in the new clothes.

Wanda did not keep Donau waiting. She trotted down the front stairs, ignoring her protesting muscles and smiling a greeting. She let the smile fall away when she saw his face. He looked haggard, and the muscles around his eyes were tense.

She gestured him towards a small meeting room and opened the door for him.

"Neil Thompson said you wanted to see me, and your insistence made it sound important. I guess he was right. We can talk in here. Do you want coffee or something stronger?"

Donau walked through the door, followed by his canine shadow. "Coffee, yes," he agreed, going straight to one of the circle of armchairs.

He waited for her to sit before speaking, but all the while she was arranging for coffee, a morning snack and a morsel for Alex, she felt Donau's eyes on her. She was thankful that whoever had ordered the clothes had been highly efficient. He would be seeing the same efficient, businesslike State Department Investigator, he'd met yesterday. It was a good thing he couldn't see the bruises, or feel the soreness.

"I saw in the paper that you caught that jewel thief. Quick work." Wanda hoped to get him talking.

"We had an anonymous tip," Donau admitted, looking across the room at the paintings of New York that was the theme of the room.

"The address we were given led us to the Carson woman."

"Is that why you are here?" Wanda asked.

"One reason. There is no doubt in my mind that she is the same woman that I caught at Alpha Prime, even though that woman had black hair. We compared prints taken from her room with one lifted from the car she jumped from."

Wanda nodded, giving no indication that she was thinking back to that moment. Perhaps she had not covered all her fingers. She asked what she really wanted to know. "Did you find the diamonds?"

"Yes," Donau admitted, sounding slightly less depressed. "But we did not release that to the press. Did you read about the intruders that went there before us?"

"Not all of it - I don't read your language as well as I speak it," Wanda lied calmly. "It sounded to me like they were after Carson too."

"That whole business is confusing. There's no doubt that she left in a hurry, and had intended to leave. Her case had everything just thrown in, but she didn't take it. We have a witness who saw her go out over the roof, after the raiders left and not long before we arrived."

"Decidedly odd," Wanda agreed, "It makes it look like she was in league with those intruders, and they fell out."

As soon as she said the words, she regretted it.

"An idea that is supported by this morning's events." Donau's face tightened, and Wanda guessed he was thinking of the injured police officers. "A similar group of armed men attacked the cars taking her to Spielsburg. They helped her to escape."

Wanda considered that uneasily, when she said, "So, what do you hope I can do?"

The coffee arrived, and Donau fell silent. Wanda took the role of hostess, pouring coffee and offering him a plate of American style cakes. She put a plate of dog treats on the floor. Alex inched forward and sniffed them, but did not eat.

"Ah, have I done something wrong? Won't he eat them?"

Donau gave a command that did not sound like German. Alex woofed and began gobbling.

"This is good," Donau said appreciatively. He saw she wasn't drinking and asked, "Aren't you having coffee?"

"I think I will stick to water," Wanda decided. "That very nice coffee smell is doing nothing for me."

It was actually making her queasy...like when she was pregnant with Davy. She did take a cake.

"So, like I said, what can I do?"

"I want to find that group. Vienna is a quiet city. We don't tolerate violent gangsters."

"Are you suggesting that they could be American," Wanda challenged.

"Carson is American," Donau countered. "How does it look to you?"

"As a surname, Carson is American enough, but Tatiana is not a name that is common there. It sounds more Slavic, or Russian."

"She knew the Wexford's and she had garments taken from their apartment. She must have gone straight there from the hospital after talking to me. She must have known where to go."

Wanda didn't quite know what Donau was leading to so she said, "I recall you saying that the apartment had been entered before you got there - was it her, then?"

"The apartment was cleared out, and cleaned thoroughly." Donau's face was stony, but he admitted, "Finding those garments might help us find the child. We have put photos of Wexford and his daughter in the newspapers."

"Carson did tell Nicole she would be looking for them. It seems that she was."

"If she was, why did she go and rob a diamond trader?" Donau asked. "Nothing is making sense."

"You don't have all the facts yet," Wanda said, considering that an understatement. She still didn't know why she had taken those damn diamonds. "Do you have Carson's passport?"

She knew he did, but not officially as herself.

He took it from an inside pocket of his jacket, and Wanda rose to take it. She opened it and studied it as if looking for signs that it was a forgery.

"It looks genuine. If it isn't I want to know who made it."

"Could I compare it to yours?" Donau sounded official, but he was aware that he was on 'foreign soil'.

"That won't be possible," Wanda told him, still looking at her other passport.

"Oh?"

"Sorry Inspector, official reasons. And it is a diplomatic passport, so it is different to normal ones."

Wanda changed the subject. "Mr Thompson said there were road blocks around the place this morning. Did you find any trace of the men or your prisoner?"

"No."

"I read there were injuries," Wanda said with sympathy.

Donau met her look and nodded. "Bauer, who works with me, was driving the car that had Carson in it. He is in a serious condition. The officer that was in the front passenger seat is critical. The one that was next to Carson, took a bullet in the shoulder. He is lucky he didn't get one in the neck. He said that the woman pulled him down. He believes she was expecting the attack, for he heard her say, 'get the bastards'."

Wanda could guess what he was thinking from the tightening of his jaw muscle. Logically, and to put him off from that idea, she said, "If she wanted her escorts dead, why would she pull him down - or was she merely ducking?"

"No, she definitely pulled. I can't decide what to make of her," Donau admitted.

"When you find her, ask her," Wanda suggested, hoping that he would never find out that Carson was herself. "If your department sends Carson's prints, I can arrange for the FBI to run them through their files." It was safe enough even if he took up the offer. She knew her prints were not on file, and hers as Wanda Dean had been removed.

"We sent her photo and prints off to Interpol. They are sending an agent here on the belief that Carson is a particular thief that they have been seeking for a while."

"Good. They might have some other information." Wanda wasn't worried about Interpol, and they might prove to be a red herring. "When is the agent due?"

"Soon. I have to be back at the office for a meeting at twelve thirty, to explain why I let the woman escape."

Wanda winced in sympathy.

"Do you want to be present when I meet the Interpol agent?" Donau offered.

"I don't think I have any real need to be," Wanda considered. "I have to follow up on some former acquaintances of Wexford, from when he lived here some years ago. He and his daughter are my priority. Carson as knowing Wexford is an interest, not Carson as a jewel thief."

Donau gave a dismissive gesture, a flick of his wrist. "Who is it you intend to speak to?"

Wanda hadn't actually planned anything, but she had an instant answer. "I was researching the companies on Wexford's agenda, and came across an oddity. The PA of the man in charge of the Scientific Glass place, used to work with Wexford at Vienna Trade Inc."

She had Donau's interest. "I think I might come with you. Anyone else?"

"Names, that I still have to track down. But I was hoping you would offer to come with me."

"And why is that?" Donau was studying her.

"Well, you are a representative of the police. And well, there's a bit of mild paranoia." Wanda added quickly, "I was about to go up and talk to Nicole again."

"Let her wait for a minute," Donau became official. "What did you mean by paranoia?"

Wanda hadn't thought before saying that, and she considered her instinct to mention the men who had followed her. It was brushing close to her Carson activities.

"After I got back yesterday, I had to attend to some other business, with people living outside Vienna. I had the feeling that I was being followed."

"Can you give me any details?"

"No, and my feeling may be unfounded. It just seemed like I was seeing too many youths, dressed like those hovering outside of here. I did tell myself that the style of clothing might be the in thing for young men here."

"Why would they be interested in you?"

"Good question - but I am trained to notice things and this began after I was with you asking questions about Wexford and finding that house."

Wanda sensed Donau was shrugging off her 'feeling' as a minor matter to consider later.

"How is Nicole this morning?" He took the subject back to his business.

"I haven't seen her yet. Do you have questions for her?"

"Yes, about Carson. Do you have others?"

"Some. I hope she will be more forthcoming today. I'm...maybe planning to use hypnosis on her if she starts to get upset." Wanda wasn't sure what Donau would think of the idea, but time was running short. Jim's deadline was less than a day away.

"Are you allowed to do that? Did she give permission?"

"Mmm," Wanda temporised, then admitted, "Officially, no, and no. But I think that she may know things that we need to know now."

"This is your territory," Donau said neutrally. "Who am I to question your methods here?"

Wanda smiled wryly. "Just so you know."

Nicole, now occupying the Oregon suite, was glad to see Wanda, but became apprehensive when Donau followed her in.

"Have you found them?" was the first thing Nicole said, she had opened the door for them, but quickly retreated to a chair.

"Not yet, but the Inspector has some questions if you are up to it?" Wanda spoke quickly, as Donau moved a chair so he could sit facing Nicole.

Nicole's nod was cautious, Wanda decided as she moved to stand behind the other woman and once again rested her hands on her shoulders in a gesture of support. However, through the touch, she would also monitor Nicole's state of tension.

Donau started with, "You spoke to Tatiana Carson in the hospital."

Nicole nodded, but glanced back at Wanda.

"Do you remember meeting her before?" Donau went on.

"No, but she said she knew Charles and Vera and was working for the US State Department.”

Donau looked at Wanda and saw that she now had a serious expression on her face.

“You don’t know her, Frau Martin?”

“No.” Wanda hoped that Nicole would not betray that blatant lie.

Donau went back to his questions. “Charles and Vera...who are they?”

Again Nicole turned to Wanda, “You know them, don’t you?” She was tacitly asking how much she should say.

“Yes,” Wanda confirmed, and then went on to explain, “Vera is Nicole’s sister-in-law. Her husband is California Senator Charles Willard. I came out in response to their request to the relevant places.”

“I’d like to question the Senator about Carson. Can you arrange that?”

Wanda nodded.

“Frau Wexford, you mentioned that you knew little about your husband’s business here. Perhaps you could tell me how you were spending your time here while he worked.”

Nicole spoke of tours, shopping, walking around the tourist sites.

“Of course you knew roughly what your husband was doing,” Donau suggested.

“He had some important trade negotiations, some were very hush-hush, but vital to US interests.”

“I see,” Donau accepted the answer, and seemed to consider his next question. He rubbed his jaw, “I understand that your husband spent some years working here...in Vienna.”

“He did. He returned home after his first wife, Rachel’s mother, died in a car accident.”

“You met him in America? After his return?”

“Oh, I knew him years ago...in high school. Vera knew I had been sweet on him back then, so when he came home, she invited me to a family get together. Vera said he was grieving, but that he had a darling little girl.”

Donau smiled, then recalled that the ‘darling little girl’ was missing.

“Did your husband make plans to catch up with old acquaintances?”

Wanda knew the importance of that question, but it sounded casual.

"He didn't say that he had, but soon after we arrived, we had a visitor."

"Oh?" Donau invited her to say more.

"Yes...Theo something. Allan said they used to work together."

"Nice of him to call in," Wanda inserted. "I wonder how he knew Allan was here."

Nicole shrugged. "They disappeared into the office bit of the suite after Allan had introduced Rachel and me. They talked for a couple of hours."

"How was Allan after that?" Wanda asked, idly rubbing Nicole's shoulders. "Keen to be back living here?"

"He didn't say so, but they were drinking. He was a little drunk, and the vodka supply took a hit."

Wanda sensed that she was hiding something and began massaging Nicole's shoulders.

Donau stayed silent, wondering what Wanda was leading up to. He knew she was speaking softly in the woman's ear, but could not make out what she was saying. He became alert when Wanda asked another question.

"Was he a happy drunk?"

"No. He was annoyed. When that Theo guy left, he stomped around and wouldn't talk to me."

Donau glanced at Wanda, who merely shrugged. He tried again, "Did your husband mention anything about his talks?"

"He said one night that he had been offered a high paying job. One that would let us live much better than we do. He didn't say who offered it, just that when he finished the negotiations, he'd discuss it."

Wanda made a statement that she wanted Nicole to answer. "Allan reported to his bosses that he thought that some of the people he spoke to were trying to defraud the US. Did he mention that to you?"

"I heard him saying something like that on the phone. It was the day before he mentioned the job. I had the idea that the job was a bribe, but Allan laughed and said if it was, he wouldn't touch it. But, he seemed different after that."

Wanda asked, "How?"

Nicole couldn't really explain, "I think he was actually considering it."

"Is that why you are afraid to talk to the police?" Wanda asked.

Nicole visibly shuddered. "No, it was those men. They told me not to or I would never see Rachel and Allan alive. They said Allan would dump me if I didn't stay quiet."

Wanda glanced at Donau, an implied, "Do you have any more questions?" She did wonder if he were going to mention finding her handbag.

"Could you describe those men?" he asked.

Wanda whispered, "Take your time. You can see them, but they are not here. Tell us what you see."

Donau's expression turned grim, as Nicole gave a description.

"That's all I have for now," Donau decided.

Wanda tapped Nicole on her shoulder, and spoke quietly. "We will let you rest now, I expect you are very tired."

Nicole yawned, and agreed. "I am rather tired."

Wanda glanced around the room and then asked Donau, "Where did your furball get to this time?"

"Don't step backwards," Donau warned. "He seems to think that you need comforting today."

"Silly hound," she muttered, but leant down to scratch between his ears.

Chapter 17 - Captured again

Wanda was glad enough to have Donau accompany her when she went to visit Heidi Lowenbach. However, she intended to leave him before his appointment with the Interpol agent.

Before they left though, Wanda put through a person-to-person call to Senator Charles Willard. She knew if she was formal with him, her father would treat the call as business. So she used her formal designation, and briefly explained that Inspector Donau wished to speak with him.

Donau, she discovered was fluent in American. He asked if the Senator knew Tatiana Carson, which he wouldn't, Wanda knew. She heard, through the phone receiver, that he understood that a Mrs Martin was on the case. Then he was asked if his wife might know of her. He handled that one well, by saying, "My wife knows a great many people, Inspector. However, I am unable to ask her just now."

Donau asked how long he Senator had known Wexford. After saying they were brother's in law, Willard explained he had known Allan since he had returned from Vienna. The man had not been able to attend his sister's wedding. Wanda ignored the next few questions. She already knew the answers.

"Thank you, that was quick work," Donau spoke to Wanda. "Now, if I were to send a copy of Carson's prints here, how soon could I get an answer?"

"That, I can't predict, but if I speak to Neil Thompson, he could probably contact the FBI and arrange for you to send them direct."

"Yes, would you do that please?"

"Do you have one of your cards? I'll see about it now."

Donau took one of his cards from a pocket and handed it over. He stayed in the little room, looking around, until Wanda returned. Then they left.

Donau had Christian ring Heidi Lowenbach at work. He was told that she had the day off and would probably be at home. He wrote the address down and gave it to Donau who checked a map on the wall of his office, and fingered a spot across the Danube in the 22nd district.

"Alex," he summoned as he led Wanda down to his car.

He drove to the address with Alex trying to breathe down Wanda's neck.

Their destination was a large house, set back in a large block that backed onto forest. A brick and ironwork fence stretched along the road, broken only by the gate that was standing open.

"Fraulein Lowenbach must have money," Donau commented as they drove in along the curved driveway.

"I wouldn't call it a mansion," Wanda gave her own opinion, "But I certainly like the location."

The house was a large two storey affair, with a portico entrance way, but they didn't need to ring the bell, for Heidi was kneeling next to a flower bed with a pile of weeds beside her.

She seemed oblivious to them, for she was listening to something with earphones in. It was when Donau's shadow fell on her that she reacted and turned to see them.

As she reached for a pocket to turn her radio or music device off, Donau brought out his ID, and introduced himself, but merely referred to Wanda as an assistant.

"What can I do for you, Kommisar Donau?" she asked.

"We have a few matters that you could help us with," Donau began, as he clipped his badge back on his belt. "Perhaps we could talk inside?"

"Kommisar, it is really too nice a day, though if you would prefer to sit, I have some chairs around the side on a porch."

Donau agreed, and let Heidi lead the way. Alex was running here and there, sniffing everything. Wanda was watching the dog, but also saw the hand gesture that Donau made behind his back. The dog stopped moving, held his head at an angle, and when only Wanda was watching, took off under some hedge bushes.

Heidi paused, but Donau said easily, "He won't damage anything except butterflies or rabbits."

They continued to where several chairs were placed around a table - Wanda had the sense that they had been carefully placed, ready for them. Donau waited for the women to be seated before sitting back and asking his first question. Heidi Lowenbach seemed to be completely at ease, and admitted to knowing Allan Wexford, as well as being surprised to meet him again some days before. There were things that Donau wanted to know, and he asked successive questions, but Wanda learnt nothing that David hadn't already told her. However, she couldn't help feeling that Heidi was hiding something, and they were being carefully kept outside.

During a brief pause as Donau was thinking what else to ask, Wanda spoke, "If I am not needed here, I will go and hunt up that silly hound." Donau merely gestured her off.

With Heidi's eyes following her, Wanda kept in view for a while, whistling and calling for Alex by name. She slowly moved out of sight, back around to the front of the house. As soon as she was out of Heidi's sight, she ducked down below the level of the windows, and ran around to the back of the house. The door there was unlocked, and not completely latched.

Without too many qualms, she pushed the door further open and sidled in, holding it until the auto closer brought it to a rest. She knew at once that she was not alone in the house, and while she knew that Lowenbach lived alone, she couldn't rule out her having a house guest. However, she had a strong hunch that she knew who the guest was, and edged silently towards that sense of a presence. She moved towards where the porch was located, and came to a room that looked like a sitting room. A faint breeze from the window within, gave her the next clue. The window was open, and someone was listening to the conversation outside.

She knocked quietly on the doorframe and Allan Wexford spun around. He had let his brown hair grow longer than it had been in his family photo, but his face was recognisable.

"What are you doing in here," he hissed accusingly but in a muted tone.

"Hoping to talk to you," Wanda told him, equally quietly.

Wexford came over, shooed her out of the room and closed the door. "You're that woman from the US State Department. What do you want?"

Wanda was receiving the sense of guilt, fear and anger from the man next to her, and wondering how he had learnt of her. She acted as if her identity was no secret, "I came to find you. The State Department is concerned by your silence."

"I told them that I needed to check out the people I was dealing with," Wexford sounded annoyed. "I felt they had criminal tendencies. I told them I would be out of touch."

"Out of touch with your wife, too?" Wanda accused softly.

"I told her that I would be away for a while," Wexford insisted. "I am often away."

"She is hysterical with worry."

"Tell her I'm fine," Wexford directed. "Look, I've got those people to trust me, and I have been invited to a meeting tonight, and I will be able to find out for sure if they are crooks or not. I didn't want to bring them or my kid into it."

"Have you read the papers over the past few days?"

"No. Why?"

"While you have been playing amateur sleuth, your wife was abducted and severely beaten up, and your daughter is missing."

Wexford grabbed the lapel of Wanda's business jacket and hissed, "What?"

Wanda went on with deliberation, "She was told if she said anything, then she would never see you again, or Rachel either."

"I'm sure that she thinks you are up to something questionable, Mr Wexford. So what would make your new friends threaten her and Rachel. Maybe because they know you are trying to expose them?"

"Is Nicole alright? Who's looking for Rachel?" He gave Wanda a little shake.

It was a convincing act, Wanda decided, but still an act. She sensed no anxiety. You snake, Wanda thought to herself, then said, "The police are looking for Rachel, her photo is in the papers. Your wife is under medical care at the US Embassy."

"Please, tell her that I am fine," Wexford urged. "Tell her that after tonight, I'll be able to come and see her."

"And Rachel? Mr Wexford, your wife needs you."

Wexford ran a hand through his hair as if he was undecided. Wanda decided to turn up the tension. "Look, I don't care if you are two-timing your wife, but don't you realise that someone took your daughter, and that someone might use her to force you to do something unacceptable.”

“That crack about two timing my wife is slander,” Wexford threatened.

“It's between you and me,” Wanda told him, unruffled. “But you need to go out and talk to the Inspector, and find out who might want to use your daughter against you.”

“What makes you think that I am having an affair?” Wexford changed tacks, trying to act shame faced and failing.

“You are here, hiding. American cigarette butts next to Heidi in the ashtray on the porch and by the weed pile. You have dirt on your trousers and Heidi's apron and hands were too clean.”

Wanda sensed the man begin to calculate. He deliberately backed down his stance and looked away.

“Alright, you are right. My family is not worth risking, and my department won't fault me if I don't finish the deals, but this was only going to be until tonight. I didn't expect to meet Heidi again, we were lovers once, before I met my first wife.”

Wanda thought, “Spare me.”

“Wexford, like I said, your private life is of no interest to me. Now I know that you are safe, I am relieved of one problem. However, I still have to find your daughter.”

That statement of intent caused an unexpected surge of emotion in Wexford. Wanda suddenly knew, that he knew where his daughter was, and that she was safe...and that was interesting.

“Okay,” Wexford sounded defeated, but he wasn't. “I'll talk to the policeman, but I really need to be at that meeting, with no police smell about me, or they will turn on me.”

Wanda decided that she had Wexford rattled. He was contradicting himself.

“You're a damn fool, you know. If you knew this business was getting dangerous, why didn't you send your family home? Then your damn affair probably wouldn't have been found out.”

“Nicole wouldn't leave,” Wexford tried to insist, but Wanda knew better.

“Come on.”

Alex caught up when they were coming out of the front door. Wexford's appearance startled Donau, and completely stunned Heidi.

Wexford spoke first. "Inspector, I am really sorry. I told Heidi that I needed to keep a low profile for a time, but I cannot keep doing that. I have just learnt about Nicole and my little Rachel."

Donau stood, while Heidi just stared at Wexford as if he had suddenly turned green.

"Herr Wexford, I am indeed glad to find you well. Have you any idea who might have taken your daughter?"

"No, Inspector. I am completely at a loss. Your associate here seems to think it might be one of the people I am negotiating with, but I don't think so. They want to drive a hard bargain, but then so do I."

Wanda let Donau question Wexford and she simply listened to the five star performance Wexford put on. He might have convinced Donau to let him continue to meet those he was negotiating with, but only after giving the policeman the location of the meeting and a promise to come to the police office, first thing in the morning. She was convinced that Wexford would bolt as soon as she and Donau departed, and if he had been truthful when saying the meeting would be at Alpha Prime, then she was certain that the location would be changed before that evening.

There was little more they could do, and Donau called Alex to heel, and walked back to the front of the house. Wanda kept pace with him.

"What made you think he was in the house? Hunch?"

"Later," Wanda put him off. "Can you arrange for a cordon around here? I am sure that Wexford is going to bolt."

"You don't trust him?' Donau asked, increasing his pace.

"He's a two-timing snake," Wanda said in a low voice. "He's having an affair with the blond Heidi, and I will bet my travel allowance that he knows where Rachel is and is intending to dump Nicole."

"My, the venom shows," Donau remarked, as they reached his car. "I'll make the call."

He drove off slowly, and spoke on his car radio at the same time.

When they were out of the gate, Donau turned left, sped up until they came to a road leading towards the forest and stopped as soon as they were hidden from the main road.

"Wait here. Alex and I will go back and see if your theory is right."

She stepped out of the car too, and watched him disappear, noticing that when he wanted to, he could move as quietly as she could. Staying in the car was to be a sitting duck, and that was not her intention.

Wexford was definitely up to something, and whatever it was he had gone to pains to keep it secret. He had betrayed himself in a dozen different ways. For one, he knew she was a US agent, where Donau had merely called her an 'associate'. Heidi had not met her before, discounting as the courier, since she had been disguised then. Someone had told him about her, and must have described her. In her mind, it was odds on that someone was involved with the masked gunmen, and she was sure that those masked men did not work for the cartel that Jim was manipulating. While he was listening and watching them talk to Heidi, he could easily have called for backup.

If she were Wexford, in that case, she would not want a certain policeman and a certain State Department investigator to learn anything else. And those masked gunmen were skilled indeed...

Wanda listened to all the little sounds around her, and only the sudden silence of the birds indicated the approaching menace. It was unlikely that she would be able to run away, even if that was her intention. The people approaching would not underestimate her, but they did not know her, as well as she knew them. She had an experience of how they worked, and was ready for a two or three-pronged attack, and the probable use of their knock out drug.

And, no matter that she had kick boxed a man twice her bulk, those that were approaching would still see a slight, short female, and subconsciously regard her as little of a threat.

They wouldn't know of the intense training she had received from extremely skilled marines, or of her rigid determination never to be as helpless as she had been once.

She stood with the car at her back, but not so close that someone could leap onto the car and grab her from behind. The voice in her mind, of David saying that he wasn't there to back her up, she squashed by saying her mental mantra to the powers that be, "Let me control this situation. Let me aim their weapons where I want." Then with a thought for Donau, she alternated that with, "Don't let Donau die," and "Don't let Alex be hurt."

From some distance away, in the direction of the house, she heard barking, but she could not be concerned about Donau. She had to concentrate, had to judge the movement of three men. She could do this - the three men would get in each other's way.

They had guns, each aimed at her, but if they had wanted her dead, they would have shot immediately. The weapons, hand sized automatics, were to intimidate her - make her too frightened to move. They would not expect her to rationalise that they wouldn't shoot. This area of the city might be less densely settled than most of Vienna, but it was by no means deserted. Shots would be heard.

Let them think she was petrified, as she looked both ways as if trying to look for an escape route. But with one coming from in front of her and one from each side, it wasn't meant to be possible. She settled on watching the one in front, he had something in his left hand, in addition to the gun in his right. Moreover, his eyes were glittering with something akin to rage.

The masked men were moving in step with each other. Wanda feigned a movement to the left, and then dived right, just as the front man got within arm's reach. He grabbed her right forearm and squeezed. Wanda tried to wrench it free, as if desperate to escape, but he dropped her. She had a brief glimpse of the tiny syringe in his hand, gave him a look of shock, closed her eyes and let her body go limp.

One man checked her eyes, but he would only have seen them staring straight ahead. Another gave her a kick in the side. Even though it hurt, and awoke all of her other bruises, she did not react. They were convinced that she was unconscious, because they would have no conception of how well she could control her body.

She was tossed over the shoulder of one of the men, and he

carried her into the forest. The air became cooler and it smelt of tree resin, and under the man's feet, pine needles rustled. Behind her, she heard four explosive pops, and the sound of air escaping under pressure. She guessed they had punctured the tyres of the car. Then there were various metallic thuds, and the sound of glass breaking.

After about five minutes, Wanda felt the sun on her again, and her guess that they had reached another road was confirmed when she peeked though slitted eyes. A small black car, sat on a dirt track, and a fourth man was opening the luggage compartment in the rear. The man carrying her, moved her into a carrying position in front of him, and then lowered her into the low well, positioning her so that they could close the cover. It was a very cramped position. She hoped they might talk, and give out a clue to where they would take her, but all she heard was, "We wait for the others."

Wanda eased her position into a slightly more comfortable one, and in the absolute darkness, began to feel along the waist band of her slacks. Then cursed silently; she had not had time to add her usual little tools to her new clothes. Not discouraged, she felt around the cramped space, to learn about her prison. After a short time, she heard and felt the engine start, and then she was bumped up and down as the car drove along the uneven road. She spared a thought for Donau. Had anything happened to him? He should have known the risks, and he had Alex to protect him.

However, if her guess was correct, Wexford, Heidi and whoever was in charge of the masked men, would want him out of the way until after that meeting.

After that, if Wexford was planning to leave Nicole, what had he planned? Was everyone supposed to think that the cartel or the masked group had taken him?

David had suggested that the unidentified group might be a branch of a Russian crime syndicate known as 'The Family' that she and he had encountered the previous year. If that was the case, how had Wexford become involved with them, and did they trust him or were they just using him?

She let the idea just sit in the back of her mind as she carefully worked an arm into position for her hand to explore the locking mechanism of the cover.

She breathed easier - if she had to, she could get it open easily. Then she worked her other arm into a position so that her left hand could feel her right forearm. Her jacket sleeve was slightly damp in the place where she had felt the man's hand grip her arm - where he thought he had injected her.

Thanks to the tough plastiskin, most of the syringe's contents was either soaked into the sleeve, or trapped between the true and fake layers of skin. The question was, how long did they expect her to be out? If it was the same drug they had used last evening, it hadn't affected her for long, but did they know that?"

A change in the movement of the car, the sensation of turning, and the smoother ride, let Wanda know the car was now on a made road. She only had a rough idea of how far they had gone, and in what direction. She estimated that they travelled about ten minutes on made roads, before they slowed, and turned into a driveway. She heard the tyres crunching on gravel for a distance, felt another turn, and then the car stopped.

Four car doors opened and shut, and a voice spoke nearby in Russian. "Any trouble?"

"Not with this one. Stood there like a spotlighted deer."

"You have the woman?" The speaker had a cultured, educated voice.

One of her captors must have nodded before asking, "Where do you want her? She's had the drug and is out cold."

"In the shed, but bind and gag her before you lock her in. She can't have been out very long last night, and may not be again. Check her for tools and weapons too. She might be an American agent, but she is also a thief. I do not trust that combination. Watch her, and tell me when she wakes up."

There was a grunted assent, and the sound of someone walking away over gravel.

Wanda closed her eyes and made her body limp again, but the cover of her prison wasn't opened immediately. She was poised to attack whoever opened that lid, hoping to have the advantage of surprise, and a startled 'what in hell...' rewarded her. However, the man had instant reactions, and punched her hard in the face, sending her head back against the metal surrounding the luggage well. While not quite unconscious, Wanda had no chance to try again, for the man wrapped her wrists with wide tape, slapped another piece across her mouth, and trapped and bound her ankles.

"Let's see you get free of that, you little freak," he muttered. "Now I know you were faking, the boss won't have to wait so long to make you talk."

Blackness overcame her as the man dragged her from the car, and once again put her over his shoulder.

Chapter 18 - Police under pressure

Donau woke to feel Alex licking his face. He pushed the brown snout away and felt where his head throbbed. His fingers came away bloody.

"Where's Frau Martin?" he asked his dog. Alex flicked his ears. "She's at the car. Go find her!" Alex only whined softly.

"Stubborn dog!" Donau came to the conclusion that he would have to help himself. He pushed to get himself up in a sitting position, and saw the split log of wood that had probably caused the bump. He had to wait for a bout of giddiness to subside, and then, while supporting himself with one arm, he checked his watch. He read the time, but could not think how long he had been out. Then his mobile phone rang, and he almost fell over while trying to take it out of his jacket pocket. He flipped it open one handed.

"Donau," he spoke into it.

He heard, "Thank God! Where are you? The chief wants you. Your meeting was meant to start an hour ago. The Interpol agent is here..."

"Slow down, Christian," he managed to get in.

"I had to tell the Chief that you were not answering your phone. Are you still out at the Lowenbach place?"

"I think somewhere near there," Donau said slowly. His head was beginning to pound like a drum.

"How soon can you get back?"

"About fifteen minutes - once I find my car."

"Otto! What is wrong?"

"Christian, I'm fine. Have you heard from the units covering the Lowenbach house?"

"No. Why were they there?"

"Wexford, the missing American, was there. I went back to see if they tried to do a flit and I ran into a little bit of trouble."

"Stay where you are! I will call those units to look for you and your car. I will drive out there."

Donau stood up in slow stages, waiting after each gradual rise, for the giddiness to subside. Once he was on his feet, he took two steps and nearly collapsed. He looked down, and saw that his head wound had bled freely.

"I think, Alex that you need to let people know we are here."

Alex began to bark, not wildly, but alternating 3 barks, a pause, and two barks and a pause.

Within minutes, two uniformed officers raced into his view from the trees all around him.

"Are you Inspector Donau, Sir? We were told to listen out for your dog."

"Yes. Can you help me back to my car?"

"Excuse me, Sir, but you look to be in no condition to drive. We will arrange to have you driven to the hospital."

"Later. What's happening here?"

"Very little. The people we were told to look for were not here when we arrived. We checked the house, as the doors were open, and there is no one inside. Only indications that a woman lived there. If I may ask, Sir, what happened to you?"

"I met the rearguard, I think," Donau pointed to the log of wood. "My car was parked in the trees on the edge of the property."

The other officer spoke into a radio, sending someone to look for the car, and reporting that they had found Donau. When the group began to stride back towards the house, Donau's unsteady progress brought an offer of support from the senior of the two uniformed officers.

Shortly after, the on-scene commander requested to speak to Donau. The radio was handed over so Donau could speak, and their progress to the house was halted.

"I have been trying to reach you for three and a half hours, Sir," the voice explained. "What are your instructions? The house is deserted. Do we still need the cordon around the area?"

If the two people had gone, it was unlikely they would come back. "No, just keep a patrol at the house until tomorrow, and have the forensic techs go over the house to see if they can find traces of the people that were there."

Back at the house, the on-scene commander reported, "There is no sign of your car yet."

Donau refrained from nodding, and merely gestured towards the trees. "It was through there. Frau Martin from the US Embassy was waiting there."

He had the idea that Wanda Martin may have driven off with it, possibly after Lowenbach and Wexford. It would explain why she had not come looking for him, but still, it had been over three hours...he began to have a very bad feeling. He was helped to one of the chairs at the side of the house.

A call came over the radio a few minutes later. Donau heard that his car had been found, covered in tree detritus and would need a tow truck.

His concern escalated. "Was there any sign of Frau Martin?" He gave a brief description.

The question was posed of the officer that reported.

The voice on the radio came through clearly, "No, Sir. The vehicle is empty. It has been pushed about twenty metres from the track, and the ground around it is all messed up. There are no clear tracks."

"I'll head that way," Donau began to stand up.

"Sir, you should stay sitting down."

"I have too much to do," he said stubbornly and Alex woofed an agreement. "If Mrs Martin is missing, Alex may find her scent."

The on-scene commander could not fault the logic, nor disobey Donau who was his superior, but he did have the last word. "Officer Eggar will go with you."

Christian trotted into view as Donau was still getting over the shock of seeing his Audi all over smashed and dented. He already knew that his radio and other accessories had been wrenched out.

"They sure did a proper job of your car. Were you in it?"

"No, but Mrs Martin was here. She's missing. There is a call out to look for her, but take Alex and see if he can pick up a scent. She was sitting in the front passenger seat. Be careful though, I want the car dusted for prints - just in case."

Donau refused to leave until Christian returned.

"Alex followed the scent to a dirt road about 300 yards through there. There had been a car parked there, a small one, but that is all I could tell."

"We will have to get a message to the US Embassy," Donau grimaced. The throbbing in his head was threatening to make him black out.

"Come back to my car," Christian told Donau sternly. "Officer Steiner can take care of things here. You are going to the hospital."

As the doctor was applying a dressing to his head wound, Donau's superior walked into the treatment room. He was followed by a tall man, who was dressed in an expensive Amani business suit.

"I hope you are not intending to stay on duty, Donau," Kolbe remarked.

"Sir, I..."

"Christian has filled me in. We have an alert out for the American woman, as well as Lowenbach and the American, Wexford. You need to rest."

"No, Sir! That's what they want." Donau moved abruptly, causing the doctor to tell him to stay still.

"Who wanted?" Kolbe demanded.

"Wexford is meeting with some people tonight to discuss an important deal. Frau Martin and I both believe that it is a criminal deal. Wexford was insisting that he must attend, and it was more important to him than the health of his wife, and the safety of his missing daughter."

Kolbe spoke an aside to the man with him. "Frau Wexford, the wife of an American trade consul was abducted and beaten up. Her daughter is missing."

The man nodded gravely, but said nothing.

"Oh, Donau. This is Interpol agent Derek Mont Pelier. Since you didn't make it to the meeting, I brought him to meet you."

"Good of you, Sir," Donau managed to say.

"Doctor, how is he?" Kolbe asked bluntly.

"Nothing broken," the doctor began, as he finished covering the wound and sticking the plaster down. "He has a mild concussion, and should rest for several days at least. I will prescribe something for the headache."

Kolbe did not need to be told how much pain Donau was hiding. His face was white and strained.

"You can come back to your office and tell Mont Pelier everything you know about that thief. Christian can take over the search for the Americans and Fraulein Lowenbach. If he has questions, he can call you. If I have any report of you being on duty before Friday, I will have you suspended for your own good."

"Understood," Donau acknowledged. He was looking forward to lying down.

"I will send a car and driver to get you," Kolbe stated before giving Mont Pelier a sharp nod, and striding out.

"He must know you well," Mont Pelier remarked neutrally.

Donau forced a smile. "Probably, but at least I still have a job. I have been having a very frustrating time."

"Losing high profile villains, I believe," Mont Pelier remarked, without censure. "I would find that frustrating too. However, it seems as if you have achieved more than I have. I had not even considered that the 'Diamond spider' might be a woman."

"Whoever coined that name was particularly intuitive," Donau admitted.

The doctor returned and interrupted them. "I have your analgesic medication. You should take two now, and take one or two no less than six hours apart. They are very strong and will probably make you drowsy. After 24 hours, you should only need regular pain relief."

At the police office, a solicitous Alex sat next to Donau's chair, and refrained from his usual antics. Mont Pelier had fetched a chair for himself and sat opposite Donau, and was comparing the photograph of Tatiana Carson with the sketch made from Donau's description of the woman caught in the building next to Alpha Prime.

"Incredible," Mont Pelier remarked. "All that is the same is the hair length and eye colour. You did not find the diamonds on her though."

"No. We searched both buildings, but we did not find where they were stashed," Donau admitted.

"Then you cannot be sure that the woman was the one who took them," Mont Pelier suggested.

"She was seen climbing back to the other building," Donau defended his belief. "There were no other intruders in that building. One of the Alpha Prime guards tripped the rope she was on, releasing the end tied to Alpha Prime. She fell, but stayed with the rope. It was a skilful save. And then she freed herself before we could question her."

"So I heard," Mont Pelier murmured. "You had a tip off about this Carson..."

Donau described the events of the next evening, up to finding the woman up a tree.

"We went back at daylight and found what she had stashed in the tree. The diamonds were pushed into a hole in the trunk and her backpack was higher up."

In a folder on his desk was a glossy photo of the diamonds, and he passed it to Mont Pelier. "The actual stones are in an evidence locker."

"I will need to examine the actual stones, but tomorrow will do. However, these do indeed look like the stones stolen from a French collection two weeks ago."

Donau could sense the excitement in the manner of the Interpol agent. "What was in the bag you found?"

A list, and more photos were passed to Mont Pelier. "That tablet, according to our experts, has a high level encryption algorithm protecting all files. It has wi-fi capability and can access the Internet. It is possible she used it to hack into the security system of Alpha Prime."

Mont Pelier tapped the desk next to the photo of the diamonds. "Yes, the French police believed that the thief had a means to compromise the electronic security about these diamonds, to get in to take them." He pointed to the photo of the unrolled tool kit. "That is a high class set of lock picking tools, and the small pieces of cable are probably used with the cards to trick the electronic locks to open them."

"Or to hack into computers," Donau added. "I cannot help wondering how she knew where those diamonds were."

Mont Pelier dismissed that question with a gesture. The thief had uncanny ways of finding out such things. He was more interested in how someone had found the thief to call in a tip off.

"So how did Carson escape next time?"

Donau leant back in his chair. Thinking about that morning's events made him angry, and he thought that he should have stopped in to see Bauer while he was at the hospital.

"The car taking her to the remand centre was ambushed by men in black coveralls and face covering, who wielded high powered weapons. Once they had disabled the car, they dragged her out. However, she didn't seem to make any attempt to escape from them."

Mont Pelier kept his opinions to himself. On first sight, it seemed the men were rescuing her. However, if they were not, compliance was better than being shot.

Still, he had overheard things while waiting in the police building that made him ask, "What happened to you to cause this?"

"A case that I thought was unrelated," Donau said slowly, he had an idea flitter through his mind, but could not focus on it. Why did he think that? Carson was a link. The masked men were a link.

"We've been looking for a missing American Trade consul. The one whose wife was beaten..."

"Yes, your Chief mentioned them," Mont Pelier was paying attention.

"I was working with a woman from the American State Department, a Frau Martin. We found Wexford hiding with a woman in a place out near the forest. Frau Martin is sure he is up to something illegal. He claimed to be ignorant of the attack on his wife, or that his daughter was missing. In spite of hearing about them, he insisted that he had to attend some meeting tonight. He promised to see us tomorrow, but he and the woman left the house. I was going back to see if they did flee." Donau gave a faint shrug. "I was knocked out, and it appears that they snatched Frau Martin. I am most concerned. I fear they are the same people who took Frau Wexford, and possibly those who freed Carson."

Mont Pelier considered what he had heard, and carefully questioned Donau to elicit all the evidence the Austrian had, and all he surmised. He didn't like what he was hearing.

"I don't remember hearing of any terror cells, or crime groups moving into Austria, but I will request a search of our database for any indications."

That reminded Donau, "We sent through some finger prints, taken from Carson's guesthouse room."

"There were no matches. However, that is not surprising, and the Diamond Spider has never yet left prints."

"It was a long shot, but I have also made the request of the Americans to check their database. I asked if the masked men might be American, since Carson's passport is American, and she claimed to know Frau Wexford - actually identified her to us."

"Interesting indeed," Mont Pelier admitted. "Have you any ideas about how the two cases, are linked?"

"None that seem relevant after this morning," Donau said, stifling a yawn.

"If you do not object, I will keep you company until you are driven home."

"I am not ready to go home yet."

"Then tell me what you know of this man Wexford and his business."

"Not enough," Donau admitted. "I have a list of the people and places that he was meant to visit. Every person on his agenda has an impeccable business and public reputation. I find it hard to believe any of them are criminals, although Frau Martin suggested it. Apparently, Wexford suggested it to his superiors. His reason for attending this meeting is to find proof."

"You want to be there," Mont Pelier deduced. "You have organised to have the meeting place watched?"

"Wexford said the meeting was to be at the Alpha Prime building," Donau revealed. "There security is the most up to date of any building in Vienna."

"However, it is apparently not secure enough if the Diamond Spider got in," Mont Pelier countered softly. "What do you know of their security?"

Donau had asked that question of the night guards, and was able to provide details.

"Wireless connections could be interfered with or blocked, or if the thief could infiltrate the computer system in the building, the security could be an open book," Mont Pelier suggested. "Do you think the meeting will remain there?"

Donau considered that. "If everything is above board, there will be no reason to change it. I don't think Wexford will mention anything, but the woman he was with is the secretary to of one the men who will be at the meeting."

"And if it is not, they won't go there," Mont Pelier guessed what Donau was about to say. "Perhaps, you should contact the group and offer your services."

For a moment Donau didn't seem to understand, and then he smiled and reached for the phone. "There is a watch already on Alpha Prime, and I know where most of the men are at the moment. We can see what will happen."

Mont Pelier leant back and steepled his long fingers in front of his lips. He listened to the one sided conversation between Donau, and the man on the phone - Wessler of Alpha Prime. He waited to hear the result of the conversation.

"Herr Wessler tells me that the planned meeting has been postponed until tomorrow, due to some unforeseen matters. He thanked me for the offer, but sees no reason for trouble."

Mont Pelier murmured, "We will see, won't we. Why don't you go home and rest. Reports may be rung through to you there."

Alex's head came up and he woofed.

"Not yet," Donau insisted. "However, I will send for coffee and sandwiches."

While they sat within Donau's office, he received a number of reports, to which he had listened, given a few directions, and either sent the messenger off if it came via a police officer or aide, or hung up the phone. Then the phone rang yet again. He listened at first, and muttered terse acknowledgments, and then he suddenly exclaimed, "What?" Whoever was on the other end of the phone kept talking. Donau finally spoke a thoughtful, "Thank you," and ended the call.

Mont Pelier waited to see if Donau would explain his reaction.

"It's impossible!" Donau said aloud, prompting a question from his companion.

"What is?"

"They found Carson's prints in my car! The only other prints that were clear were mine. They should have found those of Frau Martin."

"If it is so, it is not impossible."

An idea that was totally astounding had leapt into his mind, and he did not want to contemplate it.

"Mrs Martin has been helping me with finding Wexford, but she gave me a contact for the America's FBI, so I could run Carson's prints through their records. But what my people are saying was that I was in the car with Carson."

"They cannot be the same person. The Embassy records had Mrs Martin at the Embassy when I had Carson at the hospital. I cannot see any reason for the US Embassy to lie to us."

Mont Pelier was less trusting of that point, but he remarked, "Setting aside that possible option, there could be other interpretations?" He had Donau's full attention. "If Frau Martin is not also Fraulein Carson as you prefer to believe, and she did not disappear of her own will, those that took her may be out to discredit her. It would not be hard to wipe the car clean of prints and for another to handle the places where the first must have touched."

Donau felt his body relax, and the sudden increased pain in his head eased. That idea made more sense than his first irrational thought. Then he recalled, "Mrs Martin mentioned to me that she thought she had been followed yesterday evening. That was after she had helped me to find where Nicole Wexford had been taken."

Mont Pelier merely inclined his head as if to say, "That fits my theory."

Chapter 19 - Drug reactions

As soon as she woke again, Wanda sensed the man moving away from the door. She opened her eyes and tried to look around the dark place in which she found herself. The only light came through a filthy window that would be about head height if she could stand. She tried to get her bound wrists close enough to her feet to work at the tape, but she could not reach around the back of her ankles.

Instead of giving up, she rolled onto her stomach, feeling the roughness of the concrete floor, and tried to move worm-like towards the window - hoping to find something to help her sever the tape.

Before she moved more than six inches, her head hit solid metal bars, and she realised that she was in some kind of cage.

"Damn you for a stupid arrogant fool," Wanda cursed herself mentally. She couldn't even get to her last ditch tool kit, or the slender and flexible knife she had taken from her reversible slacks and inserted in the lapel of her jacket. That was assuming the man hadn't found it. He had been told to search her.

She stopped cursing and used all her senses to investigate her prison. The light didn't show her much, and she knew she was on concrete, and in a cage. The shed where the cage was smelt of urine, though the concrete she had crawled over had been washed. The cage had probably once housed someone's hunting dogs.

To relieve some frustration, she promised her captors, "You locked up the wrong bitch!" And then rolled again and tried to sit up. It was her intention to examine the lock that secured the cage.

She reached the door by inching across the concrete on her backside. When feeling for the lock, she felt the lower hinge, and tried to scrape the tape against it. It wasn't rough enough to fray the tape.

Her danger sense warned her that someone was approaching. She rolled back onto the hard floor, to pretend she was still unconscious.

"No use pretending, bitch," a voice announced in German, but it had an odd accent. "I know you're awake. I didn't hit you that hard or I'd have broken your face. Boss wants you." He unlocked the cage and Wanda felt him grab her and start dragging her out.

She opened her eyes and was almost blinded by the sunlight that streamed into the shed. When she turned her head away from the light, she caught a hint of movement. Then she saw there was another cage next to hers, but separated by about three feet. In the glance she had, it looked like the other cage was full of junk, except that what she thought was a roll of carpet - moved.

She had no time to consider the oddity, for the man had drawn a sharp knife and slashed at the tape on her ankles. Then he dragged her to her feet and ordered, "Walk!"

He kept a fierce grip on her arm, and shoved her in the direction of a large elegant house that would only have been fifty feet away.

Wanda only had a glimpse of the man, who was not masked now. It was enough to fix his features in her mind. She also noticed his clothes, and that was enough to identify him as one of the masked types she had encountered. He was not wearing the casual but uniform like attire of the youths she had been wary of, but his clothes reminded her of a military uniform - dark fabric shirt and trousers with the cuffs tucked into boots.

She studied all she could see, of the house in front, and then risked a stumble, to get a glance of where she had come from. Behind the shed was a high cyclone wire fence, but a windbreak of even taller trees grew beyond it. She was dragged to her feet again, and that gave her an instant to look along the gravel drive to the road. The house was set well back from the road, with gardens laid out in front. Her destination was the back of the house, where there was an open courtyard, where several cars were parked, including two expensive late model Mercedes, and a small car which she suspected was the one she'd arrived in. She saw an overgrown garden beyond them, which merged into a sparse forest of fruit trees.

Her captor dragged her to a door, reached around to open it, and shoved her in. The dimness inside, after the bright light outside, left her near blind until her eyes adjusted. She was pushed along what felt like a passage, but only a short way, and then into an almost empty room.

The only object was a single chair, but it seemed it wasn't for her. She was shoved hard enough to make her lose her balance and fall, while the man stood between her and the door.

Wanda studied the arrogant hulk, as he kept punching his right fist into his left palm. His message was clear enough - try to leave and you'll get beaten up. But she could take him...even with her hands tied in front of her. She was just trying to get to her feet when more people entered. Two more of the military types, who moved to each side of the door, and a tall, aristocratic man with dark hair and pale blue eyes who went to the chair and sat down.

It had only taken one glance for her to identify the man as dangerous. There was a perceptible sense of menace about him. Still, she finished getting to her feet, making the process look more awkward than it was. She returned her attention to the seated man, but her stance was subtly defiant.

The man issued a quiet command in Russian. Wanda did not let on that she understood, but was ready when her escort came close and ripped the tape from her mouth. She returned her attention to the man on the chair, he studied her and demanded, in a sharp tone, "What are you? Are you a thief? A con artist? Or a United States agent?"

Wanda remained silent, but answered only in her mind. "Wouldn't you like to know?"

"Why are you here?"

Wanda's mental retort was, "You tell me, pal! Your thugs dragged me here."

"I am told you are an investigator. What are you investigating?"

Wanda knew that the man would not tolerate her silence much longer, but she still did not answer, except to think, "My, my, you do have a guilty conscience."

No matter what she said, the man would use it against her. If he truly wanted her to tell him things, he'd keep her alive until he had what he wanted. The question was, would he have his men use brute force, or would he try drugs?

After waiting for a long moment, when it was obvious to him that he was not going to be answered, the elegantly dressed man rose gracefully and seemed to prowl like a cat. He circled her, stopping behind her, and whispered in her ear. The tickle of his breath on her cheek sent a shiver running down her spine.

"I am a busy man. I have asked you questions, politely, you are out of time."

He completed his circle, and glanced at the man who had moved behind her.

Wanda expected to be hit, and when she was only grabbed, she decided she had her answer. He was going to try drugs to get her to talk. As she watched, he took a slender tin from the inner pocket of his jacket. It might have been a cigarette case, but from it, he took a circular object with a sharp point in the centre. He slipped the tin into a side pocket and walked towards her again, positioning the object on the palm side of his hand.

"Compound A," he said, as if continuing a conversation. "Is a powerful truth serum."

He reached out like a snake striking and slapped the side of her neck, injecting the solution. Then he massaged the site.

"If you were not such an annoyance, I might have decided to employ you," the man told her. "But before I do, I want to know why you are so interested in Herr Wexford. I think you are doing more than trying to find a philandering husband."

He was watching Wanda, waiting for some sign that the drug was taking effect. After five minutes of mutual staring, he began to grow uneasy.

Wanda had already begun to feel the effect, and although it was unpleasant, it amused her that the man had outsmarted himself. Her body had gone rigid. She could not move now, even if she wanted to, nor could she speak. They would soon discover that, but they would not know that her mind was unaffected.

They thought she was being stubborn, and gave her several solid punches to her back. When that and several kicks to her legs elicited no sound, and no reaction, they began to look at each other uneasily. They had never seen a reaction like that. They began to speak amongst themselves, assuming that she was also deaf.

The three lesser men expressed their disbelief to "Father Theo". Amongst themselves, they spoke in Russian.

"Quiet!" he ordered. "We cannot take risks. We will try again when the drug wears off, and if she still won't talk we will have to silence her. We have invested too much in Aleksi's plan to have it ruined. Tell Aleksi to come here."

One of the men left.

"What do you want done with her, Father Theo?" one of the others asked.

"Dump her back in the cage. The shed is soundproof and secure - even against this thief. I think Aleksi was right. She must have had inside help."

Wanda smiled inwardly. She had just learnt some minor details that fit nicely into place. This man, Father Theo, must be the Theo that Nicole mentioned. The one who had visited Wexford soon after they arrived and put him in a foul mood. He must be controlling Wexford in some way, perhaps forcing him to do some illegal, anti- USA deal.

Was his mention of criminals to his bosses a cry for help? Was the abduction of Rachel, and the assault on Nicole, done to ensure his compliance after all?

But, having thought that through, Wanda asked herself, "Who was Aleksi?"

The two remaining muscle men had to carry her - like she was a solid statue. She knew the effects would wear off in time, and realised that the attempts to make her talk had actually helped. Even though she hurt, dreadfully, the punches and kicks had woken the places where she had been hurt the previous day, endorphins were spreading through her body and the pins and needles effect of her muscles relaxing and the blood beginning to flow, had already begun. Or, it might have been the surge of adrenalin that came when she outsmarted dangerous people.

They returned her to the shed, and had to stoop to carry her into the cage, far enough to set her down. They muttered between themselves, complaining of having to take that much trouble. After they retreated and locked the cage, they glanced at the other cage before leaving the shed and locking it.

Wanda was glad of the return to darkness. As she was now, her eyes were ultra-sensitive to the light, and she could not close her eyes. She thanked the powers that they had not simply stood at the cage door and tossed her in. It meant that Theo wasn't ready to kill her yet.

The returning of sensation was becoming extreme, but she could endure it. Soon, she would be able to move. After a while the pain diminished to a point where she was aware of a hoarse voice talking to her.

"Hey, you. You got any booze? Got any vodka?"

"What..."

"Vodka. Did they give you any? Can I have it?"

"No..."

"Too bad."

The voice fell silent. Wanda tried to speak. "Who?"

"Me? Nobody."

"Why..."

The voice guessed what she meant. "I killed my wife. This is penance. Father Theo says when I am truly repentant I will go free."

Wanda thought on that. If that Father Theo was a priest, he was a priest of the devil.

"You? What did you do?" the voice asked.

"Nothing..."

"Must have."

Wanda wasn't able to explain yet, but she was getting movement back in her limbs. In the past, when she had tried this kind of drug - under medical supervision - she had found that if she forced herself to move, the effect ended sooner.

She still had her hands tied, but her legs were free, so she rolled and tried to push herself up. Failing at first, she pushed herself towards the bars, inching her way there and then using them to help her up. When she was sitting, she let herself lean back against the bars, to rest.

Wanda hadn't forgotten the man, but his silence she had taken as his losing interest, but he hadn't.

"What they do to you?"

"Drug," she said. "Bad reaction."

After a while she added, "I'm getting out."

"How? I've tried. Every one of 1831 days."

"What?"

Wanda wondered if the man's mind had gone. Her mind calculated, if he was right, he had been a prisoner for five years.

"Who...are you?"

"I don't remember," the voice said after a while.

"Do you want to get out?"

"Father Theo will have me beaten if I go out."

Wanda decided it was probably true. But she wasn't going to let that man beat her.

"Do you have an empty bottle?"

"Huh?"

Wanda was feeling more movement now, and able to speak more freely. "I have to get out."

"He'll beat you up, lady."

"Not if he can't catch me. I need something sharp to cut this tape."

There was silence for a moment, and then the hoarse voice said, "Wait a minute."

Wanda heard the sound of someone guzzling from a bottle, and finally a loud burp.

"Keep talking lady, so I can tell where you are," the voice asked. "Can't see in here."

"I'm in the other cage," Wanda told him. "Do you know where that is?"

"No."

"Do you know where the door is?"

"Yes."

"Look that way. I will be on your left."

Wanda listened to the man shuffling around, moving stuff out of his way. He was coming closer, as she kept talking to him.

"Do they ever let you out?"

"Sometimes, at night."

"Do they feed you?"

"Yeah. Can you reach the bottle?"

Wanda could only vaguely make out the man's shape, and tried to get her hands through to take the bottle in the outstretched hand. However, while she could have made one arm reach further, with them tied at the wrists, she had no hope.

"Toss it to me," Wanda suggested, and she sensed the bottle moving the short distance through the air, before it smashed against the bars of her cage.

"Sorry, lady, really sorry."

Wanda didn't respond, she twisted so she could reach her bound wrists through the bars, and felt on the concrete beyond her space. When she felt nothing, she drew her hands back and put them through the next gap.

"Yes!" she hissed when she felt the sharp edge of a piece of glass. Carefully, she drew it closer, and into her cage. Then she held it between her shoes, and began to work on the tape.

The man had fallen asleep, and was snoring by the time she had her hands free. She didn't rip the rest of the tape off, but began to scratch at the edge of the plastiskin on her arms. It was then that she realised that she had nicked herself several times while getting the tape cut. She felt the stickiness of blood on her fingers, and pressed both wrists against her trousers to stop herself bleeding. She realised that she was lucky that she had not nicked an artery. After a few minutes, she felt for the plastiskin again, and began to tug it up. The synthetic skin was ragged, having been scraped by the glass, but it came up in one piece.

Wanda felt for the tool she needed, it lay against the skin as two flat pieces of metal, each flexible until locked together. Then they became rigid. With care, she joined the pieces, and slid the tool into her pocket. The skin, she pressed back into place, and hoped it would stick well enough.

Her fingers were still tingling, and had not yet regained their sensitivity, so Wanda kept flexing them to get the blood flowing. She recalled that she had her knife in her lapel, and felt to check it was still there. It was, so she eased the two pieces out, and joined them. The now rigid knife, slid back into the hidden sheath.

She was all too aware of the passage of time, and decided that tingling or not, she was functional. She pulled herself to her feet, and moved unsteadily to the cage door. Being short, meant she did not have to stoop. Her hands felt the lock, and she laughed softly. Two decisive movements with her tool, and it snapped open. The cage door opened with a creak, but Wanda had heard that the shed was sound proofed, so she kept moving. The door to the shed was locked with a deadbolt, and that took more time, since she needed to find and join the pieces of tools that would form a saw.

Once she had cut through the bolt with the ultra sharp blade, she inched the door open, just enough to let the afternoon sun provide light for her to see the other cage. She unlocked it and gingerly stepped in. She saw the man, old looking with tangled whiskers and unkempt hair, on his back against a crate of some kind. One touch told her that he was deeply asleep - drugged.

There was nothing more she could do for him yet, and things she needed to do. Through the gap in the door, she was hearing voices, and estimated they were near the back of the house. She opened the door just enough to get a glimpse of what was around. She recalled the relative position of the house and the shed. The door opened towards the back of the property, not the road, and was hinged on the right, so she could look towards the house. But the shed was set back past the back of the house, so she could not see it unless she was right out. The advantage was, they would not see the door opening. Before she opened it further, she looked around to see if there was a security camera overseeing it. Her eyes scanned the fence nearby, and the trees, and saw nothing to indicate the shed was observed. She sensed no human guards either. It seemed that they were sure of their locks. Foolish, Wanda mentally reprimanded them. They were effective against weak old men, who they kept on drink and drugs. She was another matter.

A glance at the angle of the sun told Wanda that more time had passed than she had realised. It was coming on evening. The sun had dipped behind the tall trees, and was throwing shadows her way. It gave her an advantage as she edged to the corner of the shed.

The talkers were two of the 'hired muscle', men clad in the military style dark uniform. They were lounging around, smoking. They weren't toting guns but she assumed they were still armed. When they became suddenly alert, and moved to look down the driveway, Wanda heard the crunch of gravel as a car came up it. She used that as a diversion to dash towards the trees that formed the rear of the property. Then she slipped from tree to tree to get nearer the door. By the time the car pulled up, she was crouched behind one of the wide older trees, screened by some scrubby undergrowth.

A dark haired man stepped from the car; Wanda could not see his face.

"You took your time, Aleksi," one of the men said in Russian. He crushed the butt of his cigarette into the gravel with his boot. "Father Theo has been cursing you."

The door on the far side of the car opened, and Wanda saw the blond hair, and heard a woman speak. "We had to keep clear of the police patrols."

Wanda stared - the voice had been familiar, and now, as the woman turned, she recognised Heidi Lowenbach. The man was walking around the car.

"What the..." Wanda began the thought, and then she heard a high pitched, "Daddy!" She couldn't see the child, but the newcomer gathered her up and gave her a hug.

"Hiya, Squirrel," the man said.

"Aren't you meant to be with your nurse?"

That voice was Father Theo's, and Wanda risked a better look. The child clinging to the man, looked like she was holding on as tightly as possible. The man turned, and Wanda saw the face of the child.

What the hell? "That's Rachel Wexford!" Wanda said in a quiet voice, but she did not dare go closer.

The man holding Rachel, said, "Give Grandpa Theo a hug and kiss, and then you'd better go to Nurse. Or you will miss your supper."

The child obediently freed her arms and twisted towards the older man.

"And that sounded like Allan Wexford!" Wanda told herself. Considering she had last seen him with Heidi Lowenbach, who was right over there as well, it probably was him - and he had darkened his hair. She wished intently for the man to turn around, and it seemed the powers she prayed to heard her. The dark haired man, started to walk into the house with Rachel, but suddenly set her down.

"In you go, Squirrel. I have to get something from the car."

Wanda only needed that one moment to see the face. "It is Allan Wexford, and he is chummy with that pack of Russian thugs. The slimy, stinking snake." She squatted back down and considered what she had seen.

"They called Wexford, Aleksi! That guard spoke in Russian to him. When I spoke to Wexford, and he insisted he get to that meeting, it made no sense. Now it makes too much sense. Those Russians are planning something. They have someone dressed up like Wexford. I have to warn Jim."

For a moment, she was undecided. She had found Rachel Wexford, and getting her away was a priority, but it was odd that she thought that imposter was her father. The guy must be really good.

Wanda was as close to the house as she could safely be. Being seen now, out and free, would be a death sentence. She had to wait and watch until the two guards went inside, and hope they were not replaced. She thought they wouldn't be, for the two were not acting like they were on duty, more like they were bored. It gave her time to plan.

She thought of the disguises that Nick Black could create - duplicating faces using plastiskin.

They must have Wexford somewhere, Wanda realised. Probably in the house and somewhere Rachel wasn't likely to find him. It meant, rather than just sneaking in to get Rachel, she needed to search the house. And once she had the little girl, she had to get away and find a phone to warn Jim.

Wanda waited until it was becoming dark, and let a subtle instinct guide her timing. When she decided to move, she ghosted towards the back door and put her ear to it before continuing. Hearing nothing, she tried the door and found it unlocked. She went in, and in that moment, she became the essence of stealth. All pain, all stiffness vanished as she began to search the house. This sort of thing brought her truly alive, fully alert.

She had diffuse light coming from various rooms to show her the way, but she proceeded carefully, locating all the people. Sounds to her right suggested the kitchen was there, and a man and woman were talking. A little further along a passage, and she heard several men talking, and a woman. Theo, Aleksi and Heidi and maybe some of the guards.

Another room contained the rest of the guards, eating an evening meal. The talk from that room was louder, less refined. Bottles or glassed clinked. Wanda kept moving.

On the ground floor she counted twelve rooms, in addition to the kitchen and eating rooms. A formal reception room took up a large section, a fancy suite, which she decided was used by Theo. A second suite, had a double bed, and men's clothes. She guessed Aleksi used it. She also caught a trace of Heidi's perfume, and guessed she would be sharing it with Aleksi.

Two rooms had bunks, and had dark clothes hanging over cupboard doors, and other signs that they were used by the guards. Six of the eight beds looked to be used, two were bare. So, potentially six guards. An equal number of rooms and suites were empty, none were locked, and there was no sign of a prisoner. That left upstairs, and Wanda found the stairs and silently ran up the carpeted steps to the second floor.

Most of this floor was in darkness, only one door had light showing under the door. Wanda decided that would be where Rachel Wexford was sleeping, and spending time with her nurse. To be absolutely certain, Wanda checked each door, opening it and letting all her senses examine it. All the rooms but one were empty and unoccupied.

"Where do they have Wexford?" Wanda paused for a moment's thought. They put her in that shed with that poor sod, why did they not put Wexford there? She would consider that later. Now she needed to get Rachel away from her nurse and out of the house.

Now she approached the occupied room, and listened at the door. Vague splashing sounds suggested the child was in the bath, and as Wanda silently entered the suite, she heard the nurse scolding her charge, and then the sound of a slap.

"You will not splash water at me," was the next comment.

Wanda took an instant dislike to the nurse, and took a few moments to investigate the room, and take in everything that could be useful. She ghosted to the partly open door to the bathing room.

The child suddenly yelled, in English, "You are a horrid old woman! I want my mommy!"

The nurse answered in German, "You will learn to be obedient or Father Theo will order me to smack you hard - ten times. Do you want that? Do you want your Papa to be disgusted with you?"

Rachel began to snivel, "No, Nurse, I don't want to be smacked."

"Then come here then, and I will only smack you five times and that will be the end of it."

There was a pause, and the Nurse hissed, "Come here!" And Rachel's crying increased, and Wanda waited no longer.

Grabbing a lamp of a nearby table, and yanking out the cord, Wanda moved swiftly into the next room. The nurse was so intent on twisting a squirming Rachel over a chair, that she was oblivious to Wanda coming up behind her. The lamp hit the back of her head, and the nurse dropped.

Rachel, suddenly free, ran to a corner and curled into a ball. She would not know if the stranger was a friend or a worse kind of person.

Sensing the child's fear, Wanda ignored her while she found a towel, and used her knife to slit it into strips with which she proceeded to bind and gag the woman. During that process, she checked the woman's pulse. It was still strong.

Then she looked around for somewhere to hide her. If people came to this room, she wanted them to think the nurse had taken the child somewhere. The big wardrobe in the room with two beds, caught her eye. It had two doors, she tried the right hand one and found the lower half contained drawers. The left hand side only had hanging clothes. It would be big enough to hide the nurse.

When she returned and began dragging the nurse, Wanda was aware of Rachel watching her furtively, but still in her curled up position.

The woman was solid, but Wanda knew how to use leverage to achieve her intent. Within a few minutes, the still unconscious nurse was folded into the cupboard - in a sitting position with her knees at her chin. With a moment of vindictiveness, Wanda used the key that was in the door to lock the wardrobe. Then she went back into the bathroom.

"Rachel?" she asked gently, without approaching the child. "Are you alright?"

The little girl curled up tighter; she was still completely undressed and wet from the bath, and too afraid to speak.

"Um," Wanda said, as she began to look at her feet and scuff the floor with one toe. "I'm kinda not meant to be here, but I came to see if you wanted to sleep with your mum tonight."

The girl lifted her head, "Grandpa said I was not allowed to go back. That my mommy was bad."

Wanda shrugged. "Can you dry yourself?"

"Course I can! But nurse wouldn't let me. She had to check that I dried everywhere."

"Be quick then, and dress in your day clothes. Shoo."

The girl stood and ran into the bedroom. Wanda moved to listen at the door that led to the passage. She was hiding the rage she felt at the nurse. It would serve her right if Theo punished her for letting Rachel get away.

The girl was longer than Wanda expected, and she was just about to go and see what she was doing when she appeared, dressed and with her coat on.

"What took you so long, sweetling," Wanda asked, but she saw a ring of white around the child's mouth, and recalled a passing glance of a glass of milk on a table beside the smaller bed.

"I was thirsty, so I drank my milk."

Wanda suddenly had a very bad feeling.

"Come on. Keep with me and keep very quiet."

Before they had even reached the stairs, Wanda had to carry Rachel. The sudden thought that the drink was drugged, had proved to be true. Her anger increased. These Russian bastards were going to pay! However, that must wait. Right now, she had to get the girl out of the house unseen, and away to somewhere safe. Then if she could return, she wanted to get the old man out of the shed.

Wanda crept downstairs and got out of the house unseen. It seemed like the whole household was still having their evening meal. She made a line for the trees, and began to move around to the driveway - intending to keep off the noisy gravel, and edge down to the road. The occasional car went along it, with headlights lighting the trees until they passed.

She briefly considered waving down a car, but she was too afraid that she would pick a car with people who knew Theo. She would have to carry Rachel and keep out of sight.

As she was edging past the shed, a light went on at the back of the house and the door slammed open. Her immediate instinct was to hide, and she went behind the shed, in the narrow gap between the fence and the shed. She put Rachel down, and felt for some of the tree cuttings piled there to make a tough lean-to over her, and piled more in front to hide her.

She heard two men calling a name, and wondered if it was the nurse they were seeking. Then she heard Theo's voice. "If the brat ran off again, she will have gone towards the road. Find her! And find Helga! I want an explanation of how this happened."

To another man, he ordered, "Check the prisoner!"

Wanda had an instant to react. She must not be found, and must move away from where Rachel was hidden. She slipped along the fence line, following the men who were racing down the gravel. Her own movements were almost silent. As she moved, she removed her jacket, took out the knife and slipped it into her pocket, then she paused and tossed the jacket partly over the wire fence. She was going to continue to the road, but the men began to return. They had torches, and were checking the shadows. Wanda withdrew, slipping back the way she had come.

Another yell, told her they had found her gone. She was right at the shed, albeit the back, the side nearest the road. In an instant, she scrambled onto the roof and lay very still. They found her jacket and removed it from the fence.

Wanda saw movement near the car, Aleksi was opening the door.

"Father! I need to be going," Aleksi, the fake Wexford, was insisting.

Theo was torn between the activity at the fence and what Aleksi was saying. He answered sharply.

"Drive your car so there is light on the fence!"

Aleksi paused a moment before obeying.

Wanda saw an opportunity, and when all attention was down the driveway, she slid off the roof, coming down on the side with the doors, and slipped soundlessly to the back of the car. She had the luggage compartment open in moments, and she held it open just enough for her to climb in, and then pulled it shut.

She was sure that no one had noticed her. The car was running, their night sight would be ruined by the cars lights, and Aleksi had stepped out of the car and was standing a few feet in front.

From her new listening position, she heard Aleksi getting angry. "Father, I have to get to that meeting. The deal goes through tonight. Once I have signed the papers, its official and the US will have to abide the terms. I'll go from there to the airport."

"Very well. I will send the men out to kill that bitch. However, we will have to leave. If she does get to the authorities, she'll send them here. I will see to things here, and we will be gone within the hour. Ring the pilot before you go."

Feet crunched on gravel, Wanda assumed it was Theo leaving to start packing. Aleksi, got into the driver's seat, causing the chassis to rock very little. Wanda hoped this car, which was a recent model Mercedes would give her a better ride that the little car that brought her to the house.

Aleksi voiced a selection of Russian curses, before the pilot answered his call.

Wanda listened as Aleksi told the pilot to submit a flight plan to take the plane to Hamburg. He had just started to move the car when he braked hard.

This time Wanda heard Heidi's voice. "Don't hang around after the meeting! I will see you at the airport."

"I won't, but you make sure everything of mine is out of the house."

Wanda doubted that Aleksi gave Heidi time to give him a kiss or any other kind of going off gesture. This time the car took off with the wheels spinning too fast to get an immediate grip on the gravel.

The movement gave her a sudden surge of nausea that was made worse by the realisation of what she was doing. She was leaving Rachel alone, hidden yes, but what if she woke up and wondered down to the road. What if Theo found her? Would he just take off and not care?

Damn! Wanda thought. She should have stayed, she could have hidden from the hunters, up a tree or over the fence.

But not carrying a drugged child. Then another alarming thought occurred to her. What would they do to the old man, their prisoner of five years? They'd kill him! But she could not have taken the drunken sot, he was drugged too, and even as emaciated as he was, she could not have helped both him and the child.

When Aleksi got to the meeting, she would have to get out, find a phone and warn Jim. Then he could get the police to the house...

The car accelerated once it was on the road, Aleksi was betraying his anger by speeding. Wanda was feeling inexplicably nauseous, but she persisted in trying to think what she needed to do.

Jim would be at the meeting, she could get ideas to him when she was close. She had to warn him not to approach Wexford. He would have no idea that the man he saw as Wexford was a Russian criminal. If he approached the man and tried to talk to him - they might think he was onto the switch and kill him.

If she found where the meeting was and called the police that might queer Jim's plan. Then the idea surfaced, tardily, that she didn't even know where the house she had just left was. What was wrong with her? What was she just thinking? Yes, she had to warn Jim.

Wanda felt herself getting drowsy, and wondered if the compartment was airtight, and she was running out of air...

She dropped into a waking sleep, her mind filling with times when she was in danger of being caught. None of it was applicable to now. She would wait to emerge when all was quiet. No one would find her.

Her mind drifted again, to some nebulous time when she was being chased by dogs. It seemed so real that her body jolted, and tried to sit up. She felt her head hit the metal above her, and she seemed to see bright points of light.

That she was in a small enclosed place, she knew, but now she could not recall where she was or why. Panic froze her mind as the memories she had thought well locked away paraded through her mind. Truly horrible memories of inhuman torture, imprisonment in a dark noisome place - that even now she could not talk to anyone about. They would think her insane - creatures such as she would describe did not exist on Earth.

Then as now, she called out with her mind to the only one she could hope to reach, "Lisbeth! Lisbeth! Help me!"

Chapter 20 - Criminals fall out

At Vienna Airport, David waited for his luggage to emerge through the plastic slats and onto the carousel. He looked around, hoping to see Wanda. If she was there, she would have found him by now. Belatedly, he remembered to turn on his phone - perhaps she had tried to leave him a message. Nothing. Then it occurred to him that he should check his emails as well. Wanda didn't have a phone - she wouldn't risk it ringing when she was trying to hide. Once again, nothing.

He had hoped Wanda would be there. If she was, it would tend to disprove Elisabeth's insistence that Wanda was in trouble - that she had triumphed yet again. Maybe she had, anyway. Maybe her mission required her to be elsewhere...and he knew her mission would have priority. Yet he couldn't help feeling apprehensive - increasingly so.

What to do? He dare not call Jim, so who could he call? Donau? The name of the Viennese policeman popped into his mind. Wanda said she trusted him, and given him a number to call him. He hadn't expected to need it, and he would have to wait until he had his luggage to find it on his tablet.

When his case appeared, he grabbed it and went across to an empty seat so he could open it, just enough to slip his hand between layers of clothes to where he had packed his tablet.

He didn't even bother to re-zip his bad before turning it on.

His fingers flicked the screen and found his contacts. He memorised the number and punched the numbers on his phone. He spoke in German asking for Donau, but a polite voice told him that Kommisssar Donau was not in his office.

David quickly offered to call back and disconnected. He knew it was late, but he had hoped the policeman would be there. Damn. There was the message drop Jim always had...

He punched those numbers from memory. He left a terse message. "Jim. David. I am in Vienna. Wanda is in trouble."

There, he'd admitted it. He hoped that Jim would get the message.

Moments later, his phone rang. He thought it was Jim, but the voice was female, and frantic.

"David!"

He recognised the voice.

"David, oh thank God. Wanda's in bad trouble - really bad."

It had to be; Elisabeth sounded frantic. It meant that he needed to be calm. He drew in a deep breath and asked, as calmly as he could, "What can you tell me?"

He knew from experience that Wanda, his wife, his soulmate, and Elisabeth's sister, could always tell when the other was in trouble. Freaky, most people would think, but he was used to it, and now it was an unexpected source of information.

"I am only getting panic, darkness and her mind is like it was back when she was missing."

That seriously worried David, he hadn't been able to forget that time, when he had been helpless to help his wife. She had been tortured and her mind had been full of dark emotions.

Still, he had to stay calm. He told his sister in law, "She survived back then, and she is even smarter now. I'll find her."

It was true, and he needed to remember that. He couldn't give up on her.

"You'd better, David, and soon," Elisabeth said before ringing off.

Feeling as if he had to do something, he tried the number for Donau, and this time he left a message with his name and phone number. He decided then to get some coffee and something more to eat than the meagre fare that was the in-flight meal on the plane.

He wheeled his case towards the shops and sat at a table where he could watch the flow of people, deciding that he would call the Embassy and arrange a pick up.

Wanda was barely aware when the car stopped. She knew she had curled into a ball, to hide from something dangerous, and that something was very close.

"Go away! Go away!" she kept thinking, over and over. The feeling of peril went away. The creature that wanted her, was stalking her, had moved away. The other creatures she could sense knew nothing of her, weren't looking for her. Now was her chance to get out of this hole, get away...

It was instinct, not conscious thought that made her fingers unlatch the lock, and then raise the door of the hole, very slowly. The enemy was gone, but he might return...

Wolfgang Wessler, was in the reception room of his mansion, which was on a large block on the outskirts of Vienna, but still on the city side of the Danube. His small staff had prepared tables with glasses and wine, and had trays ready to bring in small dainty savouries.

Though his guests were not due for another half an hour, Wessler helped himself to a drink of his finest brandy - much better than the quality wines he had for his guests. He was filled with fierce anticipation, knowing he was about to close a multimillion Euro deal, and at the same time, be able to legally rob the government of America. The expectation was making the bouquet of his brandy smell even finer.

His head servant entered and bowed slightly. "Sir, Herr Lunn is here, and wishes to have a private word before the meeting."

Wessler glanced at his watch, it was eight thirty; his other guests were due at nine.

"Bring him through, Pieter," Wessler directed. Suddenly, the taste of his wine seemed to sour. He put the half-full glass down on a table.

Lunn only waited until the door was closed behind him before blurting out, "What is going on? I had police watching me! I had to lose them. Two of our colleagues have told me the same."

That news alarmed Wessler, and more so when Lunn added, "They also have Alpha Prime under observation. I didn't dare go into the office. It has to be because of those damned diamonds. I regret ever arranging to get them for you."

"You must have betrayed something to someone," Wessler accused, righteously sure that he had not mentioned them to anyone. "Or maybe the thief talked."

"No way, Wessler. He...and I stress the gender...knows better. He has not got so good, and lasted so long, by talking about his work."

"Well I have mentioned them to no one."

"You must have! Only you and I knew about them and I sure as hell did not call the police to get them to come to where that woman had them."

The argument kept in low hissing tones, grew more heated as other 'misunderstandings between them, were aired.

Both men stopped talking when Pieter knocked, entered and announced another arrival.

"Mr Wexford is here, Sir."

Lunn glared at Wexford when he entered; the man had changed his hair colour. Wessler slipped a hand into his jacket pocket.

"You're early," Lunn growled at the new arrival. Then he heard a muted pop and felt a searing pain in his side. He felt his legs giving way, and an exclamation from Wexford.

Aleksi, pretending to be the American Wexford, was startled by the sudden development. "Are you mad? You have everyone coming here in less than twenty minutes. You have to leave!"

"None of us will talk, Wexford. And you certainly dare not," Wessler said calmly. "I see you are planning on disappearing, or why have you coloured your hair?"

"True, but I have personal reasons. However, I feel there are some amongst your precious cartel who are not as expedient as you. They will not want to hide a murder. And you have that South African, Lushing, coming. He is a virtual unknown. Or do you have him blackmailed too?"

Wessler saw the point. "I will go and have Pieter call the others to postpone the meeting. Can you drag him to the next room?" He indicated a door that led to his office.

Aleksi glanced into the room and decided it was a good choice. They could say they thought he was an intruder. It was also convenient that Lunn had fallen on a thick mat. He was bleeding, onto it, but the blood would not go through it quickly. Not caring that the man might still be alive, Aleksi dragged the mat into Wessler's office. At least now, if anyone else turned up, they would not see the body.

The man was not a great loss, and had been as much of a danger to the deal as a benefit. If only the police had caught him with the diamonds. Then he would have been too busy hiding all his crimes to interfere in the deal.

Aleksi retreated from the office, just as a disturbance began outside the door to the reception area. He recognized Heinrich, but not the struggling figure that he was dragging into the room.

"Look what I found crawling out of your car," Heinrich announced when he looked and saw the man he knew as Wexford.

Aleksi swore, remembering to speak in American. He knew who the woman was alright, and knew more about her than he had let on to the cartel members. "Will you quieten that bitch!" He wondered whether to mention she was the jewel thief or that she was an American spy.

"She's an American spy." Aleksi, decided that would frighten the man more, and in saying it, he thought of a way to use her. "Drag her in to the office. Wessler is calling off the meeting."

Heinrich kicked the legs from under his prisoner, and hit her hard with a punch to the jaw. The woman fell in a heap, and Heinrich reached down for a handful of clothing to drag her.

He stopped halfway into the room, when he saw Lunn on the floor, his shirt soaked in blood.

"What happened?"

Aleksi shrugged, in the direction that Wessler had gone. "It's under control. Wessler is calling the others. You need to go outside and if any of the others arrive, stop them coming in and tell them to leave."

Heinrich took one more horror filled look at the faintly moaning Lunn and dropped his hold on the woman, nearly running out of the house.

Aleksi looked dispassionately at the woman on the floor, knowing the trouble the bitch had caused. He should kill her, but she was his key to solving two major problems, or maybe three. He removed his jacket, and took a pair of thin leather gloves from inside it, and leant down to search the woman's clothing. He expected to find little, because his father's men would have searched her, then his hands felt something odd. He grinned, when he pulled out the thin flexible knife from the woman's pocket.

When Wessler returned moments later, Aleksi was calmly wiping a bloody knife on a relatively unbloody section of Lunn's jacket. The man had stopped moaning, and if not already dead would be within moments. The knife wound was at an angle that the woman might have stuck him.

Blood was spurting as Aleksi lifted the woman by her arms and held her over Lunn's body. He lowered her for a moment, as he pressed the knife into her hand, and ensured blood would be on her hands.

Aleksi was aware that Wessler was simply staring in disbelief, but he continued his setting of the scene. He took Lunn's now limp hand and forced the fingers into a talon, and raked them down the woman's face, drawing blood from her.

"What are you doing?" Wessler's voice was almost a hysterical shout.

"Quiet you fool. I am covering your tracks. Give me the gun and lock the doors!"

"What for? I cannot stay here."

"Idiot! I am making it look like Lunn disturbed an intruder - this American agent - and they fought, she stabbed him, he pulled his gun and tried to get her, they wrestled, she took it and shot him. For anyone to believe it, the gun needs to be here. You don't need to have it on you."

Wessler stood transfixed, shocked and unnerved by the callous planning. He had thought the American trade consul was a walkover, but here he was showing a completely unexpected side. Without a word, he handed over the gun, and watched Wexford clean it of his prints and press it into Lunn's right hand, and then into the woman's hand.

The woman was lying on her side next to Lunn, and when Wessler drew the knife out of the dead man, and put it down as he searched the pockets in the woman's trousers.

"They won't believe she did it," Wessler said, with a tremor in his voice. He wanted to be sick.

"Oh yes they will," Aleksi, assured him. "Agent she may be, but she is also the thief who stole those diamonds. Lunn could have told you that. He had people following her. Somehow, he found out. This woman is slick. I think she even has the US Government fooled."

Aleksi was mixing truth and lies, wanting only to keep Wessler on the edge of panic. It worked, Wessler suddenly turned on the spot and went to his office safe. He had the door unlocked in moments, and began taking things out and sorting them on his desk, before stuffing them into a case. His concentration was so focussed, that he did not notice Aleksi straightening up, or creeping up behind him. He felt the arm come around him, and when he tried to turn, felt a knife plunge into his stomach. Wessler gave an exclamation, and his hands dropped the papers he was holding, and went to press on the gaping wound. The light faded from his eyes as he sank to the floor.

Aleksi let him fall, and then swore when he saw he had blood on his sleeve. It meant he would have to get blood on the woman's arm. He lifted the woman, and pressed her arm around Wessler as if it had been her that stabbed him. It was no matter that some of Lunn's blood was now on the back of Wessler's suit.

He was glad that the woman was so light, and that she was still alive. He dragged the woman out of the way, and roughly shoved the knife in her pocket. He realised that he had cut her, but, he didn't care. She deserved it for all the trouble she had caused.

Casting a last look over the scene, he paused to wonder if he should take Wessler's files. Surely the man would have been taking the most valuable information...

Aleksi stepped over Wessler, and glanced in the safe. He saw several bundles of high denomination notes, and another which showed the gold rimmed edges of valuable shares. He reached in carefully, and took them. That was all, he decided. The thief was supposed to have been caught in the act. He glanced down at the woman and caught a slight movement. She was beginning to come around - he needed to leave.

With his jacket hiding the blood on his sleeve, and the bundle of share certificates, Aleksi calmly walked from Wessler's office. He regretted that the deal he had worked for was beyond redemption, but the shares might make up for some of that. Yet, with both Wessler and Lunn out of the picture, and no clear leader to take over the cartel, he could support Heinrich to take over, and the Austrian could be his front man. Certainly he would be more malleable that Lunn or Wessler.

However, he would not offer his support right away. He would wait and see what the police turned up. The entire cartel might be arrested and that would be even better. There would be a vacuum, waiting for him to step into it.

Aleksi turned and closed the office door behind him. Pieter, Wessler's manservant was hovering outside in the reception room looking uncertain.

"Oh, Herr Wexford, would you know if Herr Wessler is finished with his private discussions? I have messages for the master."

Aleksi frowned, glanced at the closed door, and suggested, "I think not. I was told to get out. Heinrich bought in a spy. Your master and Herr Lunn are asking her questions. They want to know who she is working for. If I were you, I would be scarce for a while, until they call for you."

Pieter looked startled, glanced at the door, and nodded. "I will come back later."

Aleksi watched the man vanish towards the back of the house, and thought to himself. "Obviously, he knows what that means."

Outside Aleksi saw the luggage compartment of his Mercedes was up. He closed it, and saw Heinrich emerging from the shadows, and coming over.

"Only the South African showed," Heinrich told Aleksi. "I only had to mention the smell of trouble and the man was off like a rocket."

"Good. Let's go. I will get in touch in a few days. I think you will be the best man to take over, and you would be wise to forget everything you saw."

"Yes," was Heinrich's agreement. He went to where he had parked his own car, and sank into it with relief. While waiting for the American to come out, he had begun to shake like a leaf in the wind.

Jim Phillips, posing as a South African arms dealer, hadn't gone far. He had seemed to take off in his car, but had only gone out to the street and two houses along. Then he trotted back on foot, and hid deeper in the shadows than Heinrich. The Austrian was in such a state of nerves that he could not keep still. He was pacing and scuffing the concrete of the driveway, and the noise was drowning out Jim's own voice as he spoke softly by phone to his team who were waiting nearby, ready to leave.

"Nicholas? Something is up. I think Wessler and Lunn have had an argument. I am going back to check the result."

He heard the 'be careful' admonishment, but his ears had caught the sound of a door shutting and he ended the call and edged closer to the house. He saw Wexford, closing the boot of his car. He'd seen it open and had thought it odd. Then he saw Heinrich come out of the shadows and the two men spoke for a few moments, and then went to their respective cars.

Once both had passed him, he called Nicholas back. "Wexford and Heinrich have just left. Wexford is in the blue Mercedes. Follow him and see where he goes."

He heard the acknowledgment and closed his phone. He then kept to the shadows and circled to the back of the house and found an open door that led into the laundry. Moving quietly, he avoided the kitchen where two male servants were talking and one was pouring a drink. He continued through to the front of the house and found himself in the reception room, noting that it had been set up for the meeting. He stopped and took a careful look around, and listened. If Wessler and Lunn were arguing, it was too quiet. He noticed the closed door, and guessed this led to Wessler's home office. He'd seen plans of the mansion, but none of the rooms had been labelled.

He walked closer, keeping to the edge of the room, as he pulled out some latex gloves. Before trying the door, he put an ear to it, but no sound came through. He squatted, and peeped through the keyhole, part of his mind alert for the approach of servants. He saw the light was on, but caught no sound through it nor saw any movement. He gently pushed on the door, surprised that it opened easily. Rising, he looked into the office. Clear in his view was the blood covered body of Wessler. He ventured in a short way, he saw the opened safe, the files on the desk, the open case...as he turned to leave, he saw another pair of legs. Another person was lying beyond the desk. He had on a suit, in the shade of brown that Lunn preferred, and the carpet around that body was thick with blood. He'd seen enough. More than enough. He retreated, pulling the door closed like he had found it, and wasting no time slipping out of the house and into the shadows. His mission to destroy the cartel was complete, now he needed to follow Wexford and find out what the trade consul knew. Had he seen anything?

He did not know that Wanda had been there, and that he had missed her by mere minutes.

Wanda came back to awareness, instantly wary. Awareness of a throbbing headache and a burning sensation down her thigh followed instants later. She reached up to feel her head, and her fingers came away bloody. She looked down at her thigh, but saw the blood on the front of her blouse. She was transfixed, but gradually realised that the blood was not hers. She felt her leg, touched the outline of her knife and cursed. She must have fallen on her knife. She felt the trousers, they were black, though some of the blood showed. Still, there was not a lot - she had been lucky - only a shallow wound.

She did not recall how she had come into that room, and when she tried to recall anything, she saw darkness and recalled the nightmares - the memories of those alien creatures...

There was no one with her now, and scrambled up, nearly falling again as her leg felt boneless. Her eyes looked for what she had heard skitter across a section of polished floor, and saw the body and the blood. She drew out her knife, it had blood on it, and she never considered it might be hers.

Backing towards the door, the other body came into view. Her gorge rose, and she swallowed hard.

"Oh no!" she said in a small voice. The hallucinogenic dreams of fighting and killing those alien creatures, must have been her doing this. She had done this, she must have - no one else was around.

Her mind went into panic mode; she turned and stumbled towards the door, pushing it open, and then pushing it closed to hide her crime. The front door was right there, and she began to run. Outside in the still, night air, she heard a car start up, not far away. She instinctively turned away from the road, and went deeper into the landscaped garden behind the house. Her mind was convinced that someone had seen her, and was even now, calling the police.

Aleksi returned to his father's rented mansion, it was less than ten minutes away from Wessler's place. He saw that all the lights were still on, and guessed his father had not yet left.

His Father looked around in surprise when he heard the quick footsteps in the hall.

"Why are you here?" Theo demanded.

"Later. I found that woman and she won't be a problem," Aleksi announced. He told his father what had happened. Neither father nor son had any qualms about killing to achieve their goal.

"Quick thinking," Theo approved. "She will be too busy with her own trouble to come after us. We are almost finished here."

"I need to change. I have blood on me. Where are my clothes?"

"Your Heidi packed them into a case; that one, by the door."

"Where is she?"

"I sent her to the airport to wait for us," Theo told him. "There were things here I did not want her to see. Be quick."

Aleksi didn't need telling. He wanted to be out of Vienna before the murders were discovered.

He returned wearing a complete change of clothes, and put the blood stained ones in a suit bag. He would dispose of them at the airport.

Two of his father's men were dragging the prisoner from the shed. The real Wexford, was so pickled by alcohol and addicted to drugs, that his mind was almost destroyed. Still, he would now have a purpose.

He could disappear, and the real Wexford would be found, dead. No one would come looking for him.

Theo spoke, "What about Wexford's brat? Do you want to keep her?"

"She is no kin to me, and a spoilt American brat," Aleksi spared not a shred of concern.

With equal lack of emotion, Theo agreed, "It will make this seem like the work of the cartel if they are found together."

"They believe I didn't know where she was," Aleksi warned.

"And when you went to the meeting, they betrayed your trust and abducted you," Theo countered.

Aleksi nodded in agreement. "She will have had her milk."

"Yes, Helga is thorough and took it up before you left."

"Does she know that you are leaving?"

"That whore is no doubt dead drunk already," Theo predicted. "I have no more use for her. Are you ready?"

Aleksi nodded. Theo gave one of his men quiet orders, and gestured Aleksi out. He grabbed his case and headed for his car. His father's driver was waiting with the door of the other car ready for Theo to enter.

Jim called Nicholas Black as soon as he was clear. "Wessler and Lunn are dead," he said tersely. "We need to find Wexford. I think he saw it."

"He's just pulled in at a house across the river. One of those luxury ones on a huge block. It sure doesn't look like he was forced into anything."

"Is he alone?" Jim asked.

"From where we are, it looks so. Do you want me to go in closer?"

"Yes," Jim said decisively. "Put Max on."

"Yes, Jim," Max Hart acknowledged. "If Wexford leaves, follow him. I think he is up to no good. I am going to hint to those who need to know, that he should be investigated."

"Right!" Max agreed, and ended the call. He turned to another of the team. "Grant, do we still have the extra pair of night glasses?"

The binoculars were pulled from Grant's overnight bag, and Max began to scan the near side of the house. They had an opportune line of sight through the trees screening the front of the house.

He caught sight of Nicholas racing back.

When he arrived, he panted, "Two men came out. Neither of them is Wexford. They both had black hair."

Max immediately dialled Jim and reported, and Jim gave new orders. "Get inside, look for Wexford and for a child."

Max shoved the phone at Casey Randall and gestured to Nicholas and Grant. They ran through the darkness towards the house.

"What's up, Jim?"

"Have those men Nicholas saw gone?"

"Yes, they just passed us. Why?"

"I have a horrible feeling that those men, whoever they are, were using Wexford. Wanda thought he was shady, but had no proof. Wexford told his department boss that he thought the cartel were crooks, I think they have double crossed him. If he didn't leave with those men, they may have killed him and left him in the house. His daughter might be there too."

"Oh, no!" Casey murmured, worrying now about the child.

"Be ready to leave quickly - those men may have left a rearguard. We can't afford to get involved further, but Wanda was looking for the Wexfords."

"Ok Jim, I'll have...God!"

"What?" Jim demanded, hearing the shock in her voice.

"Fire, Jim! One end of the house just exploded."

"Where are you?"

"Grant said the 22nd district. I don't know the street."

"Where are the others?....Casey...Casey!" Jim realised he was talking to an open line, and that Casey had rushed off.

Casey had been looking through the night goggles, when the house exploded. Her eyes took time to readjust, and when they had, she saw someone running, someone who was burning like a torch. She feared that it was one of her friends.

She met Grant and Max, carrying a body that reeked of burnt flesh and other vile odours.

Max, saw her and insisted, "Case, help Grant with this bloke. I'm going back to look for Nicholas."

He gave her no time to answer, but went off again at a fast sprint. The man in Grant's arms moaned.

"Who is he?" Casey asked, her concern for the poor man coming to the fore. "Can you carry him to the van?"

Grant shrugged the man into a fireman's hold and followed Casey back. "I don't know who he is. The house exploded and he came running out the door, we had to help him. There's almost no weight to him."

In the van, Casey lay several of her spare outfits on the floor before Grant put him down. They had a light on, and could now see the man's gaunt blackened features. His hair was shrivelled, and he didn't seem to be anyone they knew."

"Is it Wexford?' Casey asked.

Grant shook his head. "Wexford's a solid bloke. This smells like some hobo."

Casey began first aid, wetting down strips of cloth she made from one of her shirts, with the spare water meant for the radiator. Grant was placing these on the man's face and hands.

Max and Nicholas returned at a run. Nicholas climbed in the back, while Max went to the driver's seat.

Nicholas told Casey and Grant, "We found a kids room, but no kid. The bed wasn't slept in, but there was an empty glass of milk. It tasted like there was something in it. Where's the phone?"

Casey looked around, recalling she had dropped it. "There! I dropped it when I saw this poor man on fire."

Nicholas tried Jim's number. It rang once then stopped. He waited to see if Jim would ring back.

When it rang, he answered immediately, saying only, "Nick."

Jim's voice was audible to the three in the back of the van. "The police are at this other mansion in force. I had to move. What did you find?"

"The house blew up, and this old hobo came running out, on fire."

"Was it Wexford?"

"No, he's little more than skin and bones. Smells of vodka, and urine, and he's got some nasty burns."

"What about a child?" Jim asked urgently.

"Signs one was there, but we didn't find her. The bed wasn't slept in. Other than that, I would say that at least nine other people had been staying in the house."

Jim swore softly. "The two you saw - did they have a child with them?"

"Not that we saw," Nicholas told him, he glanced at the others for their confirmation.

"Fine, get out. Get that hobo to the hospital and get out of Vienna. I'll follow later."

Jim, still keeping one eye on the police activity at Wessler's mansion, had more than a bad feeling. He was reminded that Wanda Martin had not called him for over twelve hours. That in itself was not unusual, for she was on her own mission, but she had told him that she had a lead on Wexford. He needed to know what she had learnt, and to warn her of seeing Wexford at the mansion, and of the situation. After telling his team to get out of Vienna, he rang the number for his message drop and the first message he heard was, "Jim, its David. I'm in Vienna! Wanda's in trouble."

For a moment, he was at a loss. Then he began to think through what he knew of Wanda's plans. She was going out with the Austrian policeman. Did he know anything?

He dialled the number for the American Embassy and asked for Neil Thomas.

Just from the man's voice, he knew there was trouble. "Wanda and Donau ran into trouble. They saw Wexford. He promised to come here after some meeting tonight. Wanda is missing, and the police have units out looking for her."

He wish he knew what the police knew, but Thompson would have passed it on if he had been told. It seemed that the people who had targeted her the previous night had succeeded. He had to consider if Wanda was even alive. If she was, she'd get in touch. She had yet to meet anyone she couldn't handle - but there had been four masked men the first time and only one of her.

Then he realised, that she had to be alive. If she wasn't, David would know. Elisabeth Willard would know.

He checked through the rest of the messages. Two were call backs with information he had requested. Then he heard, "Jim! It's David. I've seen Wexford! Here at the airport! He was with an older man, going onto a charter flight. It's him! I'm sure! He's dyed his hair black, but it's him!"

Jim checked the time of the message - it had come in less than two minutes ago. He dialled David's number.

"Watch him! Call the police. Do you have the number for them?"

"Yes, they went into the charter lounge. Where's Wanda?"

Jim said quietly. "I don't know, David."

Chapter 22 - Fallout

When darkness fell, Derek Mont Pelier quietly insisted that he and Otto Donau went out to eat.

"If anything of importance comes in, they can call you. In the meantime, we need to sustain ourselves."

Alex woofed in agreement. He had been sitting quietly beside his human friend and refraining from his usual games. He had sensed that his human was ill and worried.

"I too know how helpless one can feel - not knowing - when we are worried about someone."

Donau met the Interpol agent's eyes. "You're right. We should eat." He rose and went to a small handbasin and filled a glass with water. Then he shook out two of the pain tablets and used the water to wash them down.

"I am surprised that you aren't feeling that you came here for nothing," Donau suggested. Though he didn't say it, he was grateful for the company. With Bauer in hospital, and himself out of action, he hadn't seen Christian who was following up leads they all should have been on.

"Not for nothing," Mont Pelier managed to sound sincere. "It never hurts to listen to the flow of crime somewhere. Occasionally I have gained helpful information that way."

"In that case, let me introduce you to my favourite restaurant - where they spoil Alex shamefully."

On their return, they met Chief Kolbe in the passage leading to Donau's office.

"I thought I told you to go home," he challenged the younger man.

"I have been resting, overseeing Christian and the officers out looking for Wexford, and Frau Martin."

"And answering a lot of questions for me," Mont Pelier added, sounding grateful. "I believe there is to be a meeting of some importance tonight. I requested to be allowed to monitor what is discovered."

"The business that involves Herr Wessler? I think the American was misled, or out to cause trouble. It will turn out to be nothing, and important men will be angry. What about that Carson woman? Any word on her? I want her found, and either locked up or deported. I do not like that kind of person in Vienna."

"I quite agree," Mont Pelier said politely. "I am sure your men will soon find her. Meanwhile, I will keep your Kommisar from doing too much."

The first of the reports came through. There was no indication that a meeting was to be held at Alpha Prime. Wessler, it appeared, was still in his office. According to the switchboard he was in conference with one of the other CEO's who worked in the building. If that were the case, he had told Donau the truth earlier.

Watchers on the other men on Wexford's list had three of them heading out towards the 22nd district. Four more had been observed going into restaurants with their wives or escorts. The others had gone home and apparently stayed there.

Donau was listening to the voice of the police dispatcher when his personal phone rang. He answered it with his name, listened and then snatched up a pen and began to scribble furiously.

When he ended the call, he used his phone to call the dispatcher, to mobilise a squad to go to the airport, and to get the airport police to hold a charter flight. He turned to Mont Pelier, a grin on his face, and his headache forgotten.

"That was the US Embassy, they just had a call from one of their citizens, who identified Wexford at the airport. He was with another man and about to board a charter flight to Hamburg. They had the flight details and it is due to leave in 15 minutes."

"Do they know who arranged the charter?" Mont Pelier asked, his interest just as keen. "Can we get the passenger list? I will call my colleagues in Hamburg."

Donau got busy on the phone. He spoke to the airport and wrote down the answers to his questions.

As he wrote, he was speaking aloud, "Three passengers. Theo and Lenka Alekseev and a Heidi Lowenbach. The woman was the one I spoke to this morning."

He ended that call and started another to the dispatcher. "Have the security film scrutinised at the Air Vienna charter desk for the American, Wexford. He may have darkened his hair."

Covering the mouthpiece while he waited for a reply, Donau told Mont Pelier, "The man who initiated the call mentioned that, and if Heidi Lowenbach is part of the group, it is very likely he is right."

Donau stood to collect his coat.

"Going home?" Mont Pelier asked.

"No - the airport. I was put in charge of finding Wexford."

Mont Pelier stayed seated. "By the time you got there it would be too late. Either he will be caught or the plane will have taken off. Besides, if he was still there, and saw you, he is likely to be spooked. If he ran this morning and is fleeing now, he has something to hide."

"What?" Donau muttered, frustrated. The Interpol man was sharp, and his own mind was fighting a throbbing headache.

"If they catch him, they will bring him here and you can question him."

Donau still seemed intent on going, so Mont Pelier asked a question to distract him. "Is it the missing child that bothers you so?"

He got Donau's attention. "Yes, and the missing American agent."

"I see. About the agent - a woman I understand. You haven't actually told me much about her. A Frau Martin, I believe you said."

"Wanda Martin," Donau supplied the name. "She was also helping me with the Carson case. She has a really sharp mind."

"What is she like?" Mont Pelier was not as casual in asking the question as he looked.

"About 5 foot 4 inches, light brown hair, blue eyes. Competent. Has scars on both wrists, but wouldn't say how she got them and I don't believe she is the sort to try suicide."

"And Carson?" Mont Pelier prompted for his own reasons.

"Brown eyes, about the same height, foul mouth," Donau summarised. "Had white streaks in her hair the first time I saw her, and dark hair the night of the robbery. Are you trying to say they are the same now?"

"No. I was wondering if you have confirmed that the Wanda Martin who arrived here is the same one that left America?"

"How can it not be? I picked her up from the Embassy. And she organised a call to a Senator that Frau Wexford knows."

"By phone, you rely on information given," Mont Pelier said quietly. "Who was it that you spoke to?"

"Senator Charles Willard, from California," Donau supplied, as the Interpol agent reached for the phone. He then added, "Dial o for an outside line."

He listened with envy as Mont Pelier went through a series of contacts and finally reached the senator at his home.

From Donau's perspective, Mont Pelier explained his call and then asked a series of questions, starting with, "How well do you know Mrs Martin? Can you describe her? And I believe you requested her help?"

Then he listened for a time and then finally said, "Why do you ask?" After another pause to listen, he concluded with, "Thank you, Senator."

Mont Pelier was extremely thoughtful.

"Can I ask what you learnt?" Donau spoke after a while.

"I was consideringing with the idea that Carson might have been impersonating Martin - since eye colour is easy to change, and scars - realistic looking ones, can be created."

"And?" Donau prompted.

"How was Frau Martin this morning as compared to yesterday?"

Donau shrugged. "Much the same. Perhaps a bit pale. Why? They can't be the same. Carson was in hospital until six thirty in the morning. I caught up with Frau Martin at nine-thirty. The Embassy said she'd been there since the night before."

"Did they say if Frau Martin had been out that morning?"

"I can ask," Donau offered.

Mont Pelier shook his head. "It may not tell us anything. The Senator tells me that Frau Martin and her husband are very good at what they do. The former has many unconventional methods and is apt to go off on her own...hunches."

"Yes...I'd agree with that," Donau spoke slowly. "There was more?"

Mont Pelier smiled faintly. "The senator also said, that she has the devil's own luck. However, he is personally grateful to her for finding his wife last year."

That was all that Mont Pelier was going to divulge. He was still trying to make sense of some of what the senator had told him and he hid his concern after hearing the rest.

As soon as the senator had named Wanda Martin's husband, he knew that he had met them both before and he too was personally grateful to both of them. The only difference was, back when he had met them, they were using the surname Davis.

The rest, about Wanda Martin being a very close friend of his daughter, and that daughter being highly agitated and saying that her friend was in trouble...known by some classified means, was worrying him. Now, he felt as edgy as Donau in wanting to get out and be doing something. However, he too had his feet tied. He was working in a foreign country, and his mandated authority was only in the Carson/diamond thief matter.

The phone rang yet again, Donau answered it. "What is it Christian?" Then he listened, and finally directed, "Head back here, leave the details to the airport police."

Donau filled Mont Pelier in. "The plane left early. The pilot refused to turn back. It headed towards Hamburg, but the radar lost it. You can try calling your colleagues, but again, there is no guarantee they were actually going there."

Mont Pelier made the calls anyway, and assured Donau, "They have been alerted and will be looked for."

Donau began to pace restlessly. "Where are you staying tonight?"

"Your chief arranged a room at a hotel just down from here."

"I suppose I ought to go home," Donau admitted. "Soon though. I will wait for Christian to get here."

"I am surprised you are still capable of standing," Mont Pelier chided mildly. "Do you think..."The dispatcher's radio came alive again, and Donau gestured peremptorily for quiet so that he could listen. He went back to his desk and flicked through a file.

"That address they just mentioned is owned by Wessler, the CEO of Alpha Prime," Donau stated, staring across the room for a moment.

"I am not familiar with the code they used," Mont Pelier commented.

"There's been a murder. Wagner is in charge of the murder team. I'm going out there." He was daring his 'minder' to object.

"I will come along, and do the driving."

Alex, sensing a chance to be outside, suddenly came awake, and wagged his tail.

Chapter 23 - Murder most foul

The scene was lit by portable floodlights and the stark picture of death was hideously revealed. Mont Pelier stayed back as Donau spoke to Wagner, explaining his interest and the connection to cases he was working on. He drew Wagner back to the door to introduce Mont Pelier.

The other officer, gave a passing nod to the foreigner, and went on talking to Donau. "The butler found them. There was meant to be a meeting here, about 9 pm, but fifteen minutes before then, Wessler came out and told his man to call the guests and tell them to return home. He had let in Herr Lunn, the other victim, and a Herr Wexford, an American. Sometime before 9.30, the American came out, said he'd been sent out because Wessler and Lunn were questioning a spy that Herr Heinrich had found outside. The butler said he was told to keep away whilst they questioned her."

Donau pounced on the pronoun. "Her? Did he see the woman?"

"No, but he saw both Heinrich and Wexford leave. And he said that there was a fifth man outside, who never came in."

"Do you mind if I assist, Rudy? I think I know who that woman might have been. I will put a call out for Heinrich. He, Wessler and Lunn were all people who were having negotiations with the American."

Donau glanced at Mont Pelier and wondered if he should say that Wexford had fled the country. This must have been the reason why.

Wagner didn't give him a chance to speak further, but went right on, "This is a really nasty case, I'll have any help you offer. We haven't found the knife that was used on both men. Lunn was also shot, but we have the gun. Forensics are on the way."

They had not moved far into the room, but Donau looked around. "The safe is open..."

"It looks like Wessler was emptying it into a briefcase when he was killed. We can't tell if anything was taken. Hey! Can you keep that blasted dog of yours out of here?"

Donau looked at his dog. "He's found a scent."

"Do you think you can get him to check outside for the weapon?

We are looking for a narrow blade of some kind. I will let you know what we find out here, and have the lab concentrate on this. We need to have answers before the press are all over us. They have to come from a fatal house fire. Though fortunately for me, most of that other work will be done by the fire lab and the coroner's office. The coroner will come here as soon as he is finished there."

Donau knew the procedure all too well. "When you can, Rudy. But I would like to have that brief case and the safe contents," he requested. "If they tell me anything I will let you know."

"Deal, Otto," Wagner agreed. "Now get that twitchy nose out of here."

The fact that Alex was already out the door and whining softly, forced Donau to agree. Alex had not been asked to find a scent, so he had recognised a scent he had followed earlier. Not sure what that would be, Donau gave the quiet command to seek, and Alex, with a quiet woof, trotted off.

Donau had to trot to keep up, but now the fresh air and the adrenalin surge had cleared his head a bit. Mont Pelier, wasn't dressed for running, but he was fascinated by the behaviour of Donau's dog, and decided to forego dignity and follow. The trail that the dog followed was not perfectly straight, more like a drunks meanderings, but it led fairly directly to the wire fence at the bottom of the property. The dog was growling faintly and looking at his master.

"This is like de ja vu," Donau muttered, only this time he was not going to help Alex over, for that would mean he had to scale the fence to follow. "We'll find a gate. Alex, come!"

"What's beyond the fence?" Mont Pelier asked, as he kept up with the Austrian.

"Probably the river. If this is the killer, it would be a good place to ditch the knife."

Alex picked up the trail again on the other side of the fence and he led them through a maze of dark, narrow spaces, until they had travelled two miles and they were down near the river, in a park like area with footpaths and a wall along the river's edge. Once there, he trotted directly towards the source of a commotion, one they had been hearing getting louder.

A figure was standing on the retaining wall, back to the river, screaming obscenities at a group of milling youths. They were chanting, "Jump, jump, jump," and some were close enough to reach out and try to unbalance her. The figure kicked those ones in the face, forcing them back.

Donau tried to run, but he had little energy. He saw glint of light on metal, as the figure slashed at arms that came too close. He was sure it was a woman, and she sounded out of her head - high on something. He whistled a command to Alex, and the youths turned, saw the men approaching and began to move away.

As they approached the woman slowly, an older man emerged from the trees. He approached and asked, "Are you police. I called the police."

Donau stopped and turned to the man, "Yes. Donau, Investigative Bureau." He produced his badge.

"This woman is mad, Sir. She is covered in blood. I think she is trying to kill herself."

"Thank you," Donau responded. "You can leave this woman to us. Please wait by the road and when other officers arrive, have them come down here quietly."

Mont Pelier had not taken his eyes off the woman, she was inching along the fence, moving away from them, watching them. However, once the youths had moved away, she had stopped screaming.

"Otto," Mont Pelier said quietly, to get his attention.

Donau saw the woman's movement, whistled softly and gave an arm gesture. Alex trotted to the fence, jumped over it. There was a narrow section of bank along the far side.

"What is he doing?"

"Getting behind her," Donau explained softly. "Wait back here."

Mont Pelier stopped, but kept watching the scene. Donau was walking slowly, towards the woman, making no threatening moves, but when he reached a certain point, the screams began again.

He took a step back, and another until the woman stopped again, and he could try to talk to her.

"I am not going to hurt you. I am here to help you."

"No! Stay away! Please, stay away."

Donau tried, "Tell me what the trouble is."

Alex gave a tiny woof, and the woman spun around, nearly losing her balance but regaining it instinctively and beginning to run along the fence as if it were the footpath. Donau gave another whistle, and Alex leapt, pushing the woman off the fence and landing on her. Donau was already running, and seeing the knife flashing in the glow of one of the lights along the path. He whistled Alex off, but the dog whined a protest. He backed off when the whistle was repeated.

The woman struggled to her feet, and began to run. Alex leapt again, closing his mouth on the arm with the knife. The woman tried to shake him off, or drag him along, but his weight was too much.

Donau threw himself on the woman, and drew out his hand restraints. He managed to capture the flailing arms without being thrown off by the frantic struggles. He kept some of his weight on the woman, as he drew out his phone, and dialled the police dispatcher.

"Donau! Can you send an ambulance to Stanza Park, down near the river? I have a psych case. I also want the forensic pathologists to attend at the hospital. The prisoner is also a murder suspect."

Mont Pelier was watching silently, and guarding the knife that the woman had dropped. He wondered why the dog was trying to lick the woman's face.

"Alex! Stop that!" Donau said sharply. He wasn't about to turn the woman over to identify her, but he had his suspicions.

"This is what Carson was like last night," Donau told his companion. "I don't know what brought it on then. The doctor said she'd had a high dose of a knock-out drug, and by rights should have been unconscious. If she was being questioned by Wessler and Lunn, who knows what they tried."

Mont Pelier was thoughtful. "So this is Carson, the thief? She used that fence like a footpath, and had instinctive balance, even zoned out like she is."

"And for some insane reason, Alex likes her," Donau responded, in disgust.

The police reinforcements and the ambulance men arrived together. Donau let the uniformed police take over restraining the still struggling woman. He stumbled unsteadily to his feet and took a plastic bag out of his pocket. He moved back next to Mont Pelier, who picked up the knife he had been guarding and dropped it into the bag. He was careful not to destroy any prints on it.

The ambulance men had come prepared, and with the police to help, soon had the woman on the stretcher and restrained.

"I don't want anyone to tend to her until the forensic pathologist has seen her," Donau instructed. "This woman is a murder suspect." He made a move to follow them, but Mont Pelier gripped his arm and held him back.

"Let the officers take over. You need to go home."

Donau cursed him softly, under his breath, but the other man ignored it.

"Or I can take you to my hotel which is not far from your headquarters. If you like, I will then go to the hospital. She is, after all, also my suspect."

"Your hotel," Donau conceded. After the adrenalin surge of the past half hour, he was suddenly exhausted and about to die from a headache.

By the time the ambulance reached the hospital, the woman's struggles had abated to feeble. The blue eyes that had glittered with manic fury had become like cold blue marbles, un-reactive, unseeing, and fixed.

Despite the orders to delay treatment until the police doctor arrived and examined her, the emergency doctor took vital signs, and overruled the police. He set to work to stabilise the patient.

Mont Pelier arrived as the police forensic pathologist was introducing himself and asking for details of the patient. He made no complaint about the situation, agreeing that the woman had needed immediate attention. He did ask for a blood sample for his own use, and a copy of all blood test results. Then he worked with the other doctor, until the patient was stabilised.

"Where is she to be taken," the police doctor asked. He was told the psych ward.

When the patient was moved, Mont Pelier quietly inserted his presence into the group.

"I expect you are aware, that the murder investigation has precedence over that of theft," the police doctor remarked. He was a man in his sixties, with a lined face.

"That is understood," Mont Pelier agreed. "I can perhaps take notes for you while you work."

"Well, that's a kind offer. It will save me time, as I still have to attend to the victims that this one left behind."

"Are you not making presumptions, Doctor? The blood might be her own, considering the state she is in, and we did find her standing on a fence, a mere step away from the river."

"Yes, you are right," the doctor sounded like he was clearing his throat. "It has been a very busy night." The doctor spoke to the on-duty nurse. "We'll pull the curtains around. Mont Pelier, you will need to stay outside."

Mont Pelier took out a note book and a pen, and gave an affirmative. He pulled a plastic chair closer to the curtain, but not where he expected to be in the way if the doctor moved around.

He heard the doctor instruct the nurse, "I need to bag all of the clothes this woman is wearing. Use gloves, please and place them in this plastic bag. We can remove the restraints for now." He made a note, of instruction and time.

As the doctor went ahead with his examination, he noted all the doctor said, including details of various samples he had taken and their identification number.

The doctor was thorough, taking hair samples, swabs from hands, face, and arms. Mont Pelier realised with relief that the man was not just out to prove the woman guilty, but to try to understand why. It seemed he was also looking for signs of recent abuse for he remarked on the deep scabbed over nicks around the wrists and the traces of adhesive there. The latter was more noticeable on the backs of the hands than the palm side, where the cuts had been.

His itemisation was interrupted when he saw the long, shallow cut up and down the right thigh. He called for butterfly sutures and took swabs, and remembered to speak for the benefit of his note taker. "Slide 19, blood from long shallow incision on right thigh. I am dressing that wound."

He continued with his itemisation, noting multiple bruises on back, chest, ribs and shins. After continuing down to the woman's feet, having noted that there was no sign of sexual penetration, he moved his attention back towards her head, looking for less obvious signs. He found the red mark on her neck where something had been injected, and then called Mont Pelier inside the curtain.

His patient was covered by a sheet, up to her neck, but her arms were uncovered.

"This might interest you." The doctor indicated an oddity about the skin on the forearms. He began to tug at something that looked, at first glance, like a bloody flap of loose skin.

Mont Pelier's eye brows went up in surprise as the doctor peeled off a layer of skin toned material. He drew in a breath when he saw that the side nearest to the real skin had flat plastic items adhering to it. They were the same substance that the distinctive knife had been made from. There were two nearly identical narrow indentations that were empty, and he would wager the knife had come from there, and it had once been in two pieces.

On the other arm, when the false skin was removed, the tools were all thin and tapered to points.

"Well, dual purpose - tools and a way to hide a possible prior suicide attempt."

Derek Mont Pelier studied the scars, and studied the woman again. He did not speak of the knowledge that had just profoundly shocked him. He knew the woman, and when he had met her before, her name was not Carson. He had suspected it, when Donau spoke of Wanda Martin. He had known of her as Wanda Davis, and knew she was an American agent, knew with equal surety that she was no murderer.

He kept silent, and would refer to her as Tatiana Carson until he knew why she was in Vienna, or until she admitted her true name. It was possible that she was in Vienna for an important and vital purpose.

The doctor had not noticed his abstraction, and was continuing with his work. Mont Pelier hid the sympathy he felt. He would wait to see what the tests showed, and the other evidence that was found. In his own view, he was afraid that Wanda Martin had run out of luck.

Chapter 24 - Friends Rally

Jim Phillips went out early to get a newspaper, working to blend into the trickle of early risers, on their way to work. He should have been half way home by now, his mission successfully completed. He had seen his team off to the airport, but he had told them he was staying. They knew he was worried about Wanda Martin, and they shared that concern. All knew she was another of Jim's cadre of specialist operatives as they had all worked with her before, and hoped all would turn out well.

For Jim, his instinct was that she was deep in trouble. It wasn't because she had not been in touch with him for over 24 hours. She had no requirement to report to him. That she had was more of a professional courtesy, a politeness, because she knew that her mission was linked to his.

His concern now, was personal. He cared about all of his operatives, but Wanda was more than his protégé, and her husband, David, was more than his apprentice. They were like the children he had never had.

That David had come to Vienna, leaving their son in the care of friends, could only mean one thing. Wanda was in more trouble than she could handle. He knew she could handle a lot - she had been in trouble before, and in deadly peril before, and each time she had survived and overcome it. Once, it had been with his help, and it seemed she needed his help again.

The paper seller was proclaiming the headlines to the passers-by, and Jim stopped and smiled at her, requesting a paper. As he produced the coins to buy it, he began a conversation with the woman, not worried if his American accent was evident, because it gave him reason to discover the woman's feeling about the story behind the headline about two murders.

She was angry, because one of the murdered men was a great man who had brought profit to Vienna and used it to help people. Her wish was that Vienna had the death penalty and even that would be too good for the bastard who had killed the men.

Jim gave no sign that he had been responsible for orchestrating a feud between the two victims, or that he knew that the public image of the two men had been fabrication and their real selves had been evil. He had no remorse about their death, even after seeing the aftermath.

He smoothly ended the conversation by murmuring agreement with her, and turned to return to the hotel. Once the police began to look into the victims lives, they would find the truth.

He had not wanted the paper for news of that matter, though the article would be of interest. He wanted to see if there was a report about the hunt for a jewel thief. And he unfolded the paper with that intent.

A picture on the front page almost stopped him in his tracks. Right under the headline about the double murder, was a picture of Wanda Martin, called by her alias of Tatiana Carson, and she was named as the chief suspect for the killings.

He quickly refolded the paper and increased his pace back to the hotel, his mind working at high speed, trying to make sense of the connection. How could they possibly think it was her? She wasn't there! He had seen the murder scene mere minutes after it had happened, or had the gap been longer than he had thought?

His mind went to the last report Wanda had sent him. She had said there was another group moving in on the cartel. That group had located her, taken her diplomatic passport, and set Lunn and the police onto her. He knew that she had escaped from them and returned to the Embassy. He had told her to stay there, but she had gone off with Donau - continuing her mission.

Beginning to work on a strategy to help her, he was back at the hotel before he knew it, and was not fully aware of the people around him. He began to trot up the stairs, glancing up instinctively as he sensed someone coming down. He quickly averted his face, when he recognised Inspector Donau. The representative of the Investigative Bureau, had walked in on Wessler, when Jim's character of Lushing, the South African, had been talking to the CEO of Alpha Prime.

"Don't I know you?" Donau asked, after moving down a few more steps and turning around.

Jim emphasised his American accent and said, "Why, I don't think so, Sir. I am Jim Phillips, visiting from the US of A."

Donau wished him a pleasant day, and continued downstairs. Jim began continued up, lost again in thought, his head watching his feet. He almost collided with a well-dressed man.

His head came up and with a shock, he recognised Derek Mont Pelier. From the brief flash in the taller man's eyes, the recognition was mutual, but Mont Pelier merely made a hat doffing gesture and continued on. Jim hurried back to his room, unsettled by the encounter.

David Martin, who had arrived the previous night through the courtesy of Neil Thompson, was awake, and only refraining from pacing because he was holding a cup full of hot coffee. He wasn't alone. Max Hart was leaning against the wall, where he could also see out the window. Nicholas Black was making himself coffee, while Casey and Grant were lounging in two of the chairs.

Jim met four pairs of eyes in turn and then remarked, "I thought I told you all to go home."

"No way, Jim," Nicholas Black spoke for all of them. "Tell us what we can do."

The other three faces were equally resolute. Max Hart, Casey Randall, and Grant Collier were waiting for him to make a plan. Their loyalty heartened him.

"I don't know yet. Have you seen the paper?"

"We have," Max agreed.

Jim glanced at David whose face was practically bloodless.

Max added some extra information. "Somebody died in that fire last night. The one we rescued the hobo from. The papers reckon he caused the fire to start."

"And I reckon it was a set up," Nicholas stated. "There was a whole crate of vodka in the room."

"Steady a moment," Jim requested, sensing the indignation that Nicholas was controlling.

"Go over what you saw when you searched."

Max spoke up. "We only found the hobo there, all the other rooms were stripped bare. Except the nursery upstairs. There had been a kid staying there. We found clothes, and damp towels and a glass that had recently contained milk. David said that Wanda had been looking for a kid, as well as that Wexford bloke."

"And I said I had seen him at the airport," David snapped. "And he didn't have his kid with him."

"I saw Wexford at the house where Wessler and Lunn died," Jim drew the topic back to the important one. He came out and told Heinrich and myself to leave."

"So why did he take off? Did he think he would be a suspect, or was he afraid?" Casey asked.

"The impression that I got was that the two men were still alive then," Jim said slowly, deciding not to mention how they were supposedly questioning a spy. Perhaps that had been a lie...

"Why didn't Wexford go and talk to his wife? He's a pathetic coward," David snarled. "And what about his missing kid?"

Jim spoke quietly. "I am going to the hospital, to see if there is a chance that I can speak to Wanda or Tatiana Carson as she is being called. Nicholas, can you make me look different? As I was coming up the stairs, I ran into Donau, the policeman. I think he recognised me as the South African who had been talking to Wessler."

"I am going too," David insisted. He put his untouched coffee on the small table, and straightened his clothes.

"No." Jim said firmly. "It is not a good idea until we know all of the circumstances. And there is another possible complication."

"What?" David demanded.

"Derek Mont Pelier is here."

David slumped onto a stool. "He knows Wanda!"

"And Donau knows her as both Carson and herself," Jim reminded him.

"But he didn't know they were the same," David tried to insist, tried to believe.

Jim interrupted his agonised thoughts, "We don't know the full facts, and whatever they are, we still have a problem. Rachel Wexford is still missing."

"Do you think she was at the house?" Max asked, with concern. He stared at Nicholas, "Could we have missed her?"

"No, and if they were leaving why would they leave the child there? What makes me think is why half the rooms in that place had never been used," Nicholas thought aloud. "But the people were still there until last night - how would a hobo have known he could move in? And I don't think they would have invited him while they were there."

Max subsided, quelling his doubts. "Jim, we're here to help."

Jim nodded, and let the many questions in his mind settle into a pattern of action. "Grant, see if you can get into the CCT records at the airport. David, if he does, see if you can spot the men you saw. I want to know if they met anyone else and confirm they got on that flight."

Grant rose at once and went to retrieve his laptop from the table. David put his coffee down, followed Grant like his shadow, but colour had returned to his face.

"Nicholas, Max, see what you can find out about that fire. If the police don't have it blocked off, go and take another look. Talk to any reporters, try to talk to the neighbours - whatever you can. I want to know who the people were who lived there and anything about them."

"Casey, I want you with me. When we get to the hospital, see what you can find out about the hobo you rescued. If you can, try to talk to him. He might have seen something. Perhaps you might say you think he might be a relative."

Nicholas had fetched his theatrical make-up kit and when Jim stopped talking, gestured for him to sit. He quickly made some subtle changes to the lines of his boss's face, so that he no longer looked so like his Lushing character. Once Jim was satisfied, the four of them went out. Jim and Casey to get a taxi, and the others to fetch their hired car.

Jim sent Casey off before he made the attempt to get past the cordon of security. He claimed that he was a lawyer hired on behalf of the prisoner. The guards however, had no orders to let a lawyer through, and were stoic in their refusal to let him go past. He was as insistent in waiting nearby.

He suspected that they thought him another reporter, like the five men and two women who were also loitering nearby.

It served the purpose of keeping their attention partly on him, and away from the attractive woman who had caught their eye, who had arrived with him.

Before they had come up, they had looked at the hospital map to see where the burns ward was located. It was on the same floor as the psych ward, which according to the news report, was where the murder suspect was being held. Casey had planned her approach and was now speaking to a nurse at a desk down the corridor.

"Excuse me, but I was sent up here to see if I could help identify the man brought into the burns ward last night."

She knew that the man was still unidentified, for the nurse looked at her more intently.

"Why do you think you might know him?"

She had devised a story about a lost relative, but added at the end, "Even if I don't know him, I want to help the poor man. Somebody must be missing him."

The nurse knew the police were interested in the man, but had been given no orders to keep people out. She responded to the concern in the visitor's manner.

"I will let you in for a short time, but you will need to gown up, and wear a mask," the nurse instructed, as she was fetching what was needed.

Casey followed the nurse into the private room, and noticed the lack of clutter. The bed stood amidst an array of medical equipment, but most was not in use. The patient was lying on his front, for it was his back that was badly burnt, and he had a drip running into his right arm, to give him fluid and the painkilling medication. The man's face angled towards them.

The nurse checked his chart, and said, "He will be due for more medication soon, and he may wake up. Don't go too close."

Casey wrinkled her nose at the smell of burnt flesh that still lingered about the man. She studied the pale, loose flesh, on the side of his face, and decided that he had lost a lot of weight. It was hard to determine his hair colour, for most of it had frizzled and burnt.

"Do you think he is your uncle?" the nurse asked, referring to Casey's story.

"It is so hard to tell? Is he able to speak?"

The nurse said with sympathy, "When he is conscious, he is in a lot of pain. He was raving about the fire. There are indications that he is an alcoholic, and when he came in, he had high levels of valium. So he may also be an addict."

"Do you think he was trying to kill himself?" Casey asked. "My uncle was not himself after my aunt died."

"It may have been an accident, but he was in the room where the fire started. I am afraid the police believe he started it. They have been unable to question him."

"I can't really tell if it is Uncle Mark. Do you think I can sit with him, and try to talk to him?"

The nurse glanced at the door, and back to the earnest face of the woman. "Just for a little while."

Casey drew a chair closer to the bed, and studied the face once more. After a time, one eye opened and stared at her.

"Anna? Am I dead?"

"No," Casey said softly. "But I need your help."

"Do you have any vodka?"

"You are better off without that,"

"Yes, bourbon is better," the voice trailed off, and Casey thought he had drifted off to sleep again.

That last comment made her thoughtful, and she asked in American, "What is your name?"

The man answered in American, "I don't have a name." His eyes were closed, but then he switched to German, and added, "You asked me that before."

Casey didn't say that someone else had asked the question, only, "Where was I before?"

The man didn't answer immediately, his voice was slow, and probably his mind was working slowly.

"In the cage, don't you remember? You asked me for a bottle, and I tossed one to you."

"I have forgotten what I wanted it for," Casey said, reacting to what might sound like raving to some people.

"To go free..."

Once again, it seemed that the man had dozed off, but once again he spoke. "Did Father Theo punish you?"

"I didn't see him," Casey said. "Did he let you out?"

"He told me I was free. I had been forgiven for killing my wife, my Anna, and little Chel. My poor little baby."

The man was racked by a sob, and Casey spoke another question, hoping to distract him. "Is that why you were in the house?"

"Yes, he gave it to me."

The nurse returned and gestured for Casey to leave. She was removing her gown and gloves when a big man walked up and flashed his police badge.

"Rudy Wagner, Homicide Bureau." The man stared at Casey, as if she was a suspect. "What are you doing here? That man is a murder suspect, no one should be talking to him."

Casey took exception to his attitude. She looked him in the eye and said, "That poor man is in no condition to tell you or me anything. I asked to see him, fearing that he might be my uncle. I cannot tell, and when I tried to ask him who he was, he murmured something that sounded like Anna and Chel. If they are names, they mean nothing to me. Perhaps they will help you to identify the poor man."

"We will check it out, Fraulein," Wagner promised, although Casey doubted it. "What is your name?"

"Casey Rowan," she claimed. Then, before the abrasive policeman could ask, she repeated the story she had told the nurse.

Wagner scrutinised her, as if he didn't believe her claim, but she met his eyes and he looked away first. "Leave your details at the desk. I may want to talk to you again."

Casey nodded, not promising anything, and moved off as Wagner demanded gown and gloves and groused at the need to cover his shoes. She went to the unattended desk, and pretended to write her details, but it was an excuse to watch what Wagner did. She heard him speak loudly to the man, and decide then and there that she would not help the policeman. However, her sympathy was for the poor burnt man, and she did want to help him.

Jim was looking out for her to return, and gave her the hand sign for stay clear. So she waited at the desk as if waiting to ask a question, and watched the activity down near the psych ward. A man in a suit, more casual than a business suit, strolled past Jim's position, looked at the loiterers, before showing his ID to the guards. Several of the watchers moved to watch as he entered the guarded room.

Chapter 25 - Working with the police

Donau entered the secure psych ward, as he made a mental note to get rid of the reporters outside. The duty nurse glared at him, from her place beside the patient's bed.

"Donau, Investigative Bureau," he introduced. Sensing the nurse's antipathy, he guessed that Wagner had rubbed her the wrong way. He gave her a smile, and asked, "How has your patient been during the night?"

It seemed to be the excuse the nurse needed to vent her displeasure. "She had finally settled and had barely slept, when your colleague came in like he was God's angel of vengeance - upsetting her again. I am afraid that if you wish to question her, you should wait. She is in no condition to answer questions. Wagner has insisted on an immediate psychiatric assessment, and I would like him to have one. This woman has exhausted herself and I am hoping that she will sleep now."

Donau glanced at the pale face of the woman, recalling how she had been the previous night.

"Do you know the results of the drug screen they did last evening?"

The nurse checked the chart and the doctor's notes. "It was inconclusive. There was nothing they could identify. Maybe it is some new drug, or one that was contaminated. All I know was that the woman had multiple psychotic episodes during the night, and as you can see, she is restrained to prevent her harming herself. Some of the episodes were violent enough to upset the bed."

Donau wanted to form his own opinion of her condition. "When I found her last evening, she was screaming obscenities and threatening anyone who came near her. Is that how she has been?"

The nurse had eased her hostility, and answered, "I have only been on since 2am. But, yes, she has been screaming, but I could not understand her words. I believe that she has strained her voice, since your colleague did not get the full volume."

"As a nurse, what is your opinion of her mental condition and her current state?" Donau wanted to see if she agreed with him.

"I doubt that she is fully aware of her surroundings," the nurse advised tactfully.

"Has the doctor restricted further questioning?" Donau asked.

"No, he will be coming shortly. However, she would be better if she were allowed to rest."

"I'll be brief, and I will try not to upset her."

The nurse frowned, but did not have the authority to refuse.

Donau moved to the side of the bed and pulled a chair closer. The woman turned her face away from him, but not before he saw the trace of tears in her eyes.

"How are you feeling," he asked gently, infusing sympathy into his voice as a contrast to his colleague's abrasiveness.

He heard no answer. He tried, "Are you feeling better?"

This time, he heard a faint, "No."

He walked around to the other side of the bed and looked into blue eyes and saw fear and helplessness. He reached out to take one of the restrained wrists. The woman tried to jerk it away, but couldn't. He gently traced the scars with his finger, and the face turned away again.

"Who are you? Tatiana or Wanda?"

"Both," was the faint admission.

"Did you tell Wagner that?"

"No."

"I can't withhold what I know."

"I know."

"Can you tell me what happened to you?"

"No."

"Why not?"

"It's not there."

"Not where?"

"In my head. Nothing is clear."

"I see," Donau didn't like the ideas that were occurring to him. "Can I do anything for you?"

Wanda looked back at the policeman that she had come to like. "I want to sit up. I feel sick."

Donau patted the hand that he held, releasing it as he stood up.

He hid his swirling thoughts as he spoke to the nurse.

"We cannot maintain the restraints if the bed is slanted," the nurse said practically. "I will talk to the doctor."

"I may be wrong, but I think that some of those episodes were the result of an inability to communicate a need to you," Donau suggested.

"She hasn't been coherent," the nurse countered.

"I don't know about earlier, but I spoke to her just now and had rational answers. She said she felt sick and needed to sit up."

The nurse gave no reply and walked over to talk to the patient. When she returned, she admitted, "You seem to be right, she has improved, though it did not seem so a short while ago. She asked me for some dry biscuits, but not anything to settle her stomach. I will see if I can arrange that."

"Before you do," Donau spoke before she went off. "Were you on duty the evening before last?"

"No, I was on days off. Why?"

"This woman was brought in two nights ago, with different symptoms than she exhibited last night. I am thinking that drugs do not have the expected reaction on her."

The nurse checked the patient chart again. "There is no mention of that in the patient history. I will ask about that, thank you."

Donau went out of the ward to where Mont Pelier was waiting.

"Did you learn anything?" Mont Pelier asked.

"Yes." Donau did not explain. He added as an afterthought, "I do not think we can question her yet."

"Will that mean that she will be staying here?"

"No. This is not a suitable place. She will have to be moved to the prison psych ward. We will ensure that there will not be another attempt to free her."

Mont Pelier did not comment on that statement, instead he made a request. "There is someone here that I think you should meet."

Donau was in the midst of thinking uncomfortable conflicting thoughts, and the request startled him. "What?"

Mont Pelier repeated his request, and Donau asked, impatiently, "Who is it?" He was forced to follow the Interpol man, since he walked towards the guard cordon. He spotted the light haired man and asked, "Was he the man I saw at the hotel?"

"Yes, I want to introduce you. However, it might be better if you had these reporters moved away.

Since it was something he had intended, Donau spoke to the senior guard - a police officer - and waited until the listening ears were further down the passage. Only then did he join Mont Pelier and the stranger.

"Otto Donau, this is Jim Phillips. Sent over by the US Embassy. He is with their State Department."

Donau took the proffered hand and shook it, using the time to form an opinion of the man.

"Why are you here, Herr Phillips."

"I would like to speak to Tatiana Carson."

"No, that won't be possible," Donau said immediately. "She has not yet been questioned."

"Then I insist on being able to represent her," Jim said.

Donau repeated his answer, but added, "The restriction is procedural. Unless you are a lawyer, accredited in Austrian law. Are you?"

"No, I guess I am not."

"Fraulein Carson is a suspect in a particularly horrific crime, Herr Phillips. In the interests of fair and thorough investigation, the suspect will be sequestered until she is fit to be questioned, and her statement is investigated. If you wish to help Fraulein Carson, you might employ suitable representation."

Jim showed no sign that the refusal of his demand was a setback. "I certainly will. We will not allow US citizens to be..."

"To be what?" Rudy Wagner's voice broke in. "To be tried and receive just punishment?"

Jim controlled his instant dislike of the newcomer. He kept his voice firm as he continued, "...denied their right to be considered innocent until proved guilty."

"And if that woman is found to be guilty of the murder of two prominent business men," Wagner challenged, "What then? You whisk her away to some American jail?"

"That is not in my power," Jim admitted, not showing how the attitude annoyed him.

"Too right it's not!" Wagner agreed. "That woman is pretending! I saw her face when I told her she was to be tried for what you Americans call first-degree murder. She is guilty alright!"

Wagner stalked off, and Mont Pelier remarked, "I wonder if he got any sleep last night? Otto, why don't we go back to the hotel. I am sure there are things you wish to discuss with Herr Phillips."

"Why not my office?" Donau demanded.

"Officially," Mont Pelier stressed the word, "you are meant to be off duty."

"So you think this meeting should be off the record?" Donau glanced between the two men, feeling he was about to be coerced into something.

"For now," Jim requested quietly. "I assure you, I am not trying to subvert justice. Quite the opposite."

"I need to go by my office and catch up on reports," was his answer, which was only half true. He wanted time to sort out why he had no wish to reveal the Carson/Martin co identity. "Where can I find you? At the hotel?"

Jim confirmed it and added, "Room 209."

"Give me an hour," Donau said, striding off. He glanced back to see if Mont Pelier was following, but saw him in conversation with the American.

Jim watched Donau walk off and asked Mont Pelier, "How does it look, your Highness?"

"Please, just Derek," the other insisted. "It looks extremely bad for your young friend. Is there anything you can do?"

Jim shrugged. "As your colleague said, get a lawyer. Apart from that, no. Wanda was here, acting in a private capacity."

"Do you have a car here?"

"I took a taxi," Jim told him, as he turned and caught Casey's attention.

"Let me drive you back to the hotel," Mont Pelier offered, bowing slightly in surprise as Casey joined them.

All the while that Jim had been away, David had tried to keep busy, working with Grant to attempt to spot Wexford on the airport security camera records. He was edgy and alternately ready to give up the idea they would find anything, and being determined to succeed. But all the time, he was desperate to know how his wife was.

When he heard the door being unlocked, he spun around and began to walk to meet Jim. Casey came in first, and gave him a look of sympathy, Jim followed, but on his heels was another man, and David stopped in his tracks and the blood ran from his face again. However, the well-dressed man, tall and familiar, came directly towards him.

"David," Mont Pelier greeted, holding out his hand, and saying with genuine sympathy, "I wish things were different."

It was only because David had a great deal of respect for the Interpol agent, that he forced himself to return the handshake, but he couldn't speak, so he merely nodded.

"Have you been here long?" Derek asked, trying to put the younger man at ease.

"No. I came in last night."

"May I ask what you are working on?" Derek tried, this time glancing at Jim, the person he knew was the group's leader.

David snarled, "Trying to find out what that bastard Wexford is up to. Wanda came here to find out what had happened to him and his kid, and he's damn well done a bunk."

"Ah, so it was you who called the police about him?" Derek sounded pleased. "It was luck indeed that you were at the airport."

"Luck!" David snarled again. "When someone is trying to..."

"David," Jim chided gently.

With a glance at his team leader, David subsided, "Sorry. Since Wanda is...unavailable...we are still trying to find his kid."

"Have you any ideas?" Derek asked. "Kommisar Donau is also looking out for the little girl."

"We have nothing positive," Jim commented, cautiously.

Since Derek was well aware of the kind of work that Jim and his group did, he understood that caution. "Let me clarify my position here," he said with deliberation. "My mandated authority is to question Tatiana Carson about the jewel robbery three nights ago. I cannot interfere with any other local investigation."

"And what if you learn anything of interest to local investigators?" David asked, with a remaining trace of belligerence. He was not quite facing off with Mont Pelier, but was glaring at him. "Are you obliged to pass them on?"

Jim spoke into the pause. "Why don't you sit down, Derek. Casey can make you some coffee, if you like? David, sit down and stop acting like a bouncer at a club."

David relaxed his stance, only then realising how tense he was. He dropped his head and went to pull another chair over, and gestured to Derek, before sitting himself.

"In the usual situation, yes," Derek went on smoothly, "However, if revealing information on one matter, would interfere with an Interpol investigation of another matter, then I have a degree of discretion."

"Which means?" David asked, with more civility.

"I have authority to question Tatiana Carson. If she has information pertinent to other matters, and my revealing it will help her case, then I can pass it on."

"What if she says something incriminating?" David asked. "Will you tell her to keep her damn mouth shut?"

"As to the first, as I said, I have a degree of discretion. As to the last, will she listen?"

He managed to force a faint smile from David. "I don't know. I really don't know."

"Do you think she is acting oddly?" Derek asked carefully.

David looked to where Jim was perched on the edge of the table before answering. "I don't know enough of what is going on."

Jim smoothly inserted, "I was aware of what Wanda was doing, in outline, and her activities were...a useful distraction."

Derek glanced up at the ceiling, understanding, but finding it annoying, to need to phrase ideas so carefully.

"There is little doubt that Tatiana Carson stole diamonds worth several hundred thousand dollars from a safe in Alpha Prime," Derek kept his voice matter of fact. "Was this part of any pre-made plan?"

"No!" David said forcefully.

Jim covered this outburst with, "Until we can talk to her, we cannot know her intent." He knew that it hadn't been, but wasn't going to admit that Wanda still didn't know why she had.

"I will accept that," Derek compromised. "There is talk that the thief that stole the diamonds from Alpha Prime, had to have known that they were there." He saw David about to protest, and shook his head so he could finish. "Do I have your absolute assurance, that Wanda was nowhere near France two weeks ago?"

David looked at him with some relief. "Yes! Davy had chicken pox. So did half his playgroup. Wanda was minding two other kids as well."

Derek gave a wide smile. "Then I am relieved on one concern. I do not have to arrest her for being the 'Diamond Spider'."

"The what?" David almost laughed.

"Never mind. I think I would like to enlist her aid to find that person." Derek waved the subject aside. "I mentioned that only because of the talk that the two robberies were linked. However, assuming the robbery was meant to be a distraction, and the diamonds were there by chance, the outcome gives me new avenues to explore."

"Alpha Prime," David guessed aloud.

"Indeed, and I hope you all will treat that information as confidential." Derek turned to take the cup of coffee from Casey, and smiled in thanks. She blushed.

"You can be assured of that," Jim answered for the four of his group that were there.

Derek sipped the coffee as he considered how he could make this group open up to him.

"I am going to entrust you with some information that I learnt by being with Otto Donau. Last night, Wessler and Lunn were said to have been 'questioning a spy'. A woman they found outside the house. Your American, Wexford, told the butler this as he was leaving."

Jim fixed his attention on Mont Pelier. He had gone in; mere minutes after Wexford had come out. He had seen the bodies there, and Wanda had not been there. He hadn't seen anyone leaving, but he wouldn't have if they went out the back way. All that carnage, could not have happened in the short time.

Derek Mont Pelier seemed to see something in Jim's face. He added, "Donau told me that Carson had, on the previous night, suffered an unusual reaction to a knock out drug. He feels that if

Wessler and Lunn were questioning her, they might have given her some other kind of drug."

David collapsed further into the chair. "Gods!"

Derek turned his attention to David. "What concerns you?"

David swallowed, took a deep breath and said, woodenly, "Wanda has weird reactions to most drugs. That time, when we were helping your brother, they tried a truth drug on us. It would have worked on me, except she can impress her thoughts on me at times. She experienced the effect of being unable to move or speak, but her mind stayed clear."

"That is interesting," Derek mused. "Describe how she reacts to knock out drugs."

There was no mirth in David's laugh when he answered. "Maybe you can check me on this. They work on her for a short time, way shorter than anyone would expect. Then she wakes and seems normal and that lasts for a while, but then...she's hyper. She tried it with a doctor supervising, because she wanted to know. That doctor concluded that she metabolises the drug quickly, but the metabolic by products that her body produces, cause the secondary reaction."

"Either way, it would be unlikely that Wanda killed those two men," Derek suggested. "I don't see her as a killer."

"If she were there, and able to move freely," Jim pointed out. "She would have disabled them, not killed them. Don't let her size fool you. She convinced a marine special ops sergeant to teach her what he knew."

"Even killing?" Derek had to ask.

"No! To avoid killing," David stated flatly. "Did you see her last night?"

Derek nodded.

"How was she?"

After describing how Wanda had been before Donau had restrained her, Derek asked, "How do you read that, David?"

His immediate answer was, "If she was there, and saw someone kill those two men..." He paused, mentally considering the first scenario that had occurred to him. "No, that doesn't seem right... she freaked out, and didn't want anyone to come near her...she was afraid..."

"She had a knife, like the one used to kill both men," Derek said bluntly. "An unusual one, made of two layers that fit together. And which would fit into two of the shaped depressions in a layer of false skin that she had on her forearms."

None of the other people in the room reacted to that statement, and that told Derek that they all knew about the knife and the false skin.

Jim changed the subject. He had seen David's look of utter horror and he was certain that Wanda's husband believed that she could have killed.

"Wexford came to Austria to talk to various business people, and in one of his reports he implied that he believed that there was a criminal conspiracy involved. He felt it could seriously impact the US economy and trade relations. It was also implied that it could destabilise the government and the value of the Euro."

"Indeed..." Derek's attention was riveted. "Donau has requested the folders found in Wessler's house, which he was taking from his safe and putting in a brief case. I will also request access to them on the grounds that his building had those diamonds in it."

Derek was thoughtful, and added, "If what Wexford suggested is true, and Wessler and Lunn were involved, perhaps the leaders, their demise is fortuitous. The conspiracy might break down."

He saw no reaction to prove he had guessed truly, for Jim replied, "Except that Wanda was convinced that a second group is trying to move in on that cartel."

"That's a leap of logic. Do you have proof?"

David leapt up and went to where Grant was still concentrating on the airport security films.

"Grant, can you bring up the best of those saved photos?"

Aware that the Interpol agent had come to look over David's shoulder, Grant complied.

"Can you enlarge that?" Derek asked, pointing to one of the montage of six images.

David pointed to one of the men in the images. "That is Wexford. He's made his hair black, instead of fair, but it is him! I don't know who the other man is, but Wexford isn't being coerced. Do you know him?"

"Have you a photo of Wexford?" Derek asked.

"I can get one," Jim confirmed.

"Can you print out that photo? Where is it from?"

Grant spoke up, "It's from the airport CCTV. We don't have a printer, but I can attach it to an email."

"Yes, that will do. I will tell you where to send it. I need to contact my superiors."

"Do you know who that other guy is?" David asked, intently.

"I might," Derek said briefly.

"Go for him," David invited, as his energy waned again and he returned to the chair. "It still doesn't help Wanda, or us to find the kid."

Derek took out a business card and handed it to Grant. "If you could send the image to that email address, it should arrive before I get through to Paris. I will try to get back before my Austrian friend gets here."

David waited until the door had closed before blurting, "Is he on our side?"

Jim answered with, "He is receptive to our concerns. He has to walk a narrow path..."

"Quit with the spook speak," David grumbled.

"Fine! Then tell me why you think Wanda did kill those men."

Leaning forward to emphasise his point, David said, "Jim, I don't want to believe it. But if she had that knife, and it is the murder weapon, then all that screaming to keep people away - I think she does believe she did it."

"She could have picked it up," Casey suggested. She had taken the seat vacated by Derek. "And if she were given something - she may not be thinking clearly."

"We don't know," Jim told David. "I am going to talk to the Embassy and get them to recommend a lawyer. Anything we can find out to help Wanda, we will pass on to him. I think, at worst, there is a good case for involuntary action under the influence of non-self-injected substances."

David snarled, "Yeah, right!"

Jim glanced at Casey. David needed a distraction - something positive to do. "Did you have any luck?"

"Yes, Jim. The nurse let me talk to him. She said that when he was awake, he was raving, but I am not so sure."

"Why is that?"

"The nurse suggested that he was an alcoholic, and also said that when he came in he had a high level of Valium. So, what he said may not have a great deal of value but..."

She told Jim what the man had said.

Jim went quiet, thinking. Then summarised, "He thought you were someone called Anna, and asked if he were dead. Later, he said he was forgiven for killing his wife Anna and daughter Chel."

An idea was stirring in Jim's mind. "He asked for vodka, said bourbon was better, and understood American. Run the rest by me again."

Casey did. "He was in a cage, next to another cage with a woman in it. She wanted a bottle to get free."

"I must find out if Wanda had cuts, like from broken glass - if she was trying to get free of rope or tape bindings. What else?"

Casey went on, "The person he called Father Theo must have been punishing the man, but forgave him, freed him, put him in the house with a crate of vodka."

"A proper set up," David stated. "That sod wanted him dead. Put an alcoholic in a room full of booze - and he won't move."

"I agree. I think we need to mention this matter to our friend, Derek," Jim agreed. "Considering that the house that burnt, was where Wexford went after leaving Wessler's place."

"Jim, try another idea for size," David blurted. "Father Theo - the Family - like that Russian crowd Wanda and I met with last year. I suggested it to Wanda."

Chapter 26 - A new point of view

"I am going to have to find out what the four of you know," Derek Mont Pelier startled everyone, for he had slipped quietly back into the room. "David, how do you know about the Family?"

After hearing a very abbreviated report, of events David and Wanda had been part of the previous year, Derek revealed, "You are actually correct. Theo Stephanovich is one highly wanted man, believed to be part of that organisation. My superior agrees that the man in the photo might be him with his grey hair disguised, or it may be a son. I now have an expanded mandate to investigate what Theo was doing here. Therefore, I am appointing the four of you, and the rest of the group, as confidential informants and Wanda Martin is now a prime witness in this matter."

"I hope you can argue jurisdiction with that arrogant man, Wagner," Casey said meeting the gaze of the Interpol agent. "The old man I spoke to needs protection, not persecution."

"Old man? Who are you meaning?"

Jim nodded to Casey and she repeated what she had told him. To put the matter in perspective, Jim mentioned that Wexford had been seen at that house, before the explosion.

"Jim! I've found something," Grant announced. Derek and Jim went over to look over Grant's shoulder at the images on the screen. David stayed slumped in the chair, staring at their backs.

"This is from the camera in the airport carpark. See there...the two men, both have cases and one has a suit bag over his shoulder. They came from a Mercedes, and went out towards the passenger terminal. Note the time."

"Go on," Jim instructed.

"Okay, this film is from the terminal. They have met up with a woman, but now there is no bag, but they still have the cases. There is an eight-minute time gap. When we walked from the terminal to the hire car desk, it only took us five minutes."

"They might have been talking," Casey suggested.

"Not likely," David argued. "They couldn't leave fast enough."

"Do you want me to get the police on it?" Derek offered as a knock sounded at the door.

Jim didn't answer him, going instead to see who was at the door. When he opened it, he invited Donau in. Alex, the faithful shadow, followed, sniffed the air, trotted to sniff each of the occupants of the room in turn, and chose to flop next to David's chair.

Donau had made his own swift survey of the room, nodded at Mont Pelier and asked abruptly, "What is all this about?"

Jim simply said, "Justice, and the life of a little girl."

"Very well. What about it?" Donau sounded annoyed.

"Why don't we all sit down," Jim suggested, and without being asked, Casey stood up and moved aside, and David decided to vacate his chair, and sit on the floor beside Alex.

As he sat, Donau challenged Jim, "How exactly, do you propose to find Rachel Wexford?"

"You need to speak to Tatiana Carson," Jim said evenly.

Donau sat back and studied the American, as he considered the suggestion.

"Why don't you quit playing games, Herr Phillips? I know that the jewel thief and your so-called investigator Wanda Martin are the same person, and I think the jewel thief was being more honest."

David's hands clenched on Alex's fur, and the dog turned and licked his cheek.

"Were you involved in that deception, Herr Phillips? Is this leading up to a trick to get her out of prison - so that you can spirit her away?"

Jim took a slow breath and said, "I have known Tatiana Carson for many years. Early on, during that time, she was working for some very evil men, and learning to commit robberies with the skill you have seen for yourself. In spite of that immoral streak, she would not, ever, stand for murder. When she agreed to speak against her employers, it was an extremely brave move. And she did it because those men had killed people who meant something to her. I will make no secret of the fact that I do not believe she is guilty of murder now. And no, Tatiana Carson is not her original name. It was a name she took when she went into witness protection."

Donau had not expected that, and did not know what to say, so he brushed it aside. "Leaving that point, why do I need to talk to her?" He was further surprised by the answer.

"Because I think she has discovered some criminal dealings and the perpetrators have tried to discredit and punish her for interfering."

"Who are 'they'?"

"Otto," Derek interrupted, "I believe that they are a group of foreign criminals who are trying to buy into an Austrian crime cartel."

Donau shook his head and said, "You are going to have to explain this to me one step at a time."

Jim nodded and began, "Tatiana's interest in this matter was personal. Her help was requested by Senator Charles Willard, of California. Last year, his wife was abducted, and Tatiana and her partner found and rescued her. I will add that the Senator's wife is Allan Wexford's sister. Tatiana agreed to come and help find Allan Wexford and his daughter, Rachel."

"So where do you come in?" Donau spoke into the pause.

"I was assigned to confirm claims made by Wexford that he had encountered a criminal conspiracy."

"And did you?"

"Yes. Wessler and Lunn were the two leaders."

"Your Wexford was talking to them. He told me he was playing along to prove his belief. Now I hear he has fled the country."

"Leaving you with an intense headache," Derek commented. "And Wanda Martin missing. I intend to look at Wexford more closely."

"That is needed," Jim agreed. "But I think Wanda/Tatiana might have the missing puzzle pieces."

Donau felt impelled to admit, "I am somewhat constrained in this matter, right now."

"Oh, I see," Derek looked at Donau with sympathy. "Your Chief stood you down."

"Yes!" Donau snapped. "I can liaise with you, but take no active part in the investigation."

"Excellent!" Derek said, sounding pleased. He ignored the Austrian's scowl and went on, "I need for you to arrange for me to speak with Tatiana Carson."

"I heard that Wagner is having her analysed by two of our top psychiatrists. He doesn't want her to be able to use insanity as a plea."

"Is she still at the hospital?" Jim asked.

"No, the prison." Donau looked from Jim back to Derek. "What do you think you can do? Wagner said she was struggling like a wild creature, screaming insults. They had to tranquilise her."

David asked a question. "Was she speaking American or German?"

Donau was momentarily silent. Finally he said, "I don't think that Wagner speaks English, so I would guess she was speaking German - unless he was judging by her tone of voice? Does that matter?"

Derek had his own question. "How was she when you spoke to her this morning?"

"Lucid and weak. She admitted that she was both Carson and Martin, and admitted that she had not told Wagner that."

From the floor, David put that admission into context. "She trusts you, Inspector. I dare say that was because you listened to her. I have heard your colleague can be both arrogant and abrasive. And unless he lets her talk, and listens to her with an open mind, hell will freeze over before she cooperates."

"She won't do her case any good if she doesn't..." Donau warned.

David twisted his words. "She won't do it any good if she does. Anyway, shouldn't she have a lawyer present if she is being asked questions?"

Donau wondered at the younger man's intensity. "I have looked at the lab reports. There isn't much doubt of her guilt." He went into detail of the findings and concluded, "She is still insisting that she remembers nothing."

David stood up from his position on the fawn short pile carpet, and told the policeman, "Then I think you should accept that statement and work from there." He turned his back on the group and walked out of the room. Alex stood up and watched him leave.

Jim glanced at Grant, who left his computer and followed David out.

Derek smoothly distracted the policeman. "Otto, my mandate has been expanded to include investigating why Russian crime lord Theo Stephanovich has been in Vienna. Since he was identified leaving from Vienna airport with your missing American, Allan Wexford, there is a lot of interest in my finding out. It was David who recognised Wexford and alerted me to Stephanovich. Now, I want to see Wanda Martin, alias Tatiana Carson, as soon as I can. If there are objections, I will ring my superiors and have them talk to yours. I will require several sessions and later I will bring an assistant with me."

"Assistant? Who?" Donau glanced around the room.

"I will be attaching David to Interpol, on a temporary basis."

"I don't know if that will be allowed," Donau warned.

"Leave that to me. Now why don't you take something for that headache of yours so that your mind will return to functioning at its normal efficiency? I need your help."

Casey went, without being asked, to fetch a glass of water. She handed it wordlessly to the Austrian.

After obeying the suggestion by taking two pain relief tablets, he asked, "What do you want me to do?"

"Listen," Derek said. "You are off duty, forbidden to work on official investigations but still a dedicated investigator. Will you listen and accept the providence of what you hear as truth?"

"Go on then."

Jim spoke from where he sat in his chair, and met Donau's gaze. "Your perception in thinking that you had met me before was correct. I was speaking with Herr Wessler when you came to speak to him. I had convinced him that I had goods that were of interest to him. As a result, I was invited to a meeting at Wessler's house. I arrived early, but I was met by Herr Heinrich and warned that there was trouble. I pretended to leave, but when I was out of sight, I crept back and watched."

He could see how Donau's mind was working, sizing him up as a suspect. Jim went on speaking. "Heinrich was still fidgeting outside when I returned, and it was a fair while before Wexford came out. The two of them spoke and then went off in their separate cars."

Donau moved in his chair, and Jim paused. "How long do you think you were waiting before Wexford came out?"

Jim thought back and estimated the time. "From when I drove off to when I got back, maybe ten minutes. Then another five to ten minutes."

"I don't know how this matters, but when Herr Wexford was leaving, he told Wessler's manservant that his master and Lunn were questioning a spy." Donau watched the American, looking for a reaction. "The woman was alone with them. They must have been alive."

Jim shook his head. "No, I don't think so. I went in as soon as Wexford and Heinrich were down the drive. Both men were dead, and I assure you, there was no one else in the room. Had they been alive and questioning someone, the someone would have been restrained, and even if not, there was not enough time for that someone to overcome both men and commit all the carnage and escape in that short time."

"She could have been helping Wexford, and that is why he took off," Donau suggested. "She had both Wessler's and Lunn's blood all over her, and the murder weapon in her pocket. How do you explain that?"

"I can't yet," Jim admitted. "However, to get back to my report - I had several of my people close by as back up. I had them follow Wexford's blue Mercedes. He went to a house not that far away, and went inside. Later, two men came out - my people said both had dark hair and neither looked like Wexford. Thinking that Wexford might have been incapacitated inside the house, I told them to go in and check. The house exploded, and my people rescued a man from downstairs, and checked the rest of the house. They found no one else, but did find a room where a child had been. The bed had not been slept in."

Donau swore softly, confused by the story, half convinced it was a trick to get Carson released, but this man knew things that the media had not revealed. "In that house, the fire investigators found a woman, tied up and gagged, in the wardrobe upstairs. She suffocated from the smoke. I hope your people didn't miss the child."

The door to the room opened and closed, Donau glanced around and saw a tall muscular blond haired man and a shorted dark haired man enter.

Jim spoke to them. "Find anything?"

Max Hart glanced at the two strangers, recognised one and decided it was okay to talk in front of them, and said, "The neighbours saw a child there, once or twice. Each time she came near the boundary fence, one of those wire ones, a nurse came and marched her back. One of the neighbours said he heard the kid being smacked hard, for running off."

Nicholas added, "The house was rented on a long term lease, from about a year ago. The agent was paid in cash and the name given for the renter was Schmidt."

Derek jotted the information down in a small notebook as Donau turned back to Jim.

"So where is this man you rescued?"

From where she stood, back against the wall leading to the inner rooms of the suite, Casey spoke softly. Donau looked around in surprise. He hadn't noticed the attractive woman when he came in.

"He is in the hospital, with very bad burns. The nurse let me in to talk to him. She warned me that he was in great pain, and had been given medication to ease it. She said too, that when he was conscious, he was raving. But I don't think so. He said something about being in a cage, next to one with a woman in it. She wanted his bottle, so she could cut the tape on her wrists and feet and go free."

"Wanda had nicks on her wrists that might have come from glass," Derek confirmed, glancing at Jim to see him nod thoughtfully.

"Yes, I saw that," Donau admitted. His preconceived ideas changing, but he still could not refute the evidence.

Max Hart commented again, "There is a shed out the back, with two cages bolted to concrete. The place reeks. But I saw traces of a broken bottle."

"I saw nothing about that in the report," Donau said. "The arson investigators did not look there."

"Would you agree that you should take Alex out there and look around?" Derek suggested.

Donau did agree, he stood up quickly was about to leave, but an idea came to him. "Why did Frau Martin or Carson, take some of the child's clothes from the apartment?"

Jim shrugged. "Hunch, I expect. Will that be an issue too?"

"I'm off duty, so I will say it was a valuable foresight. After she went there, someone emptied the apartment - completely. One person could not have done that in the time."

Max drove Nicholas, Donau and Alex to the house where they had rescued the hobo. The Austrian used his phone to talk to his superior to provide authorisation for the Interpol agent to talk to Tatiana Carson at the prison. In response to a query about his own intentions, he merely said he would be taking Alex out for a run and would keep in touch with Mont Pelier by phone.

After the return call, confirming Donau's request, he called Mont Pelier and warned him that he might have to deal with Wagner.

Jim waited at the hotel to hear back from David and Grant. He restrained himself from pacing by will power alone, and tried to think through all the information he knew to try to find a way to help Wanda.

Casey brought him a coffee, made with the kettle and supplies in the room. "I have never seen David so…"

"Irritated? Angry, intense, edgy?" Jim supplied the words Casey couldn't find.

"Yes, all of that. Should he be here?"

"If this was the middle of a mission…no. However, if Wanda is in trouble, or being trouble, he knows what to do. That is why Derek plans to take him to see her."

"Do you really think Wanda is innocent? No one would believe it from the evidence."

Jim didn't chide Casey, he just asked, "What does your feminine intuition say?"

"I don't believe she killed anyone."

"Then consider what Wanda is trying to tell them. She doesn't remember anything of it. If she was unconscious, she could have been set up. The real assassin might have found the knife on her and made use of it. Remember, there was also a gun used."

Casey nodded. "Did Wanda have a gun?"

"No. She refuses to use one."

"If she was unconscious, why didn't they find her there?"

Jim forced a faint smile. "It would look a little suspicious if the killer were found - conveniently unconscious with the two bodies. Wouldn't it?"

"Then what about the state she was found in?"

"David said, she freaked out," Jim reminded Casey. "And the drug tests picked up an unknown substance. How would you feel, if you woke up covered in blood? How might your mind be if it were hallucinating or something?"

Casey shuddered at the thought. "Jim, can we help her? It sounds like no one will believe her. It sounds impossible."

"We've done that before," Jim reminded her. "And I think we have begun to change Donau's mind."

Derek was met at the gate of the high security women's prison and escorted to the observation room. This was a room where one wall was made of one way glass, and the chairs and tables were set up to be able to watch a prisoner in the adjacent padded cell. After a glance around when he saw a computer that controlled monitoring and recording equipment, sitting on a table so that the operator faced the room, he turned his attention to the woman in the padded cell.

He was aware of his escort leaving and Wagner edging closer. Two men who were dressed as guards, stood near the door, ready to go into the adjacent room if needed. They were both relaxed, since the woman slumped against one of the padded walls, was only twitching spasmodically.

Derek saw that Wanda had been changed into the shapeless brown dress worn by the women prisoners, and no attempt had been made to ensure it wasn't hitched up indecently.

"You have had a very long night," Derek remarked as Wagner came close enough to bump his elbow.

"Oh, I'm off to bed soon," Wagner admitted. "I was just waiting for you to arrive, Sir."

"Kind of you," Derek said, pretending he didn't hear the sarcasm in Wagner's remark. "I believe that she has been difficult."

"Yes, they had to go in and give her something to calm her down. I am afraid that you have had a wasted trip. They don't expect her to be awake for some hours. At least you missed the screaming harridan."

Derek decided that he didn't like Wagner, but he was too polite to say so. "I will see if I have any luck, but I expect that I will need to come back later. Thank you for filling me in."

Wagner didn't make a move to leave when Derek asked to taken into the prisoner. The guard stayed inside by the door, while Derek strolled closer. The padding on the floor made his approach nearly silent, and he was able to study the prisoner without her seeming to be aware of him. She was hugging her knees, and her head was resting on them, but when he was within a metre of her, she looked up. He didn't speak immediately, just watched as her head moved from side to side, like an animal testing the wind. She didn't seem aware of him, even though her blue, bloodshot eyes, looked right past him. He saw tears there too, and felt pity. He walked closer and squatted down to talk to her.

"At least it is quiet in here," he remarked in a gentle voice.

He saw Wanda start, but she answered immediately. "No it's not. You are damn well in here! GET OUT!"

"I wanted to talk to you," Derek persisted, his ears ringing from the shout.

"I am out of talking."

"Wanda, I need your help," Derek tried, speaking too softly for the monitoring microphones to hear.

"Pull the other leg. It plays a symphony."

"Do you know who I am?" Derek tried.

"Another damn policeman. At least you aren't that bastard Wagner, or those cursed shrinks," Wanda didn't care if her insults were overheard. "You have a minute to leave before I start screaming again."

"I think you have done more than enough of that," Derek advised, as he waved a hand in front of Wanda's eyes, and got no reaction. "Can you see me?"

"Of course I bloody can!" Derek saw the tears leaking down the pale face.

Only then did Derek realise that she couldn't wipe the tears away because her wrists were restrained by manacles attached to the floor.

"Talk to me, Wanda," Derek spoke softly again. "Did you find Rachel Wexford?"

He thought then, that Wanda had passed out with her eyes open, as all trace of life had gone from them. He waited a long two minutes before he heard a reply.

"I can't make sense of what I remember."

"Will you tell me what you remember? You don't have to make sense of it. Tell me the images. Where did you see Rachel?"

"I took her," Wanda said, oblivious to the fact she was being overheard. "Hid her. Hid the witch in the wardrobe."

Derek stared at the floor in frustration. This was not the Wanda Martin he knew. The tranquiliser had to be muddling her mind, but she had not started screaming, perhaps on some level she did recognise him.

"Where did you leave her? Did you hide her in the house?"

"Why do you...want to know?"

"Wanda! Stay awake. Where did you hide her?"

'Bysh...ed....drugged..." The blue eyes closed, and the head dropped back to the knees.

Derek stayed squatting, controlling a slow burning fury at whatever had made Wanda this way. Finally, he stood up and gestured to be let out. He went back to the observation room and found Wagner still there.

The Austrian Inspector shrugged. "No luck then? I made a transcript for you. Don't like the idea that she took that child." He was trying to sound concerned, but in Derek's mind, he was gloating.

"You have it wrong, Inspector," Derek chose to misinterpret the statement. "There is no way that Frau Carson could have taken her. She wasn't in your country when the child went missing."

"Must have been," Wagner argued. "We found no record of her entering, and anyway - she had to have known where the kid was to be able to take her again."

"As for when Frau Carson arrived, you cannot have looked in the right place. She came to find the child, because has been successful in such cases before. Unfortunately, in her current state, I cannot get her to help me. Please leave word that I am to be advised when she is awake once more."

"Yes, Sir," Wagner agreed, a shade too readily. "Let me lead you out."

Derek accepted the escort, and studied the Austrian as he walked. He had the feeling that Wagner did not want him to question the prisoner when he himself, was not present. Not that the attitude was unusual. Many policemen considered Interpol a kind of mean big brother.

Outside, he politely thanked Wagner, and parted to walk to his car. He didn't leave right away, deciding make some calls and let Wagner get away first.

He called Donau, who was still at the half burnt mansion house, and reported what little he had, then admitted, "They had her tranquilised, and I can't be sure that what she said helps."

"Well," Donau spoke through the phone. "She 'hid the witch in the wardrobe' - must refer to the woman we found. Alex found Carson's scent in the house. What did you say she said about the child?"

"Bysh...ed...drugged."

"Bysh," Donau repeated, trying to make sense of it. "Was she talking German or American?"

"American," Derek confirmed. "Have you had any luck?"

"Half the place is too dangerous to walk in, but I am checking everywhere else, using the garment that Carson took from the Wexford apartment. The child was definitely here, and had free run of the house. Her scent is everywhere too."

"At least Carson is helping that much," Derek reminded Donau before ending the call.

Derek checked and saw Wagner's car still parked near the gate. He decided to call Jim.

"Jim, in the odd reaction to drugs theme, how does our friend react to tranquilisers? Can you ask David?"

"He's not here. He is with Grant out at the airport. I will ring Grant and have him ask. How is Wanda?"

"Frankly - not good. She was just given a dose of tranquilisers, and was very dopey, and she couldn't see properly. Certainly - she didn't recognise me. I am going to call in a completely neutral doctor for an independent examination. That Wagner is making things worse."

"An Interpol doctor?" Jim asked, hoping he knew Derek's idea.

"Close enough, and she will be by the time she gets here," Derek promised, sure that Jim knew who he meant.

"One that Wanda won't try to bamboozle?"

"Indeed," Derek agreed. "The psychiatrists at the prison think she is mentally unbalanced. Wagner wants to prove she isn't. Not a pleasant situation, either way."

Jim didn't need to be told. "I will call you as soon as I hear from David," he promised.

When Derek drove off, he was aware of Wagner following him. He decided to drive to the police building, and if necessary, have the police chief order the man home. Though part of him considered charging the man with obstruction of an Interpol investigation.

His phone rang, and he pulled off as soon as he found a safe place. Wagner's car went past, but Derek ignored it, but as he dialled Jim back, he saw it pull in a little way ahead.

He forgot all about Wagner when he heard what Jim had to say. He glanced at the clock on the dash and said, "I'll meet your people at the airport."

Once he ended the call, Derek checked the traffic and made a fast u-turn, and when he checked in his mirror, Wagner was waiting for traffic, to do the same. However, Derek had taken a few turns, to get onto the road to the airport and he believed that Wagner had lost him.

Jim had said that Grant and David had found something, and needed official back up. That had immediate priority. The message from David about Wanda and tranquilisers, translated as, he had time. If, as he was told, Wanda would wake up after an hour, not the four or so most people took, he could go back and talk to her without Wagner expecting her to be awake.

Derek parked near the terminal in a spot reserved for police. He placed a laminated sign on the dashboard, which showed the Interpol badge. He found the security desk and spoke to the guard in duty.

"I need your help on an official matter. Can you arrange a replacement?"

Feeling important, the man called his superior, explained the emergency, and asked to be relieved.

His request was approved and the man told Derek, "My replacement will be along in a moment, and then I can assist you. What do you require?"

"I need to go to the area between the carpark and the terminal."

"That is not a problem. The stairs are just over there." He gestured and was about to give further directions when Derek interrupted. "Not the pedestrian walk over, I need to be at road level."

"Passengers and visitors are not allowed there," the guard began to explain, and then realised that Interpol, like the police, were not mere visitors.

Derek did not have to wait long before his guide was free to take him out through doors marked, 'Airport Staff only'. After explaining where he needed to go, the guard set off at a fast walk, leading the way along the outside of the terminal building, around a corner and along a road.

When they reached a junction in the road, where it split so a road went into the lowest level of the multi-storey car park and also went on ahead, the guard became aware of a standoff about 100m away. He saw two figures facing off against one of the rubbish removal trucks and one of the dog handling guards trotting towards the group.

David and Grant stood two arms lengths apart, balancing on the balls of their feet, ready for a fight. They were standing between a large dumpmaster full of rubbish, and the truck that had its prongs down to come in and empty it. The driver was swearing at them in German, getting angrier and angrier at being delayed. He was just climbing down out of his truck as the guard and dog arrived.

The dog's snarls were ignored, as was the demand from the guard that they leave the area.

"No," Grant said. "Not until the police arrive."

"I'll have you arrested! This area is off limits unless you work for the airport."

"Perhaps you should see what is keeping the police," David suggested. "We called for them to come here."

"You did what? They get angry when people make false calls."

"We had an excellent reason," David explained, as he glanced along the road. He had seen more people approaching, and was relieved to recognise the tall figure of Derek Mont Pelier.

David met Grant's glance and shrugged to his right. Grant saw what David had seen and spoke again.

"We will explain our actions to the tall gentleman now approaching. This is an official matter."

As soon as Derek arrived, both Grant and David relaxed from their tense 'at the ready' stance, as the Interpol agent showed his ID to the guard with the dog. It didn't appease the man, but he ordered his dog to sit and be quiet.

"What is the situation here, Herr Davis?"

David responded to the alias he had been using when he and Derek had first met. "We found more than we were looking for, Sir. You will need to call the local investigators."

Grant gestured, moved back to the dumpmaster and lifted the lid a short way. Derek glanced in and saw what was within. He took control with practiced ease.

Of his guide, he requested, "Summon the airport police to come here, please."

Then he spoke to the rubbish-truck driver who had alighted from his truck, but stayed back when the guard had confronted the two trespassers. "How often is this receptacle emptied?"

"Every Monday," the man rumbled. "You going to let me empty it?"

Derek ignored the request. "Is this bin always here?"

"Yeah, it's so I can get in and out easy," the man challenged. "The boys who empty the bins in the carpark dump their filled bags here."

"I would like you to wait here, please, and give your name and contact details to the police. I might have to talk to you and find out your regular schedule. Do you empty this bin at this time every week?"

"Yeah."

Derek made a mental note to check the security footage for this area, as he turned to David.

"And how did you get to be noticed, Herr Davis?" That he sounded as if he was chiding a subordinate, made the two guards less hostile.

"When we discovered what was in there, we called the police. They told us to wait here, but the truck driver here began to insist that he empty the bin." David reported without any trace of hostility. "I did not think it wise to advertise our discovery."

The guards were moving in to see what the fuss was about, but Derek said, "I advise you not to touch the bin, and you will need to organise to keep people well away from here."

"Did you find what you were looking for?" Derek asked, speaking to David again.

"No Sir," David admitted.

"Well, you had better get on with it." Derek sounded like he was chiding when he added, "You might try lost property while I wait here."

David and Grant knew they were being given an out, so they would be gone before the police arrived. If the police needed a statement about the finding of the body in the dumpster, they could come forward privately.

"Lost property!" David spoke aloud, in disgust. "Why the hell didn't we think of that? We tried all the lockers." And they had been checking the rubbish bins too, to see if a suit bag had been discarded between the carpark and the terminal.

Grant had stood watch while David had opened the locked lockers and glanced in the unlocked ones."

"It could be possible," Grant considered. "The lockers are all short term. When the time runs out, anyone can get in and re-use them. Perhaps the stuff is taken to lost property then."

"We looked just in case," David reminded his fellow agent. "If someone wanted to get rid of something, he'd throw it away!"

Which had been David's initial idea, and why they had followed a worker to the dumpmaster.

"So, perhaps they did," Grant compromised. "And they miscalculated. Perhaps they dumped it in there, like they did the woman, and someone saw it there and did the good citizen thing?"

"Who'd bother?" David asked, derisively.

"This is Austria, not America," Grant pointed out.

"Well, do you have any idea where we need to go?" David asked, just before they entered the building below the main concourse.

Grant grinned and pulled out a small tablet. Within a minute, he had up a small map of the airport buildings. David, decided to admit to himself that he wasn't working at his most efficient.

The lower floor was the province of the maintenance and catering departments and was generally accessible to employees only. David and Grant were not wearing any of the staff uniforms, but they both walked purposefully, as if they knew exactly where to go and had the right to be there. As they walked, they both looked left and right, automatically noting details.

"At least you seem to have worked off most of your aggravated energy," Grant remarked.

"Don't be deceived, I am still spoiling for a fight. Wexford had better watch out if I see him, but yes, I am not so twitchy."

"So how come?"

"Have you noticed that Wanda and I seem to know how each other work?" David glanced at his friend.

"Are you psychic too?" Grant asked. He knew of some of Wanda's special talents.

"I'm not, but Wanda and I are...close, I suppose you could say. Sometimes I get spillover from what she is thinking. We don't usually mention it, but anyway, I think at the present, Wanda has finally zonked. Up until a little while ago, it has been like bees buzzing in my head, or as if I expected to step into a still pond and walked into a spa instead."

"So, what was that question about the effect of tranquilisers in aid of?"

"Well, I think they might have given Wanda one. If so, she will be expected to stay unconscious for some hours, but they usually don't work on her for long. I think, in this case, Derek wants to talk to her before anyone else expects her to be awake. That looks like the passage up ahead."

Grant quickly checked his tablet, and agreed.

The door with the "Lost Property" sign was locked, but while Grant kept watch, David seemed to be trying the door. In fact, he was forcing the lock using a technique Wanda had taught him.

"We're in," David said softly, and he opened the door, and going in. He automatically looked for security cameras, saw none and gestured to Grant.

Grant went in but stayed by the door to listen for the clerk to return. David ducked under the counter flap and began to check the shelves. Ten minutes later he acted on a whistled warning, and when the clerk returned, they were both outside the counter, Grant leaning against it with his arms crossed, and David impatiently tapping his fingers on the counter top.

"There you are!" David spoke in German. "We've been waiting here for a very long time."

The clerk glanced from them to the door, as if thinking that he had locked the door, but then shrugged and asked them what they wanted.

David had only enough time to glance at the shelves in half of the room. So he described what he was looking for. The man nodded, and went not to any of the shelves, but to a door at the rear of the room. He returned, with a black suit bag that reeked of rotten rubbish. The man had his face averted from the bag, and a grimace on his face.

When he came closer, Grant and David involuntarily mirrored his expression.

"Is this your missing item?"

David compared it to what he had seen in the camera footage and said, "It looks like it. May we look inside?"

He received a curt nod, and the clerk placed it on the counter.

Since there were traces of rotten garbage on the outer surface, the clerk did not seem surprised when David used a handkerchief to unzip it, nor did he try to get closer to look inside. Instead he watched as David opened it and glanced inside.

"This is the bag," David announced, hiding his elation. He looked at the clerk and requested, "I need you to notify your security police and ask them to get a message to Derek Mont Pelier of Interpol."

The man gaped, and groped for the telephone that was somewhere under the counter. He rang, babbled the message, listened and hung up.

"You are to stay here until he comes," the clerk passed on the instructions he'd been told. Then he couldn't resist asking, "What's in there?"

"Clothes," David said with a faint grin. "I suppose that you didn't try to find the owner because of the smell?"

A very fervent nod, showed his agreement.

"You might need to say who brought it in, if you can recall," David suggested, deciding not to say he might have to be fingerprinted, since he had been touching the bag.

The clerk stood still for a moment, and then said, "It was one of the maintenance guys. He thought it might have fallen from the walkover. He said he had left it there, but someone tossed it in the bin. He brought it in later."

David didn't press for more details, but he guessed the man would be going over the event, and the police would question him further.

Two members of the airport police arrived soon after, and one asked directly, "Is this the item you were looking for?"

David answered him, as Grant kept back out of the way. "I believe so. Has Agent Mont Pelier briefed you on its importance?"

The same officer nodded, "It is evidence in a murder investigation."

The other officer remarked, "We could have looked for this, Sir."

David grinned and shrugged. "Orders, sir. We do as we are directed."

He made no move to leave. He was not letting the bag out of his sight until Derek took charge of it.

Derek Mont Pelier slipped into the room in his usually quiet way, nodding at Grant before speaking to the Airport Police officers. He requested how he should proceed, to handle this evidence, and accepted the suggestion that he should wait for the forensic team to finish with the earlier incident. He then glanced from David to Grant and directed, "One of you needs to stay here, the other come with me."

David nodded his agreement to stay, and Derek took a card holder from his pocket and took a card from it to give to him."

"Please advise the technician that this is an Interpol matter and he is to talk to me before working on this item."

The Airport police officer that seemed to have the role of spokesman, assured Derek, "We can handle things from here. We have been asked to cooperate with you, and we will see that you receive copies of all statements and reports."

When David arrived back at the car, almost an hour later, he was glad to be away and to let Grant drive them back to the hotel.

"That was a worthwhile day's work," David said with satisfaction. "Wexford might have got away, but he was seen with the victim, here, and there is no way that they can claim that Wanda stiffed that woman. And I will bet a month's pay that the suit has Wessler's and Lunn's blood on it."

Grant did not try to dampen David's improved spirits.

Chapter 28 - An unexpected ally

She tried not to sleep again, for when she slept, the nightmares came. The memories of a time she thought she had forgotten. But with an eidetic memory and perfect recall, nothing she had seen, heard or experienced was ever truly forgotten. She felt now, as she had back in that time, when inhuman creatures tortured her and debased her, and she had killed them to survive.

Yet she wasn't there now, so why had she killed. The aggressive voice told her that she had, and it had to have been her. She had been covered in blood. She had a bloody knife in her pocket, her unique knife, and blood on her hands. She had been sitting in the blood of two men.

That policeman, the horrid one, his face was brick red, and he almost yelled at her, she remembered how he had described the murder scene in graphic detail. He thought to torment her, shock her, but he had only sickened her. Yet he kept demanding that she tell him why she did it.

She didn't remember, told him that, but he didn't believe her, and his logic was too strong.

She was the inhuman monster now. She had killed and she didn't know why. And she didn't want to live if she was going to kill again for no reason. But now, like then, she couldn't give up and die. There was something she had to do - hadn't finished. If only she could remember...

If she could stand up, walk around, the fogginess would clear. She tried, but her hands were tied to the floor...like she had been tied up back then. Had they been able to see what she truly was? Was that why they had kept her tied up?

Admit it! Admit it! The words echoed in her mind. She couldn't think with him demanding she admit it.

No! Back then, she had killed to get free. Killed because the creatures were killing innocents, and she had to help the innocents. Like now?

Like now...she had something she had to do...she couldn't stay locked up.

Admit it! No.

"No you effing son of a bitch," she remembered yelling. She cursed him, finally pleading, "Why won't you believe me."

Then her mind had blanked out again - no controls, no memory, only the desperation to get away.

The sharp jab of the needle had jerked her back to awareness. Two hefty men were holding her down on the floor, clamping her hands into something. She jerked her arms, felt the manacles, saw the policeman watching, vindicated, gloating...believing this was her natural self...

"No!" she screamed, but the chemical was already flooding her system, mixing with the dregs of others. She had to stay awake, must not fight them.

The weight lifted off her arms, and she understood, "She'll be quiet for now," and all the people withdrew, thinking her docile, tractable.

How long ago had that been? The memories and the nightmares were swirling together, making her sick...she needed to sit up. This time she forced herself, inch by inch, backwards until her head touched the padded wall. She held her head up, and inched some more. The ties on her wrists swivelled, and she could, finally, sit up and rest against the wall, but she mustn't sleep again. She had to think.

It was quiet, with no one yelling at her. The movement had helped some of the fog to clear. She remembered a snippet of a soft voice. How long ago had that been? She been tied then too, but someone had spoken gently to her, listened to her, hadn't acted like she was a monster.

But that was just one voice, the others were more numerous.

Her eyes filled with tears as she thought of the tiny new life within her. So new that it was still a secret, did that tiny little innocent baby girl deserve to be the child of a murderer? Perhaps she would be better off not being born...

The breath of air moving made her go rigid. Someone was in the room with her. She looked towards the door, in the direction her other senses were telling her that someone was. She saw only a grey blurred outline against the white padding of the walls.

"At least it is quiet in here," she heard, and the words made sense. But she didn't want company. She wanted to be alone.

"No its not! You are bloody well here and talking. Get out!"

"I wanted to talk to you," the voice sounded hurt.

"I'm out of talking."

"Wanda! I need your help!"

He had the wrong person. She was Carson - Tatiana Carson - jewel thief and murderer. They had kept telling her so.

"Pull the other leg! It plays a symphony."

"Do you know who I am?"

The question stopped her mind's endless circling.

"You are not that bastard Wagner, or those incomprehensible shrinks, so you can have another minute before I start screaming again."

"I think you have done enough of that. Do you really want to bring everyone back again?"

She had, and no, but it had forced the others away, so she could try to think.

"Can you see me?"

She looked to where she sensed the person to be - at the blurred shape. "Of course I bloody can."

She couldn't though, and she dare not let anyone know, or they would sneak up on her like this person had, and then she'd kill them.

"Talk to me, Wanda!" The voice was sharper now, more like those others. "Did you find Rachel Wexford?"

What? Did I ... find Rachel? Images came into her mind - partial memories.

"I can't make sense..."

The voice didn't demand an instant answer, and after a moment, she recalled the trusting little hand in hers. "I took her..." a memory of carrying a sleeping child down stairs, "hid her." Where had she hid her? A memory of moving branches, blocking a hole, covering it…so no one would find her. Oh, gods, had she killed the little girl too? There'd been a horrible woman, about to beat the child…she hit her, tied her up and, "hid the witch in the wardrobe." Had she killed the woman too?

"Where did you hide Rachel? Was it in the house?"

Why did it seem like he was afraid that it was? "Why do you… want to know?"

"Wanda! Stay awake! Where did you hide her?"

The voice knew her! It needed to know and wasn't trying to hurt her or dominate her.

She tried to say, "By the shed," but her mouth couldn't form the words. Then her mind suddenly recalled why she had carried the child. Drugged. The child had been drugged. She hadn't killed her. There was something more…there had been danger…she had to remember…

Her eyes opened onto whiteness, her mind was quiet, and for the moment, lucid. The dreams had gone, her memories were locked away. Her body felt like it was floating.

It wouldn't last - this was the eye of the storm - the backlash of the last drug would begin soon, and the horrid memories would return.

A shadow drew her attention to the door, now a black square - but she couldn't escape - a shadow moved away from it and the square disappeared.

"Not again," she said, more to herself. She didn't want the blissful moments to end too soon.

"You still have a job to do!"

"I can't. I have to stay here. I don't want to kill anyone else…"

"I don't give a damn about dead criminals!"

Wanda tried to focus on the face of the speaker. He was squatting down in front of her now. She knew him. Knew him from…

"Prince Derek?"

She heard his sigh of relief, but her own moment of relief was momentary. She remembered where she was and why. The bliss vanished, the illusion of peace crashed. Derek was Interpol, police;

he couldn't help her. She looked down, afraid of him, but unable to move. Then a gentle hand lifted her chin, speaking to her.

"I do not think that you have turned into a purposeful, deliberate assassin," Derek spoke in English, not German. "Have you?"

"But I ..."

"Listen, Wanda Martin," Derek urged. "I am not here to help condemn you and I won't pretend that you are not in a very serious position. I have no authority to interfere with local investigations. Do you understand?"

She nodded. He couldn't help her, but he wasn't going to make things worse.

"I am here," Derek went on, watching Wanda's eyes to see if she was comprehending, "to investigate a jewel theft and..."

He felt the shivering increase. "Wanda, you don't have to fear me. I just need your help again."

"What?' Wanda whispered.

"Russian criminals. I think you know things that I need to know."

"Everything is muddled...and distorted."

"When you can, try to remember," Derek asked. "But my most urgent question is if you saw Rachel Wexford. You said something about it when I was here before."

Derek saw Wanda's eyes 'blank out'. He waited, releasing her chin, and not pressing her.

"Yes...I took her...outside. They had drugged her milk."

There was a sigh from Derek and the sense of relief and hope. "Where did you take her? We need to find her."

The blue eyes unfocussed again, and Derek waited once more for the flicker of intelligence to return.

"Behind the shed, between it and the fence. I blocked it with tree bits."

Derek felt a surge of elation, but he had one last question. "Why did you leave her there?"

"Looking for us."

"You led them away from her?"

"Tried..."

"Who was looking for you?"

This time the pause was longer, and Derek was afraid that the period of lucidity was over.

"Theo. Aleksi."

Derek lifted Wanda's face again. "Wanda, listen to me...don't fight here..."

"I have to," Wanda said before her mind blanked out again.

Derek stood up, and looked down with sympathy at the woman who had once helped his family. He glanced up at the monitor and gestured to be let out.

Back in the room where the warders kept watch on the prisoner, he asked, "Was our conversation recorded?"

The warder on duty told him, "No, Sir. You did not request it."

"I see," Derek said politely. "Thank you."

He called Donau from his car. "Have you found the child yet?"

The policeman's voice in his ear said, "We are still searching through the house."

He asked, "Is there a shed outside?"

"Yes. We looked in there."

"Have your dog check behind it, between the shed and a fence. Is there a fence?"

"Yes...but there was a pile of tree cuttings there."

"Move them!"

Donau caught on at once, "I'm on my way."

Derek hoped that Wanda had not been muddled when she told him that, but it seemed that place had not been checked. Donau had Alex, and the clothes that Wanda had taken. He could do no more there. He had other matters to follow up, and some international calls to make. He slipped his phone back inside his jacket, and started the car, heading it back to the police building in the first district.

He had been allowed the use of a desk in Donau's office. It was usually occupied by Johann Bauer, but he'd been injured when the black masked men had 'rescued' Carson. Leonard Christian, the third member of Donau's team, was at his desk.

"Good day, Sir," Christian greeted. "Can I help you with anything?"

"Not at the moment. I need to make some international calls."

Derek sat at the desk, and pulled the phone closer. He dialled the number of his superior, who was at Interpol headquarters in Paris.

While he waited for the call to go through, he asked Christian for the fax number of the machine on a bench in the office.

He spoke in French when one of his colleagues answered, and passed on his request for information on Theo Stephanovich, Aleksi, and the crime group known as 'The Family". He already had an outline, but now he needed more details. He received a promise of having it faxed through to the Vienna Police within the hour. He also requested permission to co-opt assistants and a doctor. For this, he was transferred to his superior, to explain his reasons, but permission was quickly given. An official confirmation would be emailed to his phone.

His next call was to a number in his own country - the tiny kingdom of Weisboden.

His call was to the Free Hospital in the Capitol, and when the switchboard answered, he asked to be put through to Dr Renee Du Pont.

The phone seemed to ring for a long time before it was answered. "Renee DuPont speaking."

Derek recognised the voice of his youngest sister, and merely answered with, "Derek." She said nothing, just waited for him to continue. "I have need of a totally discreet, totally independent doctor."

"Is this family business?" Renee asked at once.

"No, official. Can you come to Vienna? Now?"

"Why does Interpol need a doctor, and why can't you find one there?"

"I will explain if you come, and if you do I will have a document granting you a limited medical licence here."

Renee made a guess, "You have a particular reason for asking for me specifically?"

"Yes." Derek confirmed her guess, but did not try to force her choice. She worked in the emergency department of a very busy hospital.

"Give me five minutes to check if I can be released and call me back."

Derek ended the call and used the time to look up flight details on Bauer's computer. When he rang back, Renee said, "I can come."

"Good...there is a flight leaving from there in an hour, to go to Hamburg, and there is a connecting flight from there to Vienna..."

"Slow down, what's the rush?"

"That's confidential. I will arrange tickets for you..."

"If there is that much urgency, why don't you charter a direct flight and give me a chance to pack a change of clothes? And if your travel allowance won't cover it, you and I can split the cost."

"Fine, I will do that. Get to the airport. I will call on your mobile to give you the details."

"This had better be very important, Derek," Renee warned.

Chapter 29 - Repaying a debt

"Alex, come!" Donau said, as soon as he had ended the call. He told his civilian helpers to, "Keep checking in here."

Donau found the rear door of the half fire gutted house, and ran towards the shed. Alex trotting after him. The shed had been examined and then sealed by the forensic team. Someone, possibly two people had been imprisoned in there, but neither had been Rachel Wexford.

Donau continued around to the back and began tossing branches out of the way; the smell of pine resin was very strong. Alex watched, but after a while, began nosing at the pile. He barked and began digging out smaller branches. He had caught a scent, and as soon as there was a hole big enough for his head, he nosed into the pile. When he drew it out, he had a child's shoe in his mouth.

Donau began to work faster, and began to see glimpses of pale fabric. Alex, had not gone into his 'statue' stance, so the child was not dead, even though she had been out all night. He moved only enough so that he could reach in and lift the child out. She was alive, but her skin was very cold. He took off his coat and wrapped it around her and began to walk quickly towards his car.

Before he reached it, the two Americans came racing out of the house.

"You drive," he told the blond one, Max. "You get in first," he told Nicholas. "I will hand her into you. We will go straight to the hospital. I will warn them we are coming."

"How did you know where to look?" Nicholas asked as he settled the girl on his lap and held her firmly.

Donau sat beside him and tucked his coat in around the girl. Max was driving down the driveway, ignoring Alex who had happily taken the front passenger seat, when Donau answered. "Mont Pelier spoke to your friend. He must have caught her in a lucid moment."

He then dialled the hospital and warned them of the girl's condition. Then he called Mont Pelier back.

"We found her, where you said. We're on the way to the hospital now. Once I know how she is, I will call the US Embassy."

Mont Pelier had another idea. "I will come by and pick you up. We can both go and get the mother. I should have time to do that before I need to be back at the airport."

"Fine," Donau agreed. Then he asked, "Did you find anything there?"

"Yes. A body and a suit bag. I will fill you in later."

At the Embassy, Derek merely observed, when Donau spoke to Nicole Wexford and gave her the good news. He was certain that her near hysterical relief was genuine. She insisted on going to the hospital as soon as she had her handbag.

In the car, she asked about Tatiana Carson, and Donau fended that awkward moment by saying, "I will pass on your thanks."

"Have you found my husband?" was the next question, but again, Donau handled it by saying, "I spoke to your husband, yesterday morning. He was upset at hearing of your troubles, and about his daughter. He did however, have some imperative appointments today, to finalise his work."

He didn't say that Wexford had promised to be in touch, or that it seemed sure that he had left Austria.

Nicole's worried expression tightened, and if she was angry with her husband, she wasn't going to admit it. Her concern just then was for her daughter.

Having had the chance to evaluate Nicole Wexford, Derek let Donau shepherd her into where her daughter was. He waved at the two Americans who were leaning against Donau's borrowed car, keeping Alex company, as he left to return to the airport.

As he walked along the walkover from the carpark to the terminal, he noticed people watching some activity below. Being tall, he was able to glance over several shorter people. He saw that the police had the area cordoned off, and the forensic officers were busy at work. He continued towards the charter lounge, and arrived as his sister's flight was on final approach.

Renee Du Pont walked out with the flight attendant, spotted her brother and walked over. She smiled up at him, but greeted him formally, since this was business not a family gathering.

"Thanks for coming. I will brief you in the car," Derek responded. His sister understood the need for discretion.

Once in the car, Renee challenged him. "This isn't all business, is it?"

"I do have a witness that I need to question on agency business," Derek told her. He had the car keys in his hand and made no attempt to start the car. "She is on remand on some very serious local charges but currently reacting very badly to various illegally and legally administered drugs."

He briefly described the witness's behaviour and finished with, "I cannot question her if she is still under the influence of those chemicals."

"I see that, but why me?" Renee faced her brother and watched him fiddling with his keys in a most uncharacteristic manner.

"You know the witness," Derek admitted, glancing at his sister. "It's Wanda Martin."

Renee felt her jaw drop, and said quickly, "And I am supposed to be unbiased?"

Derek gave her a wry grin. "Independent, I called it. You will have no trouble examining and diagnosing her condition without bias."

"So she has annoyed the local police, is that it? What is she charged with?"

"Nothing yet, but the Austrian police have a solid case against her for a jewel theft, and I know she is guilty there. However, they believe they have an equally excellent case against her for two murders."

Renee swore softly, using words their father would not approve of. "I don't believe that."

"Nor I, but I cannot help her there. They have had two psychiatrists attempting to evaluate her and I don't think she is choosing to, or can, cooperate with them. I am certain that they have a pre-conceived bias. They prescribed tranquilisers, since she was uncontrollable, but I believe they are reacting with traces of a knock out drug and a truth drug, in her system."

"You don't give me an easy one do you? What was Wanda doing

here in the first place?"

"Looking for a missing US trade attaché and his daughter," Derek explained. "However, I think she fell afoul of a group of Russian thugs. They are my interest, but I need Wanda able to talk to me, and I didn't want just any doctor to help her. I wanted the best."

Renee murmured, "I'll do my best, Derek. We, our family, owe her too much. However, the behaviour you described is quite unusual for the types of drugs you mentioned. There must have been something else."

"Well, I spoke to her husband, and he says that she reacts to most drugs in unexpected ways."

"David is here too?"

"Yes. He came in last night and he is worried out of his mind. He and those he works with, are working hard to clarify Wanda's movements."

"Do you think they can help?"

Derek shrugged. "It doesn't look good, and Wanda herself cannot remember what happened. I am hoping she might when the drugs wear off, since she has recalled some things. And I cannot interfere in the murder investigation."

Renee slumped in the seat and thought on what she had just learnt. She did not believe that Wanda Martin would murder anyone - not even in self-defence. It was equally obvious that her brother felt the same way and was very much aware of the life debt that their family, the Royal family of Weisboden, owed Wanda and David Martin. If not for them, and their friends, their brother, the current monarch would have died in disgrace.

Derek started the car, and began to ease out of the parking space. "We need to get to the prison before they try to tranquilise her again. I have official documents attaching you, pro tem, to the agency and specifying the limits of your authority. You will report exclusively to me, and I will deal with the local police."

Derek went directly to the monitoring room, and had the prison director summoned. He introduced Renee, and explained why she was there.

"I doubt that the good doctor will be able to do much with that one," the man gestured to the prisoner in the room below. The voice pick up was turned to low to mute the screams and shouted obscenities.

Renee was already studying the woman prisoner, who had been quiescent until the heavy built man had entered the padded cell. He had become immediately threatening and verbally abusive, standing over the helpless prisoner and demanding answers.

The prisoner, in turn cursed the questioner, and jerked at the wrist restraints, as if she had wanted to hit the man. That had made the man even more threatening.

Renee returned her attention to the Director, after glancing at the three others in observation room. No one seemed to think that the man's actions were excessive, or that the wrist and ankle restraints were out of place.

"You will let me go to my patient immediately," Renee spoke to the Director, infusing every bit of 'presence' that she knew how to muster. Her voice and manner, Derek recognised, were an excellent imitation of their father.

"Inspector Wagner has asked not to be disturbed, unless he summons us," one of the observers commented.

"That woman is in no state to be questioned. Anything she says at this point may be considered as being obtained under duress," Renee stated.

When no one made a move to accompany her to the prisoner, Renee turned and took herself out of the room and headed to the cell door. Derek followed her, and then the Director decided to comply with the orders Derek had presented. He overruled the orders that Wagner had given the guards, and demanded they open the cell.

Inside the padded cell, Wagner had been joined by two of the med techs from the prison hospital ward. They were advancing towards the hissing, struggling, screaming wildcat that wore the guise of a woman.

"Stop!" Renee spoke in a loud, carrying voice.

Wagner and the med techs all turned. The former, retorted immediately. "I ordered no one to interrupt me! Get out! I will see that you are reported for this!"

His anger was forced to cool, when he saw Derek Mont Pelier

entering next, followed by the prison Director. Behind them, the woman continued to struggle, although the screaming had stopped when Wagner's attention had turned from her. It seemed she was reacting to Wagner's hostility and was now beyond helping herself.

"You will allow the doctor to examine the woman and provide appropriate treatment," Derek stated. "This woman is also required for questioning in relation to an agency investigation. We require that our own appointed specialist doctor be allowed to evaluate her and ensure that she is fit to be questioned. If not, anything she says will be invalid."

"The bitch is pretending," Wagner insisted. "Pretending to know nothing so as to try to escape justice."

"I will decide that, Herr Wagner," Renee stated. "Please step away from the woman."

"Our doctor prescribed a tranquiliser, to calm her so that the Inspector can question her," one of the med techs insisted. He had a syringe in his hand and had been about to inject it into the prisoner.

"I am sorry gentlemen, but you will have to let her wear herself out, and let all medication work out of her system. Then I will be able to evaluate her."

Her upper class voice and how she stood facing the bigger or taller men, told them all that she had perfect faith in her ability to handle the prisoner.

The med tech shrugged and took the syringe back to a small trolley that was just inside the cell door. He asked then, "Is there anything you need, then?"

"Yes, I would like you to bring a trolley, so we can take this woman to the hospital section."

"You don't want to go handling this woman out of here," Wagner insisted. "She'll escape as soon as look at you."

"And I will not get her quiet with all you vultures looking on," Renee said with a degree of harshness. She turned to the med tech who hadn't left yet, and emphasised, "Please get the trolley and warn the ward that we are bringing the prisoner there. I will want to make use of a quiet corner, away from any other patients."

"Quiet!" Wagner muttered. "Won't be that once you get there."

Derek allowed Wagner to mutter comments until the trolley

arrived. Then he commented, "Doctor Du Pont has had a great deal of experience with patients such as this. She will not be deceived by her behaviour, if it is self-imposed. That is what you wish, is it not?"

Wagner took his eyes from the struggling prisoner and glanced at the Interpol agent, who had been calmly assessing the prisoner from where he stood. "It is," he admitted. He started to move towards the woman, to help the med techs, but Derek calmly suggested, "Let the doctor and the techs manage her."

Despite the struggles, the prisoner was released from the floor restraints, which were deftly replaced with normal handcuffs, and hoisted into a standing position. However, the prisoner slumped in the grip of the techs, who merely dragged her towards the trolley. As the woman got closer and saw the trolley, the struggles increased and she began kicking, since her arms were restrained.

Wagner emitted a faint chuckle as one med tech deftly swiped the woman's feet from under her, and in the follow up movement, helped lift her to the trolley and hold her down. He saw the doctor secure the chest and leg restraints, and waited as the trolley was wheeled out before following. He decided not to say that the whole farce was like a carnival sideshow. He was annoyed that his questioning session had been interrupted, but not that the prisoner was getting handled. He had every intention of staying with the prisoner and checking on what the doctor did.

He stayed back as the woman was transferred from the rattling and unsteady trolley, onto one of the ward beds, where she was held down while the hand cuffs were removed and her hands secured to the side of the bed, and her feet in a similar manner to the foot of the bed. That bed was sturdier but the sides rattled as the prisoner struggled.

When the techs moved away, Renee drew a curtain around the bed, blocking the prisoner from view of the Austrian policeman, the prison director and Derek.

"Thank you. I will handle things from there."

The med techs were happy enough to go back to their other work, but Wagner looked like he intended to stay.

"Agent Mont Pelier, Inspector Wagner, please wait elsewhere.

The process will take time and cannot begin until the woman is calm."

"That one is only calm when tranquilised or exhausted," Wagner muttered, turning to leave with ill grace.

Derek merely glanced at Renee and tilted his head slightly as he gave a 'good luck' hand gesture, as he followed Wagner out of the ward.

Renee waited for the clang of the door shutting before returning behind the curtain.

She watched her patient's struggles for a moment before speaking in a tone loud enough to be heard over the noise.

"The policeman has gone, Tatiana, so are the med techs, and nobody here is impressed by your antics."

The degree of struggling abated, but didn't stop. Renee was joined by a young man in a white coat.

"I'm Wilhelm Grosz, the doctor assigned here. How can I help?"

"I need to hook up pulse, respiration and blood pressure monitors," Renee told him, wanting him away so that she could talk privately to her patient.

When the doctor's footsteps indicated he was out of earshot, Renee gently placed her hand on her patient's face and asked, "Wanda? Can you hear me?"

The struggling eased further, and the woman's eyes tried to focus. It seemed however, that some of the struggling was involuntary, and Renee decided that she needed to help her patient relax. With very gentle hands, and while speaking in soft soothing tones, she began to massage Wanda's temples and the sides of her face. She recalled how it had seemed that Wanda could pick up on the thoughts of others, hoped this was still so. She wanted to exchange her own calmness for the agitation caused by Wagner's abrasive personality.

When Grosz returned with the monitors. He was surprised by how much calmer the patient was. He saw what Renee was doing and asked, "Can you do that with all raving lunatics?"

"The woman is not a lunatic, and I would not try this on all violent patients. It works on some patients when some chemical might be the cause of the body being out of control. In this case, I do not wish to give the patient more drugs, and this massage helps the body relax."

As they were attached, the monitors began their recording of vital signs. Renee watched the figures and graphs. Wanda's heart rate and pulse were elevated, her blood pressure as well, and the respiration rapid - not surprising, considering her recent struggles, but what was most alarming was the oxygen levels.

"We need to give her oxygen," Renee told Grosz. "Not a mask."

Grosz returned with the tubing to attach to the oxygen cylinder, and gently arranged the prongs that released air into each nostril. He was wary whilst doing it, expecting the patient to relapse at any moment. Yet he took his cue from the calmness of the foreign doctor.

Chapter 30 - Facing the inevitable

Wanda felt the throbbing headache subsiding and with it the painful muscle spasms. The sense of mindless panic that had overcome her when the evil one had repeated the evidence that would condemn her for murder began to recede too. No matter how often she told him that she truly did not recall being in the house with the dead men, he didn't believe her. He accused her of lying, of taking some drug so she could be thought insane, had invented reasons for her to want to kill the men.

Part of her believed herself guilty. She had remembered being in a room, covered in blood. She'd had blood on her hands, her clothes spattered with it, her knife was bloody, she couldn't fault the evidence, but she could not recall going to the house.

She could have done it; had killed before. Then, as now, the memory sickened her. However, then she had killed for survival and because many others would die if she did. She had sworn never to kill again, had learnt ways to disable people without killing them. But her mind had been recalling that horrible time, had turned ordinary human people into the inhuman monsters who had tortured her. Had she thought herself to be threatened? That she had to live, because she had something important to do?

The gentle hands she felt massaging her head were banishing the evil thoughts, making her feel safe and bringing back some self-awareness. People were talking, softly, gently.

"Dr Grosz, could you prepare an IV drip with normal saline and…"

"Don't you effing dare," Wanda spoke to warn the gentle presences around her. She did not want to freak out again, and maybe hurt them.

Footsteps, merely the faint squeak of rubber soles on vinyl floor tiles, moved away.

"Do you always have to make things harder for yourself, Wanda Martin?"

Wanda tried to focus on the figure that stood next to her bed. The voice was tantalisingly familiar. She should know who it was. All she could see was an outline – someone in a white coat.

"Eff off! Effing release me." Wanda jerked her wrists, making the bed railing rattle.

"Not just yet. The drugs are making your movements uncontrolled. I want to put in a drip to help flush the drugs from your blood. Do you understand?"

"Damn you!" The woman was right, whoever she was.

"Call you tell me how you are feeling?"

"Effing awful."

"I am not surprised," the calm voice commented, neutrally. "When did you eat last?"

Wanda tried to recall. "I don't know. But I don't want anything, I'll throw up."

"Are you nauseous?"

"What do you think?"

The squeaky footprints returned with a trolley that rattled and screeched. The wheels needed oiling.

Wanda heard the sounds of the drip being prepared, and then the woman sent the other off again.

"I think we need to have a glucose drip as well. Then I will need to take blood samples for analysis. I want to know exactly what drugs we are dealing with here."

When Wanda felt the tourniquet snap on, her body began to struggle again. As the doctor had said, that reaction was unintentional.

"Wanda, lie still. I am trying to help you."

This woman knew her real name, Wanda realised, and her body began to tremble violently. She tried once more to get her eyes to focus, but all she saw was still a white coated blur.

"You can't help me," Wanda said, thinking of what the police thought she had done.

"I can help you begin to think straight..."

"I don't want to think..."

"I know you are scared, Wanda, its natural. But you are not helping yourself this way."

Once again, Wanda felt she should know this doctor. This person who was concerned for her. She let her finish inserting the drip and bandage the site.

"Do you want a drink?"

Wanda felt herself wanting to lash out with a rude retort, but this gentle person didn't deserve it.

Instead, she nodded.

The woman went away, not far, and then there was the sound of water splashing into a plastic cup.

Wanda sensed her return, and felt a straw placed near her lips.

"Take it slow," was the warning, and Wanda felt her parched mouth absorbing the moisture, and her throat easing its grip of soreness. It was painful, just sipping, but she tried not to show more weakness than she had betrayed already.

Renee saw the tightening of the face muscles, and guessed that merely drinking was painful. She went back to stroking the sides of her patients face, and studying the healing scratches on both cheeks. The blue bloodshot eyes were returning her gaze, but there was still no sign of recognition. There was a tinge of black in the skin around the eyes.

"I'm going to take some blood to be tested," Renee told her patient, knowing that the Wanda she had met over two years before, would respond to logic.

She tightened the tourniquet once more and requested the things she needed from Grosz, who was following her orders with no sign of resentment. "We will repeat the tests at hourly intervals, but in between you can rest. I think we should insert a catheter and test the urine output too."

"B....off," Wanda muttered.

"I won't ask for a translation of that. It is good to know you are aware of what I am saying."

True to the promise, the doctors moved away from her after they had finished their initial setting up and testing. Wanda was fighting the need to sleep, afraid that her nightmares would start again, but no longer afraid for her own safety or that she would turn into a monster again. It was how she had told herself to consider the restraints as a good thing.

Without realising it, she slipped into a deep sleep, waking again when they were taking the next lot of samples from the cannula they had left in her right arm. While the woman worked, she spoke softly, speaking of what she was doing, and Wanda recognising the concern was content to let herself drift, half awake, and for the moment, pain free. She closed her eyes, feeling relaxed, but didn't immediately return to sleep. She heard voices, the kind woman, and a male voice – not the other doctor, but another she knew...had heard recently.

"The lab is waiting," that voice was saying. "They are the best in Austria – and right here in Vienna. They have access to the forensic database..."

Wanda allowed herself to relax, and once again drifted off into a deep sleep, this time not waking until the room was lit only by dim light from a light beyond the curtain wall.

Voices roused her, even though they were quiet.

"I have the results of the first samples," the familiar male voice said. "I hope you can make sense of their report. I only know that they identified a number of substances, and feel many others that are in high levels, are metabolites."

There was a rustling of paper, silence for a moment, and the man asked, "How is she?"

"Sleeping, and her vital signs are starting to normalise."

"Fit for questions?" the male asked, in a hopeful tone.

"Not yet. She was exhausted and dehydrated, probably hadn't eaten much for a couple of days, add that to the drug reactions going on and the effects of being beaten, or whatever gave her all the bruises and grazes...after that she is doing well enough. I have not tried to test her memory, but I do not think she is able to remember much...Give me some good news."

"I don't know about good... except that Rachel Wexford is alive, and that I am sure is all due to your patient."

"What else?"

"Nothing positive. I do need a separate blood sample from her."

"May I ask why?"

"One of the dead men had traces of blood and skin under his nails. They think he tried to fight her off."

"Oh," the woman sounded unhappy, and the man hadn't seemed to enjoy the request either. "That is more likely to be a woman's reaction than a man. I would think a man would tend to punch rather than scratch."

"I will get what you need, Derek. Has nothing turned up that can help?"

"Like I said, nothing positive. They consider the case tight."

"They should try looking at it from the point of view of the little Wanda has said. There has to be another explanation."

"I agree, but there is little I can do. Will you tell me as soon as you think I can question her?"

"Of course, but she still hasn't recognised me. It will help if you keep that arrogant beast Wagner away from her."

"I had a chat with his Chief. Wagner told him that he had been on the verge of getting a confession from her. I explained her condition, and he agreed that such a confession would have no weight."

"That is something. Have they charged her with anything yet – or still talking about it?"

"If you are hoping for a reason to get her out of here, Renée, it won't work. She is to be charged with the jewel theft. The paperwork for that has been approved. As soon as she is coherent, they will make it formal."

"Damn."

"I don't think they will wait much longer for the other charges."

"Can you find a way to get David here?"

"Hmm. Perhaps you need an assistant to relieve you. Not another doctor, maybe a paramedic. I will see to it."

The fragments of memory fell into place, and Wanda recalled the voice of Derek Mont Pelier. Remembered that she had spoken to him during a period of lucidity. Now she understood why the woman's voice had made her feel safe. He said he couldn't help her, but he had. He had brought Renee, his sister, the doctor, her friend.

Now she wanted to call out, see if this new revelation was true, or just another kind of dream. She willed the woman to come to her, deciding that her silence was a safer response, or those others might force her to go away.

She had started to doze again, when she sensed the woman return and take a seat beside the bed. Then she turned her head as much as she could, with the restraints holding her on the bed.

"Renee?"

"Finally!"

"I couldn't see anything clearly," Wanda admitted. "I thought I should know your voice, and then, I thought of you, but I did not know how it could be. I thought I was hallucinating."

"Have you been" Renee asked, as if idly.

"Yes...at least I hope I was."

"You've been subjected to several strong illegal substances, so it is possible. Tell me how you are feeling now?"

"Now," Wanda echoed. "Weak...nauseous, and my muscles are still aching something fierce. If I stay lying here tied up for much longer, this prison is going to have a human statue. All in all, I am not quite functional."

Renee recalled a comment made by Wanda's husband, David. He had explained that her idea of functional was most other people's ideas of too sick to get out of bed.

"What about your mind? Is it clearer?"

"Yes, but it is still feeling weird. I can't block the minds out – well not completely. I am feeling emotions. You are blissfully calm, not like that Wagner."

"Anything else?"

Wanda decided she needed to be completely frank with Renee. "I can ignore the dark shadows I see in my peripheral vision. I am not having visions of evil creatures, and I can't seem to recall more than flashes."

"Do you know where you are?"

Wanda looked away. Of course she did. It was inevitable – Wagner had made sure she knew.

"I really wish, that you were not seeing me this way."

"Human, you mean?"

"No. Here in prison. You must think I am vile."

"My opinion of you has not changed," Renee said passionately. "I know what you are able to do and I have known others who were criminals. They are all simply fallible human beings.”

She saw her patient flinch at the description of criminal and said quickly, “You are a level above, you do what you do to help others.”

“I am not handling this as well as I did last time,” Wanda admitted.

“Last time?”

“I have been in prison before. I swore I would never go back. There was a time that I nearly had to, but Jim helped me then. He needed my skills and now I help put bad people away.”

“Can’t the US State department help you?”

“No. I am like any normal US citizen. If I commit a crime overseas, I have to abide the local punishment. And, I have always known the risks, but...”

“You never expected to be caught,” Renee finished for her. “Why did you take those jewels Derek told me about?”

“I don’t know.”

“Or don’t remember?”

“No, that incident is clear. I wanted certain people to think that was my target, not their private computer files. And I hadn’t known what was likely to be in that safe. I was hiding, in what I thought was a storeroom. When I flashed the torch around briefly, I saw the safe. There had been one in the main office too, but I hadn’t even thought of opening that. That’s when I had the idea of a diversion.”

“So, what happened? You opened it and took the stones...”

“Yes, but there were several bags, and I was pulling them out, intending to leave them on the floor as if I had been disturbed. Most had small stones in – probably diamonds. Then I pulled the last one out. The stones were bigger, but I didn’t even try to look at them. I would have sworn I put them down, but I found them later, in my pocket. And I really meant to send them to the police, but somehow I never did.”

Renee could not offer any hope of avoiding the charge for the robbery, so she decided on distraction. She stood and began to undo the restraints.

“I think you need to get up and walk around. Are you up to it?”

“Yes, I need to move.”

Wanda sat on the bed until the initial vertigo eased, and then allowed Renee to help her to stand. The soles of her feet were tender, and she knew that was a bad sign, Still, she knew she had to get her blood moving and held the drip stand for support, and took the catheter bag in her spare hand.

It was bad, moving just at the hobbling pace, and she tried to hide how much merely walking hurt. She knew she had failed, when Renee said with sympathy, "I don't want to give you any drugs…"

"They won't help," Wanda told her.

"Is there anything else that will?"

"A hot spa, a massage, and a damn good argument with that sod, Wagner."

"Are you sure that you would be up to that?" Renee meant the option of fronting Wagner.

"No, but I will make an exception," Wanda promised.

Renee chuckled, relieved that Wanda was beginning to show some of her true mettle. "Were you deliberately riling him before?"

"At first, because he just refused to listen to me. Then, I just let myself go. I was feeling awful."

"You did more than let yourself go," Renee remarked.

"I knew I wouldn't be able to fight the effect much longer anyway, so I didn't try. He was insisting I admit to something I don't remember doing. I let the darkness swallow me, and I didn't care what I did until I was exhausted."

Renee saw the look of fear on her patients face. She wanted to offer comfort, but did not speak. Still, it seemed that Wanda could sense that.

"No. I can't be soft. And I can't stay in here either." She was making a noticeable effort to regain control, standing still and taking deep breaths.

"You are not going to be a fool and try to escape from here…"

"I have to get out of here. I have things to do, things I haven't finished."

Renee guided Wanda back to a chair. "Your friends are working for you. Derek is using them as informants and they found the little girl. Derek said she will be fine."

"How did they find her?"

"Apparently you told Derek where you had put her. He said you saved her life, because the nurse was still in the child's suite, and she died there."

A swift vision of hitting the nurse and tying her up, passed through Wanda's mind. She began to tremble. In a whisper, she asked, "How did she die?"

"I don't know," Renee admitted.

"I killed her!" Wanda's voice was full of horror. "Oh, Gods! I am never going to be allowed out. I will never see Davy grow up or get to see my little girl." She buried her head on the side of the bed.

It took Renee a moment to understand. "I thought you only had one child. Are you pregnant?"

Wanda nodded. She was sure.

Renee slumped onto a second chair, feeling suddenly weak. What a complication. It would explain part of Wanda's behaviour, possibly the nausea. Not knowing what else to say, she left Wanda to her thoughts and went to add details to her notes.

Derek Mont Pelier returned very late with his 'assistant'. David wore white trousers and tunic, and would be taken to be a male nurse. The relevant documents stated that he too was on temporary attachment to Interpol. To the warders at the prison, it seemed that everything possible was being done to make the prisoner fit to be questioned.

Renee took David behind the privacy curtain, where Wanda was still hiding her head. She watched as David knelt down beside her and drew her face towards his. She withdrew as these two friends of hers clung to each other as if it were to be their last hour together.

With a gesture, Renee directed her brother to the far end of the room so that they could talk.

"You have the last lot of lab results?"

She used the excuse of examining them to delay answering his question.

"How do they look?" Derek asked.

"They are fine. The levels of both the drug and the metabolite have dropped to baseline. I cannot delay things anymore."

"She is lucid?"

"Lucid, yes, but I am not sure about her memory."

"David thinks he can help. He said he had learnt some 'focussing' strategies that might help." Derek stared at the curtain around the only occupied bed. "He also said that he could do massage if she is stiffening up. He didn't really explain, just said it is some genetic thing that blows up on her at times."

"Wanda mentioned something like that, obliquely, and she was in some pain when she was walking before, but that wasn't why I asked for him." Renee caught her brother's eye and said, "They need to take strength from each other."

Derek nodded, understanding. "The warrants are to be served in the morning," he murmured.

In an equally low voice, Renee commented, "I think, now, that she will be strong enough. But I think someone needs to make her understand that she needs to be polite, especially with Wagner."

Nodding again, Derek agreed. "Somehow, he has found out her real name. He is out to crucify her as a spy as well."

With a grimace of distaste for the policeman, Renee said sharply, but quietly, "As if murder is not enough. What has Wanda done to deserve this?"

"More good than harm," Derek murmured. "I am convinced of that. We just have to prove it."

Renee looked sharply at her brother. "You are not doing anything to get into trouble?"

"No, I am being careful, even though trouble seems to be a tradition of our generation. Actually, I have had Wanda's friends out helping Donau and looking for other clues. All in line with me finding the two Russian criminals seen here. Jim, who we met back home, has engaged a very capable lawyer. He will be here tomorrow."

"So, when do you want to question her?"

"When will you let me?"

"How about when those two have had a few more minutes together?"

"Fair enough. I don't want her relapsing before I get what I need."

Renee decided not to ask why he wanted to question her without a lawyer present. Instead she spoke of something that had confused her.

"She told me something, and ethics don't allow me to repeat it, but ask her why she took those diamonds."

"What do you mean?"

"Her reason was most odd." Renee abruptly began to walk back towards the curtained off bed.

Before she moved the curtain, she heard murmuring, and then, audibly, "David, promise me, when I am sentenced, go home. Go back to Davy, don't try to see me."

"No! I couldn't be with you when you were in that other place. I won't desert you again."

"You know it is going to happen, Dav. And I can't do this if I can't picture you at home with Davy. I don't want him losing two parents."

"I don't want to leave you to face this alone."

"I know, just like I knew the risks when I went into that damn building. David, I have been in prison before and survived. I survived that other place. I can handle things, but I have to do things my way. I can't show weakness. I have to pretend it is just me."

"But it isn't just you, this time," David had his soul, pleading in his tone. "How will I know that you are all right?"

"Because I promise you, David Martin, that you and I are going to die together in extreme old age. Anything that happens before that is ephemeral. Promise me, David, please?"

There was a moment of silence before David said, with some difficulty, "I promise. But you had better stay functional."

Renee coughed quietly, before she moved the curtain. David had risen from beside his wife and was looking away from everyone.

Derek poked his head around the curtain and said, "Wanda? We need to talk. Are you up to it?"

He saw the way she straightened, and stood up and looked straight at him.

"Yes." Her eyes were red rimmed and moist, but she was resolute. "Where? Here?"

Derek nodded, and came closer, pulling the second chair nearer, and seating himself.

Wanda, sat back on her chair, and sensed that Derek was a little diffident, not quite the confident, assured agent he had been in Weisboden when they had first met. "You will be recording this?"

Derek nodded. "This is for my own personal use. Though if necessary, I will have to play it for others."

"I understand," Wanda told him. "I'm sorry if this is difficult for you, but I don't expect you to do anything different for me that you would do for any other witness or suspect."

She saw his sympathy and knew she had read his feelings correctly. "I trust you, Derek. Ask me anything you need to know, I will not hide anything from you. I will tell the truth, and if you have to share it, I know it will be because it is the right thing to do. I have accepted that I am most likely going to prison. I am not...looking forward to it. And I know I cannot be an exception."

Derek in turn, made his own reading of Wanda. Her resolve, was not quite solid yet.

"You will probably have to answer these same questions tomorrow when they come to serve the warrants," he warned her.

"She will have a lawyer with her," David stated, coming to stand behind his wife. The traces of his own emotion were still evident in the red watery eyes, but he was resolute. "Who will, I hope, tell her when to keep her mouth shut."

Wanda's hand went up to touch his where it rested on her shoulder.

"There is no lawyer here now, so ask away."

Derek reached into his jacket and brought out a slender device and switched it on. He took a moment to adjust his thoughts. His voice was calm and unemotional as he gave the time and place, before asking his first question, "Are you, Tatiana Carson, prepared to voluntarily and truthfully, answer the questions I put to you?"

Wanda gave the requested oath, calling herself Tatiana Carson as he had. She relaxed slightly, knowing that he intended to call her by her alias.

His next question was, "What was your purpose in coming to Vienna?"

Wanda spoke calmly, answering in detail, from the initial contact with Senator Willard – she didn't say he was her father – giving his reasons for asking her, and the information he and Vera gave her.

Derek's questions probed for her reasons, for doing everything she had done since coming to Vienna. She gave him her observations at each place she visited, and during all her movements. At times he made notes in a small book, as prompts for further avenues of investigation.

He talked her through all her movements in Vienna, including her correspondence with David, who he referred to as her 'researcher'. When she finished, he knew as much as he would if he had been living in her head. He turned his recorder off.

"That...is impressive. I wish I could co-opt you permanently for the agency."

With more than a hint of wry amusement, Wanda said, "Anytime you want to spring me from prison..."

The amusement was short lived.

Derek decided to offer Wanda some advice. "Renee is going to have to tell the people here that you are fit for questions."

"I expected that," Wanda admitted, as David gently kneaded her shoulders.

"I don't know who will be doing the questioning. If it is Donau, I know you will be reasonable. I suggest that you be polite and reasonable even if it is Wagner. It may be that half of his antagonism to you is from your attitude to him."

"He started it," Wanda muttered, but stopped saying more when David squeezed her shoulder a little more firmly.

"Persistent politeness, can be as aggravating as constant crudeness," David proposed.

Wanda thought for a moment, "And it would be a contrast - to emphasise the nice normal me – versus the doped up horror..."

They came for Wanda at half past nine, a solid woman guard who looked to be in her fifties, and a younger man.

By then, Wanda had slept fairly well, after David had massaged away the muscle aches, and Renee had removed both the drip and the catheter.

Derek came in early with a fresh set of casual clothes for Wanda, and Renee had groomed Wanda's hair and tied it back so it resembled Tatiana Carson's style. They could do nothing about the eye colour, except hope that the subject didn't come up.

The legal representative, one of Vienna's brightest upcoming lawyers, had arrived an hour before and discussed her case. He had tempered Wanda's insistence on 'telling the whole truth' with the notion of 'if they want to know everything, let them give you some benefit in return'.

Wanda heard an echo of Jim Phillips in his words and subsided. In her mind, she couldn't see the difference, and knowing how smart Jim was, had to admit to herself that her mind might not be at one hundred percent efficiency.

David and Renee had stood back as the warders handcuffed Wanda, and led her from the room. Neither betrayed any emotion, and both had said their good wishes and David was thinking hard at his wife, "You will be fine."

For the walk to the interview room, the warders held her by the arms, and Derek and her lawyer, Jurgen Hauser, followed behind. Wanda remained docile and compliant, and refrained from speaking.

The interview room where she was led was a large one, and even then, it seemed crowded. Wanda sat where directed, allowed herself to be secured in place, and then gave one sweeping glance around the room. Of those present, she recognised Jim, Donau and Wagner. There were six others present, not counting Derek and Hauser. In her mind, she classified the extras as senior policemen, prosecutors and note takers.

Their first concern was her identity. The man who identified himself as the district Prosecutor, called her Tatiana Carson when serving the warrants, and he was made uncomfortable by her direct return gaze, and by her refusal to look at the papers. He made her status quite clear. That he used her alias relieved her but only for five minutes.

Wagner's intent gaze was unnerving, as if he were waiting for her to admit her real name. However, Wanda was letting Hauser speak for her on the matter of her identity. Donau knew the truth, but if he had mentioned it to anyone, his neutral expression betrayed nothing.

One of the men she had tagged as a top policeman, was the one demanding proof of her identity, and as Hauser spoke, Wanda had the oddest thought that the masked men who had invaded her hostel room, had unintentionally done her a favour. They had taken her diplomatic passport, so that the police only had her Carson one.

Jim Phillips, acting the part of the official representative of the US, gave her a passing glance as he stood to answer the question. She gave no indication of knowing him, and merely moved her gaze to study her hands on the table. Yet she was aware of Jim opening a folder and taking a document from it. He began to speak. "A search of our records showed that a passport was issued to Tatiana Carson on the 23rd of August...." He gave details of the year and place, as well as Carson's personal information at the time. It all sounded perfectly official, and perhaps that passport wasn't a fake. He went on to claim that no official record existed of a Wanda Martin, no passport in that name.

The real Wanda Martin permitted herself an inward sigh of relief. She had no doubt that should anyone check on Jim's report, they would find exactly that, even though her diplomatic passport was genuine.

The Austrians might know of her claim to be a State Department Investigator, but Wanda Martin was not officially on their books and the reasons for that were none of their business. What mattered now was that they now considered her an ordinary US citizen who had committed crimes in Vienna. She would not be the source of a major diplomatic incident and she would not have a criminal record in her own name.

Once the matter of her identity was settled, Jim moved back next to Derek Mont Pelier and listened unobtrusively to the proceedings. The lawyer handled the formalities and confirming his appointment to represent her.

Wanda had the distinct idea that Jim had given him some information that she had not been told. Her first reaction was irritation at him. It was a stupid one, for she had not seen him since they had met several nights ago. And if Derek knew things, he was not obligated to tell her anything either.

She kept her expression bland, and after a moment of thought, realised that irritation was the reaction Jim had intended to provoke – to remind her to think before she spoke, and on another level, to provoke her 'survival' instinct.

Jim was standing just within her peripheral vision, watching her. She flicked a quick glance at him, so that he knew that she understood, and that she knew he was trying to help her.

When she was obliged to speak, and permitted by her lawyer, Wanda kept her tone one of seemingly bored indifference – no swearing, cursing or screaming. Her reactions were controlled, and Hauser had told her what she could say and where to stop. In effect, she was telling the police very little that they didn't know already, and that new knowledge was intended to provoke further investigation – into Wexford, Heinrich, the mysterious masked men and a criminal conspiracy based in Vienna.

Her biggest silence was about matters that occurred after she had been abducted from Heidi Lowenbach's property. Another silence was about her intentions in the Alpha Prime building, and any ideas she had about the masked men.

Donau had questions, and from their wording, Wanda knew he had found a lead to the criminal conspiracy and she guessed he wanted conformation of certain points before the matter leaked to the press. She wanted to help him, but most of what she knew had been obtained illegally. Surely though, the police would think to check the business computers, Wessler's at least. Hadn't they found Lunn's laptop?

Wagner, when his turn came, was still wanting to pound her about the two knife murders. Wanda repeated exactly what she had told him before. She was expecting him to bring up the subject of the nurse.

Hauser had advised her on this and she simply stated, "I did not kill her."

Wagner accused her of hitting the woman and tying her up, and causing her to suffocate from the smoke. Wanda stayed silent, even though she was mentally retorting that she was going to call the police and had no reason to suspect that the house would catch fire.

Then he was harassing her about leaving Rachel out in the cold, insinuating that she might have died.

Since she had admitted her reasons for coming to Vienna were to find Wexford and his daughter, while remaining silent about her methods, she stated, "Returning Rachel to her mother was my priority. I needed to hide her whilst I led those who abducted her away. Her bedtime milk had been drugged and she was unconscious when I carried her from the house. I had every intention of returning quickly. And if you are fair minded enough to admit it, I saved her life. If I had not brought her out, she would have died."

Hauser whispered a warning, to say nothing further on that subject, and when Wagner asked further pointed questions about why she hadn't returned, he was met with a wall of polite silence. Wanda knew the man's anger at being unable to get an admission, was simmering within him still. With all these others present, he could not be his usual overbearing self.

One impression was indeed clear in the minds of Donau, Wagner and the other police officials.

Renee had reported that Tatiana Carson was now clear of the illegally administered drugs. The Tatiana these men saw now was calm and reasonable – not screaming and irrational. It reinforced the idea that what she had done under the influence of the drugs was not her normal behaviour.

Wagner saw it and did not want to believe it. Donau, who had worked with her, was more thoughtful. He knew her as thief, and as investigator. She had helped him as Martin, and given him useful leads, but they had led to him getting a mild concussion and her disappearing. That might be construed as her planned intention. He still didn't want to believe it.

Of all those present in the room, only Jim Phillips recognised the 'shutters' that came over her eyes, as she was answering questions. He had seen it before, and knew that his protégé was not as calm as she appeared.

Wanda stayed silent and inscrutable as Hauser bargained for a reduced sentence for all charges if she cooperated and provided useful information that helped their investigations. Hauser hinted at what she could reveal, but gave no details. The prosecutor did not want to agree, but did so in the end, reluctantly.

Once the officials, including Jim and Derek Mont Pelier, left the room, and she was alone with her lawyer, Wanda visibly slumped in her seat, and rested her weight against the table.

"What use is that bargain, Herr Hauser? So they give me twenty years instead of life for murders I did not commit. It is still a lifetime away from my son. And it is still way longer than I would get for being a thief."

"It is better than the rest of your life!" Hauser told her in a quiet voice that still had the force of a slap. "I am going to do my best to get you off all charges, and you have some very good friends who are helping me. I believe there is a very good chance of throwing sufficient doubt on you having committed deliberate, premeditated murder. I will not claim to do better, just yet. I am more concerned with that jewel theft charge. You were caught to rights there and that case is airtight. You have admitted to me that you are guilty of that, and what your intention was."

Wanda recalled his reaction to her, "I don't know why I took the jewels" statement. He had accurately pointed out that if she had not gone to that office, and opened the safe, she would have got away clean.

Hauser toned down his comments. "Please cooperate with me."

"I intend to, I promise," Wanda assured him.

"Good, because I don't think you realise just how high profile this case is. The death of two prominent businessmen has roused a lot of anger. Part of that is that there is now doubt about the stability of their business empires. So far, the media have not learnt of the criminal conspiracy that you helped to uncover. Donau has read some of the records and files that Wessler was taking from his safe when he died. It seems he was about to abscond. From comments he made, those records are damning. How the public mood will swing when that comes out, I cannot predict."

"But you don't think that I will be considered a public benefactor," Wanda murmured. "You think it will be more like I am the fan that spread the shit."

Hauser shook his head at her analogy, but said, "You begin to see the picture. Austria is not like America where theft and murder is common place. What you are accused of has shocked people. The things that you have helped to bring to light has further shocked them."

"Perhaps my warning of the Russian thugs taking over will change their minds?" Wanda muttered, sarcastically, since she felt the truth of what Hauser was saying.

"Mont Pelier, and Donau are working on that matter, but the men you saw appear to have left the country."

Wanda wanted to slump back on her chair, but the restraints kept her leaning towards the table.

"Do your best, Herr Hauser. I will do what I can to help you, and I am grateful for all you are doing, and you have my thanks – no matter the outcome."

Hauser stood and closed his briefcase. "Don't lose hope."

"I'm a realist," Wanda countered. "What happens now? Do you try to get me out on bail, or doesn't Austria work that way?"

Hauser sat down again.

"I want you to consider this advice very carefully," he said, making sure Wanda met his gaze. "You have angered a lot of people. Donau is going to have to work very hard to build cases against the other members of the cartel. Some have already tried to leave the country, some may try to get at you for purposes of revenge or to stop you talking – if they think you have learnt things about them."

"O...kay," Wanda agreed reluctantly. "There was more?"

"Yes. Those Russian thugs — have you stopped to think about what sort of game they have been playing with you?"

Wanda subsided. She hadn't, and Hauser was right — she needed to. They were directly responsible for her being caught.

"Don't you think that being held here is the safest place for you?"

Put that way, Wanda had to agree. "I guess I haven't been thinking as well as usual. But I still don't want to be here. Any idea when you will know if your bargain is accepted?"

"When they finally realise that you might know things that they need to know, and then I will have more leverage to try for a better deal. However, don't expect it to be too soon."

"I hope you get their deal in writing before you let me talk," Wanda told him. "I had the distinct feeling that the Prosecutor wanted me exterminated. And what I have to say may not please him."

Chapter 32 - Not enough facts

Derek Mont Pelier sat at his borrowed desk and scanned through some files that Donau had received from the safe at Wessler's house. He already had half a page of details he wanted to check through Interpol files.

"Have you been able to get a warrant to look through the computer files at Alpha Prime?" Derek asked the Austrian.

"I have requested it, but nothing yet. I also asked about the computer files of the other places that American visited. I suspect that I do not have a high enough position to demand them. If the approval is ever granted, it is likely that any suspect files will have been erased."

Derek tapped his pen on the desk. If he told Donau things that Wanda had told him, he might get to learn what he wanted, but it would only get Wanda in more trouble.

Donau stopped his own perusal of Wessler's files and sat back on his chair. His right hand dropped to where Alex sat beside him, and he felt Alex's moist tongue licking it.

"It is not making sense," Donau admitted. "We have an American official, visiting a list of people in Austria, who all turn out to be members of some criminal enterprise. That same American tips off his government and then disappears. Now, it seems that he disappeared on purpose, and is allied to a Russian criminal."

Donau tapped the arm of his chair with the hand that wasn't idly scratching Alex's ears.

"Put that way, it seems like he wanted those people investigated," Derek proposed.

"Maybe so, but then we have Carson. She claims to have come to look for Wexford, as a personal favour..."

"Which I have confirmed," Derek inserted.

"We have another official come to confirm the conspiracy claims," Donau continued. "One to work openly, questioning each of the contacts Wexford visited, and one that works illegally by entering places. What I want to know, is what Carson was looking for when she came across those diamonds, or was that always her intended target?"

Derek murmured, "I do not know how she could have known of the diamonds, or where they would be. That they were stolen, was not widely known."

Donau looked at Derek. "Phillips admitted that she was a highly skilled thief. That safe, the one with the diamonds, was probably not the only one she looked at. I want to know why the Americans would use a thief."

"I think you have probably worked that out already," Derek deflected the subtle request for his opinion.

"If the people were dishonest, they would hardly admit it," Donau proposed. "But even so, they could not use any information found that way."

"Not legally," Derek agreed. "It might have been they simply wanted to confirm the claims Wexford made so that the United States didn't sign off on deals with criminals. On the other hand, it might have been to look for confirmation of Wexford's movements as a means to trace his whereabouts."

Donau was considering that idea when his phone rang. He sat up and reached for his phone and after a terse, "Donau," he listened for a while and finally gave a "Yes, Sir, I will have everything boxed and ready by the time he arrives. Thank you, Sir,"

He rubbed his face and said, "That was the Chief. They have decided to form a task force to investigate the list of names we found. A colleague will be around to collect these files and I am to make a report containing everything I know about them and the affair at Alpha Prime. The task force will have the power to search the company premises that Wexford was to visit, and to seize records."

"Are you to assist them?" Derek asked delicately.

"No. I am to continue to liaise with you on your case and with Wagner on the murders of Wessler and Lunn. They also want to talk to that American."

"Who, I believe is not an American," Derek said. "Are they still interested in that jewel thief?"

"Very. I am to pass on anything I learn about her."

Derek was thoughtful. Donau was intelligent, and on the verge of believing Carson had been looking in many safes – not just at Alpha Prime. He worded his suggestion subtly. "You don't know that Carson was looking in other safes…"

"No…" Donau began to consider that idea, and it put a rotten taste in his mouth. He looked down at Alex, who inexplicably liked the thief. "At least the case against her for the jewel theft is tight."

He didn't want his face to betray his mixed feelings about Carson. In that persona, she had tricked him, and that had annoyed him. As Martin though, he had liked her. Very much. She was intelligent…brilliant at piecing things together, and she had come through and found the child. Yet in the back of his mind, he couldn't help feeling that it was too convenient, that maybe she had her own hidden agenda, that the ambush at Lowenbach's house had been expected and she had disappeared on purpose, and that she had been in league with those who attacked him.

His head came up and he asked, "Phillips, the Embassy representative, said he'd known Carson for a long time. Were they working together on this Wexford thing?"

Derek considered his answer. "They knew each other, certainly, but I believe they began investigating independently, and met by chance. What are you thinking?"

"Wondering," Donau corrected. "I would like to know how well Carson knew Wexford, and if she is or was, also working with the Russian group you hypothesized."

Derek's first thought was to firmly quash the idea, but he said instead, "What might indicate that?"

"Those masked men rescued her when we were taking her to prison."

"Rescued or abducted? Similar men invaded her hostel room," Derek pointed out.

"She was gone when we arrived after the tip off," Donau countered.

"Someone had given her a knock out drug. Why would they do that to an ally?"

"She might have gone against orders…tried to keep the diamonds."

"You told me," Derek said, "that someone else came just before she fled. Did you find that man?"

"No, but he might have drugged her."

Derek shook his head, Wanda had told him otherwise.

Donau stated, "We know she was at Wessler's place as was Wexford, and at the place where the fire was. The place you believe was the headquarters for the Russian gang. If Wexford was a Russian in disguise, maybe Carson was trying to protect him, and the masked men are Russians as well."

"Then why did they have her tied up at the house?" Derek focussed on the conflicting detail in a plausible theory, that he knew wasn't true. "And why, if Wagner's theory is correct, did she kill the two business men? If you keep to the protecting Wexford idea, why did she have all the drug effects? I cannot see Carson letting herself be caught, so I do not believe she drugged herself."

"She could have angered them and they were teaching her a lesson," Donau proposed. "And catching her that time was a fluke."

"They could have been using her as a distraction," Derek proposed, to get Donau thinking.

"And they had her tied up...why? Was she a risk of some kind? No longer useful?"

"A perfect scapegoat – if she were a US agent, and they thought she was onto Wexford..."

"Are you saying that Wexford might have killed Lunn and Wessler?" Donau sat up straight, startled by the idea. He hadn't liked the idea of Carson's guilt, but the evidence was convincing.

Derek hid his grim satisfaction, he now had the perfect lead in to get Donau looking at the suit bag from the airport and he reminded him about it.

"The one your informant claimed the man resembling Wexford had?"

Derek passed a file with the preliminary lab results to Donau. "Early results. Wagner forced them to stop and work on the murder evidence."

"Two different blood groups found on the clothes," Donau remarked aloud. "Neither match Carson's blood type. I will have the rest of the work hurried up, and I will have the lab cross reference the results with the samples from the Lunn-Wessler case. This puts a new slant on things, but how can we prove the garments are actually Wexford's? We might be lucky to get traces of DNA, but we don't have Wexford."

"Have your people go over the Wexford's apartment. It is still sealed off is it not?" Derek suggested. "Or perhaps the Lowenbach place. Wexford was there too. Surely we will find hairs, or fingerprints or something."

Donau got busy, dialling the extension for the forensic lab.

Derek said, "I'll start looking at Wexford's background. To see if his prints are on record anywhere."

He also intended to follow up on the reference to 'Aleksi'. Wanda had identified Wexford and heard him called that. If someone called Aleksi was impersonating Wexford, then that was probably the reason why he had walked out on Nicole. The question became, was Wexford still alive?"

Two officers came to collect the files from Wessler's place – Donau pointed at the box and then waved them off. A short time later Donau's colleague, Christian accompanied Wagner into the office. Alex stood up and went to sniff Christian's pocket.

Wagner stated, almost belligerently, "I'm told we have to work together on this double murder,"

"Yes, it seems my case has merged into yours," Donau agreed. "Who is leading on the airport case?"

"Felix has it. But how does that fit into the double murder?"

"The dead woman was the personal assistant to Heinrich, one of the people being investigated by the new task force. Both Lunn and Wessler are alleged to have been part of the same crime cartel."

"That you say exists," Wagner pointed out.

Derek decided to settle the point. "It exists, Inspector Wagner, I have had confirmation through my sources."

Wagner, thought better of arguing the point. "So, Otto, why did you tell the lab to drop the work on my team's cases in favour of some suit bag?"

Donau explained the providence of the suitbag, and saw Wagner's face turn thoughtful.

"Wexford might be a witness to that murder," Wagner said.

"And he might be involved in the death of Lowenbach. He was at her house before I got hit on the head."

Wagner chuckled, "Lucky you have a hard head."

Donau wanted to mention the death at the fire damaged house, but needed to speak to Derek's 'informants' before claiming to have witnesses. So he used the knowledge that Carson had told Derek where to find Rachel Wexford, to place Carson at the house.

Wagner didn't stay much longer. He left, fired up with the thought of finding more evidence against the American woman.

Derek watched him go, satisfied. A man hell bent on some kind of vengeance, missed few details.

Wanda saw Jim as she was led into the small interview room. She was still unsettled by the intensity of the interview the previous day. Her mind had been running in circles, trying to probe the blank period when the police claimed she killed two men.

She didn't greet her friend and mentor, for only a select few people knew they were not strangers. Her escort freed one of her hands from the restraints, and once again passed the free end under a bar on the table before refastening it on her wrist. He didn't bother positioning the chair for her so she jerked it closer with her foot before sitting down and staring at her friend.

Jim came and sat opposite her, and gave a polite greeting.

She didn't feel like being polite, not after the previous day. "Don't I need my lawyer present when I talk to you?"

"Not for this Miss Carson. You simply need to listen," Jim stated, as if they were indeed strangers.

"Go on then," Wanda agreed, but instead of looking at him, she adjusted her head to study the room behind Jim, looking for the video monitor and trying to see if there were listening devices. The guard had retreated and would be watching through the glass window in the door.

Jim had made the same casual scan before Wanda had arrived. Now he pitched his voice low, so it only carried across the table.

"Have you any idea where your passport is?"

Wanda knew which one he meant. "No, and I am not exactly in a position to go Russian around to find it." She gave him a quick glance and looked away again.

Jim frowned slightly at that. "Very well, I am to tell you that there can be no diplomatic intervention on your behalf. You are a private citizen and must follow the laws of this country when you are here."

It was what she had expected, but in her present mood, not what she wanted to hear.

"And that's the end of it? People rub their hands with glee and say, 'Oh, gee, that was nice of the Austrians to pick up our trash?'"

Wanda didn't keep her voice low for that, but her next words were so soft only Jim heard them. "I had already figured all that, dammit!"

Jim added softly, "The VP is keeping out of it."

Wanda relaxed, Stan Russell, who had signed off her original pardon after helping to jail the Franklin family, had attached strings to her pardon. It gave him the option to revoke it if she stole again for personal profit. "Nice of him," she murmured with a trace of sarcasm.

For a few moments, Jim studied Wanda, trying to decide how much of the 'attitude' was a deliberate act and how much wasn't.

"How are you coping?" he asked quietly.

"It's only day two, so apart from boredom, well enough," was the ungracious answer.

Jim spoke with slightly more volume. "Is there anything I can get for you?"

Wanda finally turned to face him. "Yes, if you would oblige. I need some personal things – brush, comb, soap, a change of clothes. I am tired of this doctor outfit. It needs a wash."

Jim stood and walked so that his back was to the monitor, and angled himself so the guard watching through the door couldn't read his lips. "Don't cause trouble," he warned. "We are doing all we can to help, but we can't force a deal if you don't cooperate."

"You're the one who told my lawyer to gag me!" Wanda said, hardly moving her lips.

"Full disclosure at this point will put you deeper in trouble. Derek has Donau on the idea that you might have been set up, but Wagner is still trying to bury you. Then there is this Russian group, Donau is not convinced that you are not in with them."

"Is that all?"

"No, they have created a task force to investigate the cartel, and I am sure they will want to question you further. But not until your lawyer gets his deal."

"The deal he asked for stinks," Wanda muttered.

Jim seemed to be counting to ten, before he turned to face her. "Are you reacting to hormonal effects of the nine-month type?"

Wanda didn't answer immediately, but finally admitted, "Yup. I was pissed off about yesterday, I thought it was that. Sorry, for taking it out on you, I will try to control it."

"It isn't needed for me," Jim said gently. "You don't need more trouble. Have you any more thoughts on the idea of Wexford as a Russian?"

"Nothing I didn't tell Derek. I can't even guess when the fake took over. No more than I have any idea of why those Russian guys are stuffing me around."

Jim's face took on an intent, thoughtful expression. Wanda knew that look, he had thought of a bad possibility. He didn't explain, just said, "I will have an embassy aide deliver what you requested."

He walked to the door and gestured to be let out.

Later, when Wanda had worked her way through a series of mental exercises for relaxing, focussing and calming her mind, and finished her makeshift exercise routine, she stood and looked down from the high window at the prison exercise yard. It seemed to be teeming with women dressed in the ghastly orange shift dresses. Yet as she studied the ebb and flow, she identified several groups. She saw how they seemed to gang up on the loners, and memories of her own, from when she was in prison at sixteen, came flooding back. She forced them back into memory; she wasn't that naïve innocent any more. When the inevitable happened, and she had to join those below, those women would learn...

End of part 1

Wanda's story continues in Part 2

Prisoner-Spy
Where family connections of another kind add to her troubles.

WANDA: FROM BAD TO WORSE

If she was going to die young, like her mother, Gwen Willard was determined to die rich and she had very few years to do it. Her first step was to leave home. She met Hooch, who taught her some exciting and illegal skills. She was the Draco's lucky mascot until she came to the attention of the police. Then her uncanny knack for predicting trouble, warned her to flee to the city and change her name.

Life wasn't easy. She was 15, had little money and no regular job, but her new skills came in handy. Then she crossed the path of an evil and unscrupulous man and she didn't want him to have his way.

WANDA: CHOOSING CRIME

Wanda was free. She was never going back to jail. But she was homeless, almost penniless and Harrison Franklin had a long and vengeful memory.

Jim Phillips had a long memory too, and Wanda had saved his life. Could he save her from Franklin?

WANDA: RISKING LIFE TO LIVE

The euphoria of successful heists were what kept Wanda Dean alive. At 23, she was crime boss Harrison Franklin's top agent – well paid for absolute obedience. That's all that mattered. Until she met Mike Johnston and her boss ordered him killed. For that, the Franklins were going to pay. In Risking Life to Live, justice conflicts with loyalty and the penalty for betrayal is death.

WANDA: A NEW LIFE - HIDDEN SECRETS

Even before beginning as a covert agent for the US Government, Wanda is abducted by a foreign operative. After being rescued, there are signs that she had been subjected to hypnosis. With an important government gathering imminent, her handler must ensure she is not a security risk.

Can Wanda's psychic extra senses help her recognize and resist the implanted commands and clear her for secret work?

WANDA: A NEW LIFE - FIRST MISSION
On her first covert mission for the US Government, Wanda calls on the skills that made her a skilled thief to convince a revolutionary general that she's an ideal recruit. When her team mates' covers are blown, it is up to her to ensure that two missing scientists and confidential Government documents are not smuggled out of the US.

WANDA: FULL CIRCLE
Three generations after the alien Kumatan left Earth, their own world is suffering from alien invaders. In desperate hope, one returns to Earth seeking help - little knowing they had left one of their own behind.
Wanda, a child of the third generation, answers the call.

ERIN: THE FORCING OF WISDOM
For years, Erin has used the intricacies of cyberspace to banish unwanted emotions. Others call what she does hacking, and her manipulations criminal, but now her skill was exceptional - in, out, traceless. She was wrong. Someone betrayed her.
Travis has dangerous plans. He needs an electronics expert – one he can coerce through fear. Erin was perfect.
With the inescapable threat of prison looming, Erin accepts his offer of sanctuary. When she realises his intentions, she is in too deep. But the terrifying of innocents is unforgivable. She cannot walk away. She is an empath and shares their distress. She has to help them, even if it means prison, and insanity...

ERIN: THE CALL
(including ELISABETH AND TANYA: BLOOD CALLS TO BLOOD.
Elisabeth's sister, Wanda, had been missing for half a year. Multiple authorities had found no trace of her, or her two colleagues. Yet she knew her sister was still alive and had answered a call for help from an alien who had once lived on Earth.
Elisabeth, along with her newly found cousin Tanya, have started to sense things from her missing sister. Enough to know that she is

in dire trouble, but not enough to help her.

While looking for traces of the aliens, Elisabeth makes some unexpected discoveries about her family. Yet even with the help of a second newly discovered cousin, she fears she is not strong enough to help her sister and the others to return.

ERIN: THE CALL

Convicted cyber-criminal, Erin Mason, is startled into awareness in an unfamiliar place, with no memory of escaping and only vague memories of getting there. Voices in her head were urging her to go west, and they were getting more urgent.

After a chance meeting with covert agent, Jim Phillips, when she helped save his mission, he realised that she might be the key to another, more personal quest – to find three missing state department agents.

All he must do is keep Erin safe, and hide her from an intense police search, until he can introduce her to cousins she was unaware of.

However her uncontrolled psychic gifts conflict with a logical mind that prefers the ordered intricacies of computers and electronics. She only wants to shut out the voices and the madness she sees looming.

Can Phillips convince her to help him, before the forces of the law find her?

THE SERPENT'S SHADOW

Three books in one.

Janna consorts with terrorists to protect her friend Prince Ali from assassins.

Former cyber-criminal, Erin, becomes part of the merchandise of stolen tech secrets.

Jim Phillip's team is sent to neutralise the leader of the terrorist Cobra Sect.

KORVU: THE BEGINNING

The prequel to The Wild One

Jai Ansuni was the first female Atapi sorcerer for thousands of years, but she dare not reveal it. However, when tribal sorcerer, Stacion Ansuni escalates the enmity between Atapi and Kumatan to an ominous level. Jai and her womb mate, Con, try to mitigate his atrocities but can two young Atapi, not even a score of years old, win against the powerful sorcerer?

THE WILD ONE

Sixteen year old Jai Cassidy thought she was finally free of her family until she is discovered by her other relatives...the ones that aren't human. Jai uses her natural perversity and cunning to escape their control, but catapults herself into the middle of a deadly feud between two alien races.

ATAPI SORCERESS
The sequel to The Wild One
Jai Cassidy is beginning her mission of reversing the decline of the non-humanoid Atapi. As a sorceress and an Atapi-Human hybrid, she is vehemently disliked by the male Atapi sorcerers and the humanoid rulers of Korvu. Her task is complicated by the treachery of a group of alien engineers, who are inciting insurrection and harsh reprisals.

THE TYMOREAN TRUST BOOK 1 - POWER RISING
The Tymorean Trust - When peace rules Tymorea - Peace reigns in the universe.

Chosen to be the Advocates of the mystical and incorporeal Guardians of Peace, twins Tymos and Kryslie must first learn to control and use the power rising in them - or it will destroy them.

On Tymorea, only the ruling Triumvirate Governors are powerful enough to guide the strong-willed alien-bred twins until they have mastered their power.

THE TYMOREAN TRUST BOOK 2 - GREAT ONES
The peace of the Guardian Planet, Tymorea, is in deadly peril. War there will create ripples of unrest and destruction throughout the settled universe.

Tymos and Kryslie, still adolescents, have barely mastered their power and Llaimos is still less than a year old, but they are the three chosen to be Advocates of the mystical Guardians of Peace, to safeguard the Tymorean Trust.

THE TYMOREAN TRUST BOOK 3 - RETURN TO EARTH
Even before the war on Tymorea, the Elders foresaw that Great Ones Tymos and Kryslie would have an imperative mission on Earth.

But as the Tymoreans prepare to build an Earthbase to support them, they discover that specifications for two vital protective shields are missing.

Now, nearly a century later, Tymos and Kryslie must find his work and build the generator before the base is found.

THE TYMOREAN TRUST BOOK 4 - EARTH MISSION
Just before their graduation from the prestigious WSRA Washington University, Tymos and Kryslie Ward deliberately disappear.

The Great Ones have foreseen the capture and death of the new Tymorean missionaries and discovered that the leader of the Eastern Imperium plans to undermine the United World Nations.

Tymos and Kryslie must protect their kin and prevent a potentially devastating world war.

THE TYMOREAN TRUST BOOK 5 – ALIEN CONTACT
Tymos and Kryslie Ward, hide their Tymorean intelligence and abilities while working as low ranked technicians at the WSRA's lunar base. When an alien ship arrives at Lunar One, pursued by a powerful enemy who will stop at nothing to get what he wants, only the two Tymorean Great Ones have the knowledge and abilities to overcome him, but to do so they must risk their sanity, and their souls.

THE TYMOREAN TRUST BOOK 6 – INVASION
Great Ones Tymos and Kryslie go to rescue the crew of Earth's first deep space mission – and discover that Ciriot space pirates have discovered Earth's location. When the Ciriot invade in force,

the Great Ones reveal themselves so that Earth can gain vital help. However, Kryslie becomes the victim of Ciriot, who want to control her mind and make her betray the people of Earth.

TRICKS

Tom and Jo Dwyer had a reputation for playing tricks – and getting detention. They didn't seem to care about that, so long as they made their class laugh. That was until someone began to turn their tricks against them, and it was no longer funny.